The Laughing Dragon

THE YOUNGEST OMNIBUS

Edited
by
ROSALIND VALLANCE

Illustrated by
Ruth Gervis, Honor Appleton
and others

Thomas Nelson and Sons Ltd
London Edinburgh Paris
Toronto New York

THOMAS NELSON AND SONS, LTD.

London :

35–36 Paternoster Row, E.C.4

Edinburgh :

Parkside Works, Dalkeith Road

Paris :

25 rue Denfert-Rochereau

Toronto :

91–93 Wellington Street West

New York :

381–385 Fourth Avenue

H. 50

TO

JOHN WAYFARER

THE PLAYS

CONTENTS

CONTENTS

CONTENTS

CONTENTS

ACKNOWLEDGMENTS

THE editor has pleasure in acknowledging her indebtedness to the following for permission to include copyright material in this volume:

To Mr. Rodney Bennett and the University of London Press, Ltd., for "The Sleepers," from *Whither Shall We Wander*; Mr. Hugh Chesterman for "The Paper Hoop" and "On the Lawn"; Miss Harriet Clark for "The King and Queen's Daughter"; Mr. Walter de la Mare for "The Cupboard" and "The Hare"; Miss Eleanor Farjeon for "The Waves of the Sea" and "The Artist"; Miss Elizabeth Fleming for "Bread," from *The Creepie Stool*; Miss Rose Fyleman for "The Broom" and "The Fairy House"; Miss Bertha I. Gofton for "The Lonely Little Tree"; Mr. Robert Graves for his version of "My Mother Said"; Miss Eleanor Halsey for "The Jug and the Teapot," "Watching for Trains," "The Orange-Peels," and "Cats in Mary-le-bone"; Mr. John Hampden for "Storm Fairies"; Mr. Norman Hunter for "His Majesty Comes Over All Handy-man"; Mr. A. K. Hamilton Jenkin for "The Small People's Fair"; Miss P. Laflin for "The Cat on the Dovrefell" and "The Three Billy Goats Gruff"; Miss Ella Monckton for "The Cow, the Duck, and the Pig" and "Irish Stew"; Mr. Christopher Morley and Messrs. Doubleday Doran (New York) for "The Unamiable Child," from *I Know a Secret* (Faber and Faber); Mr. Arthur Ransome for "The Stolen Turnips," from *Old Peter's Russian Tales* (Nelson); Mr. W. C. Berwick Sayers for "Fairies who are Out by Day"; Mr. James Stephens for "When You Walk"; Miss Anne Trotman for "Christmas Pies" and "Eleven and Twelve by the Clock"; Mrs. E. Lucia

Turnbull for " Aspirations " and " Spring " ; Mrs. Amabel Williams-Ellis for " The Boy in the Moon," from *But We Know Better* ; Mr. E. Harcourt Williams and Messrs. Samuel French, Ltd., for " The Play of The Three Bears " ; Mr. Humbert Wolfe for " The Blackbird " ; and Mr. W. B. Yeats and Messrs. Ernest Benn, Ltd., for " The Stolen Child," from *Poems*.

To Messrs. Ernest Benn, Ltd., for " The Bouncible Ball," from *Nine Unlikely Tales*, by E. Nesbit ; Messrs. A. and C. Black, Ltd., for " Olaf the Fair and Olaf the Dark," from *The Flying Carpet*, by Lady Cynthia Asquith ; Messrs. Basil Blackwell for " The Little House," and " The Fox and the Pot," from *Picture Tales from the Russian*, by Valery Carrick, " Toffee Boy " and " The Snow-man," by Mabel Marlowe, " Greedy Jane," by B. Peddle, " The King of China's Daughter," by Edith Sitwell, " Choosing Shoes," by Ffrida Wolfe, " The Chinese Umbrella," by Dorothy Rowe, " Next Door," by Joan Ryder, and " The Three Stones," by M. Braidwood ; Messrs. Jonathan Cape, Ltd., for " Picnic," from *Porridge Poetry*, by Hugh Lofting ; Messrs. W. and R. Chambers, Ltd., for " Conrad of the Red Town," from *The Pedlar's Pack*, by Mrs. Alfred Baldwin ; Messrs. Chatto and Windus for " Extremely Naughty Children " and " Ann's Bath," from *Green Outside*, by Elizabeth Godley, " The Christmas Tree " and " The School," from *The Spider's Palace*, by Richard Hughes, and " The Porcelain Stove," by " Ouida " ; Messrs. Constable and Co., Ltd., and the executors of the late Katherine Mansfield for " Little Brother's Secret " ; Messrs. J. M. Dent and Sons, Ltd., for Reed Moorhouse's version of " Jilly Jenkin," from *With Pipe and Tabor*, and " Carol," by William Canton ; Messrs. Evans Brothers, for " Jeremy's Big Red Ball," by Helena Mills, and " The Magic Room," by Irene Thompson, from *Child Education*, and Messrs. Evans and Miss Rhoda Power for " Gopala and the Cowherd," and " The Mannikins and the Green Peas," from

Stories from Everywhere ; Messrs. Faber and Faber, Ltd., for "The Seven Sleepers," from *Moonshine and Magic*, by Alison Uttley ; Messrs. Longmans, Green, and Co., Ltd., New York, for "The Princess Lindengold," from *Canute Whistlewinks and Other Stories*, by Z. Topelias, trans. by C. W. Foss, edited by Olcott ; Messrs. Macmillan and Co., Ltd., for "The Jelly-fish," from *Green Willow*, by Grace James ; Messrs. Elkin Mathews and Marrot, Ltd., for "The Fooling of King Alexander," from *The White Man's Garden*, by Mervyn Skipper ; Messrs. Methuen and Co., Ltd., for "Market Square," from *When We Were Very Young*, and "Eeyore Joins the Game," from *The House at Pooh Corner*, by A. A. Milne ; Messrs. Thomas Nelson and Sons, Ltd., for "The Mouse, the Bird, and the Sausage," retold by Richard Wilson, "The Robin's Worm" and "The Laughing Dragon," by Richard Wilson, "Brer Rabbit's Adventure," by Jean McIntosh, "The Chocolate Pigs," by Dorothy Russell, "Jack Seeks his Fortune," retold by Louie Chisholm, "The Run-Along Man Sells Spoons," by Agnes Grozier Herbertson, "Œyvind and his Goat," adapted from Björnson, "Bunny's New House" and "The Fire Engine," by S. G. Hulme Beaman, "The Little Wee Hairy Man," by Charles M. Campbell, "The Careless Hedgehogs" and "Things I'd like to do," by Enid Blyton, "The Lady of the Pyramids," by E. D. Hancock, and "The Five Littl'st Orphans of All" ; The Oxford University Press for "Moppety Mow," from *The Oxford Annual for Tiny Folks*, edited by Mrs. Herbert Strang, and "The Why of the Weather," by Margaret Baker ; Messrs. George Philip and Son, Ltd., for "Stories of St. Francis," from *Piers Plowman's Histories, Teachers' Book I.*, by A. M. Ramsay and M. R. Keary ; The Poetry Bookshop for "Overheard on a Salt-Marsh," by Harold Monro ; Messrs. Putnam and Co., Ltd., for "The Travelling Man," from *Seven Short Plays*, by Lady Gregory ; The proprietors of *Punch* for "Gollywog," by "Jan" ; The University of London Press for "Barnaby the Goat," by Marion St. John Webb, from *Twice Ten*; Messrs. Frederick Warne and Co., Ltd., for "Mr. and Mrs. Spikky Sparrow," from *Nonsense Songs and Stories*, by Edward Lear; Messrs. Wells, Gardner, Darton and Co., Ltd., for "The Concert," by "Brown Linnet," from *Why Why and Tom Cat*.

The editor also wishes to thank Miss Freda Holmdahl and Miss Joan Huggins for all their help, so courteously given in the preparation of this book.

THE LITTLE HOUSE

By Valery Carrick

Translated by Nevill Forbes

ONCE upon a time a jar rolled off a man's cart, and was left lying in the middle of a field. And a little mouse came running along and saw the jar lying there, and thought what a nice house it would make, and began to wonder who lived there.

And the little mouse said : " Little house, little house, who lives in the little house ? "

But no one said anything. Then the little mouse looked in, and saw no one there ! " Well then," he said, " I shall live here myself." So he began to live in the jar.

Then a frog came hopping along, and said : " Little house, little house, who lives in the little house ? "

" I, Mr. Mouse, I live in the little house, and who are you ? "

" I am Mr. Frog." " Come inside, then, and let's live together." " Very well, let's." So the frog got into the jar, and they began to live together.

Then a hare came running over the field. " Little house, little house," says he, " who lives in the little house ? "

" Mr. Frog and Mr. Mouse, and who are you ? " " I am Mr. Hare who runs over the hills. May I come in too ? " " Yes, you may ; come and live here, there's plenty of room."

Then a fox came running past, and said : " Little house, little house, who lives in the little house ? "

" Mr. Hare, Mr. Frog, and Mr. Mouse. And what is *your* name ? " " I am Mr. Fox." " Very well, then, come and live with us." " Right you are ! " So the fox got into the jar too, and all four began to live together. And they went on living there, when a bear came along out of the forest, and said : " Little house, little house, who lives in the little house ? "

" Mr. Fox, Mr. Hare, Mr. Frog, and Mr. Mouse ; and who are you ? "

" I am Mr. Bear-Squash-you-all-flat ! "

And the bear sat down on the jar and squashed it flat.

LITTLE BOY LOST

ONCE upon a time a little boy got lost.

He sat down on the edge of the pavement and began to cry.

The milkman came along. "Milk-o! Milk-o!"

He saw the little boy. He stopped his barrow.

"Hallo, sonny, what's the matter?"

"I'm lost. Boo-hoo!"

"Lost, are you? Well, let's see if we can find you. What's your name?"

"Timmy."

"Timmy what?"

"Timmy nuffin."

"That's a funny name. I never heard of any one called Nuffin."

"I'm *NOT* Timmy Nuffin, I'm Timmy."

"Oh, I see. But what's your Dad's name?"

"Daddy."

"Yes, I know; but he's got another name. What does your Mummy call him?"

" Darling."

" Well, that's not much help. Where d'you live ? "

" In a house with a face on the door."

" A house with a face on the door ! What street is it in ? "

" There's a lamp-post there. Boo-hoo, I want my Mummy ! "

" What else is in that street ? "

" Nuffin."

" Nothing ? There must be something else."

" There's a bit of white paper."

" Where ? "

" By the gate."

" Whose gate ? Your gate ? "

" No. Where the pussy-cat lives."

" What kind of pussy-cat ? "

" Red ; and she scratches. I don't like her."

" What's the name of the lady where the pussy-cat lives ? "

" She hasn't got a lady. Oh dear, I want my Dad."

" But she lives in a house. Who else lives in the house ? "

" It's a teeny house. And it goes away sometimes."

" What goes away ? The house or the pussy ? "

" The house."

" You mustn't tell stories. How old are you ? "

" I don't know. About a hundred and fifty-three."

The milkman laughed.

Along came the baker with a basket of bread.

" Hallo, Milk-o. Hallo, little 'un. What you crying for ? "

" He's lost."

" Boo-hoo, I want my Polly ; I want my Daddy ! "

" Well, stop crying then, and tell us where your Daddy lives."

" He says he lives in a house with a face on the door. That's all I can get out of him."

" How old is he, d'you think ? "

" He says he's about a hundred and fifty-three."

" Now look here, old man, if you're a hundred and fifty-three you're too old to cry."

" I want my Mummy. I want my doggie."

" Tell us how you got here."

" I come in one of them aeroplanes. I live in a house with a face on the door."

" Don't be silly. There aren't any aeroplanes here. You must have run away from home."

" Boo-hoo, I want my Mummy. I want my doggie. I want my Polly. *I want my Daddy*. I WANT MY DINNER ! "

Along came the postman, with a bag full of letters, pushing his bicycle.

" Now then, now then, what's all this about ? "

" This little boy's lost. He says he's called Timmy."

" He says he's a hundred and fifty-three."

" He says his Dad's called ' darling.' "

" He says he came in an aeroplane."

" He says his name's Timmy ' 'nuffin.' "

" He says he wants his Polly, and his Daddy, and his Mummy, and his doggie."

" He's crying for his dinner."

" He says there's a red pussy-cat in his street,

and it lives by itself in a house that goes away sometimes."

" He says he lives in a street with a lamp-post, and a piece of white paper by the pussy-cat's gate."

" He says he lives in a house with a face on the door."

" A house with a face on the door ? Why, I know where that is. It's only just round the corner. It's the only house in the town with a letter box like that."

" Boo-hoo, the face opens its mouth when you put the letters in."

" That's right, Timmy. You know all about it, don't you? Now you stop crying, and I'll take you home on my bicycle. Or shall I put him in my bag with the letters, Milk-o? Then I could pop him in to his Mummy through that big mouth. Couldn't I, Baker?"

The postman sat the little boy on his bicycle, and wheeled him home to his mother, and the milkman and the baker went home to dinner, and told their children all about the little lost boy who lived in a house with a face on the door.

SPRING

By E. Lucia Turnbull

" My dear," said Mrs. Wren, " if Mrs. Cuckoo
comes to call,
I really think it would be best to see her in the hall,
Explaining that our house it is so very, very small,
We have no room for paying guests, or any guests
at all."

By Eleanor Halsey

The Jug and the Teapot lived side by side;
The Teapot smiled, and the Milk-Jug cried.

He said that he wanted a little hat;
But the Tea-Tray said, "You *can't* have that!"

"If the Teapot has one, why can't I?"
Said the Milk-Jug, heaving a heavy sigh.

Said the kindly Teapot, "Borrow mine;"
And the Milk-Jug thought the plan was fine.

But the Teapot's hat was far too small,
And didn't fit the Jug at all!

It fell inside, and there is no doubt
That they had some trouble to get it out!

"What did I tell you?" the Tea-Tray said,
"A Jug should *not* wear a hat on its head."

THE MOUSE, THE BIRD, AND THE SAUSAGE

Retold by Richard Wilson

A Mouse, a Bird, and a Sausage kept house together. The Bird flew every day into the forest to bring wood. The Mouse brought the water from the well. The Sausage cooked the food in the pot. They were all happy, for they all did their own work.

But one day the Bird said they must all change their work.

So they cast lots, and now the Sausage had to fetch the wood from the forest, the Mouse had to cook the food in the pot, the Bird had to bring the water from the well.

One day the Sausage stayed out a very long time. The Bird flew to the forest to look for him. In the forest the Bird met a big dog.

" Have you met a Sausage in the forest ? " said the Bird to the dog.

" Yes," said the dog, " and I have eaten him."

So the Bird flew home and told the Mouse. They were very sad about it ; but the Mouse went to get the dinner ready, and she fell into the pot and was drowned.

The Bird looked for her all over the house, and he made the burning wood fall on the floor, and set fire to the house ; so he flew to the well for water. But the bucket fell into the well, and the Bird fell in with it and was drowned.

THE FOX AND THE POT

By Valery Carrick

Translated by Nevill Forbes

Once upon a time a man was going through the forest, carrying an empty pot, when all at once he saw a fox's hole.

" Hallo," he thought, " how can I keep the fox in the hole while I go for my gun ? " So he took the pot and put it near the hole ; then the wind began to moan—oo—oo—oo !

" That's all right," he thought, " now the fox won't come out ; he'll think that it's people here making a noise." And he went away.

All this time the fox was sitting in his hole, and he could not make out what was making that noise. He wanted to peep out, but he was afraid. Then after a while he looked out and saw the pot. " So it was *you* trying to frighten me, was it ? " he said. " Well, just you wait ; I'll give it you ! "

And the fox put his head into the pot, because he wanted to see if there was something there, and then he couldn't pull it out again.

He turned his head this way and that, and still the pot stuck fast. Then he said to the pot : " *Please* let me go ! " But the pot wouldn't.

"Oh," he said, "is that your game? Then I'll just drown you."

And so he ran to the lake near by and began drowning the pot. And the water came running into the pot—bubble—bubble—bubble! "That's all very well," said the fox. "You are sorry now, I know, but it's too late." Then the pot began to get full of water, and to pull the fox down. "You silly," he said in his fright, "I was only joking,

and you thought I really meant it!" And it was as much as the fox could do to pull his head with the pot on it out of the water.

Then he ran off again, back to the forest. But while he was running, he couldn't see where he was going, and went bang against a tree, and the pot broke in pieces and fell off his head.

Then the fox began to cry, and said: "What have I got to boil my porridge in now?"

And that is all!

MY MOTHER SAID

Arranged by Robert Graves

My Mother said, I never should
Play with the gipsies in the wood.

If I did, she would say,
" You naughty girl to disobey.

" Your hair shan't curl and your shoes shan't shine,
You gipsy girl, you shan't be mine."

And my father said that if I did
He'd rap my head with the teapot-lid.

THE COCK AND HEN THAT WENT TO THE DOVREFELL

By Sir George Dasent

Once on a time there was a Hen that had flown up and perched on an oak tree for the night. When the night came, she dreamed that unless she got to the Dovrefell the world would come to an end. So that very minute she jumped down, and set out on her way. When she had walked a bit she met a Cock.

" Good-day, Cocky-Locky," said the Hen.

" Good-day, Henny-Penny," said the Cock, " whither away so early ? "

" Oh, I'm going to the Dovrefell, that the world mayn't come to an end," said the Hen.

" Who told you that, Henny-Penny ? " said the Cock.

" I sat in the oak and dreamt it last night," said the Hen.

" I'll go with you," said the Cock.

Well ! they walked on a good bit, and then they met a Duck.

" Good-day, Ducky-Lucky," said the Cock.

" Good-day, Cocky-Locky," said the Duck, " whither away so early ? "

" Oh, I'm going to the Dovrefell, that the world mayn't come to an end," said the Cock.

" Who told you that, Cocky-Locky ? "

" Henny-Penny," said the Cock.

" Who told you that, Henny-Penny ? " said the Duck.

" I sat in the oak and dreamt it last night," said the Hen.

" I'll go with you," said the Duck.

So they went off together, and after a bit they met a Goose.

" Good-day, Goosey-Poosey," said the Duck.

" Good-day, Ducky-Lucky," said the Goose, " whither away so early ? "

" I'm going to the Dovrefell, that the world mayn't come to an end," said the Duck.

" Who told you that, Ducky-Lucky ? " asked the Goose.

" Cocky-Locky."

" Who told you that, Cocky-Locky ? "

" Henny-Penny."

" How do you know that, Henny-Penny ? " said the Goose.

" I sat in the oak and dreamt it last night, Goosey-Poosey," said the Hen.

" I'll go with you," said the Goose.

Now when they had all walked along for a bit, a Fox met them.

"Good-day, Foxy-Cocksy," said the Goose.

"Good-day, Goosey-Poosey."

"Whither away, Foxy-Cocksy?"

"Whither away yourself, Goosey-Poosey?"

"I'm going to the Dovrefell that the world mayn't come to an end," said the Goose.

"Who told you that, Goosey-Poosey?" asked the Fox.

"Ducky-Lucky."

"Who told you that, Ducky-Lucky?"

"Cocky-Locky."

"Who told you that, Cocky-Locky?"

"Henny-Penny."

"How do you know that, Henny-Penny?"

"I sat in the oak and dreamt, last night, that if we don't get to the Dovrefell, the world will come to an end," said the Hen.

"Stuff and nonsense," said the Fox; "the world won't come to an end if you don't get thither. No! come home with me to my earth. That's far better, for it's warm and jolly there."

Well, they went home with the Fox to his earth, and when they got in, the Fox laid on lots of fuel, so that they all got very sleepy.

The Duck and the Goose, they settled themselves down in a corner, but the Cock and Hen

flew up on a post. So when the Goose and Duck were well asleep, the Fox took the Goose and laid him on the embers, and roasted him. The Hen smelt the strong roast-meat, and sprung up to a higher peg, and said, half asleep:

"Faugh, what a nasty smell!
What a nasty smell!"

"Oh, stuff," said the Fox; "it's only the smoke driven down the chimney; go to sleep again, and hold your tongue."

So the Hen went off to sleep again.

Now the Fox had hardly got the Goose well down his throat before he did the very same with the Duck. He took and laid him on the embers, and roasted him for a dainty bit.

Then the Hen woke up again, and sprung up to a higher peg still.

"Faugh, what a nasty smell!
What a nasty smell!"

she said again, and then she got her eyes open, and came to see how the Fox had eaten both the twain, Goose and Duck; so she flew up to the highest peg of all, and perched there, and peeped up through the chimney.

"Nay, nay; just see what a lovely lot of geese are flying yonder," she said to the Fox.

Out ran Reynard to fetch a fat roast. But while he was gone, the Hen woke up the Cock, and told him how it had gone with Goosey-Poosey and Ducky-Lucky; and so Cocky-Locky and Henny-Penny flew out through the chimney, and if they hadn't got to the Dovrefell, it surely would have been all over with the world.

THE CUPBOARD

By Walter de la Mare

I know a little cupboard,
With a teeny tiny key,
And there's a jar of Lollypops
For me, me, me.

It has a little shelf, my dear,
As dark as dark can be,
And there's a dish of Banbury
Cakes
For me, me, me.

I have a small fat grandmamma,
With a very slippery knee,
And she's Keeper of the Cupboard,
With the key, key, key.

And when I'm very good, my dear,
As good as good can be,
There's Banbury cakes, and Lolly-
pops,
For me, me, me.

TOFFEE BOY

By Mabel Marlowe

There was once a boy who ate so much toffee that when he sat in the sun he melted.

He melted and melted until he was just a brown pool of treacle.

Now this treacle began to move slowly down the hill. It trickled past the school and across a meadow and under a stile, and at last it came to a little brook, running in the valley.

Now there was a plank of wood across this brook, to serve for a bridge, and the treacle trickled over this plank until it reached the middle. Then it stopped.

It was very cool over the water, and before long the treacle began to set. In a very little while the middle of that little bridge was all toffee. Some of it was like a pool of brown glass. Some of it hung over the edges like brown icicles.

Now when it was getting dark a bunny came hopping that way. He hopped to the middle of the bridge, and sat down to watch the sunset.

Presently another bunny came that way.

" What are you doing there ? " he said to the first bunny.

" I am sitting down to watch the sunset."

" I will come too."

Hop, hop, hop! The second bunny hopped on to the bridge, and sat down to watch the sunset.

Presently another bunny came that way.

"What are you doing there?" he said.

"We are sitting here to watch the sunset."

"I will come too."

The red sun went down and down, and the three bunnies sat still upon that little bridge until the last rays were gone.

"Now I will hunt for cabbage for my supper," said one.

"Yes, so will I."

"And so will I."

Then they all tried to get up.

Pull, pull!

Tug, tug!

Struggle, struggle!

"Oh dear! oh dear! I can't get up."

"Neither can I."

"Neither can I."

"I am stuck fast."

"So am I."

"And so am I."

Now just at that moment a man came along. He was a long, lean man, very weary and very hungry, but when he saw those three bunnies on that bridge he began to laugh.

"Ha, ha! Ho, ho! These will do nicely for my supper," he said. So he stooped and took hold of the plank, and pulled it hard and lifted it up, bunnies and all. He put it on his shoulder, bunnies and all, and went off home.

" See the fine supper I have brought for you," he said to his wife.

Now when the wife saw the bunnies she was very glad. Very quickly she got paper, and matches and sticks, and made a big fire.

"I will pull some turnips to cook with the bunnies," she said. So she went into the garden to pull the turnips.

"I will pull some carrots, too," said the man. So he went into the garden to pull the carrots.

"Oh dear! oh dear! We shall soon be put into a pie," said one bunny.

"Yes. I am hot enough to be roasting now. What a big fire that old woman has made!"

It certainly was a big fire. It roared up the chimney, and crackled and flamed, and the room became as hot as an oven.

"Goodness gracious me! I believe I am coming unstuck," said one bunny in a whisper.

"Yes, so am I."

"And so am I."

"Sh! Keep quiet. The old woman is coming back."

Back came the old woman, with a bunch of turnips in her hand. "Whew, how hot it is!" she said, and she threw open the window.

"Quick!" said all the bunnies at once. There were three little scuffles, three mighty jumps, and three frightened rabbits were gone through the window. In a flash their tails vanished over the hill.

"Where are the bunnies?" said the man, coming in with a bunch of carrots.

But there was nothing but a plank of sticky wood, and a brown pool of treacle on the floor.

THE CAT ON THE DOVREFELL

By P. Laflin

PEOPLE IN THE PLAY

Halvor.
A Woodcutter.
The White Bear.
A Lot of Trolls.

Scene.—*A small cottage in the middle of a wood. The door is open, and we can see that the table is laden with good things to eat. Near the cottage is a Woodcutter busily chopping wood.*

[*Through the wood comes a tall man leading a Bear by a chain.*]

Halvor [*holding the Bear tightly*]. Good-day.

Woodcutter [*staring hard at the Bear*]. Good-day, sir.

Halvor. Will you give me shelter for the night, my bear and me ? Will you give me a bit of food too ? I will pay you well if you will.

Woodcutter. Sir, I cannot, for to-night no one may stay in my house except at the risk of his life.

Halvor. How is that ?

Woodcutter. Every Christmas Eve such a pack of Trolls come down on us that we have to spend the night in the woods. I am obliged to spread a feast for them, and there they stay all night, eating and drinking. If they found any one there they would tear them to pieces.

Halvor. This is a strange business. I would

like to stay here, my bear will protect me from harm.

Woodcutter. No, no, do not stay, I beg you. Spend the night under the trees with us.

Halvor. Oh no. I would like to stay here, for I have a mind to see the Trolls.

Woodcutter. Very well.

[*The Man and his Bear go into the cottage. The Woodcutter walks slowly away through the wood. Now and then he turns round to look at the cottage. He sees the Bear lying just inside the cottage door.*

For a short time all is silent. Then the Trolls come through the forest and go into the house. Some are tall, some are short ; some are fat, some thin ; some have sticks in their hands, some have none ; some have tails which brush the ground as they walk.

They rush through the door and in at the windows. They squeal and shriek as they gobble up the good things.

One of them sticks a sausage on a fork and holds it to the sleeping Bear's nose.]

Little Troll. Pussy, oh, pretty pussy ; will you have a sausage ?

The Bear [*springing up and knocking the Trolls out of the way with his strong paws*]. Grr—grr—grrrr !

[*The Bear chases all the Trolls away into the wood. He returns and sleeps peacefully in front of the cottage.*]

Woodcutter [*running towards the cottage*]. Did the Trolls not come ?

Halvor [*coming from the cottage, and followed by the Bear*]. Oh yes, they came, but we drove them away. I do not think they will trouble you again.

Woodcutter. Thank you—thank you.

[*Halvor leads his Bear away through the woods. The Woodcutter returns to his chopping.*]

A Voice [*calling from behind a tree*]. Woodcutter ! Woodcutter !

Woodcutter. Well, what is it ?

Voice. Have you that big white cat with you still ?

Woodcutter. Yes, that I have. She's lying under the stove, and, what's more, she has five kittens, far bigger and fiercer than she is herself.

A Voice [*very frightened*]. Oh, then, we'll never come to see you again.

JEREMY'S BIG RED BALL

By Helena Mills

There was once a big red ball which could roll and bounce as well as any ball in the world. It belonged to a little boy called Jeremy, who played with it all day long.

One sunny day Jeremy was running along the big white road, bouncing his ball as he went.

" Ping ! " sang the big red ball as it struck the road. Up it bounced to meet the fleecy clouds, then down it dropped into Jeremy's hands.

" Next time it shall go *very* high ! " said Jeremy, and he flung the ball downward with all his might.

" Ping ! " sang the big red ball again, and up it bounced till it was lost to sight among the leafy branches of a large oak tree.

With outstretched hands Jeremy waited, but his ball did not come down.

Poor Jeremy! He stared upward into the green branches; he

searched the hedgerow, and he peeped among the bushes in the high, thick hedge. Where *could* it be?

"My beautiful ball is lost!" he sobbed. "I shall never bounce it again."

But his big red ball was not the least bit lost, as you shall see. It had only dropped on the *other* side of the hedge, into the short grass of a gently sloping meadow.

There it stayed for a moment, rocking this way and that; then, slowly and easily, it began to roll down the grassy slope.

Down it rolled, nearly grazing Mrs. Rabbit's left whisker, as she popped her head out of her front door.

"What monster is this?" she squeaked, and scuttled back to her cosy burrow, determined not to go outdoors any more that day!

On rolled the big red ball, past Mother Cow and her speckled calf as they munched the sweet grass.

Mother Cow took no notice, for she was old and wise, and knew that there were many strange things in the world; but the speckled calf got very excited.

"Ma-a-a! Here's an apple!" he cried.

"It is *not* an apple! Don't touch it!" mooed his mother.

But the speckled calf felt sure that such a pretty rosy-red thing must be *some* sort of apple, so he kicked up his little heels and raced after it.

The big red ball rolled faster, for now it had come to the place where the meadow sloped steeply toward a little stream. And, as the speckled calf could not catch it, and the big red ball had no power to stop itself, into the stream it went!

There it lay, shining beneath the clear, smooth water, while Jeremy wandered sorrowfully up and down the big white road, thinking he should never see his ball again.

It was a lucky thing that Farmer Cherry and his dog happened to come along.

Farmer Cherry listened to the whole sad story, and then he said:

" Perhaps your ball has rolled into my meadow. We will go in and have a look, and we will take Spot with us, for he is very clever at finding things."

They were soon in the meadow. Farmer Cherry trod slowly and heavily while he looked around ; Jeremy ran to and fro, searching eagerly ; and as for Spot, he hadn't the least idea what they were looking for, though he hoped it was rabbits! He barked excitedly and rushed madly around the meadow, so perhaps it was just as well that Mrs. Rabbit had decided to stay indoors !

" We'll go down the slope. Your ball may have rolled a long way," said Farmer Cherry.

So down they went, stopping for a moment to pat the speckled calf, who was dozing by his mother's side and had forgotten all about the strange apple.

Very soon they came to the lazy-moving stream. " Woof ! " barked Spot, catching sight of the wet, glistening ball. At last he had discovered what they were looking for !

Splash ! He was in the stream and had caught the ball in his mouth. Another splash and a shake of his coat, and he had laid the big red ball at Jeremy's feet !

" Good dog ! " cried Jeremy, and patted Spot's wet head.

Then Jeremy ran home to tell his mother all about it, bouncing his ball as he went. But he was very careful not to let it go so high again !

R. S. GERVIS

WATCHING FOR TRAINS

By Eleanor Halsey

Up and down the country,
  Everywhere you'll spy
Little boys, all waiting
  To see the trains go by.

Leaning over fences,
  And out from windows high ;
Everywhere they're waiting
  To see the trains go by.

Off they run, like rabbits,
  Here's the reason why—
To reach the level crossing
  And see the trains go by.

"What to do this morning ?"
  Hear them all reply :
"Let's wait about the station
  And see the trains go by."

GREEDY JANE

By B. Peddle

ONCE upon a time there was a little girl who would fill her mouth too full. And Mummy told her not to : but she did. And Auntie told her not to : but she did. And Daddy told her not to : but still she did. And this is what came of it.

One day this little girl was left alone to finish her tea, and she put a whole penny bun in her mouth. Just then a large bit of coal fell from the fire on to the hearth. From the hearth it jumped on to the hearthrug, and from the hearthrug it rolled into the middle of the room. And it was red-hot. So the little girl jumped down from her chair in a fright and ran to her Daddy in the next room. And she meant to say, " The house is on fire ! " But you know she had a whole penny bun in her mouth ; so what she did say was : " Thuff huff uff uffuff ! "

And no one could tell what she meant.

Now Daddy was reading the paper, so he said, " Don't bother me now, dear, I am very busy. Go and talk to Mummy." And he thought no more about it. And now the coal had burnt the carpet.

So the little girl ran upstairs to Mummy, and

she meant to say, " Oh, the house is on fire, and Daddy doesn't care ! " But you know she had a whole penny bun in her mouth, and what she did say was : " Uff thuff huff uff uffuff, uff Duff duff cuff ! "

And no one could tell what that meant.

Now Mummy was standing before the looking-glass putting on a new hat. So she said, " Don't bother me now, dear. Go and talk to Auntie." And she thought no more about it. And now the coal had burnt the floor.

So the little girl ran out into the garden to Auntie, and she meant to say : " Oh, the house is on fire, and Daddy doesn't care, and Mummy doesn't care ! "

But you know she had a whole penny bun in her mouth. So what she did say was : " Uff thuff huff uff uffuff, uff Duff dufft cuff, uff Muff dufft cuff."

And no one could tell what that meant.

Now Auntie was lying down asleep. So she said : " Don't bother me now, dear. I am very busy. Go and talk to Daddy." And she thought no more about it. And now the coal was burning the curtains, and all at once Daddy jumped up and cried, " I smell burning ! " And Mummy ran down and cried, " I smell burning ! " And when they ran into the room they found it all burnt up. And they turned to the little girl and said, " Why did you not tell us ? " And the little girl said " Uff," and began to cry. Then they said, " Never fill your mouth too full again." And, of course, she never did !

THE PLAY OF RED RIDING-HOOD

By Rosalind Vallance

In the first part of the play Red Riding-Hood is playing the game of " Muffin man " in her garden. She walks up and down, pretending to carry a tray of muffins on her head, and rings a little bell, singing :

Do you know the muffin man,
The muffin man, the muffin man ;
Do you know the muffin man
Who lives in Drury Lane ?

As she is playing, her Mother comes out of her house with a letter in one hand and a basket full of things in the other. She calls Red Riding-Hood, but the little girl is so busy walking up and down and ringing her bell and singing that she does not hear her.

Mother. Red Riding-Hood.
Red Riding-Hood [*sings*],
Ting-a-ling-a-ling-a-ling,
A-ling-a-ling, a-ling-a-ling.
Mother. Red Riding-Hood, I want you, dear.
Red Riding-Hood. Oh, Mother, I want to play !
Mother. I want you to go to Granny's.
Red Riding-Hood. Can't Granny come *here* to-day ?
Mother. Granny can't come to-day, dear,
Granny is very ill.
Red Riding-Hood. Oh, poor old Granny, I love her.
I love dear old Granny, Mother.
I'll run all the way to her cottage.
What have you got in this basket ?
Mother. Butter, and sweet new honey,
eggs, and a cake for Granny.
Carry it carefully, darling.
Red Riding-Hood [*takes the basket*. *She says*].
I'll carry it carefully down the road,
I'll carry it carefully through the wood,
I'll carry it carefully right to her house.
Mother. That's a good girl, Red Riding-Hood.
Red Riding-Hood. But when I come home with my basket empty

I'll run through the meadow, I'll run through the
wood,
I'll run down the road, and I'll run through the
gate :
I'll never stop running till I get home.

[*She puts down the basket, and gives her Mother a hug and a kiss.*]

Mother. Good-bye, little Red Riding-Hood.
Come back quickly. Don't stay in the wood
unless you see Daddy cutting down trees.

Red Riding-Hood. Can't I pick Granny a bunch of flowers ?

Mother. Well, just one bunch, then, but do not loiter,
for in the wood there are strange wild creatures.
They come out at night and prowl about,
so come back quickly. Be back by sunset.

Red Riding-Hood. When the sky turns golden I shall be here.
Good-bye, Mother.

Mother. Good-bye, dear.

[*Red Riding-Hood picks up her basket and walks off. She waves her hand to her Mother as she goes. Mother goes back into the house. That is the end of the first part of the play.*

The next part happens in the wood, full of dark trees. Red Riding-Hood comes in, humming to herself, and walking very carefully with her basket, Soon she sees some primroses under the trees, so she puts down her basket and begins to pick some for her Granny. She does not see the Sly Old Wolf come out of his cave. He watches her pick the flowers. He is thinking. At last he speaks to her.]

Sly Old Wolf. Little girl, little girl, what is your name ?

[*Red Riding-Hood turns round and sees the Wolf, but she is not afraid. She answers.*]

Red Riding-Hood. My Mother calls me Red Riding-Hood.

Wolf. That's very pretty. I like your red cloak.

Red Riding-Hood. My Granny made that. I'm going to see her,
and take this basket. She's ill in bed.

Wolf. Where does she live, this Granny of yours ?

Red Riding-Hood. In a little white house a long way away,
straight through this wood and over the stile,
across the meadow and down the road.
She lives at the edge of the great black forest.

Wolf. And are you going there all alone ?

Red Riding-Hood. Yes. *I'm* not afraid. Poor Granny is waiting.

Wolf. Shall I come too, to help with your basket ?

Red Riding-Hood. Oh no. I can carry my basket alone.

Wolf. Then will you race me, Red Riding-Hood ?
I'll give you a start because of your basket.

Red Riding-Hood. I'll race you, I'll race you, you old grey wolf.

[*The Wolf is very angry with her because she calls him* " *old grey wolf,*" *but he pretends not to mind.*]

Wolf. Race me then, race me, Red Riding-Hood.

Red Riding-Hood. One, two—— Which way will you go ?

Wolf. This way, and you go across to the stile.
When you have gone I shall count a hundred,
then I shall start. Now are you ready ?
One, two, and away you go !

[*Red Riding-Hood goes off with her basket as quickly as she can. But the Sly Old Wolf does not count a hundred. He looks after her as she dis-*

appears, and shows his great teeth, and growls angrily.]

Wolf. I'll teach you to call me "old grey wolf"!

[*Then he turns and runs off the other way. That is the end of the second part of the play.*

The next part is inside the old Granny's little

white house that stands at the edge of the great black forest. The old Granny is lying in bed with a shawl and a nightcap on. She hears some one knocking at the door. It is the Sly Old Wolf, who has found a secret path through the wood and got there long before Red Riding-Hood. He has smelt the old Granny inside the house, and he pretends to be Red Riding-Hood, and calls out in a small voice.]

Wolf. Granny, dear Granny, are you there?

Granny. Is that you, Red Riding-Hood, dear ?

Wolf. Yes, Granny darling. May I come in ?

Granny. Pull the bobbin and lift up the latch.

[*The Sly Old Wolf pulls the bobbin and bounds into the room. He rushes towards Granny's bed. Granny screams.*]

Granny. Oh, oh, oh ! It's the old grey Wolf !

[*She scrambles out of bed on the other side. The Wolf jumps on to the bed and snatches her cap and her shawl, and puts them on himself. Granny runs into a corner, crying out.*]

Granny. Help ! Oh, help ! Here's the wicked old Wolf !

[*The Wolf is busy dressing himself up and getting into bed, and does not notice that Granny has hidden herself in a cupboard. He says proudly.*]

Wolf. Don't you think I make a good granny ?

[*He finds Granny's spectacles under the pillow and puts them on, then spreads out the newspaper and pretends to read, though really he doesn't know A from B. Soon he hears Red Riding-Hood's step on the path outside. She knocks on the door and calls out.*]

Red Riding-Hood. Granny, dear Granny, are you there ?

[*The Sly Old Wolf puts on a very quavery old voice and says.*]

Wolf. Is that you, Red Riding-Hood, dear ?

Red Riding-Hood. Yes, Granny darling. May I come in ?

Wolf. Pull the bobbin and the latch will go up.

[*Red Riding-Hood pulls the bobbin, the latch goes up, and she comes in. She thinks the Sly Old Wolf is her Granny, so she goes up to the side of the bed and puts her basket on a chair. The Wolf grins at her.*]

Wolf. You kind little girl, I'm so glad you have come.

Red Riding-Hood. We are so sorry you're ill, dear Granny.

Wolf. And what have you brought in your little basket?

Red Riding-Hood. Butter, and sweet new honey, eggs, and a cake for you, Granny.

Wolf. Thank you, my dear. Come closer to me.

[*Red Riding-Hood sits down by the bed. She looks at Granny very curiously, then she says.*]

Red Riding-Hood. What big EYES you have, Granny.

Wolf. All the better to SEE you, my dear.

Red Riding-Hood. What big EARS you have, Granny!

Wolf. All the better to HEAR you, my dear!

Red Riding-Hood. And what a big NOSE you have, Granny!

Wolf. All the better to SMELL with, my dear.

Red Riding-Hood. And what big TEETH you have, Granny.

Wolf. All the better to EAT you, my dear!

[*He jumps out of bed and springs at Red Riding-Hood. She screams, and runs to the door. The old Granny calls out from inside the cupboard.*]

Granny. Oh, help! Oh, help! Come and kill the old grey Wolf!

[*And Red Riding-Hood is calling out.*]

Red Riding-Hood. Mother! Father! Come and save us!

[*The Wolf chases Red Riding-Hood round the room. Just as they get to Granny's cupboard she opens the door, pulls the little girl inside, and slams the door in the Wolf's face. The Wolf scratches on the cupboard, but he does not get in, for Red Riding-Hood's Father comes rushing in with a big axe. He cries out.*]

Father. What is the matter?

[*But at once he sees the Wolf, and shouts.*]

Father. Ah, you big brute!

[*He knocks him on the head with the axe, and the Sly Old Wolf falls dead. Red Riding-Hood and Granny peer out of the cupboard. Red Riding-Hood sees the Wolf is dead. She comes out of the cupboard and runs up to her Father and takes hold of his hand.*]

Red Riding-Hood. Oh, is he dead, Daddy? I was so frightened!

Father. Yes, he is dead. You poor little girl! But where is Granny?

Red Riding-Hood. She hid in the cupboard. Come out, Granny. It's all right now.

Granny. Not till you give me my nightcap and shawl.

[*Father takes Granny's nightcap and shawl off the Wolf.*]

Red Riding-Hood. Please carry the nasty old Wolf outside.

[*Father pulls and pushes the Wolf outside, while Red Riding-Hood takes the things to Granny and helps her to dress. Father comes back. They help Granny to get back to bed.*]

Red Riding-Hood. We'd rather have you than a *Wolf*-granny, Granny!
Oh, Daddy, you only just came in time!

Granny. Suppose the Wolf's mother should come out to find him!

Father. Don't be afraid. There are no wolves left.
That old grey one was the last of all.

Now what have you brought in your basket for
Granny ?

Red Riding-Hood. Butter, and sweet new honey,
eggs, and a cake for Granny.

Father. Give Granny her tea, Red Riding-Hood,
and then we will take her home through the wood.
The cart is outside, and the old horse Dobbin.

Red Riding-Hood. Oh, that will be fun ! Will
you drive us, Father ?

Father. Yes, if you're good. We'll be home by
sunset.

Red Riding-Hood. When the sky turns golden,
we shall be home.
Won't Mother be glad to see us come ?

THIS IS THE END OF THE PLAY.

MOPPETY MOW

MOPPETY MOW was mopping up her house one day, when she found a silver sixpence.

"What shall I do with my silver sixpence?" she said. "I know—I will go to market and buy a fat pig."

So she went to market and bought a fat pig. But when she brought him home she had nowhere to keep him except under her kitchen table, and there he would not stay. So she took the fat pig back to market and sold him for fourpence.

"What shall I do with my fourpence?" said Moppety Mow. "I know—I will buy a black cat."

So she bought a black cat and took him home with her. But when she got home she found she

had no milk to give him. So she went back to the market and sold him for twopence.

" What shall I do with my twopence ? " said Moppety Mow. " I know—I will buy a singing-bird."

So she bought a singing-bird, and started home with it sitting on her finger. But she had not gone far when the bird flew away.

" Now I have nothing," said Moppety Mow, and she went home and finished mopping up her house.

THE ORANGE-PEELS

By ELEANOR HALSEY

THERE was once a family who were bright orange colour in front and pale yellow at the back. Their names were Mr. and Mrs. Orange-Peel, and they had a little boy named Pip, and a baby. They lived in a little brown house with only one room, but it was quite large enough for them, for they were very flat and thin. The house had black painting on the outside, because it was made of a brown-paper bag from the greengrocer's shop.

This house was tucked away behind the railing of a front garden, under a privet hedge that grew there ; the family did not come out into the road very often, because there were lots of motors and buses, and people walking about, and Mrs. Orange-Peel was very much afraid that Pip would be run over.

One day Mr. Orange-Peel heard the people to whom the garden belonged say, " We really must tidy up this garden ; ever so many pieces of paper and bus tickets and paper bags have blown in and stuck in the hedge. To-morrow we will pick them all up and put them in the dustbin."

Mr. Orange-Peel did not like this ; he could not understand that his little brown house looked to other people like a paper bag ; and though he did not know what the dustbin was, he did not want to be taken off in his house and put there.

So he said to Mrs. Orange-Peel, " I think we had better move away from this place to-morrow, and find another house." And early next morning they left the garden and climbed down the kerb-stone, which was very steep to them, into the road, and started off down the street. It was so early that nearly every one was in bed, and they got along very well: directly they saw any-body coming, they all lay down quite still in the road, and then they only looked like ordinary pieces of orange peel.

Mr. and Mrs. Orange-Peel walked along together with the baby, lifting her over the cracks and stones in the road that were too wide for her to step over. But Pip was so pleased to be out and moving that he ran about in every direction by himself. " I know that child will be run over one of these days," said Mrs. Orange-Peel nerv-ously. " Pip," called Mr. Orange-Peel, " if you don't behave yourself you will end by being made into marmalade." Now that is a thing that none of the Orange-Peel family can bear to think of ;

and for a little while Pip kept close to his people and walked quietly, but soon he forgot and went rushing along in front, looking down every turning and into every corner.

"Look, Dad!" he called, "there's a lot of green down there—is it the country?" "No," said Mr. Orange-Peel, "it must be a park, and it would be very pleasant to live there, if we can manage it." He was hurrying up to overtake Pip when he saw a man coming along, so, of course, they all stopped at once and pretended to be ordinary orange peel; and they might have been quite safe, only, unfortunately, the man happened to be clearing and tidying up the street, sweeping it and picking up the paper that was lying about; and when he saw what he thought were pieces of old orange peel, he picked them up too, and put them on the top of the rubbish in his cart. "Here! Hi! Hallo!" cried Mr. Orange-Peel, "take us off this at once—we're not rubbish, and we don't want to go on your cart—you leave us alone! I say! Hallo!" But the man took no notice whatever, and went on tidying up the road. "My dear, this is very tiresome," said Mr. Orange-Peel; "I wish now that we had stayed at home and chanced being turned out of it." "I could bear it better," said Mrs. Orange-Peel faintly, "if this old salmon tin next to me wasn't cutting my head off with its sharp edge." "Sorry, mum," said the salmon tin, "I'll roll over the first opportunity I get, and give you a bit more room ; but it is rather a tight fit, and if I'm not careful I shall roll right off on to the ground, and that will make dents in my shape."

"I wish *we* could roll off," said Mr. Orange-Peel eagerly ; "it wouldn't hurt us, and we don't want to be on this cart. We are just moving, you see, and it will probably take us out of our way."

"W-e-ll," said the tin, "it might be managed ; if I roll over suddenly and give you a good push, and you all jump as far as you can, I should think you would land at the side of the road—if that's what you want. I shouldn't like it, I should get so horribly battered ; but you might not get hurt, you're so light."

"That is most kind of you," said the Orange-Peels, both together ; "we shall be so glad of your help." "Very well," answered the tin, "are you ready ? One, two, three ! Go ! " and he rolled over quickly and came up against them with such a tremendous push, and they jumped so high and so far that they found themselves flying through the air right on to the side of the road.

There they all lay for a little while, quite breathless ; but they were not hurt at all, and very pleased to have escaped from the dustcart. But where was Pip ? "I didn't see him in the cart," said Mrs. Orange-Peel. "Perhaps he wasn't picked up at all, as he had run on so far in front."

"Now, that's just what I think," said Mr.

Orange-Peel. " Let's go straight on as fast as we can, and I expect we shall find him." And, sure enough, on the other side of the next lamp-post they found him sitting still and looking very sad. But he brightened up at once when he saw his family, and they all went on, delighted to be together again.

When they came to the Park they had to be very careful and go in when the Park-keeper wasn't looking, for, of course, if he had seen them he would have picked them up and put them into the little wire baskets for waste paper and rubbish. But he was having his breakfast, and waiting for another egg to be boiled harder than the first one, and so they managed to scuttle through the gates and down a side path in no time. " This is the place for us," said Mr. Orange-Peel, and he crept under a large laurel bush whose leaves touched the ground. " And there is a jolly little house, too, all ready for us." And there it was, quite a large cardboard box that had once held somebody's sandwiches. It was quite roomy and comfortable, and all the family were enchanted with their good fortune in finding a house that was so much better in every way than the one they had left.

" Ah ! this is much more pleasant than the old place," said Mr. Orange-Peel, as he sat at the front door in the evening, while Pip and the baby played under the laurel leaves. " I have just met some very friendly people who are living close by, and they say we shall have plenty of agreeable neighbours."

"It's most fortunate," said Mrs. Orange-Peel. "But now you must stop talking, and all go to bed early, because we have had a long, tiring day!"

And as time went on the Orange-Peel family became quite well known in the park; they are there still, and one day you may even see them yourself. Pip and the baby have grown up, but their father and mother look just the same—they have many friends, and are very popular.

But the salmon tin had gone away in the dust-cart, and they never saw him again.

LITTLE BROTHER'S SECRET

By Katherine Mansfield

When my birthday was coming
Little Brother had a secret :
He kept it for days and days,
And just hummed a little tune when I asked him.
But one night it rained,
And I woke up and heard him crying :
" I planted two lumps of sugar in your garden,
Because you love it so frightfully ;
I thought there would be a whole sugar tree for
    your birthday,
And now it will all be melted."
O the darling !

THE BOY IN THE MOON

By Amabel Williams-Ellis

Once upon a time there was a boy in the moon, as well as a man in the moon. This boy was called Fred, and was a worry to his father because he always thought that he knew best.

But really he never took the trouble to find out or learn about anything. One day he went to his father and said that he wanted very much to go down and visit the earth as the old man in the moon had once done. " I think," he said, " that the moon is a horrid little place."

So the kind old man in the moon began to explain to him how things were on the earth. Do you think that Fred would listen ? He would not listen to a word. " All that is too dull, Father. You'll see, I shall manage all right."

" But Fred, dear," said the kind old man in the moon, and shook his grey head, " you will do all sorts of silly things if you won't listen ; you see things are quite different on the earth. Once I went to Norwich when I was young, but it was far too soon, and I did not have at all a nice time, and I burnt my mouth. I should like you to enjoy yourself."

But Fred was quite rude, and said that he did

not want to hear all that stuff, and he went off, and did not listen to a word of the useful things that the kind old man wanted to tell him.

When he had gone out of the room the old man shook his head and thought to himself, " How the people on the earth will laugh at that silly Fred, who won't learn."

Well, Fred got to the earth all right in the very same flying coat that the old man in the moon had once worn. It was rather too big for him, as you can see in the picture, but he got down quite safe. He found he was in a little wood, and that it was a nice fine day. Some sheep were feeding in a field close by. Fred looked at them, but presently they walked slowly away.

Soon a farm boy came by, singing and whistling, and what should he see in the wood but a boy. It was Fred. Fred was holding on to the roots of a tree, and was looking very much frightened.

" Why do you hold on to the roots of that tree, little boy ? " asked the farm boy, who was older, " and why do you look so frightened ? "

" Of course I am frightened, you silly," said Fred, " and you had better hold on too."

" But why ? " asked the farm boy.

" Because you may fall up into the sky if you don't," said Fred in a very serious voice. The farm boy began to laugh.

Fred got to the earth all right.

" Things never fall up, you stupid," he said.

" Well, the sheep have," said Fred, and he pointed up into the sky to where there were a lot of little soft white clouds floating along.

" Look, look! there they are, all the poor sheep that were feeding here a minute ago! And if they fell up, so shall we, if we don't hold on tight."

Well you can guess how Sid, the farm boy, laughed and laughed before he told Fred what they were.

Now just as he was telling him this, a lark flew up singing into the air. At once Fred turned quite pale and held on to the roots again.

" There, there! Only look at that stone! " he said. " That's falling up, anyhow."

" That was a bird, you stupid," said the farm boy, laughing again, and he took Fred along and showed him the sheep still eating grass a little farther on and the lark walking quietly back to its nest.

Now Fred never said " Thank you " to Sid for explaining, but only looked very cross when he saw that he had been silly. But all the same Fred thought he would walk along with this boy for a bit and hear some more about the earth.

Presently, as they went along they came to two stones on the path, a big one and a little one. Sid took up the small stone to throw it. But Fred thought that big stones were always the small stones' Mothers, so he called out in a fright:

"Oh, don't touch the baby stone! Now the Mother stone will run after you and bite you. Run. You'd better run." And Fred began running down the path, looking back at the big stone and thinking every minute that it would roll along and bite Sid in the leg.

"Well," said Sid, laughing again, and this time he stood and stared at Fred too, "you're the biggest stupid I ever saw. Little stones aren't the babies of big stones! Whatever stupid thing will you say next?"

Well, as you can guess, the farm boy hadn't long to wait for Fred to say another stupid thing, for as they walked along to the farm they saw a train a long way off.

"Oh!" said Fred in a serious voice. "How dreadful! Look at that terrible dragon wriggling along and breathing out smoke and hot breath."

"Silly!" said Sid. "That's a train."

When they saw a brown cow lying down in a field, Fred thought it was a tree stump.

"What fruit grows on that sort of tree?" asked Fred. The farm boy laughed: "'Tisn't a tree, it's an animal." When she saw them the cow lowed. But Fred was quite frightened, and clutched hold of Sid's hand and said, "Save me, save me from that roaring lion!"

Sid, who was more than eleven years old, and

collected birds'-eggs and cigarette cards, thought Fred was so funny that he would like his Mother to see him. So when they got to the farmhouse, Sid called out, " Mother, Mother, I've got a boy here. Oh, such a funny boy ! Please can I bring him in to tea ? " " Yes, that you can, Sid," said his Mother, who was baking scones. So the two boys came in. " But what makes you think he's so funny ? " his Mother said softly to Sid, as soon as she saw that Fred was at the other end of the room and could not hear. So Sid told her all about this queer boy, how Fred had thought that the clouds were sheep that had fallen up into the sky, and that a lark was a stone falling up ; how he thought that a big stone was a little stone's Mother ; how he had asked what kind of fruit grew on a cow, and then, when the cow had lowed, how he had thought it was a lion ; and also how he had said that the train was a wriggling dragon. That made Sid's Mother laugh so much that she had to wait and put down the tray of scones on the table.

" Now wherever can such a stupid boy have come from, Sid ? " said his mother.

" I don't know," said Sid.

But we know.

Now although Sid and his Mother tried to be polite, and not to let Fred see what they were laughing at, Fred knew quite well. As he watched them laughing, he began to wish very much that he had waited to hear what the kind old man in the moon had wanted to tell him. He could see from the way these two laughed that he must always be saying silly things. He thought, " Very well, I won't be laughed at, so I won't speak at all." But all the same, when Sid's Mother opened the oven door to put in the scones, Fred couldn't help calling out, " Oh, mind ! the fire's going to bite you ! " And then, when she put in the scones, he cried out, " There, now, the fire has eaten all the scones ! "

He thought that the ginger cat which was sitting curled up in a chair was a cushion, and sat on the end of her tail, so that she scratched him. He thought Sid's Mother's furniture was very nice. " Does it grow in the woods, or out of the floor of the house ? " he asked. They told him that chairs and tables had to be made. Next he wanted to know if they had to keep mowing the carpet to keep it short. He thought a big photograph on the wall of Sid's Father was a real person, and said, " Why does that man keep so still ? "

But what made Sid and his Mother laugh the most was to see Fred at the looking-glass. He kept asking who the little boy was, and could not believe Sid when he told him that it was himself. " But it moves about," said Fred. " It must be alive." In the end Sid had to get the looking-glass down from over the mantelpiece and let

Fred touch its cold smoothness before he would believe that it wasn't another little boy in another room.

The scones turned out very nice ; they were brown ones with currants in them, and they were quite hot out of the oven, so Fred had a very good tea with Sid and his Mother.

Then Fred said good-bye to them, and they never saw him again, because, as soon as he went out of the house, he put on his flying coat and he went straight back to the moon, where it was bed-time.

THREE BILLY GOATS GRUFF

By P. Laflin

PEOPLE IN THE PLAY

Little Billy Goat.	Big Billy Goat.
Great Big Billy Goat.	A Wicked Dwarf.

Scene.—*A field through which runs a stream. Over the stream is a bridge. Under the bridge sits a Wicked Dwarf.*

[*The three Billy Goats Gruff are busily nibbling grass in the field.*]

Little Billy Goat [*suddenly looking across at the sweet grass on the other side of the bridge*]. I will cross that bridge. I am going to eat some of that rich grass.

The Two Elder Goats [*severely*]. If you do, the dwarf will catch you.

Little Billy Goat. I'm not afraid. He will not eat me. I am too little.

[*Little Billy Goat trots over the bridge. The two Elder Goats watch him.*]

The Wicked Dwarf [*sitting under the bridge*]. Who is that trotting over my bridge ?

Little Billy Goat. It is only Little Billy Goat.

The Wicked Dwarf. I will eat you up.

Little Billy Goat [*peering down at the Dwarf*]. No, do not eat me. I am so little. Eat Big Billy Goat when he comes over the bridge. He is much fatter than I.

The Wicked Dwarf. Very well. Run over my bridge. I will wait for Big Billy Goat.

[*When Little Billy Goat has crossed the bridge he begins to eat the rich grass.*]

Big Billy Goat [*looking enviously at Little Billy Goat*]. I too will run over the bridge. I will eat the sweet grass.

[*Big Billy Goat trots over the bridge. When he has gone half-way he stops.*]

The Wicked Dwarf [*peeping from under the bridge*]. Who is that trotting over my bridge ?

Big Billy Goat. It is only Big Billy Goat Gruff.

The Wicked Dwarf. Then I will eat you all up.

Big Billy Goat Gruff [*looking down at the Dwarf*]. No, do not eat me. Wait until Great Big Billy Goat comes over the bridge. He is much fatter than I.

The Wicked Dwarf. Very well. Run over my bridge.

[*Big Billy Goat runs over to Little Billy Goat, and they both eat the rich grass.*]

Great Big Billy Goat Gruff [*looking enviously at the two Goats, who are eating the grass on the other side of the bridge*]. I too will go over the bridge to eat the sweet grass. The Dwarf did not eat Little Billy Goat. He did not eat Big Billy Goat. He will not eat me.

The Wicked Dwarf [*who is now really cross*]. Hi ! hi ! who is that trotting over my bridge ?

Great Big Billy Goat Gruff [*with a great big gruff voice*]. It is I—Great Big Billy Goat Gruff.

The Wicked Dwarf [*looking up at the Goat*]. Ah ! I will eat you up, Great Big Billy Goat Gruff.

Great Big Billy Goat Gruff [*with a big laugh*]. Ha ! ha ! ha ! Come up here and try it, little man.

[*The Wicked Dwarf jumps on the bridge. He is rather frightened. Great Big Billy Goat Gruff stamps his feet and shakes his horns. He laughs very loudly.*]

Ha ! ha ! ha !

[*He runs at the Dwarf and kicks him right off the bridge into the water. Great Big Billy Goat Gruff calling to the Dwarf, who is in the water.*]

Now you can drink water for ever and ever.

[*He trots over the bridge to Little Billy Goat and Big Billy Goat. They all three eat the sweet grass for ever and ever.*]

THE ROBIN'S WORM

By RICHARD WILSON

ONE day a robin flew into a room. It flew round and round, and then hopped upon a table.

On this table stood a looking-glass. The bird looked into the glass and saw a robin like itself.

It looked and looked with its head on one side. It seemed to say, " Who are you ? "

The robin in the glass did the same.

Then the real robin gave a sharp peck at the glass and flew out of the window. After a time it came back with a worm in its bill.

It flew down to the table and put down the worm beside the other robin.

Then some one came into the room. The robin took fright and flew away.

The robin in the glass also flew away. Only the worm was left beside the looking-glass.

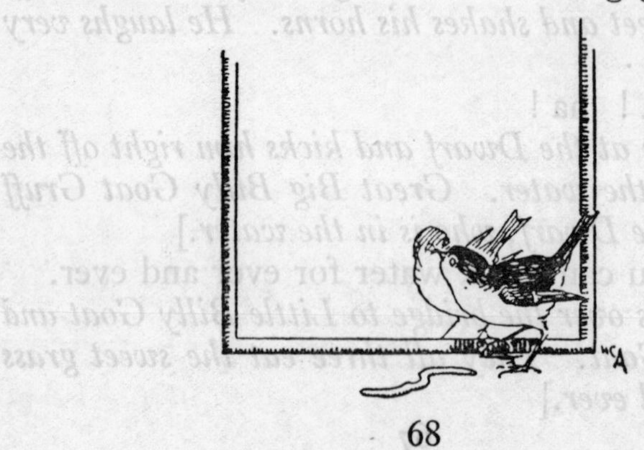

OH! LOOK AT THE MOON

By ELIZA LEE FOLLEN

OH! look at the moon,
She is shining up there;
Oh! mother, she looks
Like a lamp in the air.

Last week she was smaller,
And shaped like a bow;
But now she's grown bigger,
And round as an O.

Pretty moon, pretty moon,
How you shine on the door,
And make it all bright
On my nursery floor!

You shine on my playthings
And show me their place,
And I love to look up
At your pretty bright face.

And there is a star
Close by you, and may be
That small, twinkling star
Is your little baby.

THE CARELESS HEDGEHOGS

By Enid Blyton

Once upon a time, Hoo, the white owl, found a baby elf cuddled up in his nest.

"Tu-whit!" he said, most astonished. "Who are you, and where have you come from?"

The baby elf stared at him, but didn't answer a word.

Hoo perched on the side of his nest, and wondered what he should do with the queer little creature.

"I'll go and ask my friend Prickles," he said at last. "He is wise, and will be able to tell me."

Off he flew.

Prickles, the hedgehog, was awake, just outside his house.

"Good-evening," said Hoo politely.

"Good-evening," answered Prickles. "I hope you are well. What have you come to see me for?"

"In my nest there is a queer little elf thing, that will not speak a word," explained Hoo. "What am I to do with it?"

"A little elf thing!" said Prickles, sitting up quickly. "What is it like?"

"It is small, with yellow wings," answered Hoo.

" Have you seen the notice that the King of Fairyland has put up everywhere ? " asked Prickles excitedly.

" No," said Hoo.

" Come and I'll show it to you," said Prickles, scuttling off, with Hoo hurrying after him.

Presently they came to a tall foxglove. Hung on it was a notice which said :

" LOST FROM DREAMLAND

A LITTLE ELF BABY WITH YELLOW WINGS. ANY ONE FINDING IT WILL HAVE A GREAT REWARD

PLEASE TELL THE
KING OF FAIRYLAND "

" There ! " said Prickles. " You must have found the lost baby elf."

" But how could it have got into my nest ? " asked Hoo, very puzzled.

" Don't bother about *that* ! " answered Prickles. " Go and tell the King ! "

" Will you take care of it while I'm gone ? " asked Hoo.

" Yes," said Prickles. " I'll get all the fairy hedgehogs I know to look after it."

So Hoo flew down to the hedgehogs, carrying the elf baby gently.

" Now look after it carefully," he said, flying off to the King's palace.

All the fairy hedgehogs sat down in a ring, and looked at the baby. It lay in the middle of them and laughed and kicked.

" I think perhaps the bad gnomes stole it," said Prickles. " They are enemies to the people of Dreamland."

Whenever any one came near the baby the hedgehogs stiffened all their prickles, and made the very worst noise they could.

" Here comes Hoo ! " cried

Prickles at last, as Hoo perched on the tree above him.

" It *is* the lost baby," he cried, " and the King of Dreamland is coming to fetch it in two days. Our King says you must take great care of it till then."

" Very well," said Prickles.

" And," said Hoo, flying off, " you must see the bad gnomes don't come for it again."

So all that day the hedgehogs watched the elf baby. Prickles fetched it honey from the heather, and dew from the grasses. All through the night the fairy hedgehogs watched, and next day Prickles said :

" I'm going to fetch a special dew from the red blackberry leaves. Be very careful while I am gone," and off he went.

Then one of the hedgehogs stretched itself.

" I'm *so* tired of watching," he said, " I'm going off for a little walk."

He ran off through the grass, but in a minute he came back looking very excited.

" Come quickly ! " he cried ; " there is a fairy dance by the foxgloves, and if we're quick we can all go and hear the music."

The hedgehogs thought that would be lovely.

" We'll go to the dance till Prickles comes back ! " they cried ; " he'll never know."

Off they scampered as hard as ever they could, and were soon having a glorious time.

The little elf baby, finding there was nobody to stop it, crawled away by itself, and fell fast asleep under a mushroom.

Suddenly there was a great fluttering of wings, and down flew the King of Dreamland and the King of Fairyland: they had come to fetch the lost elf baby. At the same moment up came Prickles too, with his blackberry dew for the baby.

"Where is the baby?" cried the King of Dreamland.

"I don't know," answered Prickles, looking astonished. "It was here when I left, guarded by lots of fairy hedgehogs. Now they're all gone!"

At that moment back came all the hedgehogs from the dance. They looked very frightened when they saw the baby was gone and the two Kings had come.

"How *dare* you disobey my orders?" said

the King of Fairyland to the trembling hedgehogs. " Now the baby has gone, and perhaps the bad gnomes have stolen it away again ! "

" Please, we're very sorry," said the hedgehogs.

" That doesn't help matters," said the Dreamland King angrily.

" I shall have to punish you," said the Fairy

King ; " you haven't been good hedgehogs, so perhaps you will be good if I change you into something else ! "

He waved his wand. In a minute all the fairy hedgehogs found themselves climbing up a big chestnut tree.

The King waved his wand again. The hedgehogs climbed along the branches, turned green, and sat quite still.

" There ! " said the King ; " now perhaps they will keep the baby chestnuts from harm until they're ripe. Now, Prickles, hunt around until you find the elf baby."

Of course Prickles found him under the mushroom very quickly, and brought him back to the King of Dreamland.

But Prickles is very lonely now without the other hedgehogs. They never come down to play with him because they are so busy looking after the baby chestnuts, and they are much more careful of them than they were of the little elf baby.

And if you look at a chestnut tree in Autumn, you'll see what the King changed the hedgehogs into—and you'll find they're still very prickly !

ASPIRATIONS

By E. Lucia Turnbull

If I'd a little pair of wings
  I'd gather honey with the bee,
And learn the song the thrushes sing ;
  The butterfly would play with me.

I'd go so high if I had wings !
  My legs they keep me on the ground.
Oh ! in this world so full of things
  Can't just one little pair be found ?

THE LONELY LITTLE TREE

By Bertha Gofton

There was once a little tree that grew in a lovely garden. He was very, very happy, for he was taller than the bushes and shrubs around him, and so was able to spread his branches in comfort. He was a pretty little tree, too, and his green branches looked beautiful when the sunlight fell upon them.

Then one day a sad thing happened. The little tree suddenly found that all his leaves had withered away, and he was standing quite bare, while all the other little bushes were still covered with green. At first he thought it was autumn, and he had lost his leaves as usual, but soon he found he was wrong, for the West Wind told him he would always be bare. This made him sad, for he knew the birds would no longer build their nests in his branches, and the sweetest moments of a tree's life are when the birds are building.

All that summer the poor little tree was still unhappy. The little bushes around him all had nests hidden away in them, and the whole day long birds sang and flitted about their branches. But no bird came near the bare tree.

At last winter came, and then spring began. The birds that had left before the cold weather were now coming back again. The little tree looked sadly about him, and in his heart he envied the other bushes.

Then one day some new people bought the garden, and the flowers were surprised to see a little girl running up and down the paths. She stopped when she reached the bare tree.

" Poor little thing," she said, " I do hope you are not lonely."

The next morning she came again, and brought with her some nuts threaded on a string, and a little bird table. She fixed the table in the tree, and then fastened her string of nuts on the branches.

"Now you won't be lonely, little tree," she said. The little tree sighed, and wondered what all this meant. He soon found out. After a few minutes some blue-tits came flying along.

They alighted, and, balancing on the string, began to eat the nuts. Later, birds came to the table, and the little tree, quivering with excitement, watched the tiny feathered creatures flit from branch to branch.

So the little tree was never lonely again, for there were always birds flying about him and singing in his branches, just as they used to do before he lost his leaves. And when the birds got to know him well, they told him where they had built their nests and all about their little babies. So that, in time, he came to know more about the affairs of the birds than any one else in the garden, which made him very happy indeed.

THE COW, THE DUCK, AND THE PIG

By Ella Monckton

Once upon a time a Cow, and a Duck, and a Pig lived in a comfortable farmyard.

" Moo," said the Cow.

" Quack," said the Duck.

" Grumph," said the Pig.

Every morning early, Jenny, the farmer's daughter, brought them their breakfast.

Hay for the Cow.

Bran for the Duck.

Swill for the Pig.

And they were very happy and contented.

But one day Jenny, the farmer's daughter, was taken ill, and in her place came her little brother, Joey, to feed the animals. He was angry at having to do the work when he wanted to fly his kite on the hill, and so pretended to be more stupid than he was, and gave—

Swill to the Cow.

Hay to the Duck.

Bran to the Pig.

The Cow tried the swill and couldn't bear it. The Duck took a mouthful of hay, and it made him cough horribly. The Pig, who ate everything, bolted down the bran, but it was very dry to his taste, and it didn't make him feel fed at all.

However, they were good-tempered souls, and prepared to overlook this sort of thing for once. But the next day Joey was just as careless. He gave the Swill to the Duck, the Bran to the Cow, and forgot to feed the Pig at all.

" Bother ! " said the Cow.

" Dash ! " said the Duck.

" Bother, dash, and blow ! " said the Pig.

They met together in the yard, and decided to give Joey one more chance, though the Pig said he wasn't sure he even deserved that. But on the next day there was a lovely whirling wind playing round the hilltops, and Joey rushed away to fly his kite, and no one got anything at all.

" I am hungry," said the Cow.

" I am very hungry," said the Duck.

" I am going to faint," said the Pig.

They stood disconsolate in the yard, while the big white clouds sailed over their heads from east to west, and the leaves sang in the wind. And just at that moment a Fairy walked in through the yard gate. He didn't look much like a Fairy—in fact, anybody who saw him would have said he was a Tramp : his clothes were in rags, his flat, brown feet were bare, and his hair was full of hay stalks. But the Cow, and the Duck, and the Pig knew at once who he was, and greeted him enthusiastically.

" Thank goodness it's you ! " said the Cow.

" You have come just in time ! " said the Duck.

" Give me something to eat ! " said the Pig.

The Fairy smiled, and asked what the trouble was. " That's bad," he said when he heard. " But never mind, it's not so bad that something can't be done. Perch on my shoulder, Duck. Get under my arm, Pig. And hold on to my coat tails, Cow." They did as he told them, and then somehow or other (mind you, that Tramp really was a Fairy), they all disappeared from the farmyard and never appeared again until they reached the middle of a little forest five miles away, where there was a green grass clearing and a charcoal burner's hut. And, best of all, there was a load of hay for the Cow, a dish of bran for the Duck, and a great big, big pail of swill for the Pig. " Now stay here and eat," said the Fairy, " and I will come back for you at sunset."

" Umm," said the Cow, with his mouth full.

" Umm, umm," said the Duck, with his beak full.

And the Pig was too busy to say anything at all. So he wiggled his curly tail to show that he, too, agreed.

Then the Fairy disappeared again, and reappeared just behind a hedge on the hilltop where Joey was flying his kite. He whispered a magic word to the wind, and it immediately gave a great puff, which nearly tore the kite string out of Joey's

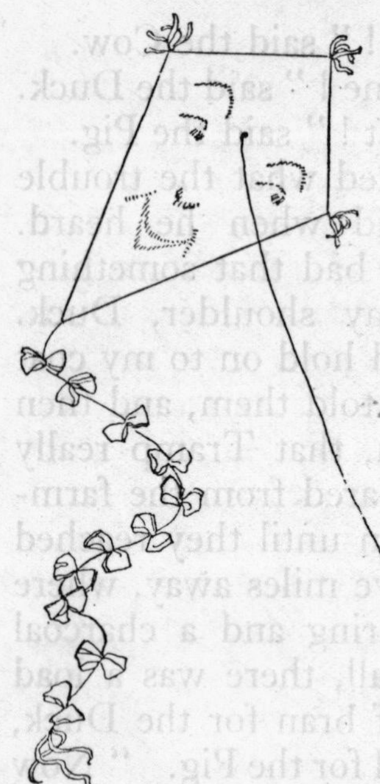

hand, and then began to pull him, willy-nilly, over the hill. He wanted to let go, but found that he couldn't, and so was forced, helter-skelter, after the kite, through hedges which scratched his face, over muddy ploughed fields which tore his shoes off, and he was finally dropped—splash! splosh!—into a green, scummy pool in the valley. He scrambled out and made his way home, and when his mother saw him she stripped off his wet clothes, spanked him soundly for losing his shoes, and put him to bed with no dinner.

"Good!" said the Fairy, who was hiding behind the kitchen door. "And now to cure poor Jenny."

He went into the

fields and picked a handful of cowslip flowers; then he went into the woods and pulled up a handful of green moss; then he went to a fairy spring that nobody knows about, and filled an acorn cup with water. With these he made a Magic (which all the Doctors in the world would pay a lot to know about), and just before sunset he slipped into Jenny's room, where she was lying, feeling dreadfully bad, and so softly that she never even felt it, he dropped the Magic on her forehead. Immediately her head stopped aching, and she fell soundly asleep.

At sunset the Cow, and the Duck, and the Pig woke up after a satisfying rest, to find themselves back in their own farmyard.

"That's funny," said the Cow.

"I thought——" said the Duck.

"Anyway, I feel much better," said the Pig.

And on the next morning, to their great delight, out into the yard, all aglow in the sunshine, stepped their beloved Jenny. She looked more beautiful than ever, and, best of all, she brought them their right breakfast.

"Moo," said the Cow.

"Quack," said the Duck.

"Grumph," said the Pig.

THE KING OF CHINA'S DAUGHTER

By EDITH SITWELL

THE King of China's daughter,
So beautiful to see,
With her face like yellow water, left
Her nutmeg tree.
Her little rope for skipping
She kissed and gave it me—
Made of painted notes of singing-birds
Among the fields of tea.
I skipped across the nutmeg grove—
I skipped across the sea ;
But neither sun nor moon, my dear,
Has yet caught me.

The King of China's daughter,
She never would love me,
Though I hung my cap and bells upon
Her nutmeg tree.
Her oranges and lemons,
The stars in bright blue air
(I stole them long ago, my dear),
Were dangling there.
The moon did give me silver pence,
The sun did give me gold,
And both together softly blew
And made my porridge cold ;
But the King of China's daughter
Pretended not to see
When I hung my cap and bells upon
The nutmeg tree.

BRER RABBIT'S ADVENTURE

By JEAN McINTOSH

SAID Brer Rabbit to his wife one day, " Oh, how I should like to see the world! It is very dreary living in this green field, and always having the same thing over and over again."

" My dear," answered his wife, " it is a dangerous world beyond the green fields, where all manner of strange things dwell, and two-footed animals lie in wait to gobble you up. *I* do not want to leave my little burrow."

And Brer Rabbit's wife tucked herself up in her little bed and went to sleep."

But Brer Rabbit kept thinking and thinking, and longing and longing to go beyond the green field in which he had his home; and one morning he popped out of his hole and ran away.

Over the fields he went, faster and faster. On the way he passed whole families of rabbits, and when they called after him, " Where are you going to, Brer Rabbit? " never a word he answered.

At last Brer Rabbit began to feel tired. It was long since he had left his home, and he had travelled many, many miles, and now felt very hungry.

" I wonder where I could get something to eat," he said to himself.

But he looked about in vain. Not a blade of nice sweet grass could he see anywhere, and he began to feel very sad.

" Oh, what shall I do ? " thought poor Brer Rabbit. " How I wish I had never left my nice home ! "

But now he was too tired to go back ; and

even if he would, he could not go, for, in his haste, he had not noticed by which way he had come.

Just then he spied a box with a lot of straw in it.

" Ah," said Brer Rabbit, " this looks a nice quiet bed. I will just pop in here and have a good sleep."

So in he popped, and curled himself up in the corner, and soon fell fast asleep.

Brer Rabbit must have been sleeping for a long time when he awoke with a start.

And what do you think had happened ?

Some one had put a chair inside the box and packed it in with more straw, and now the lid was being hammered on, and poor Brer Rabbit was too terrified to move. There he was held fast in a prison, and no one to let him out.

" Oh dear, *dear* me ! " wailed Brer Rabbit. " If only I had taken my wife's advice and never left my home ! "

But Brer Rabbit wailed in vain, for never an answer was there to his cry.

Presently Brer Rabbit felt the box being lifted and put into a train. Then the door was shut, the whistle blown, and away he went, far across the country to a strange land.

Brer Rabbit shivered and shook with fright, and he got so ill with hunger that he was forced to eat the hard, coarse straw. How he longed for some green grass and a nice cool drink !

After many hours the train stopped and the box was taken out ; then it was put into a van and taken to a big shop in a town. There, with poor Brer Rabbit still in it, the box was put into a dark cellar.

After a time a man came to the box and took off the lid ; then he took out the chair.

" I am lost now," said Brer Rabbit, " for surely this is a two-footed animal come to gobble me up."

So he huddled himself up in the corner ; but it was so dark in the cellar that the man never saw him, and he took the chair away, and left Brer Rabbit all alone, and *the lid off the box*.

" Now," said Brer Rabbit, " I am at least free of this box, but I will just wait awhile before I pop out in case any one should come in and see me."

So he waited till all was quiet, and then popped out of his prison. Oh, how weak and ill he did feel! He could scarcely hop round the floor. He looked all over for something to eat, and found some crumbs, but no water to drink.

So Brer Rabbit stayed there all that night, and the next day, until he was almost dead and had lost count of time.

. . .

" O sir," said Bob, the errand boy, to his master, " there is a great big rat in the cellar. I have never seen such a big one before, and I am almost afraid of it."

" I will come and see," said the master. And off he went with Bob to the cellar.

Bob opened the door and peeped in.

" It is still there," said he.

" Let *me* look," exclaimed the master, and he too peeped in at the door. " Why," he said, " that is not a rat ; it is a *wild rabbit*."

Bob's eyes nearly dropped out with surprise. And no wonder, for here was poor Brer Rabbit sitting in the corner, too weak and ill to run away.

" Now," he thought, " I must surely die, for I am caught at last."

But Bob's master was a kind man, and he loved animals very much.

He took Brer Rabbit up in his arms, gave him some milk to drink and biscuits to eat, and then put him into a warm basket and took him home for his children to look at.

That same day they took Brer Rabbit away into the country, and put him down in a lovely green field, and gave him his freedom.

CHRISTMAS PIES

A Christmas Fantasy

By Anne M. Trotman

Dame Alice is asleep. A crowd of children steal into her bedroom, saying :

Children. It's Christmas Day, and we want some pies. Here's Dame Alice. She knows how to cook pies, but she's asleep. Let's wake her up. We'll sing to her.

[*They sing*]. Dame, get up and bake our pies.

(*Songtime.* Martin Shaw and Percy Dearmer.)

[*Dame Alice wakes.*]

A Merry Christmas, Dame Alice. We want some pies.

Dame Alice. Certainly you shall have some pies, but you must help me make them.

Children. We shall love to do that.

Dame Alice. You shall sing some pies. Be little Jack Horners, and you can have a pie at once.

[*She waves a magic spoon, and they all become Jack Horners.*]

Children [*sing*]. Little Jack Horner sat in a corner, etc.

Dame Alice. That was a nice pie, wasn't it ? Now for a walk to meet the Pieman. Simple Simons, every one of you !

[*Again she waves her spoon over them all, and they begin to walk towards the Pieman, who comes shouting.*]

Pieman. Pies all hot—hot pies—a penny for a pie—pies all hot.

[*Children and Pieman sing their parts in " Simple Simon met a Pieman."*]

Children. Simple Simon met a pieman
Going to the fair ;
Says Simple Simon to the pieman,
Let me taste your ware.

Pieman. Says the Pieman to Simple Simon,
Show me first your penny ;

Children. Says Simple Simon to the Pieman,
Sir, we have not any.

Pieman. No pennies—no pies. Off you go.

[*Children go back to Dame Alice, while Pieman goes on crying his pies.*]

Children. Dame Alice, we hadn't any pennies.

Dame Alice. No pennies on Christmas Day ! What a shame ! Here—catch !

[*She scatters imaginary pennies amongst them. The children march back to the Pieman, singing and holding up their pennies, after the last line of their song to " Sir, we have a penny."*]

Pieman. If you have a penny, you can have a pie. [*He throws sweets for pies, for which the Children scramble.*]

[*The Children, eating their pies, go back to Dame Alice.*]

Dame Alice. Well, children, what did you think of those pies ?

Children. Very good pies. Very good pies indeed.

Dame Alice. If you want any more pies, you must turn into pussy cats. [*She waves her spoon, counting*.] One—two—three. [*The Children turn into pussy cats*.] I am your mother. [*She waves the spoon over herself*.]

[*Children and Dame Alice say their parts in :*]

Children. Three little kittens they lost their mittens,
And they began to cry.
Oh, mother dear, see here, see here,
For we have lost our mittens.

Dame Alice. Lost your mittens, you naughty kittens !
Then you shall have no pie.

Children. Miou ! Miou !
Dame Alice. No, you shall have no pie.

Children. Three little kittens they found their mittens,
And they began to cry,
Oh, mother dear, see here, see here,
For we have found our mittens.

Dame Alice. Found your mittens, you darling kittens !
Then you shall have some pie.

Children. Purr—purr—purr !
Dame Alice. Yes, you shall have some pie.

[*Dame Alice throws biscuits amongst them for pies.*] That's enough pie for one day. Now back again into good little children. [*She waves her spoon for the last time, and the Children sit up on the floor. Dame Alice looks at the clock.*] Why, it's only seven o'clock, and breakfast is at nine. I'm going to sleep again.

Children. Let's sing her to sleep. [*They sing.*]

Dame got up and baked her pies,
Baked her pies, baked her pies,
Dame got up and baked her pies,
On Christmas Day in the morning.

[*Then, all standing, they say very softly.*]

Hush—she's going to sleep again,
Sleep again, sleep again,
Hush, she's going to sleep again,
On Christmas Day in the morning.

[*The Children go off humming, more and more faintly, until all sound dies away.*]

MARKET SQUARE

By A. A. Milne

I had a penny,
A bright new penny,
I took my penny
  To the market square.
I wanted a rabbit,
A little brown rabbit,
And I looked for a rabbit
  'Most everywhere.

For I went to the stall where they sold sweet lavender.
(" *Only a penny for a bunch of lavender!* ")
" Have you got a rabbit? 'cos I don't want lavender."
But they hadn't got a rabbit, not anywhere there.

I had a penny,
And I had another penny,
I took my pennies
  To the market square.
I did want a rabbit,
A little baby rabbit,
And I looked for rabbits
  'Most everywhere.

And I went to the stall were they sold fresh
mackerel.
(" *Now then! Tuppence for a fresh-caught mackerel!* ")
" Have you got a rabbit? 'cos I don't like
mackerel."
But they hadn't got a rabbit, not anywhere there.

I found a sixpence,
A little white sixpence,
I took it in my hand
To the market square.
I was buying my rabbit
(I do like rabbits);
And I looked for my rabbit
'Most everywhere.

So I went to the stall where they sold fine saucepans.
(" *Walk up, walk up! Sixpence for a saucepan!* ")
" Could I have a rabbit? 'cos we've got two saucepans."
But they hadn't got a rabbit, not anywhere there.

I had nuffin',
No, I hadn't got nuffin',
So I didn't go down
To the market square;
But I walked on the common,
The old-gold common . . .
And I saw little rabbits
'Most everywhere.

So I'm sorry for the people who sell fine saucepans,
I'm sorry for the people who sell fresh mackerel,
I'm sorry for the people who sell sweet lavender,
'Cos they haven't got a rabbit, not anywhere there.

By Dorothy Russell

" WHAT are you going to give baby brother ? " asked Mummy. " He will be a year old to-morrow."

The twins looked at one another across the breakfast table.

" We must look in our money boxes first," said Jack wisely, " and then decide."

" Yes," nodded Daisy, who always agreed with everything Jack suggested. " We must look in our money boxes first."

Directly breakfast was over the twins scampered upstairs and turned the money boxes upside down on the floor.

Only four pennies and four halfpennies !

" Not much," said Jack sadly ; " but we could get those chocolate pigs for threepence each. I think Baby would like those chocolate pigs."

Daisy clapped her hands. " If I were baby brother I would love chocolate pigs," she said decidedly.

So Mummy's advice was asked, and the twins were allowed to run round to the little sweet-shop at the corner of the street and buy the chocolate pigs.

Jack insisted on two separate paper bags, and the pigs were put away in a top drawer in their bedroom all ready for the next morning.

That night, after Mummy had said " good-night " and turned out the light, Jack suddenly remembered the chocolate pigs, and grew so hungry he could not go to sleep.

" Daisy," he whispered, " shall we give one chocolate pig to baby brother, and just taste the other one to see how nice it is ? "

Daisy sat up in bed. " O-o-o ! Jack, shall we ? " she asked. " I'm awfully hungry," she added coaxingly.

Jack needed no further encouragement. He was out of bed in less than a minute, and in less than five minutes the chocolate pig had disappeared !

" That was your chocolate pig," said naughty Jack, while Daisy was still licking her sticky fingers. Daisy began to cry.

" So p'r'aps we had better eat mine to make it fair," he added quickly, hoping to console her.

The second pig proved just as nice as the first one, and disappeared just as quickly, and then two greedy little people fell asleep.

But next morning Mummy was wakened by

loud and despairing cries, followed by a knock on her door, and two little figures flung themselves on to her bed.

" We has no chocolate pigs for baby brother," sobbed Daisy.

" We've ate them bofe," explained Jack sadly.

Of course Mummy was very much shocked and surprised. " You are two greedy little pigs," she said gravely ; " but luckily baby brother is too young to understand how unkind you have been. The only thing you can do now is to give him one of your own toys."

The twins looked very much ashamed of themselves, and heartily wished they had never *seen* the chocolate pigs. But as for baby brother, he was quite pleased with a small ball and a tiny Teddy Bear instead.

JACK SEEKS HIS FORTUNE

Retold by Louie Chisholm

ONCE upon a time there was a boy named Jack, and one morning he set out to seek his fortune.

He had not gone very far before he met a cat.

"Where are you going, Jack?" said the cat.

"I am going to seek my fortune."

"May I go with you?"

"Yes," said Jack; "the more the merrier."

So on they went, jiggelty-jolt, jiggelty-jolt.

They went a little farther, and they met a dog.

"Where are you going, Jack?" said the dog.

"I am going to seek my fortune."

"May I go with you?"

"Yes," said Jack; "the more the merrier."

So on they went, jiggelty-jolt, jiggelty-jolt.

They went a little farther, and they met a goat.

"Where are you going, Jack?" said the goat.

"I am going to seek my fortune."

" May I go with you ? "

" Yes," said Jack ; " the more the merrier."

So on they went, jiggelty-jolt, jiggelty-jolt.

They went a little farther, and they met a bull.

" Where are you going, Jack ? " said the bull.

" I am going to seek my fortune."

" May I go with you ? "

" Yes," said Jack ; " the more the merrier."

So on they went, jiggelty-jolt, jiggelty-jolt.

They went a little farther, and they met a cock.

" Where are you going, Jack ? " said the cock.

" I am going to seek my fortune."

" May I go with you ? "

" Yes," said Jack ; " the more the merrier."

So on they went, jiggelty-jolt, jiggelty-jolt.

Well, they went on till it was almost dark, and they began to think of some place where they could spend the night.

About this time they came in sight of a house, and Jack told them to keep still while he went up and looked in through the window. And there were some robbers there counting over their money.

Jack went back and told them to wait till he gave the word, and then to make all the noise they could. So when they were all ready, Jack gave the word.

And the cat mewed, and the dog barked, and the goat bleated, and the bull bellowed, and the cock crowed, and they made such a dreadful noise that the robbers all ran away.

Then they went in and took up their abode in the house. But Jack was afraid the robbers would come back in the night.

So, when it was time to go to bed, he put the cat in the rocking-chair, and he put the dog under the table, and he put the goat upstairs, and he put the bull down in the cellar, and the cock flew up on to the roof, and Jack went to bed.

By-and-by the robbers saw it was all dark, and they sent one man to the house to look after their money. Before long he came back in a great fright, and told them his story.

" I crept back to the house," said he, " and went in and tried to sit down in the rocking-chair, and there was an old woman knitting, and she stuck her knitting-needles into me." That, of course, was the cat.

" I went to the table to look after the money,

and there was a cobbler under the table, and he stuck his awl into me." That, of course, was the dog.

" I was on my way upstairs, and there was a man up there threshing, and he knocked me down with his flail." That, of course, was the goat.

" I found my way to the cellar, and there was a man down there chopping wood, and he knocked me with his axe." That, of course, was the bull.

" But I should not have minded all that if it had not been for the little fellow on the top of the house, who kept calling, ' Toss him up to me-e ! Toss him up to me-e ! ' " That, of course, was the cock-a-doodle-doo.

THE THREE BEARS

A Play

By E. Harcourt Williams

CHARACTERS

Big Bear.
Middle-size Bear.
Little Bear.
Goldylocks.

The front of the stage is the Three Bears' kitchen. A fireplace ; a low table ; three chairs—big, middle-size, and little. In a recess at the back are three beds —big, middle-size, and little. By the side of the last is a night-light, which is the only light on the stage.

In the beds are the Three Bears. Some one is snoring. A cock crows. Big Bear grunts. Middle-size Bear turns over.

Little Bear. May I talk now ?

Big Bear [*grumpily*]. Go to sleep.

Middle Bear. Sh ! Sh ! Sh ! Daddy's very tired.

Little Bear. It must be sunrise time. I heard cock-a-doodle.

Big Bear. Nothing of the kind.

[*The cock crows again.*]

Big Bear. Ahem ! I suppose I had better get up and light the copper. [*Growls.*]

Middle Bear. Shall I do it ?

Big Bear [*rolling out*]. Certainly not.

Middle Bear. Then I'll see about the breakfast. Little Bear, draw the curtains.

[*Little Bear leaps out of bed and lets in the bright sunlight. Big Bear goes off, yawning*.]

Middle Bear. Come along, Little Bear. [*She proceeds to sponge Little Bear in a large brown basin on the floor*.]

Little Bear. Oh ! Oh ! Oh ! It's cold. No, not my ears ; you did those yesterday.

Middle Bear. Now, then, there's my brave Bruin.

Little Bear. Poohoo ! I'm not a brave Bruin.

Middle Bear [*drying him with a big towel*]. What are you, then ?

Little Bear. Little Bear.

Middle Bear. Now finish drying while I brush your hair. [*She gives him a ribbon*.] There. That's right. Now, do you tie on your ribbon while I see to the porridge ; then, if you're good, you can help lay the table.

[*Little Bear sits dreamily on the bed. Big Bear comes in with dry sticks, etc., to light fire*.]

Middle Bear [*stirs porridge with big spoon*]. Oh, this is much too thick. Little Bear, draw me some water from the pump.

Little Bear [*starting from his daydream*]. I'm not dressed yet. I can't find my ribbon.

Middle Bear. Oh, what a dreamy cub it is ! Why, there it is in your hand.

Little Bear. Oh, so it is. [*He tries, laboriously, to tie it round his neck.*]

Big Bear [*puffing at the fire with his mouth*]. Farmer [*puff puff*] Cornflour's sheep [*puff puff*] have been in the garden again [*puff puff*]. That's the second time the gate has been left open. [*He gets up for the bellows, and meets Little Bear.*] Now, who could have done that, I wonder?

Little Bear. *I* didn't, really!

Big Bear. Well, they've eaten all the young brussels sprouts plants this time, and [*very impressively*] if they go on getting in, we shall have no more vegetables, and, in consequence, we shall have no more of Middle-sized Bear's delicious vegetable pies, and as we subsist chiefly on fine vegetables, we shall get thinner and thinner, AND THINNER, and when Mother Hubbard goes to the cupboard it will be BARE!

Little Bear [*really alarmed*]. How horrible!

Middle Bear. I don't think it was Little Bear this time, because I went out last thing to see that the gate was properly latched.

Big Bear. Well, off you go and get the water.

[*He bellows Little Bear away, then bellows fire. Little Bear picks up big jug and swings it absently as he goes.*]

Big Bear. Hold it steady !

[*Exit Little Bear, holding jug very primly*.]

Middle Bear. I can't help thinking that some one comes and undoes the gate on purpose. [*She spreads cloth*.]

Big Bear [*amazed*]. What an idea ! When we are such friends with all the neighbours ?

Middle Bear. Well, you mark my words !

[*Little Bear bursts in with the jug of water*.]

Little Bear. Look what I found by the pump ! [*He holds up a pair of mittens*.]

Middle Bear [*triumphant*]. What did I tell you ?

Big Bear. Well, I never !

Little Bear. What are they ?

Middle Bear. I'm sure I couldn't say.

Big Bear. Let me have a look at them. Where are my spectacles ?

Middle Bear. I put them away safely last night, so that they shouldn't be broken.

[*Big Bear puts spectacles on*.]

Big Bear. Ah ! Yes ! Ahem ! They might be a kind of purse, only they have so many holes.

Little Bear. Stockings sometimes have holes.

Middle Bear [*taking one and trying it on*]. Or a garment for keeping the nose warm.

Big Bear [*regarding her*]. Ah ! an excellent device.

Little Bear [*taking the other*]. Or for keeping the paws warm. [*He slips it on*.]

Middle Bear. Why, bless the child, that's it.

They're mittens. [*Turning with rapture to Big Bear.*] Oh, isn't he clever !

Big Bear. To be sure ; and now I come to think of it, I have seen such garments on Farmer Cornflour's daughter.

Little Bear. Goldylocks !

Big Bear. She wears them on the things she has for paws. So she is the culprit !

Middle Bear. Bless me, I forgot the porridge ! [*She dashes to it.*]

Little Bear. Is it breakfast time ?

Big Bear. Come along. Breakfast !

Middle Bear [*pours porridge into bowls*]. Mind your fingers, darling.

Big Bear. Sit down now, sit down. You in your little chair, Little Bear. Here's a cushion for you in your middle-size chair, dear ! I don't like cushions in my big chair.

Little Bear. Oh, I've burnt my mouth !

Middle Bear. That was greedy, Little Bear. The porridge is very hot.

Big Bear. You should take a little carefully from the side and blow upon it, thus, before putting it into the mouth.

Big Bear [*he burns his mouth*]. Oh ! it is—extremely—warm.

Middle Bear. I *am* so sorry. Shall we go for a little stroll in the wood until it has cooled ?

Big Bear. A very sensible suggestion. Maybe we shall find some beech nuts.

Little Bear [*thoughtfully*]. I suppose we could never find a bun ?

Middle Bear [*tying on a bonnet*]. Get your hat, darling, and your goloshes.

[*Big Bear puts his hat on, and takes stick.*]

Middle Bear. Do put your woollen scarf on, Big Bear.

Big Bear. Perhaps it would be wise.

[*Middle Bear wraps scarf round him.*]

Little Bear [*running about disconsolately*]. Has anybody seen my hat ?

Big Bear. It's probably where you put it.

Little Bear. Where's that ?

Big Bear. Ask your mother. [*Exit Big Bear.*]

Little Bear. Oh, I know ! I left it on the bee-hive.

Middle Bear. Wait a minute. You haven't put your goloshes on.

Little Bear. Oh dear ! [*He struggles into them.*] Do help me. I *can't* get them on.

Middle Bear. Oh, what a cub it is ! [*Leaning out of the window.*] Shall I close the casement and lock the door ?

Big Bear [*putting his head in*]. Why, dear ? Nobody's going to meddle with us.

Middle Bear. Ah ! that's your good heart. You never suspect any one. [*Going to Little Bear's rescue.*] Here, come along ! Now, off you go !

[*They go out together. The Three Bears can be heard singing a song as they walk away*]—

There were three jovial Bruins,
I have heard them say,
That they would go a-hunting
Upon Saint David's Day.
Etc.

[*Goldylocks puts her head in through the window.*]

Goldylocks. What a dear little house! I have often wanted to see inside it. I wonder if the door is open. [*She disappears, and presently comes in through the door.*] I wonder who lives here? [*Looking about.*] I wish I could find my mittens. I left them in the garden last night—oh, porridge! Doesn't it smell good! I'm very hungry. I suppose I mustn't taste—just a drip, about so big. I will take it out of this big bowl. Ugh—that's too hot. What about this? [*Tries middle-size bowl.*] No, that's too cold. [*Tries little bowl.*] But this little bowl is just right. It's lovely—I must have a wee bit more, just another half spoonful. Oh, it is good!

There! I've eaten it all up! Now I think I will have a little rest before I start home. This fine big handsome chair will do. Oh! it *is* hard. Perhaps this one will be more comfortable. No. It's much too soft. Look at that weeny-teeny little one. I'm sure that will be just right—and so it is! It's a darling little chair. Oh! Oh! Oh! [*She falls through the bottom.*] Oh! I have broken it. What a pity! Well, I *must* rest somewhere. Suppose I try the bedroom. [*She goes up stage to where the beds are.*] This big bed looks inviting. [*She gets in.*] Oh dear! This is much too high. I feel as if I were sleeping on a mountain. [*She gets into the next bed.*] How very provoking! This is much too low. Whoever heard of sleeping on the floor? That would never do. I had better see what the little one is like with the crazy coverlet. Oh! Oh! Oh! How cozy! It's like my very own bed at home. I mustn't really go to sleep, but I might just close my eyes—just pretend. [*She drops off to sleep.*]

[*The Bears are heard coming near, singing the same song. Big Bear comes in humming, unwraps himself.*]

Little Bear. I am hungry.

Middle Bear. Now, my dear, do hang your hat up in its proper place.

Little Bear. And tired.

Big Bear. Who's been meddling with my porridge?

Middle Bear. Who's been meddling with my porridge ?

Little Bear. Who's been meddling with my porridge and eaten it all up ? [*He bursts into tears*.]

Middle Bear. There, never mind, my darling, you shall have some of mine. [*She gives some out of her bowl*.]

Big Bear. Bless my fur, who's been sitting in my chair ?

Middle Bear. Well, I never did ! Who's been sitting in my chair ?

Little Bear. And who's been sitting in my chair and has sat the bottom out of it ?

Big Bear. This is getting serious. We must look farther.

Middle Bear. Indeed, we must !

Big Bear. Where are my spectacles ?

[*They hunt about for them*.]

Little Bear. Why, there they are !

Big Bear. Where ?

Little Bear. You've got them on.

[*They then hunt for the intruder*.]

Big Bear. Bear's grease and honey-pots ! Who's been lying in my bed ?

Middle Bear. Clothes-pegs and wash-tubs ! Who's been lying in my bed ?

Little Bear. Baa-lambs and sugar-sticks ! Who's been lying in my bed—and oh ! here she is.

Goldylocks [*sitting up and rubbing her eyes*]. Is it time to get up ?

Middle Bear. Time to get up indeed !

Big Bear. Is there anything we can do for you ?

Goldylocks [*seeing Bears*]. Oh dear ! oh dear ! I beg your pardon. I have no wish to intrude. [*Tumbles out of bed.*] Good afternoon !

[*Little Bear stops her.*]

Little Bear. Please don't go.

Goldylocks. Please let me go, and I'll never come in without knocking again. Please, little Mr. Bear. I think you are very good and kind—really I do. [*Seeing mittens on his paws.*] Why, those are my mittens ! Do please give them back to me.

Big Bear. Then you, madam, are the culprit ?

Middle Bear. It was you who left the gate open.

Big Bear. So that the sheep got in.

Middle Bear. And ate up all the brussels sprouts.

Goldylocks. Oh ! I am so very, very, very sorry.

Big Bear. So am I.

Middle Bear. He is very fond of brussels sprouts.

Little Bear [*suddenly*]. Then you must be Goldylocks.

Goldylocks. Yes, I'm Goldylocks.

Little Bear. Oh, Daddy, do ask her to stay to breakfast.

Goldylocks [*embarrassed*]. I'm afraid I have had my breakfast.

Little Bear. Couldn't we have bread and honey instead ?

Goldylocks. But your chair ?

Middle Bear. You can have my cushion to cover the hole.

Little Bear. No, Goldylocks can have my chair. I'll use the three-legged stool.

Goldylocks. Oh, how kind you all are !

Big Bear. No, no. Not at all. We are just three ordinary bears, who like to be pleasant and agreeable to our neighbours.

Middle Bear. Even though we don't understand their ways. Come along, children [*politely*], will you take a little more porridge ?

Goldylocks. Yes, please.

Middle Bear. Little Bear, fetch the honey.

[*Little Bear staggers to the table with a huge pot.*]

Big Bear. Yes, open the honey-pot.

[*Little Bear brings his spoon down with a crash on the paper covering, which goes off with a loud report. At the same moment a May Day chorus is heard off.*]

Little Bear. Rabbits !

Goldylocks. Why do you say " Rabbits " ?

Little Bear. It's the first of May.

Goldylocks. May Day ! How could I forget,

and I'm to be the May Queen. That's my Mummy, I expect, come to fetch me.

[*Enter Mummy with a company of girls, and garlands and crown, singing a May Day carol. They crown Goldylocks, and all join in a dance—or perhaps breakfast.*]

CURTAIN

THE LAUGHING DRAGON

By Richard Wilson

THERE was once a king who had a very loud voice, and three sons.

His voice was *very* loud. It was so loud that when he spoke every one jumped. So they called the country he ruled over by the name of Jumpy.

But one day the king spoke in a very low voice indeed. And all the people ran about and said, " The King is going to die."

He *was* going to die, and he *did* die. But before he died he called his three sons to his bedside. He gave one half of Jumpy to the eldest son ; and he gave the other half to the second son. Then he said to the third, " You shall have six shillings and eightpence farthing and the small bag in my private box."

In due time the third son got his six shillings and eightpence farthing, and put it safely away into his purse.

Then he got the bag from the King's private box. It was a small bag made of kid, and was tied with a string.

The third son, whose name, by the way, was Tumpy, untied the string and looked into the bag. It had nothing in it but a very queer smell. Tumpy sniffed and then he sneezed. Then he laughed, and laughed, and laughed again without in the least knowing what he was laughing at.

"I shall never stop laughing," he said to himself. But he did, after half an hour and two minutes exactly. Then he smiled for three minutes and a half exactly again.

After that he looked very happy; and he kept on looking so happy that people called him Happy Tumpy, or H.T. for short.

Next day H.T. set out to seek his fortune. He had tied up the bag again and put it into the very middle of his bundle.

His mother gave him some bread and a piece of cheese, two apples and a banana. Then he set out with a happy face. He whistled as he went along with his bundle on a stick over his shoulder.

After a time he was tired, and sat down on a large milestone. As he was eating an apple, a black cat came along. It rubbed its side against the large stone, and H.T. stroked its head.

Then it sniffed at the bundle that lay on the grass. Next it sneezed, and then it began to laugh. It looked so funny that H.T. began to laugh too.

"You must come with me, puss," said H.T. The cat was now smiling broadly. It looked up at H.T. and he fed it. Then they went on side by side.

By-and-by H.T. and the cat came to a town, and met a tall, thin man. "Hallo," he said, and H.T. said the same.

" Where are you going ? " asked the man.

" To seek my fortune," said H.T.

" I would give a small fortune to the man who could make me laugh."

" Why ? " said H.T.

" Because I want to be fat," said the man, " and people always say ' laugh and grow fat.' "

" How much will you give ? " said H.T.

" Oh, five shillings and twopence halfpenny anyhow," said the man.

H.T. put down his bundle and took out his bag. He held it up near the man's face and untied the string. The man sniffed and then he sneezed. Then he laughed for half an hour and two minutes. Next he smiled for three minutes and a half.

By that time he was quite fat. So he paid H.T. five shillings and twopence halfpenny. Then he went on his way with a smile and a wave of the hand.

" That is good," said H.T. " If I go on like this I shall soon make my fortune." He tied up his bag and went on again. The black cat walked after him with a smile on its face that never came off.

After an hour the two companions came to another town. There were a lot of men in the street, but no women, or boys, or girls. The men looked much afraid. H.T. went up to one of them, " Why do you look so much afraid ? " he asked politely.

" You will look afraid too, very soon," said the man. " The great dragon is coming again. It comes to the town each day, and takes a man and a cheese. In ten minutes it will be here."

" Why don't you fight it ? " asked H.T. " It is too big and fierce," said the man. " If any man could kill it he would make his fortune." " How is that ? " said H.T. " Well," said the man, " the King would give him a bag of gold, and make the princess marry him."

All at once H.T. heard a loud shout.

" The dragon is coming ! " called a man who wore a butcher's apron. Then he ran into his shop, banged the door, and threw a large piece of meat out of the window. There was now nothing in the street but H.T., the cat, and the piece of meat.

H.T. did not run away, not even when he saw

the huge dragon come lumbering up the street on all fours. It crept along, and turned its head this way and that. Its face had a terrible look.

Fire came out of its nose when it blew out. And three of the houses began to burn. Then it came to the meat. It sniffed it and stopped to eat it. That gave H.T. time for carrying out his plan.

He took out his bag and untied the string. Then he threw it down before the dragon. On it came, blowing more fire from its nostrils. Soon the butcher's shop was burning. There was a noise like the noise from an oven when the meat is roasting.

The dragon still came on. When it got up to the bag it stopped. It sniffed. Then it sneezed so hard that two houses fell down flat. Next it began to laugh, and the noise was so loud that the church steeple fell into the street.

Of course it had stopped to laugh. It sat up on its hind legs and held its sides with its fore-paws. Then it began to smile. And a dragon's smile, you must understand, is about six feet wide!

The dragon looked so jolly that H.T. did not feel afraid of it any more; not in the least. He went up to it and took one of its forepaws into his arm. The cat jumped on the dragon's head. And they all went along the street as jolly as sand-boys.

A woman popped her head out of a high window. " Take the first to the right," she said, " and the second to the left. Then you will come to the King's royal palace. You cannot miss it."

" Thank you very much," said H.T. ; and he and the dragon and the cat smiled up at her. H.T. waved his hand. The dragon waved its other forepaw. And the cat waved its tail.

So they went on—down one street and then another. At last they came to a big, open, green space in which stood a big palace. It had a wall round it with four large gates in it. At each gate there was a sentry box. But not one sentry could be seen.

H.T., with his friend the dragon, came smiling up to one of the gates. Above the gate H.T. saw some one peeping over the wall. " He wears a crown," he said to the dragon, " so it must be the King." The dragon kept on smiling.

" Hallo ! " cried the King. " What do *you* want ? "

" Hallo ! " cried H.T. " I want the bag of gold and the princess."

" But you have not killed the dragon," said the King.

" I should think not," said H.T. " Why, he is my friend. He is my very dear friend. He will not do any harm now. Look at him."

The King stood up and put his crown straight. It had fallen over one eye in his fright. The

R.S.GERVIS

dragon went on smiling in a sleepy way. There was no fire in his nose now.

"But," said the King. "How do I know he will not begin to kill people again?"

"Well," said H.T., "we will make a big kennel for him and give him a silver chain. Each day I will give him a sniff from my empty bag. Then he will be happy all day and go to sleep every night."

"Very well," said the King. "Here is the bag of gold. You will find the princess in the laundry. She always irons my collars. And you can have my crown as well. It is very hard and heavy. I do not want to be King any more. I only want to sit by the fire and have a pipe and play the gramophone."

So he threw his crown down from the wall. The dragon caught it on his tail and put it on H.T.'s head. Then H.T. went to the laundry and married the princess right away.

And the dragon lived happy ever after; and so did the cat; and so did everybody else, at least until they died.

I ought to tell you that King H.T. used the bag all his life to keep the dragon laughing. He died at the age of 301 years, one month, a week, and two days.

The next day the dragon took a very hard sniff at the bag. And he laughed so much that he *died* of laughing.

So they gave the bag to the dentist. And when any one had to have a tooth out he took a sniff. Then he laughed so much that he did not feel any pain. And when the tooth was out he was happy ever after, or at least until the next time he ate too many sweets.

CHOOSING SHOES

By Ffrida Wolfe

New shoes, new shoes,
Red and pink and blue shoes;
Tell me, what would *you* choose
  If they'd let us buy?

Buckle shoes, bow shoes,
Pretty pointy-toe shoes,
Strappy, cappy low shoes;
  Let's have some to try.

Bright shoes, white shoes,
Dandy dance-by-night shoes,
Perhaps a-little-tight shoes;
  Like some? So would I.

BUT

Flat shoes, fat shoes,
Stump-along-like-that shoes,
Wipe-them-on-the-mat shoes,
 Oh, that's the sort they'll buy.

THE CONCERT

By " Brown Linnet "

(From *Why-why and Tom-cat*)

[The book from which this story is taken is all about the adventures of a little girl whose real name was Elizabeth, but her cat, who could speak, called her Why-why, because she was always asking questions. Tom-cat taught Why-why how to speak to the other animals, and to understand what they said.]

" I HAVE got a treat for you," said Tom-cat. " Would you like to go to a concert ? "

" Oh yes, I should very much indeed," cried Why-why.

" Very well ; the birds are going to give one under the beech tree this afternoon, at three o'clock, and I thought you would like to go, and so I got you a ticket—here it is," and he handed Why-why a beech leaf.

" Is this a ticket ? " said Why-why. " It looks like a leaf."

" It is a leaf," answered Tom-cat, " and it gives you leave to go to the birds' concert."

" Are you going too ? " asked Why-why.

Tom-cat looked funny.

" Nobody would sing if I was there," he said. " They would all be looking at me, and—talking about me."

"Then I think you had better not come," said Why-why. She put the leaf in a flower-pot to keep it safe until three o'clock; and then she put on her best frock and hat, and her new gloves. The frock was white, with pretty white daisies worked all round it, and there was a little pocket in it just big enough to hold the ticket.

Tom-cat looked quite astonished when she came out into the garden.

"Is it Sunday?" he asked.

"No, you silly Tom-cat—but I'm going to the concert; don't you remember?"

"Oh yes!" said Tom-cat. "I hope you'll enjoy yourself. Madam Nightingale is to be the 'prima donna.'"

"What is a 'prima donna'?" asked Why-why.

"It is the most important singer at the concert," answered Tom-cat. "They are always called Madam. The prima donna that you will hear to-day is really a gentleman bird, but they think it sounds well to call him 'Madam Nightingale.'"

"I see," said Why-why; then she said good-bye to Tom-cat, and walked across the lawn to the beech tree in a very slow, grown-up way, because she felt rather nice and grand in her best frock.

The concert had not begun; but there was a great chatting in the tree, and when Why-why arrived a big black bird flew down and made her a low bow.

"We are charmed to see you," he said in a

loud, hoarse voice. " I am Mr. Rook, the conductor."

" I'm very pleased to see you too," said Why-why; " but, please, will you say what a ' conductor ' is ? "

" A conductor is a *very* important person at a concert," said Mr. Rook. " He keeps time, and won't allow anybody to do anything if he doesn't want them to. Will you kindly take a seat on the lawn ? This big branch is going to be the platform—and now we will begin."

He flew up on to the branch, and Why-why sat down on the lawn, and struggled and struggled to get the little leaf out of her pocket, because it was her ticket, you know. When she had got it out she put it on the grass beside her.

" Silence ! " said Mr. Rook, and all the little birds in the tree stopped talking.

Mr. Rook made Why-why a grand bow.

" I regret to announce

that Madam Nightingale is unable to be present, owing to indisposition," he said. Then he sat quite still and stared at Why-why.

" Please, what does that mean ? " asked Why-why.

" It means that she is not coming," answered Mr. Rook.

" Oh," said Why-why. " What a pity that is ! "

" Our friend, Speckled Thrush, has very kindly consented to fill the vacancy," said the rook.

" What does that mean ? " asked Why-why.

" It means that he is going to sing instead," answered Mr. Rook. Then he hopped to one side, and the thrush flew down from above and settled himself in the middle of the branch which was the platform. He was not nearly so big as Mr. Rook, and he was very beautiful. He sat quite still for a moment, puffing out his soft creamy breast, which was all spotted with black, like the inside of a foxglove ; then he opened his beak and began to sing the song of the cherry tree. His song was all about the way the cherries came, how they were " white—white—white," when they were only little flowers, and how they all grew into juicy red cherries, and each verse ended up with :

"Cherry-dew—cherry-dew—cherry-dew!"

When the song was finished Why-why clapped her hands; and all the little birds fluttered their wings with pleasure.

Then Mr. Rook hopped forward again.

"Song by the tom-tits, entitled 'Dear Father, come Home.'"

Then four tiny birds perched themselves in a row on the branch. They had little yellow pinafores on in front; their backs were green, and their wings were blue, and so were the little caps on their heads.

Why-why could not help smiling at them, because they looked such darlings.

So they began to sing, and this is what they sang: "Hi—daddy, dear; hi! daddy, dear—hi! daddy, dear!"

They sang with great expression—that is to say, they sang as if they thought about the words as well as the tune, and they sang so hard that every now and then they hung upside down. They said afterwards that that was the way they got their low notes.

After they had finished, the robin sang. His song was all "trills," and he meant it to give Why-why a creepy crawly feeling down her back—as all good music should. But Robin was rather pleased with himself, and his pretty red waistcoat, and so he rather forgot to think of his words. When he had finished, Mr. Rook came forward again.

" The sparrow chorus will now sing a glee," he said. Then he stepped aside again, and a lot of little brown birds tumbled quickly on to the branch. Some of them had forgotten to brush their hair before they came, and one very thin little one had a feather sticking straight out of his wing, which looked very untidy. They all pushed each other about and fidgeted, as if they did not know how to begin; so Mr. Rook stood close to them and began to wave his beak about. " One, two, three!" he cried; and when he said " three" the untidy little sparrow opened his mouth wide and said " Squark!"

" Hush!" said the others. " You were too soon."

" No, I wasn't!" said the little bird quickly.

" No, he wasn't!" cried two more.

" Yes, he *was*!" shouted all the rest; and then they all began " wasn't," " was," " wasn't," " was," until at last they all fell off the branch together in a mass of brown and grey feathers and naughty squalls. Then the feather in the untidy little sparrow's wing fell out and fluttered down on to Why-why's clean frock.

"Well, never mind, we will go on without them," said Mr. Rook. "My friend, Mr. Bullfinch, will now give us a song."

Mr. Bullfinch was a nice fat little bird with a grey back and rosy breast, and his wings and head were very dark, dark blue, which was almost black. He had a funny hooky beak, not at all like the other birds, and when he sang his voice was very low. He was very shy at first, and turned his back; but by-and-by he forgot everything but the music that he was singing, and he swung about on the bough and bobbed little curtsies, and when he was most excited he screwed his little tail all crooked to one side. Why-why could not quite hear what the words were, but she thought it was something about the little wife and babies at home, and so she clapped very hard when it was finished. After the bullfinch came a starling.

Mr. Rook said that he was a "comic singer," which meant that he was going to be funny; and he put his head on one side and winked at Why-why before he began his song. Why-why thought he was only an ugly brown bird at first, but when the light shone on him she saw that he had all sorts of beautiful purple and green and blue colours in his feathers. He had a long sharp bill, but only a very stumpy little tail, and he wobbled about on the branch just to look funny. Then he began. There was a lot of fast talking in his song, which he explained was "patter" singing, and every now and then he made a long surprised whistle, which made Why-why laugh and laugh until the tears ran down her cheeks. So when the song was ended he had to sing it all over again, which he did not mind in the least. When he had sung it again the skylark came. He had flown all the way from the fields on purpose to sing to Why-why. He was only a little brown bird, but he looked oh, so happy, and this was because the feathers on his head all stood up in a little crest; and when a bird raises its feathers on its head you may be sure it is smiling. He had a speckled breast, and he had a very long back claw on each foot.

"I shall not be able to sit still when I sing," he said to Why-why. "I always want to go up, up; but, if you like, I will try to stay here."

"I should like you to fly up," said Why-why.

So the lark began to sing at once a loud glad song, and as he sang he spread his wide beautiful wings and began to go up, up, up, over the tree, and into the blue sky. He never seemed to want to take breath. On and on he went until Why-why could hear him no longer, and he looked like a little black speck on the blue sky.

"Now," said Mr. Rook, "I must ask Mr. Hedge-sparrow to give us a song."

"I do not like to after the skylark has sung," said the little hedge-sparrow. "My song is so dull."

"But I like dull songs," said Why-why; and so Mr. Hedge-sparrow sang what he knew. It was a very soft, neat little song; but Mr. Robin chose to get huffy.

"That song is like mine, only not *half* so nice," he said.

"That is a pecky thing to say!" said Mr. Rook.

"I don't care," said the robin, and he puffed himself out until he was just like a red and brown ball on two little legs.

"It's a very nice song," said Mr. Rook, "and I shall have it again. En-caw! en-caw!"

"I'll en-caw him!" shrieked the robin, and he spread out his wings and was just going to fly at Mr. Hedge-sparrow and peck him when Tom-cat came walking up, and began looking up very carefully into the tree.

" C-a-aw ! " cried the conductor, and clap, clap, clap, went his wings as he flew away.

" Gu-r-r-r-r ! " called a blackbird, who had not even had time to sing. " Gu-r-r-r-r !—tuck-tuck-tuck ! "

" Whatever *is* the matter ? " said Why-why.

" They are all talking about me," answered Tom-cat. " I told you they would. Tea is ready."

Why-why got up. " Well, I do want my tea," she said ; then she threw away her ticket. " I think I should like to be a bird best of all," she said.

" No, oh no ; you'd better not be that, I think," said Tom-cat quickly. " You must remember the kitten-cat, you know. She does not like—I mean she does like birds."

" Then that is all right," said Why-why.

" Oh, but she is so dreadfully rough with them," said Tom-cat. " She sometimes breaks their wings and bites them, and they get killed."

Why-why sighed. " What would you devise me to be, then ? " she asked.

" I should not advise you to be anything just yet," said Tom-cat. " Wait until Christmas comes."

THE KING AND QUEEN'S DAUGHTER

By Harriet Clark

CHARACTERS

King and Queen.	Courtiers.
Fairy Godmother.	Simple Simon.
Tom the Piper's Son.	Boys and Girls.
Princess.	Boy Blue.
Prince.	Bobby Shafto.

SCENE I

Court of the King of all England. Two thrones [*centre*], *a few chairs or stools to left and right. Courtiers* [*any number, front*] *playing marbles in a group. Ladies* [*any number, back*] *sewing, and quietly singing Nursery Rhymes.*

First Courtier. You're cheating!

Second Courtier. Oh, I'm not. You cheated just now!

First Courtier. I shall tell the King if you talk to me like that, and I shall tell him that when we were playing hop-scotch yesterday—— [*Sound of trumpets, etc., from outside.*] Here comes the King.

[*Courtiers rush to their places, upset the marbles—great scrambling in picking them up. Enter King and Queen, with Ladies and Gentlemen. The Queen sees the marbles, and shakes her finger reprovingly at Courtier who is trying to hide them. The King and Queen are conducted to their thrones, and Court groups itself round them.*]

King. This is a great and solemn occasion.

Simple Simon [*echoes*]. —Solemn occasion.

[*Court frowns.*]

Court [*all together*]. Yes, your Majesty.

King. You all know that when our daughter, the Princess Jane, was six months old, upon the advice of her Fairy Godmother I sent her away to the land of my friend, the King of Hearts, to be brought up as a shepherd's daughter.

Simple Simon. —Brought up as a shepherd's daughter.

Queen. Oh, turn that boy out.

[*Two Courtiers go behind throne towards him.*]

King. The Princess is now seventeen years old, and that is time that all Kings' daughters should be married.

Simple Simon. —Should be married.

[*Courtiers carry him out.*]

King. Last week her Fairy Godmother went to the land of Hearts to see how she is getting on, and——

Third Courtier. Does she know she is a princess, your Majesty?

Queen. Don't interrupt the King!

Voice [*from the door*]. —Interrupt the King!

King. If you'd only be patient, I could get on. She doesn't know she is a princess. The Queen and I, as you know, have been to visit her every year. She knew we were her father and mother, but we always dressed as peasants, so she had no idea we were the King and Queen of all England. When her Fairy Godmother comes back—and I expect her to-day—you shall be told what we intend to do. Now, does any one want to ask any questions? [*Simple Simon here creeps in again.*]

Court Lady. Please, your Majesty, why did her Fairy Godmother want her sent away?

King [*to Queen*]. You tell them, my dear; my throat is quite husky with talking. Bring me my royal throat lozenges.

[*Courtiers exit during Queen's speech, enter with huge tin, and put tablet in King's mouth.*]

Queen. You see, it's like this. We wanted our only child to grow up very kind and good. Her Fairy Godmother said that princesses often grow up very proud and haughty, but that if Jane were brought up by poor people she might be very much nicer; and, indeed, when we saw her three months ago we could not wish for a better girl.

Simple Simon. —For a better girl.

[*All, including King and Queen, rush at him and carry him out. As the Queen is putting the King's crown straight, enter Fairy Godmother.*]

Fairy Godmother. Oh dear, oh dear, what a lot of fuss and noise—this is the very worst behaved Court I know of. Well, well, well, how are you all ?

Queen. Quite well, thank you, Fairy Godmother. The King's toothache was soon cured with the magic spell that you sent last Friday. But, tell us, how is our daughter ?

Fairy Godmother. I saw Old Mother Hubbard last Friday, and told her to pack up her things and bring Jane to live in the little cottage near the palace gates.

King. And when are they coming ?

Fairy Godmother. They came this morning.

King and Queen [*get up*, *crying*]. Our dear daughter !

[*But Fairy Godmother waves her wand, and they are fixed where they stand.*]

Fairy Godmother. Now don't get excited, you know how I hate it. [*Waves wand.*] Sit still and listen.

[*King and Queen return to their thrones, and sit up stiffly. Simple Simon creeps in.*]

King. What are we to do ?

Fairy Godmother. Don't talk. Old Mother Hubbard says that your daughter is always singing something that goes like this. [*Sings* " *Bobby Shafto.*"] Who *is* this Bobby Shafto ?

Queen. We know. Last time we saw her she told me that she loved Bobby Shafto, a sailor boy, whose home was in the village, and that he had promised to marry her when he came home from sea.

Courtiers [*all together*]. A princess can't marry a sailor boy !

Simple Simon. —Marry a sailor boy.

[*Fairy Godmother waves her wand, and he remains fixed to the end of the scene. Laughter from all.*]

King. Now that is where you are all wrong. We decided seventeen years ago that our daughter shall marry just whom she chooses !

[*Exclamations of surprise from all.*]

Queen. Yes, and we shall be quite sure that whoever she marries doesn't want her just because she is a Princess, because no one knows but ourselves, the King of Hearts, and Old Mother Hubbard, who brought her up.

Fairy Godmother. Don't talk such a lot. She is going to live in the cottage here for six months. We shall see then whether she is true to that Bobby Shafto, for there are sure to be many young men here who will want to marry her. Now tell me, before I go, who is that boy there ? [*Pointing to Simple Simon*.]

Queen. That's Simple Simon ; he's the worry of our lives. [*Whole Court sings*.]

Simple Simon went a-fishing for to catch a whale.
All the water he had got was in his mother's
pail.

Simple Simon met a pieman going to the fair.
Says Simple Simon to the pieman, " Let me taste
your ware."

Says the pieman to Simple Simon, " Show me
first your penny."
Says Simple Simon to the pieman, " Indeed, I
have not any."

Fairy Godmother [*laughs*]. Now, Simon, go away and behave yourself. [*Waves wand, and frees him*.]

[*Exit Court in procession, King and Queen leading with Fairy Godmother ; rest follow, leaving Simple Simon alone*.]

Simple Simon [*rubbing his stiff shoulders*]. So Princess Jane may marry whoever she likes. (*Emphatically*.] Ah, I'm not so simple as I look. [*Exit*.]

SCENE II

The Village Green. Six months later. Village boys and girls sitting on the grass.

Girls [*sing*]. Poor Jenny is a-weeping, a-weeping, a-weeping,
Poor Jenny is a-weeping on a bright summer's day.
Boys [*sing*]. Oh pray, what is she weeping for ? etc.
Girls [*sing*]. She's weeping for a sweetheart, etc.

First Boy. I'm sure there's no need for her to weep for a sweetheart ; there's Tom the Piper's Son——

Second Boy. Little Boy Blue——

Third Boy. And the Baker's Man——

Fourth Boy. And Tommy Tucker——

Second Boy. And Georgie Porgy and the Muffin Man——

First Boy. All want to marry her.

First Girl. And she won't have any of them.

Second Boy. Any one would think that she was

a princess by the number of people that want to marry her.

[*The Princess*, *dressed as a peasant*, *comes out*, *wiping her eyes*, *sits on a seat at the front of the stage*, *and begins to knit*. *Some of the children call out*, "*Hallo*, *Jenny*," *to her*. *They all sit down on the grass*. *Enter Tom the Piper's son*.]

Chorus. Tom, Tom the Piper's son.

Tom [*sings*]. Curly Locks, Curly Locks, wilt thou be mine?
Thou shalt not wash dishes, nor yet feed the swine;
But sit on a cushion and sew a fine seam,
And feed upon strawberries, sugar, and cream.

Princess. I don't want a fine seam to sew, I don't want to feed upon strawberries, sugar, and cream. Besides, I couldn't marry a boy who stole a pig. [*Tom looks abashed*, *and creeps away*.]

Second Girl. I wish Tom would ask me to marry him.

[*Enter Little Boy Blue*.]

Little Boy Blue [*to Chorus*]. I've got a whole day's holiday, and I've come to see Jenny. Good-day, Jenny.

Princess. Good-day, Little Boy Blue.

Little Boy Blue [*sings*]. I will give you the keys of my heart,
And we'll be married till death us do part.
Madam, will you walk, Madam, will you talk,
Madam, will you walk and talk with me?

Princess. Oh, Little Boy Blue, I've told you before that I'm going to marry Bobby Shafto as soon as he comes home from sea.

First Boy. Come, Jenny, don't be sad. Bobby Shafto may come back any day now. Let's race to the harbour and look for his ship.

[*All exit left, and Simple Simon and the Prince enter right*.]

Prince. Oh, how I wish that Jenny were a Princess. I would marry her and make her a queen one day, but I cannot marry a peasant. Anyhow, she is rather thin, and her eyes are blue, and I like brown eyes best.

Simple Simon. If I tell you something to make you happy, what will you give me?

Prince. You can't know anything to make a Prince happy.

Simple Simon. It's about Jenny.

Prince. Here is sixpence—tell me quickly.

Simple Simon [*sings*]. I love sixpence. [*The Prince tries to interrupt him, but he sings to the end, looking all the time at his sixpence*.] That girl is the Princess Jane, daughter of the King of all England, but she doesn't know it.

Prince. Oh, good, good! I will marry her to-morrow.

Simple Simon. Ah, she won't marry you; she is going to marry Bobby Shafto. [*Exit, laughing*.]

Prince. I shall tell her that Bobby Shafto has married some one else, and then she will be mine.

[*Enter Princess with stool, curtsies to the Prince, and walks on.*]

Prince [*sings*]. Where are you going to, my pretty maid ?

Princess [*sings*]. I'm going a-milking, sir, she said.

Prince [*sings*]. May I come with you, my pretty maid ?

Princess [*sings*]. Oh yes, if you please, kind sir, she said.

Prince [*sings*]. Will you marry me, my pretty maid ?

Princess [*sings*]. Oh no, if you please, kind sir, she said.

Prince. But listen, Jenny. You are only a poor shepherdess, and I am a rich prince, who will one day be King of Barbary.

Princess. Oh, you are very kind, but I'm going to marry Bobby Shafto when he comes home from sea.

Prince [*slyly*]. Poor Curly Locks, you will never do that, for he came home three months ago and married Little Bo-Peep.

Princess [*weeping*]. Oh, Bobby Shafto! Bobby Shafto!

[*Villagers enter with the Court, and King and Queen disguised in cloaks. Cries of :*]

Villagers. What has Bobby Shafto done?

Prince. He has married Little Bo-Peep, and forgotten poor Jenny.

Villagers. Oh, shame, shame!

Princess [*sees King and Queen*]. Oh, Mother and Father, why are you here? Oh, I am so sad! Bobby Shafto has married Little Bo-Peep!

[*King and Queen take off their cloaks.*]

Villagers. The King and the Queen.

[*Sing.*]

Here's a health unto his Majesty.

Princess. Am I really a Princess? Are you the King and Queen?

King and Queen. Yes, my child—you are Princess Jane.

Prince [*sings*]. Then will you marry me, my pretty maid?

Princess [*sings sadly*]. I don't mind what happens to me now that
Bobby Shafto is not coming back.

Prince [*sings*]. Lavender's blue, diddle, diddle, lavender's green,
When I am King, diddle, diddle, you shall be Queen.

[*All sadly shake their heads.*]

Fairy Godmother [*rushes out of crowd*]. Oh, you wicked man, hie you away before I turn you into a pig. [*Prince steals away.*] Here is Bobby Shafto coming down the road. My servants told me he was coming an hour ago.

Queen. What about Bo-Peep ?

Fairy Godmother. He has never seen her. Besides, she is married to Jack Horner.

[*Enter Bobby Shafto. Kneels to Princess.*]

Bobby Shafto. O Princess, I can never marry you now. I thought you were just Jenny the Shepherdess !

Villagers. A sailor boy cannot marry a princess !

King. Kneel down, Bobby Shafto. [*Knights him.*] Arise, Sir Bobby Shafto.

Villagers. A knight cannot marry a princess !

King. Kneel down, Sir Bobby. [*Taps him with sword.*] Arise, Duke Shafto.

Villagers. A duke cannot marry a princess !

King. Kneel down, Duke Shafto. [*Puts crown*

on him.] Arise, Prince Bobby. A prince can marry a princess ! [*Cheers and shouts of :*]

Hurrah for Prince Bobby and Princess Jane !

[*All join hands and play " Poor Jenny is a-weeping." Jenny chooses Bobby. In last verse they sing :*]

If you want to know her name,
She's the King and Queen's daughter.

PICNIC

By Hugh Lofting

Ella, fell a
Maple tree.
Hilda, build a
Fire for me.

Teresa, squeeze a
Lemon, so.
Amanda, hand a
Plate to Flo.

Nora, pour a
Cup of tea.
Fancy, Nancy,
What a spree !

IRISH STEW

By ELLA MONCKTON

LITTLE MAN TODD lived in a white cottage, with green shutters and a green front door, which stood at the top of a hill. His cottage had four rooms in it, two up and two down ; one he slept in, one he cooked in, one he used to store apples in, and one he kept for best.

His bedroom was nearly filled up by a great big four-poster bed full of nice soft pillows, and covered with a patchwork quilt. In the autumn, when it started to be rather chilly before eight o'clock and after five o'clock, he crept into his bed and snuggled down and went to sleep all the winter, while the snow fell, the cold winds blew, and the world shivered and shuddered. When spring came round again a friendly swallow would tap on his window-pane and tell him that the winter was over, and that it was time to get up.

So it happened that on a spring day he woke out of his long sleep and stretched himself in every direction to make sure that his arms and legs were still in good working order. Then he yawned " Oohow ! " three times, and decided that he felt very hungry indeed. He got out from under his patchwork quilt, and felt about for his bedroom

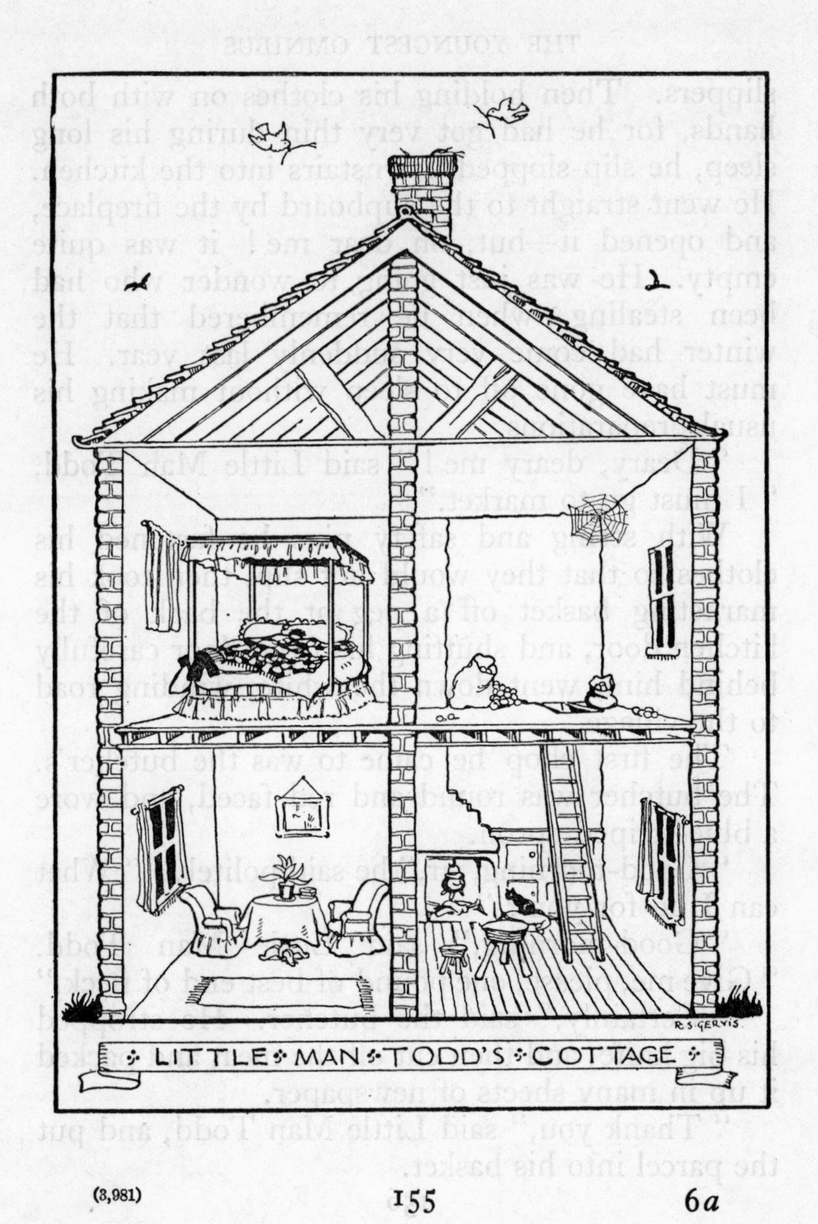

LITTLE MAN TODD'S COTTAGE

slippers. Then holding his clothes on with both hands, for he had got very thin during his long sleep, he slip-slopped downstairs into the kitchen. He went straight to the cupboard by the fireplace, and opened it—but, oh dear me ! it was quite empty. He was just going to wonder who had been stealing, when he remembered that the winter had come very suddenly last year. He must have gone off to sleep without making his usual preparations.

" Deary, deary me ! " said Little Man Todd, " I must go to market."

With string and safety pins he fastened his clothes so that they would not slip, then took his marketing basket off a peg at the back of the kitchen door, and shutting his front door carefully behind him, went down the white, winding road to the village.

The first shop he came to was the butcher's. The butcher was round and red faced, and wore a blue-striped apron.

" Good-morning, sir," he said politely. " What can I do for you ? "

" Good-morning," said Little Man Todd. " Give me, please, one pound of best end of neck."

" Certainly," said the butcher. He stropped his big knife, and then cut off the meat and packed it up in many sheets of newspaper.

" Thank you," said Little Man Todd, and put the parcel into his basket.

"Good-day to you," said the butcher.

"Good-day to you," said Little Man Todd.

The next shop he came to was the greengrocer's.

The greengrocer was short and dark, and had a pencil behind his ear. "Good-morning, sir," he said politely. "What can I do for you?"

"Good-morning," said Little Man Todd. "Give me, please, one pound of potatoes, one pound of onions, and one pound of carrots."

"Certainly," said the greengrocer. He tipped the vegetables out of their baskets, and weighed them in his big scales. Then he put them in separate paper bags.

"Thank you," said Little Man Todd, and put the bags in his basket.

"Good-day to you," said the greengrocer.

"Good-day to you," said Little Man Todd.

The next shop he came to was the baker's. The baker was tall and thin, and his hands and the end of his moustache were rather floury.

"Good-morning, sir," he said politely. "What can I do for you?"

"Good-morning," said Little Man Todd. "Give me, please, a new wholemeal loaf."

"Certainly," said the baker. He took a loaf, still warm, from the shelf and wrapped it in tissue paper, twiddling the ends to make it stay done up.

"Thank you," said Little Man Todd, and put the loaf in his basket.

" Good-day to you," said the baker.

" Good-day to you," said Little Man Todd.

The next shop he came to was the grocer's. The grocer was a big man with a pale face, and a lock of hair which curled flatly on his forehead.

" Good-morning, sir," he said politely. " What can I do for you ? "

" Good-morning," said Little Man Todd. " Give me, please, one pound of pearl barley, and one pound of the best white cheese."

" Certainly," said the grocer. He cut a wedge of cheese off a much bigger piece with a wire, and weighed it on a white porcelain scale. It was nearly right. Then he took a packet of pearl barley, already done up, out of a drawer, and put it, with the cheese, in a blue paper bag.

" Thank you," said Little Man Todd, and put the bag on the top of his basket. It was quite full now, and rather heavy.

He bade the grocer good-day, and then went back the way he had come along the village street and up the winding road to his own little house at the top of the hill. He put his basket down on the kitchen table while he lit a big fire in the kitchen stove.

Then he tipped all the vegetables into a basin of water, cut up the meat into nice little pieces, and washed a big handful of pearl barley. While he was doing this, a lean black cat came in through the window and began to watch him with interest.

Little Man Todd washed his vegetables carefully. He scraped the carrots, and cut them in slices ; he peeled the potatoes, and cut the big ones in halves ; and he skinned the onions, and cut them into rings. He got a big saucepan, and put in first a layer of meat, and then a layer of vegetables, and then some pearl barley, and then some more meat, and then some more vegetables, and so on until everything was inside. Then he put in just enough water, and just enough salt, and just enough pepper, clapped on the lid, and put the saucepan on the fire.

As soon as it was going bubble, bubble, bubble, he skimmed it with a big spoon, and drew it to the side of the fire to let it simmer very gently. At this point the lean black cat licked his lips and purred loudly.

" Oh yes, pussy cat," said Little Man Todd, " there'll be plenty for both of us."

As the clock struck ONE Little Man Todd put a clean cloth on the kitchen table, and laid the plates, and the knives and the forks and the spoons. In the centre he put a big bowl, and beside it was the cheese in a glass dish, and the wholemeal loaf on a wooden platter. The lean black cat jumped nimbly on to a chair, and Little Man Todd tied a napkin round his neck and pushed him up to the table.

The Irish stew was poured carefully into the big bowl, and oh, how good it smelt !

They each took a little, and then a little more, and then a little more. The bowl got emptier and emptier, and Little Man Todd and the lean black cat got fatter and fatter, until at last the bottom of the bowl could be seen, and the stew had completely disappeared.

" I feel much better," said Little Man Todd.

" So do I," said the lean black cat.

" Now we'll eat up the bread and cheese," said Little Man Todd.

" I couldn't eat another mouthful," said the lean black cat; " thank you very much." He got off his chair and went slowly out through the kitchen window.

So Little Man Todd ate up the bread and cheese all by himself. " I'm not really greedy," he told a spider on the wall, " but this is the first meal I've had this year, and, really, I was very, very hungry."

JILLY JENKIN

Old Ballad : Arranged by Reed Moorhouse

O MY love, will you wear red,
Will you wear red, Jilly Jenkin ?
I won't wear red ; it's the colour of my head :
I'll buy me a dillow, wear a double over dill,
I'll buy me a dillow, wear a daisy.

O my love, will you wear blue,
Will you wear blue, Jilly Jenkin ?
I won't wear blue ; it's the colour of my shoe :
I'll buy me a dillow, wear a double over dill,
I'll buy me a dillow, wear a daisy.

JILLY JENKIN

O my love, will you wear brown,
Will you wear brown, Jilly Jenkin ?
I won't wear brown ; it's the colour of my gown :
I'll buy me a dillow, wear a double over dill,
I'll buy me a dillow, wear a daisy.

O my love, will you wear black,
Will you wear black, Jilly Jenkin ?
I won't wear black. Good gracious, no, alack !
I'll buy me a dillow, wear a double over dill,
I'll buy me a dillow, wear a daisy.

O my love, you'll wear, I'm told,
You will wear *gold*, Jilly Jenkin !
Love is *love*—and *gold's* but gold !
I'll buy me a dillow, wear a double over dill,
I'll buy me a dillow, wear a daisy.

O my love, please tell me true,
I can give but my heart, Jilly Jenkin.
O yes, your heart will do ; I'll wear anything for
    you !
I'll buy me a dillow, wear a double over dill,
I'll buy me a dillow, wear a daisy.

THE HILLMAN AND THE HOUSEWIFE

Retold from MRS. EWING

By Rosalind Vallance

WHEN you have been walking on the hills in the country districts, you may have come across curious-looking mounds of earth, about the height of a small man, covered with the greenest grass. If you have put your ear to the side of one of them you may have been lucky enough to hear the echo of many tiny voices and the twang of little harps inside, for these mounds are fairy palaces (or so, at least, the people used to believe in the old days), and the fairies who live in them are called Brownies or Hillmen.

Once upon a time some Brownies were having a wedding party, and they had so many guests that there were not enough pans to contain all the delicious things they wanted to cook, so one of them ran down to the nearest cottage to ask the housewife to lend them a saucepan.

In those days the Brownies and the country people were very friendly together, and would often oblige one another. And if you were kind to the Brownies they never forgot it, but woe betide you if you were stingy.

Now it happened that the first house the

Brownie came to belonged to a very mean woman, who never gave away anything unless she thought she would get something better in return. But she had a kind-hearted little maid called Elsie, and it was Elsie who opened the door.

"Please," said the Brownie politely, grinning from ear to ear in the fairy fashion, "will you lend us a saucepan for our wedding party? I'll bring it back to-morrow."

Elsie smiled down at the funny little man standing straddle-legged on the threshold.

"Gladly," she said, and ran to fetch one from the kitchen.

But, just as she was stretching up to take down the shiniest saucepan from the shelf, her mistress came in.

"What are you doing, Elsie?"

"Oh please, ma'am, I was only going to lend this to the Hillmen. They've done us many a good turn, haven't they?"

The mistress knew this was true, for only the week before the Brownies had threshed all the corn in her husband's barn, and churned all the butter in the dairy, just out of good nature, and only taken a cupful of cream in payment. But she said sharply to the maid:

"Well, don't give them the best saucepan. See, here's an old one with a hole in it. Let them have that. The Hillmen will mend it for me, and I shan't have to pay sixpence for the tinker."

Elsie unwillingly obeyed, and took the holey old saucepan to the little man, who thanked her with a funny grimace and ran off.

When he brought it back the next day, the

mistress seized the saucepan, and, as soon as his back was turned, she examined it eagerly. Yes, the Hillmen had mended it so neatly that you couldn't even see where the hole had been.

"That's the way to manage things, Elsie," she said triumphantly. "Now you can boil the milk for the children's supper. This pan's as good as new."

Elsie put a pint of milk on the fire and turned to lay the cloth; but just as she did so the milk foamed up in the saucepan and boiled over on the coals.

"Look at that now!" screamed the housewife. "There's a whole pint of milk wasted."

"*And that's tuppence!*" cried a queer little voice.

But they thought it was only the wind crying in the chimney.

"Well, you'd better put on another pint. But scour that saucepan first," grumbled the mistress. "The children must have their supper, I suppose."

Elsie washed the saucepan and filled it with milk, and put it on the fire again. But before she could turn her back a fearful smell of burning filled the kitchen, and the second pint was ruined.

"You careless hussy!" shouted the housewife, giving Elsie a smart box on the ear, "that's a whole quart gone."

"AND THAT'S FOURPENCE!" called the same

queer little voice. But poor Elsie was too hurt, and the woman too angry, to hear or notice it.

"Here, give *me* that saucepan. Those lazy Brownies must have left their pudding sticking to it and you were too careless to clean it properly." She whisked the saucepan away and came back with it shining like silver. "Now," she said,

"this is the last pint of milk, and if you let *this* boil over you can go and get work somewhere else, for *I* won't keep you any longer."

Tearfully Elsie put the saucepan on the fire again. But scarcely had it touched the coals when "Fooz!" over came all the milk in a great cascade, and put the fire out.

"You great lubbering, good-for-nothing!"

shouted the woman in a fury. " That's three pints of new milk wasted."

" AND THAT'S SIXPENCE ! " cried a loud, saucy voice from the chimney, and flop ! a little grinning Brownie fell down on to the stove.

" So you didn't save your sixpence after all ! " He scrambled up, made them a mocking bow, and was off in a flash through the open door, and away up the hill.

From that day the saucepan played no more tricks, though the housewife was as stingy as ever.

As for Elsie, the Brownies brought her good fortune, for they never forget those who speak kindly to them.

THE CHINESE UMBRELLA

By Dorothy Rowe

Little Golden Daughter loved the rain, because when it rained she could take out her oiled paper umbrella that had yellow fishes and blue men and red houses painted on it.

Little Golden Daughter loved the rain because it made soft, pattery noises on her umbrella. It seemed as if the blue men and the yellow fishes were talking to her with the rain for their voices.

There were four little blue men and six little yellow fishes and two little red houses on this paper umbrella. The men seemed to be running very fast, for their legs were bent as if they were hurrying, and their coats were flying open. All the fishes' eyes were rolled to one side as if they were afraid of something, and their bodies were squirmed about into funny shapes. But the red houses were the funniest of all. They each had six roofs with a little place for windows between, and the four corners of each roof turned up instead of down. There were small golden bells at each corner, and when it rained the bells made sweet singing for Little Golden Daughter to hear. She liked the singing, but she never understood the words.

One rainy night Little Golden Daughter took her umbrella and walked over to Grandmother's house. All the long way she heard the little bells ringing and singing on her umbrella, and when she walked under the light from a store window and looked up at her umbrella it seemed that the little blue men were running faster than ever, and the little fishes were more afraid than ever before. Little Golden Daughter wondered and wondered about them. Why did the bells sing so loudly? Why did the blue men run so fast? And what

made the yellow fishes so afraid? She could never find out. Mother didn't know, and Granny didn't know.

At last Little Golden Daughter and her umbrella came to Granny's house.

"Oh, come in, Little Golden Daughter. Are you wet?" asked Grandmother.

"No, Granny; I carried my beautiful umbrella, and it kept me quite dry. But I am very tired, because it is a long way to your house by the Lantern Street."

So Grandmother helped Little Golden

Daughter take off her heavy, oiled shoes that are the Chinese children's rubbers, and then she said: "Come and rest on the fire bed and keep warm until Father comes to take you home. I have a new song to sing for you."

So Little Golden Daughter put her open umbrella on the floor to dry, kicked off her little green shoes, and climbed on the funny stone bed that was built over a little fire so it would be always warm. She put her head on a red pillow that looked like a big rolling-pin with no handles and was very hard, and looked at her umbrella while Grandmother sang the new song.

> "The moon shines into the old man's house,
> And I can see a rabbit
> Who eats and eats of the old man's beans,
> And will not stop when I beat him.
> The old man bought a fierce, black dog,
> But the rabbit kept on eating.
> The old man called to his yellow horse,
> But the horse was afraid of the moon."

It was very warm and quiet in Grandmother's house. The rain made soft tappings on the roof, and Little Golden Daughter's umbrella looked like a round, yellow moon as it stood open on the floor. Because it was leaning on its side, two little blue men were running downhill and the other two were running uphill on the other side. The red houses were tipped over, and three fishes stood on their yellow tails. Little Golden

Daughter wished she knew why they did such funny things.

Suddenly one of the blue men ran right off the edge of the paper umbrella and jumped on Granny's blue dress. He bowed low to Little Golden Daughter and wiped his hot forehead with a corner of his blue coat. "I'm very hot," he said, "because I have run so fast for a whole umbrella!"

"You don't run a whole umbrella," Little Golden Daughter said. "You run a mile, or an hour, or a long way."

"Beg pardon, but I said I ran for a whole umbrella. You see, I am an umbrella boy, and I have three umbrella brothers. Six rains ago we were sitting in our red houses when I suddenly heard the golden bells on the corners of our houses say, 'Run, run. Bring fish. Bring fish. For dinner. For dinner.'"

"And have you been running ever since?" asked Little Golden Daughter. "And how long is six rains ago?"

"Oh, it is just six rains ago," said the little umbrella man. "And we had to do what the bells told us, because the bells are the spirits of our red houses, and when they ring we must listen and obey."

Just then a second little blue man leaped off the edge of the umbrella and sat down near Little Golden Daughter's feet. He looked unhappy, and he said, " Goodness, I'm tired running. I've seen those yellow fish every raindrop since we left home, but I can't catch a single one of them."

" Every raindrop ? What does that mean ? " asked Little Golden Daughter.

" Oh, I can't explain umbrella talk. It is very hard to understand, and nobody can learn it," said the little blue man.

Just then off hopped the last two umbrella men. One of them sat on his own blue shoes, and the other bowed to Little Golden Daughter, and asked her very politely, " Could you do something very kind for us ? We have to catch those fish, or we will have no dinner, and can't ever go home to our little red houses, where the gold bells are. Could you help us ? "

Little Golden Daughter wriggled and said, " But I can't catch fish. They squirm so, and their tails look very rough."

" You don't have to touch the fish," said the umbrella man. " I'll whisper what you could do." So he sat on Little Golden Daughter's shoulder, and whispered in her ear, " This is the secret. You must close up your umbrella, and if you do we will bump right into the fish and catch them easily, and be at home in our nice red houses in just a minute, and have a lovely dinner."

That seemed very easy, and Little Golden Daughter was sorry for the umbrella men who had run such a long way, so she said, "All right, I will shut my umbrella at once." And the four little men ran back to the umbrella and waited.

Just then Father came in, and Little Golden Daughter sat up in bed. Granny said to Father,

"Little Golden Daughter was tired, and went to sleep while I was singing her a new song."

Little Golden Daughter smiled. Maybe Grandmother thought she had been asleep, but she knew she had not been asleep, for how could she have heard what the umbrella men said? But it was a secret, so she must not tell. She got up quietly and took up her umbrella.

The four little blue men were waiting for her, and the fishes and the red houses were there. When Little Golden Daughter closed the umbrella she saw, plain as plain, that the blue men bumped right into the fish, and caught them, and took them right into the two red houses for dinner.

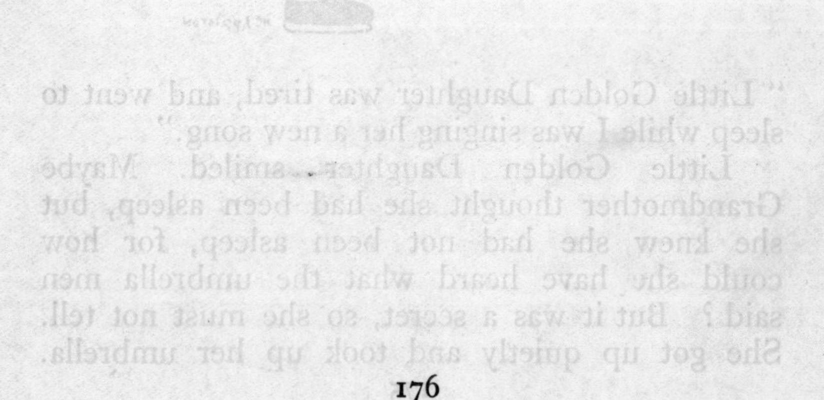

THE WAVES OF THE SEA

By Eleanor Farjeon

A Play-Rhyme for One Mother, One Child, and Nine Waves; and Any Number of Others to represent the Sea.

Don't you go too near the sea,
The sea is sure to wet you;
Harmless though she seems to be,
The sea's ninth wave will get you!
But I can see the small white waves
That want to play with me—
They won't do more than wet my feet
When I go near the sea.

Don't you go too near the sea,
She does not love a stranger;
Eight untroubled waves has she,
The ninth is full of danger!
But I can see the smooth blue waves
That want to play with me—
They won't do more than wet my knees
When I go near the sea.

Don't you go too near the sea,
She'll set her waves upon you—
Eight will treat you playfully,
Until the ninth has won you.

But I can see the big green waves
  That want to play with me—
They won't do more than wet my waist
  When I go near the sea.

Don't you go too near the sea,
  Her ways are full of wonder;
Her first eight waves will leave you free,
  Her ninth will take you under!
But I can see the great grey waves
  That want to play with me—
They won't do more than wet my neck
  When I go near the sea.

Don't you go too near the sea—
  O child, you set me quaking!
Eight have passed you silently,
  And now the ninth is breaking!
I see a wave as high as a wall
  That wants to play with me—
O mother! O mother! it's taken me all,
  For I went too near the sea!

H.C. APPLETON

DOLL IN THE GRASS

By Sir George Dasent

Once on a time there was a King who had twelve sons. When they were grown big he told them they must go out into the world and win themselves wives, but these wives must each be able to spin, and weave, and sew a shirt in one day, else he wouldn't have them for daughters-in-law.

To each he gave a horse and a new suit of mail, and they went out into the world to look after their brides ; but when they had gone a bit of the way, they said they wouldn't have Boots, their youngest brother, with them—he wasn't fit for anything.

Well, Boots had to stay behind, and he didn't know what to do or whither to turn ; and so he grew so downcast, he got off his horse, and sat down in the tall grass to weep. But when he had sat a little while, one of the tufts in the grass began to stir and move, and out of it came a little white thing, and when it came nearer, Boots saw it was a charming little lassie, only such a tiny bit of a thing. So the lassie went up to him, and asked if he would come down below and see " Doll in the Grass."

Yes, he'd be very happy, and so he went.

Now, when he got down, there sat Doll in the

Grass on a chair ; she was so lovely and so smart, and she asked Boots where he was going, and what was his business.

So he told her how there were twelve brothers of them, and how the King had given them horse and mail, and said they must each go out into the world and find them a wife who could spin, and weave, and sew a shirt in a day.

"But if you'll only say at once you'll be my wife, I'll not go a step farther," said Boots to Doll in the Grass.

Well, she was willing enough, and so she made haste and span, and wove, and sewed the shirt ; but it was so tiny, tiny little. It wasn't longer than so ———— long.

So Boots set off home with it ; but when he brought it out he was almost ashamed, it was so small. Still the King said he should have her, and so Boots set off, glad and happy to fetch his little sweetheart. So when he got to Doll in the Grass, he wished to take her up before him on his horse ; but she wouldn't have that, for she said she would sit and drive along in a silver spoon, and that she had two small white horses to draw her. So off they set, he on his horse and she on her silver spoon, and the two horses that drew her were two tiny white mice ; but Boots always kept the other side of the road, he was so afraid lest he should ride over her, she was so little. So, when they had gone a bit of the way, they came to a great piece of water. Here Boots's horse got frightened, and shied across the road and upset the spoon, and Doll in the Grass tumbled into the water. Then Boots got so sorrowful because he didn't know how to get her out again; but in a little while up came a merman with her, and now she was as well and full grown as other men and women, and far lovelier than she had been before.

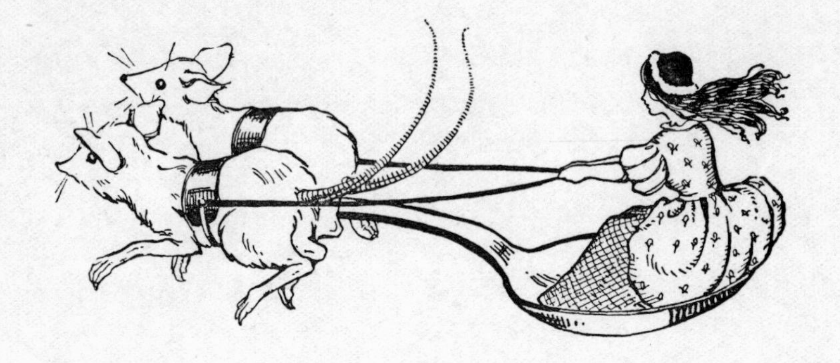

So he took her up before him on his horse, and rode home.

When Boots got home all his brothers had come back, each with his sweetheart; but these were all so ugly and wicked, that they had done nothing but fight with one another on the way home, and on their heads they had a kind of hat that was daubed over with tar and soot, and so the rain had run down off the hats on to their faces, till they got far uglier and nastier than they had been before. When his brothers saw

Boots and his sweetheart, they were all as jealous as jealous could be of her ; but the King was so overjoyed with them both, that he drove all the others away, and so Boots held his wedding-feast with Doll in the Grass, and after that they lived well and happily together a long, long time ; and if they're not dead, why, they're alive still.

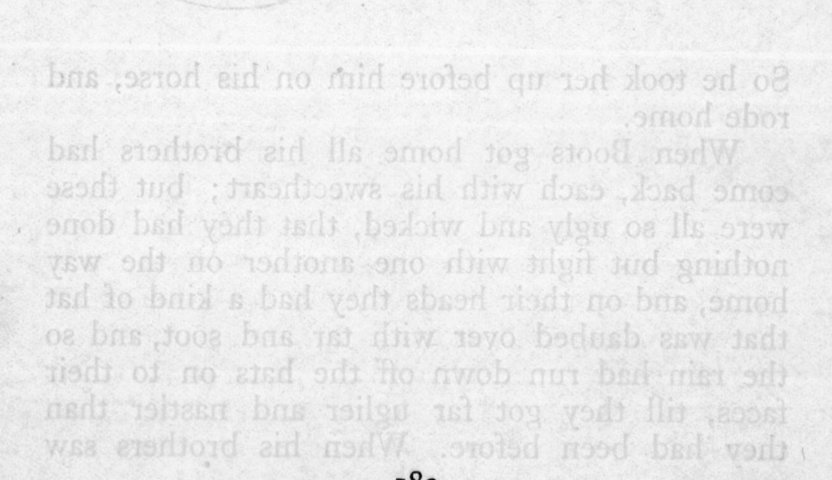

THE BROOM

By Rose Fyleman

There was once a poor crossing-sweeper whose name was Peter.

He lived rather a long time ago, when even in quite big towns the roads were ill-made, so that in bad weather they got terribly muddy and dirty.

In the summer-time he did not have much to do, but there was always dust and paper about, and even in summer it rains sometimes—doesn't it ?

He didn't earn a great deal of money.

Some people were too busy to heed him, and some were too selfish, and some too poor to give him anything.

He had, however, a cheerful heart, and managed somehow to make enough to pay the rent and to provide food and clothing for himself and his wife and his little son.

One cold winter's day he had taken rather more pennies than usual, and went to get a cup of coffee from a coffee stall not very far from his crossing, before starting on his way home.

He put his broom in a dark corner inside some railings where he often left it if he went away for a few minutes. Now, oddly enough, it happened that some one else had left a broom inside those railings. It was just the same size and shape as his own, and as it was nearly dark he never saw that there were two, and he got hold of the wrong one and went off home with it.

He put it down in the corner of the yard and went into the house to have his tea with his wife and little son.

Early the next morning, as he was getting dressed, he chanced to put his head out of the window.

There was his little son, who was only six years old, playing in the yard with the broom. He had his legs astride it, and was pretending it was a horse.

" Gee-up, gee-up," he said. And really the broom seemed to be prancing and leaping in the strangest way. " Almost as if it were really alive," thought Peter.

And just as he was thinking that, his little son called out : " Now then, up you go. Over the wall, Beauty ! "

And—would you believe it ?—the astonished Peter actually saw the broom rise up, with the boy still astride it, and fly over the wall into the next-door yard.

He rushed downstairs, half dressed as he was, ran through the gate, and into his neighbour's yard.

There he found his little boy, safe and sound

on the ground, still astride the broom, laughing with joy and excitement.

" Good Beauty, good Beauty," he said.

But Peter stood staring in utter astonishment.

" Mother, mother," he called, when he could speak. " Come quick, the broom's bewitched."

You can imagine what a to-do there was, and how all the neighbours came flocking round to see.

Every one had some different suggestion to make as to how the broom came to be bewitched.

They stood round in a circle looking at it lying in Peter's neighbour's yard, for no one dared to pick it up at first.

But presently Peter plucked up his courage and took hold of it, and seeing that nothing happened to him, his wife took it up in her turn. She turned it round in her hands.

"Why, Peter," she said, "this is not your broom at all. Don't you remember the brown burnt mark it got when it fell across the kitchen grate? That mark's not on this broom handle. You've got some one else's broom by mistake."

"It's my belief," said the little dried-up brown cobbler from the end cottage, "it's my belief it's a witch's broom. I'd have nothing to do with it if I were you, Peter. I should advise you to put it back where you got it from. Maybe your own broom is still there."

So Peter went off to look for his own broom, but he found it had disappeared.

He brought the other one home again.

"What shall we do?" he said to his wife when he came back. "I can't afford to buy a new broom; but I'm a bit afraid of this one. I dare say it really *is* a witch's broom. Don't you think it would be best to throw it away?"

But Peter's wife was a careful woman.

"No," she said. "Now we've got it, I reckon we'd better stick to it. It may bring good fortune. Who knows?"

So they kept the broom, and soon it brought them good fortune indeed, for they quickly found out that it went wherever it was told to go by the person sitting astride it.

It was really a most marvellous thing.

Peter and his father went riding on it all day long at first, then other people had a ride ; soon the whole neighbourhood knew of Peter's wonderful broom.

Presently it began to bring in money. People who wanted to get anywhere in a hurry would come in and arrange to go on the broom. They paid handsomely. It was so convenient, as you can imagine. And much quicker than any other way, for motor cars and aeroplanes were not yet invented.

Peter began to grow rich. He moved into a bigger house with a little garden in front ; he bought new clothes for his wife and the boy ; he even talked of going up to London, where he felt sure he would earn more money with the wonderful broom. He no longer swept a crossing, and they had meat for dinner every day, and a whole roast chicken on Sundays.

The whole town knew about him and his good luck.

Strangers coming into the place would stare in astonishment at the sight of somebody sailing through the air on a broomstick.

" That's Peter's broom," the townsfolk would

explain. " You can hire it out for a shilling an hour if you're lucky enough to find it idle."

One day a great scientist came to stay in Peter's town. He was a very great scientist indeed, and he spent his time finding out things about the moon. He was very much interested in the moon. And when he heard about the broom he went nearly mad with excitement.

" Now I shall be able to go and see what the moon is really like," he said.

Peter wasn't quite sure whether he liked the idea of the broom making such a long journey; but his wife persuaded him to consent.

" It will take him many hours to get to the moon," she said. " Think what a lot of shillings that will mean. And what harm can he come to ? "

So Peter consented, and the scientist set off.

It took him a good long time to reach the moon, and when he got there the very first person he saw was the witch to whom the broom belonged, for, of course, it *was* a witch's broom, as you will already have guessed.

She was sitting on the very edge of the moon in a very bad temper. You see, it's very annoying for a witch to lose her broom; it is her chief way of getting about, and without it she has to depend either upon friendly lifts or upon whatever witchcraft she can think of to help her.

And a broom is so much simpler.

The minute the scientist alighted she saw that he had come up on her broom.

"You wicked old thief," she said, "how dare you steal my broom? How dare you go riding about on it in that brazen way? And me, the rightful owner, crawling all the way up on a miserable moonbeam. How dare you! I'll put a curse on you, I will. I'll put an end to you, I will. *I'll* broom you, you wicked old greybeard!"

The scientist was very frightened indeed, for witches are alarming at the best of times, and when they're angry . . .

He backed and backed, and before he knew what was happening he had fallen off the edge of the moon, down, down, down—and then, plop into the middle of the sea.

As good luck would have it, he was seen

falling by the look-out man on a vessel, and was hauled in and given dry clothes and a hot drink and was not much the worse.

But he was bitterly disappointed.

Of course it *was* very hard.

Think of having a chance of seeing the moon at close quarters after studying it for years and years from far off, and then being chased off it by an old witch. And it wasn't his fault, either.

He was a nice old scientist. He went back to find Peter and to pay him for the hire of the broom, and to explain what had happened. Of course Peter couldn't blame him. After all, the broom wasn't really his either.

However, thanks to his careful wife, he had already saved enough money to be able to live quite comfortably ever after, so he didn't do so badly after all—did he now?

NEXT DOOR

By Joan Ryder

There's a little brown summer-house close to the wall,
There's a whole row of sunflowers and hollyhocks tall,
There's a hedgehog who rolls himself into a ball,
  In the dear little garden next door.

There's a black-and-white puppy, so jolly and fat,
There's a big tabby pussy asleep on a mat,
There's a grey polly parrot, who sings rather flat,
  In the dear little garden next door.

There's tea on the table, with apricot jam,
There's a doll on the grass, and a white woolly lamb,
There's the loveliest baby asleep in a pram,
  In the dear little garden next door.

FAIRIES WHO ARE OUT BY DAY

By Berwick Sayers

If you meet a fairy in the middle of a wood,
  Singing like a linnet or a thrush,
Pass along politely, as a nice young person should,
For fairies who are out by day are seldom very good :
  So run, my dears—and hush !

For fairies ought to sleep by day on beds of thistledown,
  Underneath the meadows green and lush ;
Only those whose naughty ways have troubled Fairy
    Town
The Queen of Fairies sends by day to wander up and
    down :
  So run, my dears—
    and hush !

THE RUN-ALONG MAN SELLS SPOONS

By AGNES GROZIER HERBERTSON

THE Run-Along Man ran over the Dimply Common every morning, wearing his silver shoes and carrying a little rumplety bag in which were silver spoons. As he ran along, his silver shoes tinkled on the pebbly path, and as they tinkled they sang, " Come and see, come and see."

Then all the fairies and gnomes and elves who lived on Dimply Common would run to their doors and look out ; and they would see the Run-Along Man with his silver shoes and his rumplety bag full of silver spoons. And quite often they would buy a spoon from him, especially if they had somebody coming to tea.

One day the Run-Along Man was thinking very much about how worrying life was when you had too much to do, so he didn't think a great deal about where he was going ; and when he reached the end of Dimply Common he didn't turn back again as he usually did. No, he ran on and on, through the Snippity Wood and past the turnstile, and at last he came to a little house where a Little Girl lived all alone.

As he ran along his silver shoes tinkled on the path and sang, " Come and see, come and see." So the Little Girl heard them, and came to her door. And she saw the Run-Along Man running past with his silver shoes and his rumplety bag in which were silver spoons. (Only one or two, for he had sold quite a lot.)

The Little Girl was much surprised, but she

was also very pleased to see the Run-Along Man; and she cried, " Wait for me, wait for me."

So the Run-Along Man waited, and when the Little Girl caught him up, he said:

"Spoons for sale. If you are willing
To give me a silver shilling,
You can have a silver spoon,
Bright and shining as the moon."

"Please," said the Little Girl, "I want to buy a spoon, but I haven't a shilling. You see, I spent the last one on Thursday."

"Dear me, that's a pity," said the Run-Along Man; "but it can't be helped. So let me say good-bye."

And he started to run on again. But the Little Girl cried, "Wait for me, wait for me."

So the Run-Along Man waited, and when the Little Girl caught him up he said:

> "Spoons for sale, if you are willing
> To expend a silver shilling.
> If you find a shilling soon,
> You can have a silver spoon."

"Please, I haven't a shilling," said the Little Girl. "Will you take a cabbage instead?"

But the Run-Along Man said, "I have plenty of cabbages, thank you. I must have a shilling."

The Little Girl thought for a minute, then she said, "Will you take a thimble instead of a shilling?"

But the Run-Along Man said, "This is a great waste of time. I have no use for thimbles, thank you."

"I happen to have one in my pocket," said the Little Girl.

But the Run-Along Man only said, "I can't help that. I must have a shilling."

Then the Little Girl thought again, and at last

she said, "Will you let me cook your porridge for you, instead of a shilling?"

The Run-Along Man was just opening his mouth to say "No," when he suddenly thought how nice it would be to have his porridge made ready for him instead of having to cook it for himself when he was weary and worn. So he said, "Oh, all right. I don't mind if I let you cook my porridge for me, instead of a shilling."

The Little Girl said, "Just wait here a minute while I run back and put on my hat."

So the Run-Along Man waited, and while he waited he noticed that he was going in quite the wrong direction, and should not be going that way at all. So when the Little Girl came back with her hat on, he said to her, "We must turn round and go quite the other way, to my little house."

"Ah, that is the way I have always wanted to go," said the Little Girl, "only I didn't like to go by myself."

So they went on together quite happily. The Run-Along Man ran pretty fast, and his silver shoes tinkled on the path and sang, "Come and see, come and see." The Little Girl ran not quite so fast, and every now and then she cried, "Wait for me, wait for me." And when that happened the Run-Along Man always waited.

They passed the door of the Shy Elf, who had been not-at-home when the Run-Along Man passed along last time.

And the silver shoes of the Run-Along Man tinkled on the path and sang, "Come and see, come and see."

So the Shy Elf came to the door. And when he saw the Little Girl with the Run-Along Man he was as frightened as frightened.

"Dear me, you need not be afraid of *her*," said the Run-Along Man. "She is coming home with me to make my porridge."

When the Shy Elf heard this he was not frightened any more. And he brought from his shelf a silver shilling, and gave it to the Run-Along Man, and in return he got a silver spoon.

Then the Run-Along Man went on his way, and the Little Girl went with him, and they were quite happy. The Silver Shoes of the Run-Along Man tinkled on the path and sang, "Come and see, come and see." And the Little Girl hurried all she could, and cried, "Wait for me, wait for me." And when that happened the Run-Along Man always waited.

At last they came to the house of Bounce the gnome, who sells caraway seed. Bounce was now at home, but he had not been when the Run-Along Man passed last time. The silver shoes of the Run-Along Man tinkled on the path and sang,

" Come and see, come and see." So Bounce the gnome came to his door.

And when he saw the Little Girl with the Run-Along Man he was as cross as cross. " She does not belong to this part of the world," said he.

" Dear me, you need not be cross about *her*," said the Run-Along Man. " She is coming home with me to make my porridge."

When Bounce the gnome heard this he was not cross any more. And he brought from his drawer a silver shilling, and gave it to the Run-Along Man, and in return he got a silver spoon.

Then the Run-Along Man went on his way, and the Little Girl went with him, and they were quite happy. And the Run-Along Man ran fast, and his silver shoes tinkled on the path and sang, " Come and see, come and see." And the Little Girl ran not so fast, and every now and then she cried, " Wait for me, wait for me." And when that happened the Run-Along Man always waited.

At last they came to the house of the Shoo-Shoo Wizard, who was at home now, but had been not-at-home when the Run-Along Man passed last time.

The silver shoes of the Run-Along Man tinkled on the path and sang, " Come and see, come and see."

So the Shoo-Shoo Wizard came to his door. And when he saw the Little Girl he waggled his apron at her and cried, " Shoo, shoo! Go away."

Then the Little Girl would have run away; but the Run-Along Man said, "Don't be frightened. He's all right, really."

And he said to the Shoo-Shoo Wizard, "Dear me, you must not try to frighten her. She is coming home with me to make my porridge."

When the Shoo-Shoo Wizard heard this he did not try any more to frighten the Little Girl. And he brought from his apron-pocket a silver shilling and gave it to the Run-Along Man, and in return he received a silver spoon.

That was the last silver spoon the Run-Along Man had to sell. So now he took off his silver shoes and put them in his pocket; and his little feet ran along the path without singing, "Come and see, come and see."

So he ran along home, but not quite as fast as before, for he was weary and worn; and the Little Girl ran with him, and now she could run as fast as he could, for she was not so tired. And they were both as happy as could be.

At last they reached the little house of the Run-Along Man, which was on Dimply Common. It had a red chimney and three windows, and the door was locked fast.

The Run-Along Man opened the door and went inside. And the Little Girl went inside too. And the Little Girl loved the little house of the Run-Along Man, but she thought the kitchen was not very tidy.

"Please don't bother about that," said the Run-Along Man; "but make my porridge." And he sat in a chair by the fire and rested—for he was weary and worn—and waited.

The Little Girl made the porridge, and while it cooked on the fire she stirred it now and again, and all the rest of the time she tidied the kitchen in the most wonderful way, so that it was soon a lovely place.

Soon the porridge was ready, and it was not burnt, but was quite delicious. The Run-Along Man ate a platterful, and so did the Little Girl. And they were both as happy as could be.

Then the Little Girl washed the dishes and the Run-Along Man dried them; so that quite soon the kitchen was again tidy.

At last the Little Girl sighed and said, "I suppose I must go home. Please give me my silver spoon."

The Run-Along Man brought a silver spoon from a drawer and gave it to the Little Girl. And as he did so he thought how nice it would be if the Little Girl stayed with him all the time, and went with him sometimes when he sold his spoons, and always made the porridge when he was weary and worn. So he said :

" I rather think you'd better stay ;
It seems so sad to go away :
Let's share this house, just you and me ;
I rather think we shall agree."

The Little Girl thought that a very good plan. So she took off her hat and hung it on a nail, and she hid her silver spoon in a special corner ; and then she brought from her pocket a thimble and began to mend the Run-Along Man's Sunday coat !

They lived quite happily together
In all and every kind of weather.
They knew each other's ways quite soon ;
And each ate with a silver spoon.

ŒYVIND AND HIS GOAT

Adapted from *The Happy Boy*
by BJÖRNSTERNE BJÖRNSON

ONCE upon a time there was a little boy, and his name was Œyvind. He lived with his father and mother in a little house beside a hill. Fir and birch trees stood on the hillside, and the wild cherry let its blossoms fall on the roof of the house in the springtime.

Œyvind had a goat. When he was not playing with it, he kept it up on the flat roof of the little house, so that it could not run away.

One day, while Œyvind was in the house, the goat looked up to the top of the hill, and he thought, " I should like to go up there." Then he jumped over to the hillside, and climbed far up the hill to a place where he had never been before.

When Œyvind came out of the house, he looked up to the roof, and his goat was not there. He looked all about, but he could not see it anywhere. He grew very warm, for he thought his goat was lost.

" Here, killy-killy-killy-goat," he called.

He heard the goat call to him from the top of the hill. " Bay-a-a-a," it called.

The goat was looking down at Œyvind with its head on one side. A little girl was kneeling beside it with her arms around its neck.

" Is he your goat ? " said the little girl.

Œyvind put his hands into his pockets, and said, " Who are you ? "

" I am Marit," said the little girl, " mother's baby, father's mouse, little fairy in the house; four years old in autumn, two days after the first frost night, I am."

" Are you ? " said Œyvind.

" Yes. Is he your goat, and will you give him to me ? " said Marit.

" He is my goat, and I will not give him to anybody," said Œyvind.

" If I give you a butter-cake, will you give him to me ? " said Marit.

Now, Œyvind had eaten a butter-cake once ; it was when his grandfather had come to see them, and he had never tasted anything so good.

"Let me see the butter-cake," he said.

"Here it is," said Marit.

She took a butter-cake out of her pocket, and threw it down to Œyvind. It fell on the ground at his feet.

"Oh, it has all gone to pieces!" said he.

He picked up every piece of it. He tasted the smallest piece. It was so good that he tasted another piece, and another, and another; and before he thought what he was doing, he had eaten the whole cake.

"Now the goat is mine," said Marit.

"Oh no, can't you wait a bit?" said Œyvind.

"No, no, you have eaten the cake, and the goat is mine," she said. And she put her arms around the goat's neck again. She tried to drag it away. It would not go, but stretched its neck and looked down at Œyvind.

"Bay-a-a-a," it said.

Marit caught hold of its fleece, and pulled it along.

"Come, Goatie dear," she said, "you shall come indoors and eat from mother's pretty dish."

As she dragged the goat away, she sang a little song to it about her pets at home.

"Come, goat, to your sire,
Come, calf, from the byre;
Come, pussy that mews,
In your snowy-white shoes;

Come, ducklings so yellow,
Come, chickens so small,
Each soft, little fellow,
That can't run at all ;
Come, sweet doves of mine,
With your feathers so fine."

Now the goat was gone.

Œyvind's mother came from the spring with fresh water, and she saw Œyvind seated on the ground. She saw that he was crying.

" What is the matter ? Why are you crying ? " she asked.

" The goat, the goat ! " That was all that Œyvind could say.

His mother looked up to the roof. " Where is the goat ? " she said.

" Oh, it will never come back," said Œyvind.

" Has the fox taken it ? " asked his mother.

" I wish it had been the fox," said Œyvind. " I sold it for a butter-cake."

" Œyvind, what do you suppose the little goat thinks of you for selling it for a butter-cake ? " said his mother.

Then she went into the house with the spring water, and Œyvind lay on the ground with his face to the grass, and cried as though he would never stop crying.

After a while he fell asleep, and while he was asleep he had a dream. He dreamt that he saw his goat up on a great white cloud.

The goat said, " Bay-a-a-a."

He wanted to come down to Œyvind, but Œyvind could not go up there to bring him down.

Just then something wet poked right into Œyvind's ear. He sat up.

" Bay-a-a-a," said a voice, and there was the goat !

" Oh, you've come back ! You've come back ! " said Œyvind.

He sprang to his feet, took the goat by the fore-legs, and danced with it like a brother. He was taking it right in to his mother, when he saw little Marit standing there.

" Oh, it's you who have come with him," said Œyvind.

" Yes, I was not allowed to keep him," said Marit.

She put her arms around the goat's neck, and cried as though her heart would break. Œyvind looked away.

" I think you had better keep the goat," he said.

" Well, Marit," said a voice from the top of the hill.

So Marit remembered what she must do. She stood up and held her hand out to Œyvind.

" Forgive me," she said.

Then she ran up the hill without looking back.

Œyvind had his goat again. But he was not as happy with it as he had been before.

But the next day, and nearly every day after that, Marit came down the hill and played with Œyvind and his goat, and then Œyvind and Marit and the goat were all happy.

EXTREMELY NAUGHTY CHILDREN

By Elizabeth Godley

By far
The naughtiest
Children
I know
Are Jasper
Geranium
James
And Jo.

They live
In a house
On the Hill
Of Kidd,
And what
In the world
Do you think
They did ?

They asked
Their uncles
And aunts
To tea,

And shouted
In loud
Rude voices :
" We

Are tired
Of scoldings
And sendings
To bed :
Now
The grown-ups
Shall be
Punished instead."

They said :
" Auntie Em,
You didn't
Say ' Thank You ' ! "
They said :
" Uncle Robert,
We're going
To spank you ! "

They pulled
The beard
Of Sir Henry
Dorner
And put him
To stand

In disgrace
In the corner.

They scolded
Aunt B.,
They punished
Aunt Jane ;
They slapped
Aunt Louisa
Again
And again.

They said
" Naughty boy ! "
To their
Uncle
Fred,
And boxed
His ears
And sent him
To bed.

Do you think
Aunts Em
And Loo
And B.,
And Sir
Henry
Dorner
(K.C.B.),

And the elderly
Uncles
And kind
Aunt Jane
Will go
To tea
With the children
Again ?

BREAD

By Elizabeth Fleming

I'd like to be a baker,
And keep a baker's shop,
And make those dumpy cottage-loaves
With muffins on the top ;
I'd set them in the windows
In rows and rows and rows,
And all the folks would laugh at me
With smudges on my nose.

I'd lean across the counter
When people rang the bell,
And say : " It's very nice to-day !
I hope you're keeping well ? "
And when my work was ended,
And all my stock was sold,
I'd go and eat new bread for tea,
And never, never old !

THE BLACKBIRD

By Humbert Wolfe

In the far corner,
close by the swings,
every morning
a blackbird sings.

His bill's so yellow,
his coat's so black,
that he makes a fellow
whistle back.

Ann, my daughter,
thinks that he
sings for us two
especially.

MR. AND MRS. SPIKKY SPARROW

By Edward Lear

I

On a little piece of wood,
Mr. Spikky Sparrow stood ;
Mrs. Sparrow sate close by,
A-making of an insect pie,
For her little children five,
In the nest and all alive,
Singing with a cheerful smile
To amuse them all the while,
  Twikky wikky wikky wee,
  Wikky bikky twikky tee,
    Spikky bikky bee !

II

Mrs. Spikky Sparrow said,
" Spikky, Darling ! in my head
Many thoughts of trouble come,
Like to flies upon a plum !
All last night, among the trees,
I heard you cough, I heard you sneeze ;
And, thought I, it's come to that
Because he does not wear a hat !
  Chippy wippy sikky tee !
  Bikky wikky tikky mee !
    Spikky chippy wee !

III

" Not that you are growing old,
But the nights are growing cold.
No one stays out all night long
Without a hat : I'm sure it's wrong ! "
Mr. Spikky said, " How kind,
Dear ! you are, to speak your mind !
All your life I wish you luck !
You are ! you are ! a lovely duck !
Witchy witchy witchy wee !
Twitchy witchy witchy bee !
Tikky tikky tee !

IV

" I was also sad, and thinking,
When one day I saw you winking,
And I heard you sniffle-snuffle,
And I saw your feathers ruffle ;
To myself I sadly said,
She's neuralgia in her head !
That dear head has nothing on it !
Ought she not to wear a bonnet ?
Witchy kitchy kitchy wee !
Spikky wikky mikky bee !
Chippy wippy chee !

V

" Let us both fly up to town !
There I'll buy you such a gown !

Which, completely in the fashion,
You shall tie a sky-blue sash on.
And a pair of slippers neat,
To fit your darling little feet,
So that you will look and feel
Quite galloobious and genteel!
        Jikky wikky bikky see!
        Chicky bikky wikky bee!
          Twicky witchy wee!"

VI

So they both to London went,
Alighting on the Monument,
Whence they flew down swiftly—pop,
Into Moses' wholesale shop;
There they bought a hat and bonnet,
And a gown with spots upon it,
A satin sash of Cloxam blue,
And a pair of slippers too.
        Zikky wikky mikky bee!
        Witchy witchy mitchy kee!
          Sikky tikky wee!

VII

Then when so completely drest,
Back they flew and reached their nest.
Their children cried, "O Ma and Pa!
How truly beautiful you are!"

MR. AND MRS. SPIKKY SPARROW

Said they, " We trust that cold or pain
We shall never feel again !
While, perched on tree, or house, or steeple,
We now shall look like other people.
Witchy witchy witchy wee !
Twikky mikky bikky bee !
Zikky sikky tee ! "

BUNNY'S NEW HOUSE

By S. G. Hulme Beaman

Illustrated by the Author

In a hollow tree-trunk on the outskirts of a forest near Toytown lived a white rabbit. He had made a very comfortable house of the tree-trunk, having built a nice door and fitted a little window made of pieces of glass bottles which he had picked up near the city. And in order that no one should see his house (for he was a very timid little rabbit) he had arranged creepers to hang over the door and window, so that a person, unless looking very closely, would not know it was a house at all.

One day the white rabbit was sitting just inside his open door when he saw a party of woodcutters approaching. They were looking at all the large trees, and presently stopped before the rabbit's house. "That's the tree we want," said one of the woodcutters; "plenty of timber there. That will do to make the King's new table; we will set to work and cut it down next week."

The poor little rabbit could hardly believe his

ears—long as they were. Cut down his house! That would be terrible! And he fell to wondering what he should do. At last he hit on a plan. He was a timid rabbit, but he knew he must be brave now; he must put on his best clothes, go to Toytown and petition the King. Surely the King would not be so cruel as to allow his house to be cut down to make a table.

The rabbit put on his hat and hurried off to see his friend Mr. Owl, quite the wisest friend he had, to ask him if he would help to draw up the petition.

"This is a very important matter," said Mr. Owl, when he had heard the story. "We must be very careful how we word this petition. Now, how shall we start?"

The rabbit had brought a pencil and some paper with him, and after sucking the pencil for some time and thinking hard, he wrote in large letters on the top of a sheet, "Dear King."

"Oh, that won't do at all!" cried Mr. Owl. "You must say: 'Your Majesty,' or 'If it please your Majesty.'"

"But supposing it doesn't please him?" asked the rabbit. "It might make him very disagreeable to see my bad writing. I shall say: 'Dear your Majesty.'"

"Oh, all right," said Mr. Owl, "if you know best."

" Dear your Majesty,

" The woodcutters want to cut down my tree, where I live, to make your new table. Oh, please do not let them. Thanking you in advance,

" Yours faithfully,

" J. Rabbit."

Mr. Owl looked at this carefully. " Well, it *may* do," he said doubtfully. " But I don't think you ought to say ' Yours faithfully.' It doesn't sound respectful. You ought to say : ' Your obedient subject.' "

" I can't alter it now," the rabbit replied, " it will look too messy." And he began to hurry away.

" Well, don't blame *me*," shouted Mr. Owl after him.

The rabbit folded the paper very carefully, and, clutching it in his paw, set off towards Toytown. He had not very far to go, but when he reached the city gates and saw the sentries he had half a mind to turn back, he felt so nervous. However, nobody interfered with him, so he passed the gates and hurried through the streets until he reached the King's palace. And on the steps stood another sentry.

" Please, officer, I want to see the King," said the rabbit in a small, timid voice.

" Have you an appointment ? " the sentry asked.

" No," replied the rabbit ; " but I have a very nicely written petition."

" Go straight ahead," said the sentry, " and wipe your paws well. The floors have just been polished."

Feeling very frightened the rabbit passed through a long hall, up some more stairs, and into a large room where a lot of people were standing about. And at one end of the room, before a doorway, stood a tall gentleman with a wand, who, the rabbit felt sure, must be the Lord Chamberlain. He walked up to him.

" Oh, sir," said the rabbit, " please can I see the King ? "

" What for ? " the Lord Chamberlain asked. " He's very busy. He's just getting ready to go for a ride."

" It's something terribly important," cried the rabbit. " I must see him ; I have a petition for him."

" Well, if you like to leave it with me I will give it to his Majesty—when I think of it," said the Lord Chamberlain. But just then the door opened and the King came out. The rabbit recognized him at once by his crown and his ermine robe.

" Oh, please your Majesty, sir ! " he cried. And he unfolded his paper with little trembling paws and handed it to the King.

" What is this ? " the King asked, staring very hard at the paper.

" Please, your Majesty, it's a petition," said the rabbit.

" But I can't read it," the King cried. " It's upside down ! "

" Perhaps if your Majesty were to turn it the other way up you would be able to read it," the Chamberlain suggested.

" Why, yes," said the King. " That is so. What's this ? Cut down the tree you live in to make me a table ? That seems very unfair, certainly. What do you think, Chamberlain ? "

" Well, your Majesty," the Chamberlain replied, " why does he live in a tree ? Why doesn't he live in a house like other people ? "

" Oh, please your Majesty," cried the rabbit, " I'm only a little bunny, and I can't build a whole house all by myself. And this was such a nice tree, and so convenient ! "

" Ah ! " said His Majesty, " I have a splendid idea, Chamberlain. We can't turn our subjects out of their homes like this to make tables. But we must have our table, so we will cut down this tree and build the rabbit a new house. How would that do ? "

" Oh, thank you, your Majesty," the rabbit cried. " It's very kind of you. I'm so sorry to have troubled you ! "

" No trouble at all," said the King.—" See to it, Chamberlain." And he went off for his ride.

The King was as good as his word, and in a

very short time workmen came and built a splendid little house for the rabbit in the field near the old tree. It was painted in bright colours, and had several windows of proper glass and a little green door with a brass knocker. And although the rabbit was sorry to see his old home cut down, he felt very proud of his new house.

Mr. Owl was quite envious. " If it had not been for me helping you to draw up your petition, and giving you advice, you would never have got this," he said. " I think I should like a house like that too. I shall petition the King myself. The only trouble is that the woodcutters have not yet said anything about cutting down my tree. I wish they would ! "

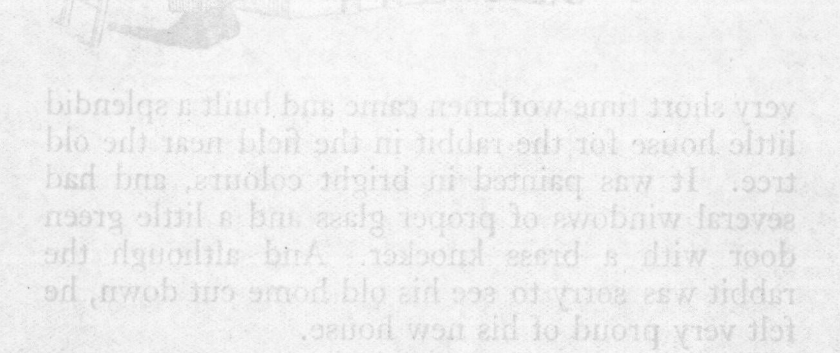

BARNABY THE GOAT

By Marion St. John Webb

In old Mr. Pounds's back garden there was a baby goat tied with a bit of rope to the iron railings. It hadn't long left its mother, and it used to cry nearly all day long. It was very lonely and there was not much to eat in the garden, but old Mr. Pounds didn't think of this when he opened his back window every now and then and roared out to the goat to stop making such a noise.

Mr. Pounds was a fierce old man. He hadn't wanted the goat, but a man who owed him money and was not able to pay had offered him the baby goat instead, and rather than have nothing Mr. Pounds had accepted the goat. And now he wished he hadn't.

"I'll have to do something about that goat if he doesn't stop his noise," growled old Mr. Pounds, thumping on the window-pane and shaking his fist at the goat through the window. At the sound of the thumping the goat stopped crying for a few seconds and looked round; then he went on crying again.

Now a little boy named Martin used to pass Mr. Pounds's cottage every day on his way to school, and he used to hear the goat crying. On the third day, as he was returning from school, he walked round the cottage and peeped over the back fence. And he saw the baby goat, with the great thick rope round its neck, crying all by itself.

" Hallo, old fellow ! " said Martin. " What's the matter ? "

And the goat cried all the harder, and tried to reach his outstretched hand, but it couldn't. Then Martin heard the window open and Mr. Pounds shouting at the goat, and the next minute, to Martin's horror, he saw the old man come running out into the garden with a big stick in his hand.

" I'm sick and tired of your noise ! I'll teach you ! " called out Mr. Pounds as he ran.

Quick as thought, Martin leaped over the fence and rushed in front of the baby goat, holding out his hands.

Mr. Pounds pulled up abruptly, rather astonished at the sudden appearance of a small boy from nowhere. Then he frowned.

" Get out of my way ! " he shouted. " I'm going to give this goat the lesson of his life ! " And he came forward.

" But he's only a baby," gasped Martin, his heart thumping vigorously. " Don't hit him. Please don't hit him."

" Out of my way, or I'll wallop you too," was Mr. Pounds's angry reply.

But Martin stood his ground, with head held high, although his knees were trembling (which is the bravest way of all).

Mr. Pounds, very red in the face and flustered, paused.

" I'll give you one minute," he said, " and if you're not out of this garden by then—my word! you'll wish you were ! "

Martin saw that he would be helpless against Mr. Pounds's strength. Then he had a sudden idea.

" Will you sell the goat to me ? I'll buy him from you if you don't want him," said Martin.

Mr. Pounds stared at him. " Eh ? " he said. " Do you mean that ? "

" Of course I mean it," replied Martin. " How much do you want for him ? "

" How much have you got ? " said Mr. Pounds.

By a piece of good fortune it happened that at that moment Martin had two shillings and sixpence in his pocket. An aunt who had been staying with his mother had gone away that morning and had given it to him as a parting gift. It was the remembrance of this that had given him the idea.

" Half a crown," said Martin, bringing it out

of his pocket, and holding it out for Mr. Pounds to see.

" Half a crown ! " growled Mr. Pounds in disgust. " Do you think my goat is only worth half a crown ? "

" No," said Martin, " but I've got another shilling at home, and I'll give you that too if you'll let me have the goat. You don't want to keep the goat, do you ? "

" That I don't," said Mr. Pounds heartily.

" I'd give you more, but I haven't got any more," said Martin honestly. " And if you let me have him now I'll bring the shilling back this evening."

Mr. Pounds scowled. " All right," he said grumpily.

And so, two minutes later, Martin found himself out on the roadway with a bit of thick rope in his hand, at the other end of which tottered a baby goat.

Until now he hadn't thought what his mother and father would say about it ; he had been so desperately anxious to save the goat. But now, as he made his way home, he thought a lot about what he had done. His father was specially proud of his garden, and Martin knew that goats weren't much good for gardens. If his father insisted on his giving the goat away—well, anyway, he could see that it went to a better home than old Mr. Pounds's.

Of course, Martin's father and mother were very surprised to see the baby goat with him. But when he had explained all about it, they understood, though his father, thinking of his cherished flower-beds, said they'd better try to get the goat a good home. But Martin pleaded hard to keep the goat.

" Can't we just give him a chance, father ? " he begged. " And if we really can't manage him, and he does eat up the flowers, then we'll give him away."

So, in the end, that was how things were arranged.

Martin made up a comfortable bed for his new pet in a shed down the garden, and then he went round with the extra shilling to old Mr. Pounds.

In the daytime the goat had to be kept on a long thin rope attached to an iron stake stuck in the lawn, except when Martin took him out for a walk in the near-by woods and fields.

" I can't bear to see any animal tied up," said Martin's mother.

" Nor can I," said his father. " I wish we had the field at the end of the garden. There's a hedge all round and a gate—the little beggar could run wild there. But you can't leave a goat loose in a garden ! "

Martin's father had long wanted to buy this field to turn it into an orchard, but its owner was trying to sell it to a man for building purposes, and was asking a lot of money for it.

It took Martin some time to decide on a name for his goat, but finally he chose Barnaby.

"Why Barnaby?" inquired his father. "He doesn't look like Barnaby to me."

"Very few people look like their names," Martin's mother reminded him.

"I know he doesn't look like Barnaby—but he *feels* like Barnaby," was Martin's explanation.

And so Barnaby he was called.

At first all went well. Young goats are not much trouble. It's when they begin to grow up and get strong that they are difficult to manage in a garden.

When Martin was home from school, he and Barnaby spent a great deal of time together playing and going for walks, and the goat seemed to be greatly attached to his young master.

"He'll do anything I ask him to," Martin told his mother, "unless he doesn't want to do it."

Martin made the shed where the goat slept very comfortable for him with constant supplies of fresh straw. And if Martin forgot the straw now and then, his father remembered it, and so Barnaby got it just the same.

As Barnaby grew bigger, Martin tried to make him understand that he mustn't break down and eat any of the flowers in the garden. But Barnaby loved eating flowers—especially red flowers. He loved eating all sorts of strange things—bits of string, the covers of books, silk scarves, gloves, cigarettes, silver paper, and once he drank a bucket of soapy water that had been left outside the back door !

While he was young the rope held him in check, but a day came when he could chew through the rope and get loose. Sometimes he would break loose and run up to the house and into the back door, and come *cloperty*, *cloperty* into the kitchen. He would snatch up anything he could reach and run outside and eat it quickly.

The sight of him always made the big fat cook quite unable to move. She would stand perfectly still, throw up her hands, and begin to scream loudly. Her screams would bring others running to the rescue, but meanwhile the mischief was done. Barnaby had seized what he wanted and scampered away. The naughty goat knew very well that cook was no match for him.

"Why don't you stop him taking the things, cook ?" Martin's mother would say. "Drive him out of the kitchen !"

"When I see him," cook would gasp, fanning herself with her apron, "I go goosey all over, and I can't move hand nor foot."

But if Martin was at home, and in the kitchen, he could always manage Barnaby. Directly the goat appeared inside the kitchen door, Martin would run forward, and, catching hold of his horns, back him gently but firmly out into the garden again, and tie him up. Barnaby always allowed himself to be backed out by Martin. He was much stronger than the boy really, but he did not exert his strength on these occasions.

At last, when it was discovered that Barnaby could chew through the thickest rope, he had to have a fine, strong chain. It was a very long one, and as he was now strong enough to wrench out the iron stake by his pulling, he was attached to the heavy garden roller. This answered well for a time ; then one afternoon Martin's father found that Barnaby had grown powerful enough to tug at his chain until he was able to pull the heavy roller along the lawn and reach a border of stock that he had long had his eye on. There were no traces left of the beautiful stock by the time Martin's father came down the garden.

Martin's father was very angry. " Martin," he said, " you must shorten that goat's chain and fasten him to the big oak tree—or he'll have to go."

So Martin did this, and for a time there was peace in the garden.

It was very unfortunate that the flowers that Martin's father prized most in the garden were some red roses. Red was Barnaby's favourite colour, you remember. This year the red roses were wonderful, and of a size and colour and perfection of shape and scent that had no equal in any of the gardens for miles around. Martin's father was extremely proud of them. The roses grew on small trees in a special bed near the dining-room window.

They were so rare and beautiful that Martin's mother and father decided to give a garden party to show the roses to their friends.

" Now we'll chain Barnaby very securely to the big oak tree," said Martin's father, and he did the chaining himself to make sure. " If he ever got at my roses—I wouldn't keep him another day."

" Do be good to-day, Barnaby," Martin whispered in the goat's ear, putting an arm round his neck.

Barnaby rubbed his nose affectionately against Martin's sleeve. " Naa-aa ! " he said.

" It sounds like no," said Martin, " but I know you mean yes."

Barnaby watched the first of the guests arrive with calm,

uninterested eyes, but when a young girl with a blue satin sash stopped to talk with a friend near by, Barnaby stretched his neck and sampled the blue sash and found it tasted good. He had taken a good bite out of it before the girl felt him, and, turning, uttered a cry of dismay. She ran off, and Barnaby saw her no more except from a distance. He felt the afternoon had started rather well. Blue satin was tasty.

Many people came and spoke to him in what Barnaby thought silly voices. He was only interested in them from the point of view of food value. Of course Martin was different ; he and Martin belonged to each other. He was fond of Martin.

There was a man he approved of because his tweed jacket tasted nice, and a lady because the glove she dropped was a palatable morsel. Then a man who had come to sing put his music down on a garden table near enough for Barnaby to reach, and Barnaby sampled a sheet of his music ; the gentleman was quite put out. His best song was ruined, he said, and he could not sing it this afternoon.

At this Martin's father strode up. " Martin," he said, " that goat must be shut up in his shed till the guests have gone ! " And he took Barnaby himself and shut him up in the shed, and bolted the door.

As Barnaby was led down to the shed he caught

a passing glimpse of the beautiful red roses. He glanced at them longingly.

It seemed to Barnaby a very odd time of the day to be put to bed. It was still daylight, and the sound of people's voices outside made him restless. He gave one or two plaintive "Naa-aa's" for Martin. But Martin did not come.

Barnaby lowered his head and butted his horns against the door of the shed. At first he butted gently—again, then again. And then he butted a bit harder, again and again and again. It was his way of protesting at being shut up. He didn't know that each time he shook the door the bolt outside wriggled and slipped, wriggled and—slipped. He went on butting.

Meanwhile, the guests had gradually disappeared indoors, where the gentleman who had had his best song spoiled by Barnaby was being persuaded to sing his second-best song. The sounds of the grand piano and the gentleman's voice floated out on the early evening air. A violin solo followed, then a lady sang, and then the gentleman again. It was all very pleasant and peaceful, and Martin's mother was happy because the garden party had been a success; and Martin's father was happy because everybody had admired his roses. And Martin was happy because Barnaby hadn't been too naughty, and the almond iced cake had been very delicious.

And all the time down in the shed Barnaby

butted and butted, until suddenly the bolt slipped right back, and the shed door burst open.

Barnaby did not hesitate a second. He ran up the garden as fast as his feet would carry him, straight to the bed where the beautiful red roses grew—and started to have his supper. Oh, how delicious the roses tasted as he tore their heads off, one after another, with his great strong teeth. He munched away.

Inside the house the guests were beginning to depart, and all of them said how much they had enjoyed the garden party, and how greatly they admired the wonderful roses. When the last guest had passed out of the front door, Martin's father strolled leisurely into the dining-room to have a last look at the roses through the French windows before the fading light made it too difficult to see. He felt well content.

But only for a moment. As his eyes fell on the rose bed outside the window he stopped dead and gave a gasp. He couldn't believe his eyes! There was not a single rose left on any of the trees!

And then he caught sight of Barnaby at the edge of the bed finishing off the last mouthful. . . . With a hoarse cry Martin's father sprang at the French windows, pushed them open, and dashed out into the garden. He was followed a second later by Martin's mother, and by Martin himself, pale and heartsick when he saw what had happened.

Barnaby, sensing danger, was not easily caught that night. He led them all a long and tiring chase. And in the end it was Martin who caught him.

" I won't go near him to-night," said Martin's father. " I'm too angry. To-morrow he must go, Martin. You understand ? "

Martin nodded ; he could not speak. He shut Barnaby up in his shed, and tried to think how he had managed to escape. But though Martin's father couldn't understand how the goat had got out, he said he didn't care about that. Barnaby *had* got out and eaten all his beautiful roses ! That was enough.

Martin couldn't sleep that night. He kept getting out of bed and standing by his window to look down the garden at Barnaby's shed. To-morrow night the shed would still be there—but where would Barnaby be ?

It was a very white-faced Martin, with dark rings under his eyes, that came down to breakfast the next morning. He saw at once that his father, who generally sat facing the French windows, sat with his back to them this morning ; he couldn't bear to look out at his mangled rose trees.

Martin's father glanced up from a letter he was reading, and saw Martin's white face. He exchanged glances with Martin's mother.

" I said, Martin," remarked his father, " that if that goat destroyed my roses he must go."

Martin swallowed a lump in his throat.

"Yes, father," he managed to say.

"Well, this morning I've had a letter from the man who owns the field at the bottom of the garden—the field I've been wanting to buy. And he has come to my terms, so I'm going to buy it. I won't have Barnaby in the garden any more, but if you like you can keep him in the field——"

Martin sprang to his feet, his eyes shining.

"Oh, father! You *are* good!" he cried.

Five minutes later he was racing down to the shed to tell Barnaby the glorious news. And Barnaby made a great fuss of Martin and said "Naa-aa!" at least a dozen times to show that he understood.

"Only, I've got to take great care you never get into the garden and eat up the flowers any more, old man," said Martin. "And I *shall* take care!"

GOLLYWOG

By "Jan"

Gollywog
Is a dirty dog :
His face is as black as a coal,
But his skin's as white
As the pale moonlight,
Compared with the state of his soul.

Who was it broke the sewing-machine ?
Who was it spilt the ink ?
Who was it pushed the plasticine
Down the nursery sink ?
Who was it pulled the horsehair out
From the seat of the best armchair ?
Gollywog did it, there isn't a doubt—
Nobody else was there.

Gollywog
Is a dirty dog ;
He's steeped in original sin
From his jet-black hair
To his set black stare
And his bold and shameless grin.

Who rubbed coal on the mantelpiece ?
Who spread jam on the floor ?
Who stuffed pellets of candle-grease
In the lock of the bathroom door ?
Who put jam in Marmaduke's hat,
And butter in Mary's hair ?
Gollywog did it, I'm
sure of that—
Nobody else would
dare.

THE CHRISTMAS TREE

By Richard Hughes

It was Christmas Eve, and the Christmas tree was all decorated ready for Christmas Day. But no sooner had every one gone to bed than the toys hung on the tree began to talk to each other.

" What fun it would be," they said, " if we all got down and hid."

So they all climbed down off the tree, leaving it quite bare, and went and hid—some behind cupboards, and some under the hot-water pipes, and some behind the books in the shelves in the library, and anywhere they could think of.

In the morning the children came down, wishing each other a Happy Christmas : but when they saw their lovely tree all bare, without so much as a cracker left on it, they cried and cried and cried.

When they heard the children crying the toys all felt thoroughly ashamed of the naughty trick they had played : but all the same they didn't quite like to come out of their hiding-places while any one was about. So they waited till every one had gone to church, and then they slipped out.

" I know ! " said the Noah's Ark, speaking in all his voices at once, " I have an idea ! "

So he led the other toys out of the house, and into the town, and there they separated and found their way into every toyshop and sweetshop there was, by the back door. Once inside, they invited all the toys and all the sweets to come to a grand party they were giving, and led them back to the house.

"Here is where we are giving the party," they said, pointing to the Christmas tree. So all the new toys climbed up on to the boughs of the tree and hung there. Indeed, there was hardly room for them all, for now there were ten times as many as there had been before.

All through church the children went on crying quietly behind their Prayer Books, and came home feeling still very sad; but when they saw their Christmas tree with ten times as many presents on it as there had been before, and ten times as many candles, all kindly lighting each other, they laughed and clapped their hands and shouted with joy, and said they had never seen such a lovely Christmas tree in all their whole lives.

ELEVEN AND TWELVE BY THE CLOCK

A Christmas Fantasy

By Anne M. Trotman

It is Christmas Eve, and the moon is full. The Common, which is chosen as the scene of the coming revels, is bathed in silver light, so that a large circular patch of turf which (perhaps by elfin rite) is found in the middle of it could be mistaken for a green lake reflecting, in its waters, the thick grasses that surround it.

Into this enchanted ground come six little elves.

Gnome the first runs in ; Gnome the second skips ; Elfin Green hops, and Elfin Green's brother golliwogs ; Imp Major turns a somersault, and Imp Minor leap-frogs. They join hands, and dance to the rhythm of " Humoresque."

From far away comes the sound of a clock striking, and the elves cease dancing to listen.

Gnome the First counts the time on his fingers ; Gnome the Second blows an imaginary dandelion clock ; Elfin Green lies on the ground and kicks his toes to the strokes ; Elfin Green's Brother stands with his hand behind his ear to catch the sounds more clearly ; Imp Major swings his cap to and fro as if it were a fairy bell ; and Imp Minor sits swinging his leg so that it resembles a bulrush swinging in the wind. When the clock ceases to strike, all the elves announce the time together.

Eleven o'clock.

They jump up, and join hands to dance and sing :

Eleven o'clock,
Eleven o'clock,
What is to be done
At eleven o'clock ?

They stop and dance in the opposite direction, repeating the song. At the last word they loose hands, and, with a spring, sit tailor-fashion on the grass. Then, nodding impishly at each other, they sing :

Eleven o'clock,
Eleven o'clock ;
(*whispered*) Some *mischief* we'll do
At eleven o'clock.
(*louder*) Some *mischief* we'll do
At eleven o'clock.

Gnome First [*questioning himself*]. But what mischief ?

[*A sound of bells is heard in the distance.*]

Gnome Second. Listen, Gnome the First, I can hear bells.

Elfin Green. They're coming this way, Gnome the Second.

Elfin Green's Brother. Elfin Green, what can it be ?

Imp Major. Who can it be, Elfin Green's Brother ?

Imp Minor. Imp Major, my lord, let us hide.

Gnome First [*standing up*]—

Not yet, friends all,
Before we go,
A spell we'll throw
Across this place.
The first to-night
That shall be seen
Within this green
Shall sleep with eyes awake.
Then of him we will make
What fun we will.

[*The five elves, jumping up*.]

Five Elves. It will be a merry night.

Imp Major. But where are we to get a spell ?

Gnome First. We must make one. We'll catch these dancing moonbeams in our hands, and, weaving them together and together, we will make an elfin net and throw it over the grass. Quickly, every one—the bells sound very near.

[*The six elves dance lightly, jumping on high toes to catch the moonbeams. Each moonbeam, as it is caught, is joined to another. When each elf has woven his piece, they all run together and make of the pieces one whole net which, as they dance backwards and outwards, is spread over the turf. This done, with finger on lip and glancing eye, they run off into the grasses.*

Santa Claus comes riding into the enclosure on his sleigh, bringing with him a large sack of toys. He at once falls under the elfin spell.]

Santa Claus. What a beautiful spot, and such a wonderful night. [*Sleepily*] I should—like—to—stay—here—but—I—— Oh dear—but I——? What was—I—going—to say? [*He says no more, but sits quite still with eyes open.*]

[*The little elves peep out from among the grasses.*

Gnome the First creeps on very high toes, and with lifted finger, to Santa Claus.

He runs back to his fellows.]

Gnome First [*in an excited whisper*]. It's a King.

The Others. How do you know?

Gnome First. He looks like one. [*He runs back on tiptoes, bows to Santa Claus, then runs back to the rest.*] He cannot see me! [*Returns to Santa Claus, bows again.*] Good-evening, your Majesty.

[*The five elves advance a little way. Gnome the First runs back again to them.*]

Gnome First. He cannot hear.

[*The six little elves now troop boldly into the enclosure and stand in a half ring in front of Santa Claus.*]

Gnome Second. He looks like a big Brownie.

Elfin Green. But his coat is red.

Elfin Green's Brother. Perhaps he's the King of the Brownies.

Imp Major. That's what you said, Gnome the First—you said he was a King.

Imp Minor. I *did* want to pull that long beard, but if he's a King, perhaps I'd better not.

Gnome First. I think you'd better not, Imp Minor. I did say we'd make fun of any one who came; but, you see, I wasn't expecting this gentleman. I'm wondering what is in his sack, and I'm going to look.

[*The elves turn their attention to the sack. Gnome the First stands aside for a while to watch the others. Gnome the Second sits astride on the sack.*]

Elfin Green [*trying to untie the sack*]. It's a hard knot to untie.

Elfin Green's Brother. Come out of the way and let me do it.

[*The two brothers pull at each other, and roll each other over on the ground. Meanwhile, Imp Major has applied himself to the knot.*]

Imp Major. I've undone it.

Imp Minor [*peeping in from the other side*]. What a lot of funny things.

[*Gnome the Second suddenly ducks his head into the sack and draws out a trumpet. He doesn't know what to do with it, and so experiments. He looks down the trumpet, but making nothing of that, he puts the whistle to his eye and tries to see the stars with it.*

Meanwhile, Gnome the First swings Imp Minor out of the way, and tries to take a fairy cycle out of the sack. He looks at the injured Minor and says] :

Gnome First. Help, you imp. This is heavy.

[*The forgiving Minor helps to tug, and the fairy cycle is lifted to the ground. Gnome the First experiments with it, using it as a jumping horse. The Minor goes back to the sack, and takes out a kite. He trails it behind him for a while, the wind catches it, and he tries to help make it fly.*

Elfin Green jumps up and draws a scooter, which he sits on until he finds it begins to move. Then he sidles on it.

Elfin Green's Brother draws out a doll, which he swings up and down.

Imp Major pulls out a drum. He rolls it on the grass, then, accidentally kicking it with his leg, he finds it makes a booming noise. He picks it up and drums on it with his fingers, then noticing the drumsticks, he unties them, and, pulling the drum cord round his neck, marches off in good military style.

(PRODUCER'S NOTE.—*The above movements in connection with the sack follow one another quickly, and are carried on simultaneously.*)

Gradually all the imps find the right use for their treasures, and enjoy themselves immensely.

Santa Claus sits in the middle, eyes wide open, unmoved by the revelry. The elves make no attempt to make fun of him, but look interestedly and inquiringly at him as they pass.

Music is played for a while as the elves play.

A voice is heard in the distance.]

Voice. Santa Claus! Santa Claus!

Gnome First. Whoever is that ? [*All the elves are stationary to listen*.]

Voice. Santa Claus ! Santa Claus !

Gnome Second. It sounds like a fairy.

Voice [*sounds clearer and clearer*]. Santa Claus ! Santa Claus ! Santa Claus !

[*A child, dressed in a long nightdress, comes sleepily into the enclosure*.]

Elfin Green. You're a big fairy.

[*The child stands still, half afraid and half stupefied by sleep*.]

Elfin Green's Brother. What do you want ?

Child. I'm dreaming.

Imp Major. What about ?

Child. Santa Claus !

Imp Minor. Who is he ?

Child. He's Father Christmas, and he puts toys in our stockings.

Gnome First. What are toys ?

Child. Why, the things you're playing with.

[*The elves look afresh at their toys*, *as though magic had touched them now that they had been named*, *and they were new creations*.]

Gnome Second. What's Father Christmas like ?

Child. He has a long red cloak, and a long white beard.

[*Elfin Green runs in front of Santa Claus*, *and looks at him*. *The child*, *seeing his movement*, *goes too*.]

Child. Why, here he is ! [*Elfin Green stands back*.] Santa Claus ! [*She pulls his cloak*.] Santa Claus—Santa Claus ! [*There is no answer*.]

[*All the elves are quite still with surprise and interest*.]

Child [*with a long wail*]. Santa Claus—Santa Claus ! [*There is still no answer*. *The child howls aloud*.]

Imp Major. What's the matter now ?

Child. I'm having a nightmare.

Imp Minor. Whatever is that ?

Child. It's the worst of dreams.

Gnome First. What's it about ?

Child [*wildly*]. I'm dreaming Santa Claus is dead, and you bad fairies have stolen all the toys.

Gnome Second. Be quiet now, we haven't stolen anything.

Imp Major. We didn't know they were toys.

Imp Minor. We've only borrowed them.

Gnome First. And who are you, anyway ?

Child. I'm one of the children waiting for Santa Claus to bring us our toys. He always does on Christmas Eve. [*Howls afresh*.] And now he's dead !

Gnome Second. Weasels and stoats !

Elfin Green. Where have you come from ?

Child. Out of my house.

Elfin Green's Brother. Then you'd better go back.

Imp Major. Where is your house ?

Child. Just near the clock on the edge of the Common.

Imp Minor. Listen, it's striking again.

Child. I believe I'm going to wake up. I must run. I'd better be in bed when I wake up.

[*The child runs away*.]

[*The elves very solemnly count the strokes of the clock on their fingers, chanting elfin nonsense*.]

Elves. Grub—caterpillar—moth—butterfly,
Jelly—tadpole—frog—toad,
Worm—grasshopper—spider—gnat,
Twelve o'clock.

Santa Claus [*moving for the first time*]. Why, I've been dreaming.

Gnome First. Another one dreaming. [*Then, as Santa stands up, he is, with the rest of his comrades, too awed to speak or move*.]

Santa Claus. All of you try to move. [*No one moves*.] Why don't you move ?

Elves. We can't.

Santa Claus. Why can't you ?

Elves. We do not know.

Santa Claus. It's because I am a King.

Gnome First [*recovering a little*]. I said so.

Elves [*in chorus*]. He said you were a King. [*Also recovering*.]

Santa Claus. I'm always King at twelve o'clock on Christmas night. Usually at this time I'm on the chimney pot ready to slide down. I don't know why I'm not there to-night. [*The elves try hard not to laugh*.] And I don't know why you little elves are playing with the children's toys. [*The elves look uncomfortably hard at the ground*.] I'm sure I don't know what the children would think if they could see you. [*The elves look at each other as though together they were remembering something*.] But I expect they're all asleep.

[*Gnome the First looks round to tell about the child who has woken up, but thinks better of it*.]

Santa Claus [*pointing to Gnome the First*]. Put that fairy cycle on the sleigh. Haven't you the wind to carry you on its back ? [*To Elfin Green*.] That scooter goes beside the cycle. Do not the slippery leaves carry you down long muddy slides ? [*To Imp Major*.] Put that drum in the sack. Haven't you the bark of trees to drum with twigs ? [*To Elfin Green's Brother*.] Back goes the doll. Haven't you acorns in their cradles ? [*To Gnome the Second*.] What do you want with a trumpet ?

Haven't you daffodils to blow, and reeds to whistle through? [*To Imp Minor.*] Cannot you make a kite of yourself? Where are your wings?

[*The elves, one after another, hasten to put back their toys. They hang about the sack.*]

Santa Claus. Come here, all of you. [*They come and stand in a half ring, staring at the ground.*] I'm ashamed of you all. Are not your games better than those of children shut up in four walls? [*The elves stare harder at the ground.*] Since you have been playing tricks, and more tricks than I know, I'm going to play a trick on you.

[*The elves fall on their knees, and wring their hands for mercy.*]

Elves. O Santa Claus, Santa Claus, we won't do it any more.

Santa Claus. I hope you won't, nevertheless I'm going to give you some *work* to do.

Elves. Oh, please, Santa Claus, don't give us any work. We don't like work.

Santa Claus. You must help me fill the children's stockings.

[*The elves jump up, and stamp and clap for joy.*]

Gnome First. Rabbits hop and frogs jump.

Gnome Second. Grasshoppers fiddle and crickets violin.

Elfin Green. }
Elfin Green's Brother. } Mushrooms and Toadstools.

Imps Major and Minor. Little stars and a big moon.

Santa Claus. So do you like work, or shall I let you off ?

Chorus. No, no, no, we do like work ; it's a lovely trick.

Santa Claus. Jump on the sleigh then, all of you, quickly.

[*All the elves, except Elfin Green's Brother, find room on the sleigh*.]

Elfin Green's Brother. There's no room for me.

Santa Claus. Then jump on my lap.

[*The elves break into song*.]

Twelve by the clock,
Twelve by the clock,
What shall we do
When it's twelve by the clock ?

Twelve by the clock,
Twelve by the clock,
We'll have real fun
When it's twelve by the clock.

[*Santa Claus and company ride out of the enclosure. In the distance Christmas bells are heard ringing*.]

(PRODUCER'S NOTE.—*The weaving of the net is done by a series of skilful and graceful finger movements, and the spreading of the net is a series of similar arm movements. All the dances and movements in connection with the spell should be accompanied by soft music*.)

CAROL

By William Canton

When the herds were watching
 In the midnight chill,
Came a spotless lambkin
 From the heavenly hill.

Snow was on the mountains,
 And the wind was cold,
When from God's own garden
 Dropped a rose of gold.

When 'twas bitter winter,
 Houseless and forlorn,
In a star-lit stable
 Christ the Babe was born.

Welcome, heavenly lambkin ;
 Welcome, golden rose ;
Alleluia, Baby
 In the swaddling clothes.

GOPALA AND THE COWHERD

By Rhoda Power

Once upon a time a poor widow lived with her little son on the edge of a forest in Northern India. The little boy's name was Gopala, and his mother loved him very dearly. She taught him to be good and truthful, and to say his prayers every night. Gopala, like many people in India, believed that there was more than one god, and the god to whom he always prayed was called Krishna.

Gopala's mother was very poor and rather ignorant, and she did not know how to read or write, so she could not teach her little boy his letters. When Gopala was five years old, his mother felt very much troubled. She said to herself, " He knows how to be good, but he must also know how to learn. I shall have to send him to school." Then she sighed and looked very sad. She was so poor, and she knew that before Gopala could go to school he would have to have neat clothes and a pen and an inkstand, and all sorts of things which would cost money.

However, she worked very hard at her spindle, and by the time Gopala was six years old she had spun so much cotton that she was able to sell it and buy the boy all that he needed. When the time came for him to go to school, she dressed him in his new clothes, put his pen and his ink-stand in his hand, and sent him off to the teacher. Then she went back to her spinning, and prayed the god Krishna to look after her little boy.

Off went Gopala to school, but the road which led there was more than a mile long, and it passed through the forest. Gopala knew that there were fierce wild animals lurking behind the trees, and he felt a little bit lonely, but he ran as fast as he could. At school he soon forgot his fear ; he was so happy that he played with the other boys until they went home for supper.

But *their* homes were quite near to the school. They did not know when they sat by their mothers, eating their bowls of rice, that poor little Gopala was running all alone through a gloomy forest.

The sun was setting, and it grew darker and darker. The wild beasts began to roar, and Gopala ran faster and faster until, at last, he reached the edge of the forest and fell down at his mother's feet crying, " I'm frightened ! I'm frightened ! I can't go to school to-morrow."

His mother took him on her knee and comforted him. Then she made him some little cakes of rice, gave him a long drink of milk, and put him to bed on a mat on the floor. She thought : " When he wakes up he'll forget all about it, and he'll go off to school quite happily." Then she

The wild beasts began to roar.

went to bed herself, and she whispered a prayer : " O Krishna, take care of my little boy ! "

The next morning Gopala awoke, but he had not forgotten the dark lonely forest and the wild beasts, and when it was time to go to school again he cried : " Oh, I'm frightened ! I'm frightened ! I don't want to go to school again."

But his mother took his hand and walked with him to the edge of the forest. She said : " You mustn't cry. Just think to yourself, ' I've got a big brother in the forest who looks after some cows,' and then, if you're frightened, call out, ' Brother Cowherd, come and take care of me ! ' "

When his mother said this, Gopala began to feel brave again. He thought : " What fun to have a brother who keeps cows in the forest ! " So he waved his hand and went off by himself, while his mother prayed : " O Krishna, take care of my little boy."

Gopala went hopping and skipping along quite happily just at first, but soon the trees seemed to be very thick, and once or twice he heard a rustle among the leaves, and he began to be a little frightened. His lower lip began to tremble, and he felt his eyes getting hot at the back, as though he were going to cry. He stood still and looked around. There was nobody there, and at last he cried : " O big brother, who looks after the cows, come and take care of me."

Then what do you think happened ?

There was a queer little whispering, rustling sound in the bushes, and from behind a shrub peeped a boy : a big boy with a beautiful shining smile. He had a golden crown on his head, and in the crown there was a long peacock's feather. He was a good deal bigger than Gopala, but he was *so* gentle. He went up to the little boy and said, " Come along ! I'll take you to school, and when you come back I'll take you home again."

So little Gopala went along with the strange boy, and he felt quite happy and safe. When he reached the edge of the wood the stranger disappeared, and Gopala ran into school.

That evening when he started to go home through the dark, gloomy forest, he did not feel at all frightened. All he did was to call out : " O big brother, who looks after the cows, come and take care of me," and from behind the bushes came the beautiful boy with the golden crown.

After that Gopala went to school quite happily every day. Every morning his mother took him to the edge of the wood, and prayed : " O Krishna, look after my little boy ; " and every night Gopala came back safe and happy, saying : " I do love my big brother who keeps the cows."

One morning, after Gopala had been going to school for nearly a year, the teacher said : " I am going to have a feast at my house next week, and I want all my little pupils to come too."

You can imagine how excited the boys were,

can't you ? They did not have a feast very often, and, of course, they made all sorts of plans, and the best plan of all was that each one should bring the teacher a present.

" I shall bring sweets," said one.

" And I shall bring a little cake made of rice," said another.

" And I shall bring a curried chicken," said another.

Then they all ran home as quickly as they could to ask their mothers to prepare presents for the feast. Gopala, too, thought : " I must give something." But when he reached home he found that his poor mother had no money and no food in the house except a few grains of rice. She could not give Gopala any supper or any breakfast, so, of course, she could not give him a present for the feast. Gopala was very sad, and that night, when she put him to bed on his little mat, his mother prayed : " O Krishna, comfort my little boy."

The next day poor Gopala went slowly through the forest. He was very hungry, and he had nothing to give the teacher. He did not want to be different from the other boys, and he knew that they were all bringing presents for the feast. At first he did not know what to do, and he very nearly cried. Then suddenly he thought : " Why ! I'll ask my big brother."

So he stood quite still and called : " O big

brother, who looks after the cows, come and take care of me." And out of the bushes came the boy with the golden crown and the peacock's feather.

Of course Gopala told him his trouble, and the beautiful stranger smiled, then he went back into the bushes and returned with a little bowl of curds. " Give this to your teacher, Gopala," he said, and disappeared.

Carefully holding the bowl between his hands, Gopala went joyfully to school, and there he found everybody giving presents to the teacher. There were cakes, and sweets, and curry, and fruit, but nobody had brought a bowl of curds.

The teacher was pleased. He took the bowl and he poured the curds into a jar.

Then a strange thing happened.

When he was giving the bowl back to Gopala he found that it was quite full, just as though he had never emptied the curds into the jar. He was very much astonished. Once again he poured out the curds into a jar, and once again he looked at the bowl and it was still quite full. He did this over and over again, until the whole school had a dinner of curds, and yet the little bowl was still full.

The teacher looked at Gopala. " Gopala ! " he said, " where *did* you get this present ? "

" Oh," said Gopala, " I got it in the forest. My big brother, who looks after the cows, gave it me."

Then the teacher said : " I want to see your big brother." Little Gopala led his teacher into the forest. As usual, he stood quite still and called : " O big brother, who looks after the cows, come and take care of me and my teacher ! "

As usual there was a rustling and a whispering among the bushes, but no beautiful stranger came to Gopala.

Gopala called again : " O big brother, who looks after the cows, come and take care of me and my teacher ! " But the boy did not come ; only a voice like a silver bell answered : " A long time will pass before your teacher may see me. But you, Gopala, are blessed, for very few boys have a mother like yours."

You know what had happened, don't you ? Every day Gopala's mother had prayed : " O Krishna, take care of my little boy ! " and Krishna had heard the prayer, and pretended to be the big brother who looked after the cows.

THE SNOW-MAN

By Mabel Marlowe

A snow-man once stood upon a hill, with his face towards the sunset. A very fine snow-man he was, as tall as a soldier, and much fatter. He had two pieces of glass for eyes, and a stone for a nose, and a piece of black wood for a mouth, and in his hand he held a stout, knobbly club.

But he had no clothes at all, not even a hat, and the wind on the top of that hill was as bitter as wind could be.

" How cold I am ! I am as cold as ice," said the snow-man. " But that red sky looks warm." So he lifted his feet from the ground, and went tramp, tramp, tramping down the slope towards the setting sun.

Very soon he overtook a gipsy woman, who was wearing a bright red shawl. " Ha, that looks warm ! I must have it," thought the snow-man. So he went up to the gipsy woman and he said, " Give me that red shawl."

" No, indeed ! I cannot spare it on this wintry day," answered the gipsy. " I am cold enough as it is."

" Cold ! " shouted the snow-man in a very growlish voice. " Are you as cold as I am, I wonder! Are you cold inside as well as outside? Are you made of ice, through and through and through?"

"No, I suppose not," mumbled the gipsy, who was getting hot with fright.

"Then give me your red shawl, this moment, or I shall strike you with my stout, knobbly club."

Then the gipsy took off her red shawl, grumbling all the time, and gave it to the snow-man. He put it round his shoulders, without a word of thanks, and went tramp, tramp, tramping down the hill. And the shivering gipsy woman followed behind him.

Presently the snow-man overtook a ploughboy, who was wearing his grandmother's long, red woollen mittens.

"Ha! They look warm! I must have them," thought the snow-man. So he went up to the ploughboy and he said, "Give me those red woollen mittens."

"No, indeed!" said the ploughboy. "They belong to my grandmother. She lent them to me because my fingers were so cold."

"Cold!" shouted the snow-man, in a very roarish voice. "Are your fingers as cold as mine, I wonder! Are your hands and arms frozen into ice, through and through and through?"

"No, I suppose not," mumbled the ploughboy.

"Then give me those red mittens, this moment, or I shall strike you with my stout, knobbly club."

So the ploughboy drew off the warm mittens, grumbling all the time, and the

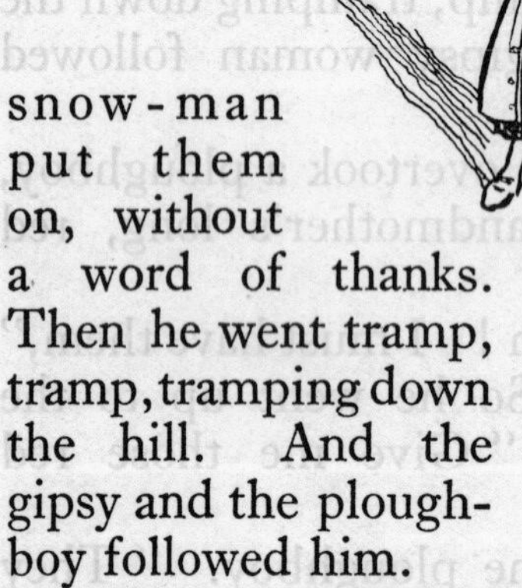

snow-man put them on, without a word of thanks. Then he went tramp, tramp, tramping down the hill. And the gipsy and the ploughboy followed him.

After a while he overtook a tame pirate, wearing a pirate's thick red cap, with a tassel dangling down his back.

"Ha! That looks warm! I must have it," said the snow-man. So he went up to the tame pirate and he said, "Give me that red tassel cap."

" No, indeed ! " said the pirate. " A nice cold in the head I should get if I did."

" Cold in the head ! " shouted the snow-man, in a very thunderish voice. " Is your head as cold as mine, I wonder ! Are your brains made of snow, and your bones solid ice, through and through and through ? "

" No, I suppose not," muttered the tame pirate.

" Then give me that red tassel cap, this moment, or I shall set upon you with my stout, knobbly club."

Now the pirate felt very sorry that he had turned tame, but he did not like the look of that knobbly stick, so he gave up his red tassel cap. The snow-man put it on, without a word of thanks, Then he went tramp, tramp, tramping down the hill, with the tassel bumping up and down. And the gipsy woman, and the ploughboy, and the tame pirate followed him.

At last he reached the bottom of the hill, where the village schoolhouse stood, and there was the village schoolmaster on the doorstep, looking at the sunset. He was smoking a glowing briar pipe, and on his feet there were two red velvet slippers.

" Ha ! Those look warm ! I must have them," said the snow-man. So he went up to the schoolmaster, and he said, " Give me those red slippers."

" Certainly, if you want them," said the schoolmaster. " Take them by all means. It is far too cold to-day to be tramping about with bare toes," and he stooped and drew off his slippers, and there he stood in some bright red socks, thick and woolly and knitted by hand.

"Ha! Those look warm! Give them to me!" said the snow-man.

"Certainly, if you want them," said the schoolmaster. "But you must come inside. I cannot take my socks off here, in the doorway. Come on to the mat."

So the snow-man stepped inside the doorway, and stood upon the mat.

"Be sharp with those socks. My feet are as cold as solid ice," he grumbled.

"I am sorry to hear that," said the schoolmaster. "But I have a warm red blanket airing over the stove. Come in, sir. Sit on that chair by the fire, sir. Put your cold feet upon this snug, red footstool, and let me wrap this red blanket around your legs."

So the snow-man came into the schoolhouse, and sat upon a chair by the glowing fire, and put his feet upon the red footstool, and the schoolmaster wrapped the red blanket round and round and round his legs. (And all this while the gipsy woman, and the ploughboy, and the tame pirate were peering in at the window.)

"Are you feeling warmer?" asked the schoolmaster.

"No. I am as cold as an iceberg."

" Come closer to the fire."

So the schoolmaster pushed the chair closer to the fire, but the snow-man gave him not one word of thanks.

" Are you feeling warmer now ? "

" No. I am as cold as a stone. My feet feel like icy water."

" Move closer to the fire," said the schoolmaster, and he pushed the chair right against the kerb. " There ! Are you warmer now ? "

" No, no, no ! I am colder than ever. I cannot feel my feet at all. I cannot feel my legs at all. I cannot feel my back at all."

Then the schoolmaster pushed the chair quite close up against the stove. " Are you warmer now ? " he said.

But there was no answer, except a slithery sliding sound, and the drip, drip, drip of black snow-water.

" Dear me ! " whispered the snow-man, in a gurgling kind of voice. " I have dropped my stout, knobbly club. My red slippers are floating into the ashpan. My mittens are swimming in a little river on the floor. My shawl is gone. My red tassel cap is slipping—slipping away. My head is going—going——"

Splosh ! Splash ! Gurgle !

" That's the end of him," said the schoolmaster, and he went to fetch the mop.

Then the gipsy woman, and the ploughboy,

and the tame pirate came in and picked up their things, and wrung them out, and dried them at the stove, and the schoolmaster put his red slippers on the hearth, and hung the red blanket over the back of the chair.

Then he picked up the stout, knobbly club and gave the fire a poke.

THE HARE

By Walter de la Mare

In the black furrow of a field
  I saw an old witch-hare this night ;
And she cocked a lissome ear,
  And she eyed the moon so bright,
And she nibbled of the green ;
  And I whispered, "Wh-s-st ! witch-hare,"
Away, like a ghostie o'er the field,
  She fled, and left the moonlight there.

EEYORE JOINS THE GAME

By A. A. Milne

[If you haven't read the book called *Winnie the Pooh,* and the second one, *The House at Pooh Corner,* from which this story is taken, you will certainly want to when you have read this.

But you will enjoy the story more if you understand that all the people in it are toy animals belonging to a boy called Christopher Robin. You can guess who Rabbit and Piglet are; but Eeyore, Roo, and Pooh, and Tigger are not so easy. Well then, Pooh is the Teddy Bear. Eeyore is the Donkey. Tigger is the Tiger. Roo is the baby Kanga*roo*.]

By the time it came to the edge of the Forest the stream had grown up, so that it was almost a river, and, being grown-up, it did not run and jump and sparkle along as it used to do when it was younger, but moved more slowly. For it knew now where it was going, and it said to itself, " There is no hurry. We shall get there some day." But all the little streams higher up in the Forest went this way and that, quickly, eagerly, having so much to find out before it was too late.

There was a broad track, almost as broad as a road, leading from the Outland to the Forest, but before it could come to the Forest, it had to cross this river. So, where it crossed, there was a wooden bridge, almost as broad as a road, with wooden rails on each side of it. Christopher Robin could just get his chin on to the top rail, if he wanted to, but it was more fun to stand on the bottom rail, so that he could lean right over, and watch the river slipping slowly away beneath him. Pooh could get his chin on to the bottom rail if he wanted to, but it was more fun to lie down and get his head under it, and watch the river slipping slowly away beneath him. And this was the only way in which Piglet and Roo could watch the river at all, because they were too small to reach the bottom rail. So they would lie down and watch it . . . and it slipped away very slowly, being in no hurry to get there.

One day, when Pooh was walking towards this bridge, he was trying to make up a piece of poetry about fir-cones, because there they were, lying about on each side of him, and he felt singy. So he picked a fir-cone up, and looked at it, and said to himself, " This is a very good fir-cone, and something ought to rhyme to it." But he couldn't think of anything. And then this came into his head suddenly :

> Here is a myst'ry
> About a little fir tree.
> Owl says it's *his* tree,
> And Kanga says it's *her* tree.

" Which doesn't make sense," said Pooh, " because Kanga doesn't live in a tree."

He had just come to the bridge ; and not

looking where he was going, he tripped over something, and the fir-cone jerked out of his paw into the river.

" Bother," said Pooh, as it floated slowly under the bridge, and he went back to get another fir-cone which had a rhyme to it. But then he thought that he would just look at the river instead, because it was a peaceful sort of day, so he lay down and looked at it, and it slipped slowly away beneath him . . . and suddenly, there was his fir-cone slipping away too.

" That's funny," said Pooh. " I dropped it on the other side," said Pooh, " and it came out on this side ! I wonder if it would do it again ? " And he went back for some more fir cones.

It did. It kept on doing it. Then he dropped two in at once, and leant over the bridge to see which of them would come out first ; and one of them did ; but as they were both the same size, he didn't know if it was the one which he wanted to win, or the other one. So the next time he dropped one big one and one little one, and the big one came out first, which was what he had said it would do, and the little one came out last, which was what he had said it would do, so he had won twice . . . and when he went home for tea, he had won thirty-six and lost twenty-eight, which meant that he was—that he had—well, you take twenty-eight from thirty-six, and *that's* what he was. Instead of the other way round.

And that was the beginning of the game called Poohsticks, which Pooh invented, and which he and his friends used to play on the edge of the Forest. But they played with sticks instead of fir-cones, because they were easier to mark.

Now one day Pooh and Piglet and Rabbit and Roo were all playing Poohsticks together. They had dropped their sticks in when Rabbit said " Go ! " and then they had hurried across to the other side of the bridge, and now they were all leaning over the edge, waiting to see whose stick would come out first. But it was a long time coming, because the river was very lazy that day, and hardly seemed to mind if it didn't ever get there at all.

" I can see mine ! " cried Roo. " No, I can't, it's something else. Can you see yours, Piglet ? I thought I could see mine, but I couldn't. There it is ! No, it isn't. Can you see yours, Pooh ? "

" No," said Pooh.

" I expect my stick's stuck," said Roo. " Rabbit, my stick's stuck. Is your stick stuck, Piglet ? "

" They always take longer than you think," said Rabbit.

" How long do you *think* they'll take ? " asked Roo.

" I can see yours, Piglet," said Pooh suddenly.

" Mine's a sort of greyish one," said Piglet, not daring to lean too far over in case he fell in.

" Yes, that's what I can see. It's coming over on to my side."

Rabbit leant over farther than ever, looking for his, and Roo wriggled up and down, calling out " Come on, stick ! Stick, stick, stick ! " and Piglet got very excited because his was the only one which had been seen, and that meant that he was winning.

" It's coming ! " said Pooh.

" Are you *sure* it's mine ? " squeaked Piglet excitedly.

" Yes, because it's grey. A big grey one. Here it comes ! A very—big—grey—— Oh, no, it isn't, it's Eeyore."

And out floated Eeyore.

" Eeyore ! " cried everybody.

Looking very calm, very dignified, with his legs in the air, came Eeyore from beneath the bridge.

" It's Eeyore ! " cried Roo, terribly excited.

" Is that so ? " said Eeyore, getting caught up by a little eddy, and turning slowly round three times. " I wondered."

" I didn't know you were playing," said Roo.

" I'm not," said Eeyore.

" Eeyore, what *are* you doing there ? " said Rabbit.

" I'll give you three guesses, Rabbit. Digging holes in the ground ? Wrong. Leaping from branch to branch of a young oak tree ? Wrong.

Waiting for somebody to help me out of the river? Right. Give Rabbit time, and he'll always get the answer."

"But, Eeyore," said Pooh in distress, "what can we—I mean, how shall we—do you think if we——"

"Yes," said Eeyore. "One of these would be just the thing. Thank you, Pooh."

"He's going *round* and *round*," said Roo, much impressed.

"And why not?" said Eeyore coldly.

"I can swim too," said Roo proudly.

"Not round and round," said Eeyore. "It's much more difficult. I didn't want to come swimming at all to-day," he went on, revolving slowly. "But if, when in, I decide to practise a slight circular movement from right to left—or perhaps I should say," he added, as he got into another eddy, "from left to right, just as it happens to occur to me, it's nobody's business but my own."

There was a moment's silence, while everybody thought.

"I've got a sort of idea," said Pooh at last, "but I don't suppose it's a very good one."

"I don't suppose it is either," said Eeyore.

"Go on, Pooh," said Rabbit. "Let's have it."

"Well, if we all threw stones and things into the river on *one* side of Eeyore, the stones would make waves, and the waves would wash him to the other side."

" That's a very good idea," said Rabbit, and Pooh looked happy again.

" Very," said Eeyore. " When I want to be washed, Pooh, I'll let you know."

" Supposing we hit him by mistake ? " said Piglet anxiously.

" Or supposing you missed him by mistake," said Eeyore. " Think of all the possibilities, Piglet, before you settle down to enjoy yourselves."

But Pooh had got the biggest stone he could carry, and was leaning over the bridge, holding it in his paws.

" I'm not throwing it, I'm dropping it, Eeyore," he explained. " And then I can't miss—I mean I can't hit you. *Could* you stop turning round for a moment, because it muddles me rather ? "

" No," said Eeyore. " I *like* turning round."

Rabbit began to feel that it was time he took command.

" Now, Pooh," he said, " when I say 'Now !' you can drop it. Eeyore, when I say 'Now !' Pooh will drop his stone."

" Thank you very much, Rabbit, but I expect I shall know."

" Are you ready, Pooh ? Piglet, give Pooh a little more room. Get back a bit there, Roo. Are you ready ? "

" No," said Eeyore.

" *Now !* " said Rabbit.

Pooh dropped his stone. There was a loud splash, and Eeyore disappeared. . . .

It was an anxious moment for the watchers on the bridge. They looked and looked . . . and even the sight of Piglet's stick coming out a little in front of Rabbit's didn't cheer them up as much as you would have expected. And then, just as Pooh was beginning to think that he must have chosen the wrong stone or the wrong river or the wrong day for his Idea, something grey showed for a moment by the river bank . . . and it got slowly bigger and bigger . . . and at last it was Eeyore coming out.

With a shout they rushed off the bridge, and pushed and pulled at him ; and soon he was standing among them again on dry land.

" Oh, Eeyore, you *are* wet ! " said Piglet, feeling him.

Eeyore shook himself, and asked somebody to explain to Piglet what happened when you had been inside a river for quite a long time.

" Well done, Pooh," said Rabbit kindly. " That was a good idea of ours."

" What was ? " asked Eeyore.

" Hooshing you to the bank like that."

" *Hooshing* me ? " said Eeyore in surprise. " Hooshing *me* ? You didn't think I was *hooshed*, did you ? I dived. Pooh dropped a large stone on me, and so as not to be struck heavily on the chest, I dived and swam to the bank."

"You didn't really," whispered Piglet to Pooh, so as to comfort him.

"I didn't *think* I did," said Pooh anxiously.

"It's just Eeyore," said Piglet. "*I* thought your Idea was a very good Idea."

Pooh began to feel a little more comfortable, because when you are a Bear of Very Little Brain, and you Think of Things, you find sometimes that a Thing which seemed very Thingish inside you is quite different when it gets out into the open and has other people looking at it. And, anyhow, Eeyore *was* in the river, and now he *wasn't*, so he hadn't done any harm.

"How did you fall in, Eeyore?" asked Rabbit, as he dried him with Piglet's handkerchief.

"I didn't," said Eeyore.

"But how——"

"I was BOUNCED," said Eeyore.

"Oo," said Roo excitedly, "did somebody push you?"

"Somebody BOUNCED me. I was just thinking by the side of the river—thinking, if any of you know what that means—when I received a loud BOUNCE."

"Oh, Eeyore!" said everybody.

"Are you sure you didn't slip?" asked Rabbit wisely.

"Of course I slipped. If you're standing

on the slippery bank of a river, and somebody BOUNCES you loudly from behind, you slip. What did you think I did ?"

"But who did it ?" asked Roo.

Eeyore didn't answer.

"I expect it was Tigger," said Piglet nervously.

"But, Eeyore," said Pooh, "was it a Joke, or an Accident ? I mean——"

"I didn't stop to ask, Pooh. Even at the very bottom of the river I didn't stop to say to myself, '*Is* this a Hearty Joke, or is it the Merest Accident ?' I just floated to the surface, and said to myself, 'It's wet.' If you know what I mean."

"And where was Tigger ?" asked Rabbit.

Before Eeyore could answer, there was a loud noise behind them, and through the hedge came Tigger himself.

"Hallo, everybody," said Tigger cheerfully.

"Hallo, Tigger," said Roo.

Rabbit became very important suddenly.

"Tigger," he said solemnly, "what happened just now ?"

"Just when ?" said Tigger a little uncomfortably.

"When you bounced Eeyore into the river."

"I didn't bounce him."

"You bounced me," said Eeyore gruffly.

"I didn't really. I had a cough, and I happened to be behind Eeyore, and I said '*Grrrr—oppp—ptschschschz*.'"

"Why?" said Rabbit, helping Piglet up, and dusting him. "It's all right, Piglet."

"It took me by surprise," said Piglet nervously.

"That's what I call bouncing," said Eeyore. "Taking people by surprise. Very unpleasant habit. I don't mind Tigger being in the Forest," he went on, "because it's a large Forest, and there's plenty of room to bounce in it. But I don't see why he should come into *my* little corner of it, and bounce there. It isn't as if there was anything very wonderful about my little corner. Of course for people who like cold, wet, ugly bits it *is* something rather special, but otherwise it's just a corner, and if anybody feels bouncy——"

"I didn't bounce, I coughed," said Tigger crossly.

"Bouncy or coffy, it's all the same at the bottom of the river."

"Well," said Rabbit, "all I can say is—well, here's Christopher Robin, so *he* can say it."

Christopher Robin came down from the Forest to the bridge, feeling all sunny and careless, and just as if twice nineteen didn't matter a bit, as it didn't on such a happy afternoon, and he thought that if he stood on the bottom rail of the bridge, and leant over, and watched the river slipping slowly away beneath him, then he would suddenly know everything that there was to be known, and he would be able to tell Pooh, who wasn't quite sure about some of it. But when he got to the bridge and saw all the animals there, then he knew that it wasn't that kind of afternoon, but the other kind, when you wanted to *do* something.

"It's like this, Christopher Robin," began Rabbit. "Tigger——"

"No, I didn't," said Tigger.

"Well, anyhow, there I was," said Eeyore.

"But I don't think he meant to," said Pooh.

"He just *is* bouncy," said Piglet, "and he can't help it."

"Try bouncing *me*, Tigger," said Roo eagerly. "Eeyore, Tigger's going to try *me*. Piglet, do you think——"

"Yes, yes," said Rabbit, "we don't all want to speak at once. The point is, what does Christopher Robin think about it?"

"All I did was I coughed," said Tigger.

"He bounced," said Eeyore.

"Well, I sort of boffed," said Tigger.

"Hush!" said Rabbit, holding up his paw. "What does Christopher Robin think about it all? That's the point."

"Well," said Christopher Robin, not quite sure what it was all about, "*I* think——"

"Yes?" said everybody.

"*I* think we all ought to play Poohsticks."

So they did. And Eeyore, who had never played it before, won more times than anybody else; and Roo fell in twice, the first time by accident and the second time on purpose, because he suddenly saw Kanga coming from the Forest, and he knew he'd have to go to bed anyhow. So then Rabbit said he'd go with them; and Tigger and Eeyore went off together, because Eeyore wanted to tell Tigger How to Win at Poohsticks, which you do by letting your stick drop in a twitchy sort of way, if you understand what I mean, Tigger; and Christopher Robin and Pooh and Piglet were left on the bridge by themselves.

For a long time they looked at the river beneath them, saying nothing, and the river said nothing too, for it felt very quiet and peaceful on this summer afternoon.

" Tigger is all right *really*," said Piglet lazily.

" Of course he is," said Christopher Robin.

" Everybody is *really*," said Pooh. " That's what *I* think," said Pooh. " But I don't suppose I'm right," he said.

" Of course you are," said Christopher Robin.

By Eleanor Halsey

When I walk along the High Street in the
morning, every day,
I see the cats who live there—white and
black, and blue and grey,
The tortoiseshell and sandy cats,
The cat without a tail,
And the little tabby kitten, sitting balanced on a
rail.

They roam about while shops are being cleaned
with broom and mop,
And every shop has got a cat, and every cat a shop.

. . . .

The cat that lives at the butcher's shop
Is fierce and sleek and bold ;
He eats up all the bones and scraps
And meat that's getting old.

The cat that lives at the dairy
Finds life a glorious dream ;
She will not touch a drop of milk
But lives on double cream !

The cat who lives at the butter shop
  Thinks times are rather hard ;
He may not eat the " very best fresh,"
  Or even lick the lard.

One cat lives at the fishmonger's
  Amid temptations sore ;
However much fish they give him to eat
  He always steals some more.

The cat who lives at the grocer's
  Is getting rather thin ;
He can't eat the salmon that's piled around,
  But only sniff at the tin !

At the rag and bone and bottle shop
  There lives the happiest cat,
For his people treat him as one of themselves,
  And they can't do more than that !

THE SMALL PEOPLE'S FAIR

By A. K. Hamilton Jenkin

When you hear the word " fairy " do you think, I wonder, of a girl in a white, spangled dress, who goes about making everybody happy simply by waving a wand ? Well, that is the pantomime idea of a fairy, and a rather dull sort of fairy, too, don't you think ?

The fairies that used to be in Cornwall were much more exciting than this, because they were so much more real. As a matter of fact, in Cornwall the word " fairy " was never used. The Cornish name for them was the *Small People*. People who have seen them say that they were the neatest little creatures imaginable, though they were rarely more than a foot high. Generally the little men were dressed in black, steeple-crowned hats, with scarlet cloaks, and underneath had tiny coats and breeches of green. Their women folk were equally stylish in an old-fashioned way. Their gowns were also of green, and frequently had long trains, whilst their high-heeled shoes sparkled with diamonds.

The Small People were always very queer and tricky in their ways. You never knew quite how to take them. Sometimes they would be friendly enough to human beings, and would come into the kitchens of the farms by night and do the housework. If the farmer's wife was sensible, she would leave them a bowl of milk the next night as a reward for their kindness.

But at other times the Small People would revenge themselves on Man by playing him all kinds of freakish tricks. Particularly was this the case with people whom they had once caught spying upon them at their fairs or revels.

Many years ago now an old lady, called Aunt Penelope, who was housekeeper to a gentleman living near the Land's End, had been into Penzance to do her weekly marketing. She stopped so long there, gossiping and drinking with her friends, that it was quite dark by the time she started back. There were very few roads in those days, and her way home lay over the rough, bleak moorlands, where it was easy enough to get lost on a night like this. She had got a good way towards home when all of a sudden she saw lights and heard the sound of sweet music playing close beside her path. Now Aunt Penelope was a lively old woman, and, despite her long walk, she felt all agog to join in the dance which she was sure was going on. So she turned aside from the path; but instead of finding a house, as she expected, she came all at once upon a smooth, level piece of grass. There, straight before her eyes, she saw a crowd of Small People holding a fair. There were dozens of little stalls, standing all in a row. These were covered with trinkets and jewellery, all on a tiny scale, but shining more brightly than you can imagine. Close by, the fairies were dancing. Hundreds of them, linked hand in hand, were whirling round so fast it made Aunt Penelope quite giddy to look at them. In the middle of the ring was a maypole. It was only about three feet high, but was wreathed around with lovely flowers. At the foot of this stood the pipers, playing the merriest old tunes. Aunt Penelope felt more than ever inclined to dance as she listened to their music. She could hardly keep her feet still. But, at the same time, she was really afraid of joining in amongst such tiny creatures, lest with a kick of her heels she should send them all flying. The girl fairies, the old woman said, were the sauciest young things she had ever seen. They were tossing up their heels higher than their heads, often kicking the hats off the men as they capered round and round. Whilst she was watching, one of them leapt right over

R.S.GERVIS

the other dancers, and landed on top of the maypole itself, where she spun round on one toe, like a whirligig or top.

Then, just as at a real fair, there were the mischievous boys rushing wildly in and out amongst the crowd. Some of them were scampering about seated astride on the backs of mice, and pretending, I expect, that they were cowboys! Others were swinging on the gossamer or long trails of cobweb which you so often see stretched between the furze bushes in summer-time.

There were lights about in all directions. Little lanterns no bigger than foxglove flowers were hung in rows along the stalls. All the glow-worms in Cornwall, too, seemed to have gathered about the fair-ground to help to light it up.

Not far from the spot where the dancing was going on there was a wrestling ring. Aunt Penelope could see the little men, with their arms locked about one another, trying to throw each other a fair " back fall." Being a Cornish woman, she knew all about wrestling, which was the chief sport of the county in those days, and as popular as football is in England now. Round the wrestling ring there were lots of little girl-fairies looking on, encouraging their brothers or sweethearts by clapping their hands and shouting applause.

Farther on again, she saw more of the Small People shooting at a target with bows and arrows. In yet another corner of the fair-ground there was a game of bowls in progress. Most of the players here were elderly-looking little men, with long grey beards. They had thrown aside their cloaks, and moved about very solemnly and sedately. They were so intent on their game they didn't seem to notice anything of the noise and racket going on around them.

All the games and sports which used to be found at old-fashioned fairs were there. But most of the Small People seemed quite content to parade up and down between the stalls, simply looking at the pretty things which were displayed. There were shoe buckles of silver and gold, sparkling with Cornish diamonds fans made out of goldfinches' feathers stuck into pearl handles, pins with jewelled heads, brooches, rings, and bracelets of every kind.

As she gazed on these, Aunt Penelope began to think how nice one of those bright little buckles would look fixed on to her own Sunday-best cap. So, very cautiously, she drew off one of the gloves she was wearing, and dropped it over the buckle. Her hand was just about to pick up the glove, with the buckle under it, when all of a sudden she felt as if her fingers had been pierced right through with millions of little sharp pins and needles. " Oh ! " she cried out in her pain, " you cussed little spirits, you ! "

That was enough ! In an instant the lights had all gone, the fair-ground had disappeared, and the Small People had vanished away among the rocks as completely as if the ground had swallowed them.

Dawn was breaking the next morning when the old woman awoke, to find herself lying stiff and cold among the prickly furze bushes on the bleak hillside. Her right hand was bleeding slightly—all that was left to remind her of the beautiful buckle she would never see again.

THE SCHOOL

By Richard Hughes

ONCE there was a schoolmaster and a schoolmistress who hadn't any school.

" This is absurd," they said. " We *must* have a school ; " so they got a brass plate, and wrote the word " SCHOOL " on it, and put it up on their gate.

The next day they rang a bell at nine o'clock in the morning for lessons to begin. But, of course, no one came. So for half the morning he taught her, and for the other half she taught him.

The next day he said, " I am going out to see if I can't find some one to come to our school." On the way he passed a toyshop, and in the window there was a fine big Noah's Ark ; so he bought it and took it home. Then he took out Mr. and Mrs. Noah, and Shem and Ham and Japhet, and all the animals, and put them in the desks in the schoolroom.

" Now," he said, " we have got a splendid big class to teach ! "

So all that day they taught the things out of the Ark.

" I do think this is a well-behaved class," said the schoolmistress. " They sit ever so still, and never make any noise at all ! "

Which was perfectly true. They never made

a sound. The only trouble was that when you asked them a question they still didn't make a sound, but just sat quiet and didn't answer.

" What do two and two make, Noah ? " the schoolmistress asked.

But Mr. Noah said nothing.

" Next ! " she said.

But Mrs. Noah said nothing either.

" Next ! Next ! Next ! " said she. But Shem and Ham and Japhet and the two lions and the two elephants and the two mice, and all the other animals, said nothing either.

" What *I* think," said the schoolmistress, " is that we've got the stupidest class that ever was ! "

So she popped them all back in the Ark and went out to look for something else.

Presently she came to a shop called " Railway Umbrellas." It was where they sell all the things people leave in railway carriages and never come back for : umbrellas, and handbags, and bananas, and babies, and concertinas, and parcels, and so on. So she went in. And sitting in the window she saw a dear little black kitten.

" Is that a railway kitten, too ? " she asked the man.

" Yes, madam," he said. " Somebody left him in a basket on the rack of a train only the other day."

" Well, I'll have that one then," she said, and bought it and took it home. When lesson-time came they took all the creatures out of the Ark and made the kitten sit in the middle of them.

" What do two and two make, Railway Kitten ? " she asked.

" Meaow ! " said the kitten.

" No, they don't, they make four ! " she said. " What is the capital of Italy ? "

" Meaow ! " said the kitten.

" Wrong ! It's Rome. Who signed Magna Charta ? "

" Meaow ! " said the Railway Kitten.

" Wrong again," she said, " it was King John ! I've never even heard of Mr. Meaow ! " And she turned round and started to write a sum on the blackboard. But as soon as her back was turned the naughty Railway Kitten began to have a lovely game with all the wooden creatures out of the Ark. He knocked them down, and sent them skidding all over the floor ; and when the schoolmistress looked round again he had climbed on his desk, dipped his tail in the inkpot, and now was swishing it about so as to flip ink all over the room.

" Oh, you *naughty* kitten ! " she cried. " If you're not good I'll send you back to your railway ! " And she took him and shut him up in the kitchen.

Just then the front-door bell rang, and the schoolmaster went to see who it was. Outside there was a little girl, with a packet of school books under her arm.

" Please," she said, " I've forgotten the way to my school ; may I come to yours instead ? "

" Certainly ! Certainly ! " said the schoolmaster. So she came in, and hung her hat and coat on a peg, and changed her shoes, and went and sat down in the schoolroom.

Now, not only was she as good as the Ark creatures, and sat perfectly still and quiet, but also when she was asked a question she answered it, and always got the answer right. And she never once let the Railway Kitten play during lessons, though out of lesson-time, of course, she played with him a lot, and gave him his saucer of milk.

When the evening came she said : " Is this a boarding-school ? Because if it is I don't think I shall bother to go home."

" All right," they said, and put her to bed.

Now, as I have told you, all day she had been good as good ; but when she went to bed there was just one thing she was naughty about : she

WOULD NOT get out of the bath when she was told. When she had been washed she just lay on her back and refused to move, and the poor schoolmistress simply *couldn't* make her. She lay there till the hot water turned her as pink as a lobster, and it wasn't till the water had got quite cold that she would come out. Then, of course, she was

cold too, and shivered, and her teeth chattered when she got into bed.

The next day she was perfectly good again; but when night came the same thing happened—once she was in her bath she *would not* move.

"I am going to count one—two—three, and then pull up the plug!" said the schoolmistress. "ONE! TWO!——"

And before she could say THREE the little girl jumped out in a terrible fright.

" That's a good plan," thought the schoolmistress, " I'll do it again."

And so she did. Every night, when the little girl wouldn't get out, she counted ONE, TWO, and before she could say THREE out she jumped. And this went on for a whole week. But when it came to Saturday night, and she counted ONE! TWO! all the little girl said was " SHAN'T! " and lay so flat on the bottom of the bath that only her nose was above the water.

" THREE ! " said the mistress, and pulled up the plug! Away the water rushed, down the waste-pipe: and alas! away went the poor little girl with it. First her feet were sucked into the hole, and then her legs, and then her body, and in a moment she had disappeared altogether.

" OH, what *have* you done ! " cried the schoolmaster. " You have lost our only child ! "

" I don't care ! " said the schoolmistress in a stern voice. " *She should have got out of the bath when she WAS TOLD !* "

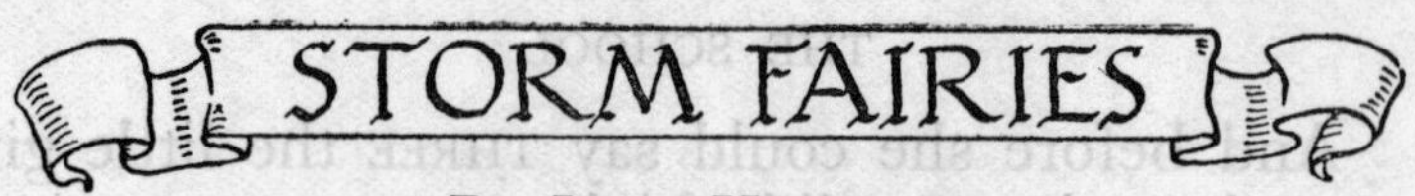

STORM FAIRIES

By John Hampden

"Won't you come in?" cried Auntie,
With the door ajar on the chain;
"Oh, do come in, for the night's so cold,
Out there in the wind and rain.

"Oh, do come in," cried Auntie,
As the candle guttered in the draught,
And no one answered a word at all;
But I think that Somebody laughed.

Then tiny feet went pitter-pitter-pat,
All the way round the house,
And there wasn't the tiniest sound after that,
No, not to scare a mouse.

"Then you won't come in?" said Auntie,
And she turned the great big key.
Now isn't it strange that they don't like Auntie,
But they'll play with you and me?

MONSIEUR SEGUIN'S GOAT

Translated from ALPHONSE DAUDET
By Rosalind Vallance

MONSIEUR SEGUIN was most unlucky with his goats. He lost them all in the same way : one fine morning, sooner or later, they broke loose and ran away up the mountain, and there the wolf ate them.

It seemed as if nothing could hold them back —neither their master's kindness nor even fear of the wolf. They were most independent goats, and cared for nothing but to be free and at large.

Good Monsieur Seguin, who did not understand his animals, grew very distressed. Every time it happened he used to say, " This is too much ; I won't keep another one." But all the same he did, and even when he had lost six of his goats in the same way, he bought a seventh. But this time he was careful to choose a very young one, so that she would more easily get used to him.

What a pretty little thing she was, with her soft eyes, her small pointed beard, her little black shining hoofs, her horns, and her overcoat of long white hair !

And she was so gentle, so loving. She would

let him milk her without moving, and never put her foot into the pail. In fact, she was a perfect little dear.

Behind Monsieur Seguin's house there was a paddock with a hawthorn hedge all round it, and it was there that he put the new arrival. He fastened her to a stake at the pleasantest end of the field, taking care to leave her plenty of rope, and from time to time he would come out to have a look at her. She was very happy, and cropped the grass so contentedly that Monsieur Seguin was delighted.

" At last," thought the poor man, " here is one who won't get tired of my place."

But Monsieur Seguin was mistaken. The goat did get tired.

. . . .

One day she looked up at the mountain and suddenly she said to herself, " How lovely it must be up there. How fine to gallop in the heather, without this tiresome rope round my neck. It's all very well to keep donkeys and cows in a paddock, but goats ought to be free."

From that moment the grass in the paddock seemed stale to her. She grew listless and thin, and seldom gave any milk.

It was pitiful to see her pulling at her rope, her eyes turned towards the mountain, her nostrils quivering, bleating all day long, " Maa—Maa-aa-aa ! "

Monsieur Seguin began to realize that there was something wrong with his little goat, and one day, when he was trying to milk her, she turned round and spoke to him :

" Listen to me, Monsieur Seguin. I am so tired of being here with you. Let me go up to the mountain."

" Oh, good gracious, you too ! " cried Monsieur Seguin, dropping his milk pail. Then, sitting down on the grass beside the little goat, he asked, " What is this, Blanquette ? Do you want to leave me ? "

And Blanquette replied :

" Yes, master."

" Isn't this grass good enough ? "

" Oh yes, master."

" Perhaps your tether is too short. Shall I lengthen it for you ? "

" That is not the trouble, Monsieur Seguin."

" Well, what *is* the matter ? What do you want ? "

" I want to go up to the mountain."

" But, you foolish little creature, don't you know there is a wolf on the mountain ? What will you do when he finds you ? "

" I will fight him with my horns, Monsieur Seguin."

" The wolf will laugh at your horns. He has eaten my other goats, big ones with much stronger horns than yours. Do you remember poor old Renaude who was here last year ? She was a strong old she-goat and a great fighter. She fought the wolf all night. In the morning the wolf ate her."

"Poor Renaude! But all the same, master, *do* let me go up the mountain."

"Good heavens!" cried Monsieur Seguin, "whatever is the matter with all my goats? Here's another one who wants to run into the wolf's jaws. But you shan't. I'll save you in spite of yourself, you rascal. And, for fear you may break your rope, I shall shut you up in the stable, and you shall stay there for good."

So he took the goat and put her in a pitch dark stable, and double-locked the door.

But, unfortunately, he forgot the window. No sooner had he turned his back than the little creature was off and away.

. . . .

When the white goat reached the top of the mountain every one was delighted. The old fir trees had never seen anything so pretty. They welcomed her like a little queen. The chestnuts bent down to the ground to caress her with the ends of their branches. The golden flowers of the broom opened to greet her and filled the air with their sweet scent.

How happy she was! Free at last, nothing to keep her from gambolling wherever she chose, and browsing wherever she fancied. And such lovely pasture—right under her feet—savoury, delicate, made of a thousand tiny plants, different altogether from the coarse grass of the paddock. And the flowers! Great blue campanulas, fox-gloves with long purple fingers, a whole forest of wild flowers overflowing with winey juices.

Half intoxicated, the white goat lay stretched on the ground with her legs in the air, or rolled headlong down the little banks among the fallen leaves and chestnuts. Then suddenly, with a bound, she was on her feet again. Hop! And off she went, skimming across the brushwood and through the little thickets of trees. No sooner was she at the top of a little hill than down she leapt into the valley again, up and down, up and down, everywhere at once. It seemed as if there were half a dozen of Monsieur Seguin's goats on the mountain.

She didn't know the meaning of fear. With one bound she would clear the great torrents which splashed her with foam and spray as she leapt over. Then, all dripping, she would lie stretched out on some big flat rock to dry herself in the sun.

Once, coming to the edge of the hill with a spray of trefoil in her teeth, she saw below, far, far below on the plain, Monsieur Seguin's house with the paddock behind. The sight made her laugh till the tears came. " How tiny it is ! " she said. " However could I have put up with it down there ? "

Poor little thing ! She was so high up she thought herself at least as big as the world.

Altogether, it was a splendid day for Monsieur Seguin's goat. Towards noon, as she was running about, she fell in with a flock of chamois who were tearing down and devouring a wild vine. The little white lady caused quite a sensation. They gave her the best place at the vine, and all the gentlemen were very gallant. Between ourselves, a young black-coated chamois was lucky enough to please Blanquette, and the two lovers stole away into the woods for an hour or so, but if you want to know what they said to one another, go and ask the little babbling brooks that trickle unseen through the moss.

Suddenly the wind freshened. The mountain grew purple. Evening had come.

" Already ! " said the little goat : and she stood still.

Down below, the mist was beginning to steal over the fields. Monsieur Seguin's paddock disappeared, and nothing could be seen of the house but the roof and a wisp of smoke from the chimney.

She heard the little bells of a flock going to fold, and suddenly she felt very lonely. A falcon brushed her with his wings in passing. She shivered.

And there came a howling on the mountain.

" Hou-oo ! Hou-oo ! "

Then she remembered the wolf. All that day the little feather-head had not given him a thought.

At that very moment a horn sounded far away down in the valley. It was the good Monsieur Seguin making his last attempt to save her.

" Hou . . . hou-oo ! " howled the wolf.

" Come back, come back ! " cried the horn.

And for a moment Blanquette longed to go back ; but when she remembered the rope and the stifling air of the paddock, she felt that she could never endure that life again : it would be better to stay on the mountain.

The horn sounded no more.

The goat heard a noise in the leaves behind her. She turned round and saw in the shade two pointed ears and a pair of shining eyes. . . . It was the wolf. Crouched on his haunches, enormous and still, he was looking at the little goat, thinking how good she would taste. He knew very well he would eat her in the end, so he was in no hurry ; but when she turned, he began to laugh wickedly. " Ha ! ha ! Monsieur Seguin's little goat ! " and he licked his ugly red chops.

Blanquette knew that she was lost. . . . For a moment, remembering the story of old Renaude, who fought all night, only to be eaten in the morning, she told herself that she might as well let the wolf eat her at once ; then, taking courage, she faced him defiantly, her head lowered and horns forward, the brave little goat of Monsieur Seguin. Not that she had any hope of victory (no goat could kill the wolf), but she wanted to see if she could hold out as long as Renaude had done.

The monster advanced, and the little horns came into play.

How bravely she went at it ! A dozen times she forced the wolf to draw back for breath, and every time the greedy little thing snatched another morsel of her precious pasture, then returned to the fight with her mouth full. All night this went on. From time to time Blanquette looked at the stars dancing in the clear air, and said to herself :

" Oh, if only I can hold out until the dawn ! "

One after another the stars faded, and still they fought on, she with her horns, he with his teeth. . . . A pale light glimmered on the horizon: the hoarse crow of a cock came up from a distant farm.

" At last ! " gasped the poor little creature.

She had only been waiting for the dawn. She stretched herself out on the ground in her beautiful white fur coat that was now all splashed with blood.

Then the wolf threw himself upon the little goat and ate her.

FOLDING THE FLOCKS

By John Fletcher

Shepherds all, and maidens fair,
Fold your flocks up ; for the air
'Gins to thicken, and the sun
Already his great course hath run.
See the dew-drops how they kiss
Every little flower that is :
Hanging on their velvet heads,
Like a rope of crystal beads.
See the heavy clouds low falling,
And bright Hesperus down calling
The dead night from underground,
At whose rising, mists unsound,
Damps and vapours fly apace,
Hov'ring o'er the smiling face
Of these pastures, where they come,
Striking dead both bud and bloom ;

Therefore, from such danger, lock
Ev'ry one his lovèd flock ;
And let your dogs lie loose about,
Lest the wolf come as a scout
From the mountain, and, ere day,
Bear a lamb or kid away ;
Or the crafty, thievish fox
Break upon your simple flocks :
To secure yourselves from these
Be not too secure in ease ;
Let one eye his watches keep,
While the other eye doth sleep ;
So shall you good shepherds prove,
And deserve your master's love.
Now, good-night ! may sweetest slumbers
And soft silence fall in numbers
On your eye-lids : so, farewell ;
Thus I end my evening knell.

OLAF THE FAIR AND OLAF THE DARK

By Cynthia Asquith

Once upon a time there lived two boys who were each called Olaf. One had golden curls clustered all over his head—curls so glittering that every woman's hand must touch their brightness: and to look into his eyes was to see the gleam of blue sky through two rounded windows. In short, he was the most beautiful child that his mother had ever seen.

The other Olaf was crowned with dark curls—blue-black as the plumage of a crow. And to look into his eyes was to see twin stars shine up through the brown depths of a mountain stream. In short, he was the most beautiful child that his mother had ever seen.

Now, these two Olafs had both been born on exactly the same day, but Olaf the Fair was the son of a mighty king, and lived in a dreadfully big palace, and Olaf the Dark was the son of a poor shepherd, and lived in a dreadfully small cottage.

When Olaf the Fair learned to walk, he staggered across a vast floor, and if he tumbled, it was only to sink into the soft depths of thick carpets.

In his nursery there was nothing dangerous—not even the corners were allowed to be sharp—so he never knew the fun of watching bruises turn from plain brown to yellow and purple and green.

But Olaf the Dark learned to walk in quite a different way; he staggered across an uneven floor of cold stone, in a small room, crowded with things from whose sharp corners Pain constantly darted out at him. The hard floor seemed to rise up and smite him, first in one place and then in another. His mother was always kissing these places to make them well. He liked these kisses, and was proud of his scarred body, especially of the red knees across which his seven skins were never seen all at once. His knees generally looked as though raspberry jam had been spread over them.

Just as you do, both Olafs hated to go to bed, but, just as you do, to bed they both had to go. Olaf the Fair plunged his bright head into a large pillow—so soft that it almost met across his nose, whilst the small pillow on which Olaf the Dark laid his dark head was so bumpy and so hard that in the morning his bruised ear would often ache.

Both boys loved to eat and drink. Olaf the Fair was fed on every sort of delicious food. You should have seen his nursery table piled high with glowing fruits, coloured cakes, and trembling jellies. Chicken came every day, and there was always jam for tea. Olaf the Dark seldom swallowed anything more dainty than lumpy porridge, black bread, and just a very little bacon. Yet he often knew a treat that was far greater than any

of the dainties in the palace, and this was the taste of his plain food when he was very hungry—so hungry that his empty place was just beginning to hurt.

His father lay all crumpled up with rheumatism, so that, almost as soon as Olaf the Dark could walk, he had to shoulder the shepherd's heavy staff, whistle to the sheep-dog, and stride forth to guard his father's flocks.

Watching the baa-ing sheep as they nibbled the short grass, their bells tinkling as they moved, the lonely little shepherd-boy shivered in the cold, wet winds of winter, and gasped in the scorching heats of summer. He would have liked to stay at home, learning to read by the leaping fire whilst his mother stirred the porridge.

The year Olaf the Fair was born his father died, so he became king, the smallest king that ever was seen. His crown was heavy, and made his head ache. His sad, smiling mother said he must learn how to be a wise king. This meant doing hundreds and hundreds of lessons. Whilst ten tutors tried to stuff figures and facts into his head, he would stare out through the windows, wistfully watching all the different sorts of weather. Oh, how he longed to be out in the hail, the thunder, or the snow !

One day, as Olaf the Dark sat by his sheep on the high hillside and played on his flute to keep himself company, a huge brown mastiff came into sight. Olaf's faithful sheep-dog pricked his ears, and low thunder rumbled in his shaggy throat. The fierce mastiff sped along the ground, and in the blinking of an eye the two dogs had flown at one another's throats. Terrified, Olaf the Dark strove with his staff to beat them apart, but all in vain. Fortunately four horsemen, who were the little king's escort, now galloped up.

" Well for thee, lad, we were at hand," said the tallest of the men. " 'Twould have gone ill with thy mongrel had he harmed the king's pet."

" It was your dog's fault ! He attacked mine ! " indignantly answered Olaf the Dark.

" Hush ! " said the man roughly. " Here is the king. Bow down to him, you saucy lad ! "

For Olaf the Fair had just ridden up. Now, Olaf the Dark had never even seen a picture book, and at the dazzling sight of Olaf the Fair he gasped in amazement. The little king was clad in velvet of shimmering blue, edged with shining silver, and on his head was a crown of gold.

" I'm glad your dog is not harmed. How long have you had him ? " said the king.

" Sentry is my father's," answered the shepherd. " He had him before I was born."

" How old are you ? " asked the king.

" I was seven years yesterday," answered the shepherd.

" Were you ? That's funny ! " exclaimed the king. " Why, I had my seventh birthday yesterday too. But, who is with you ? Surely you aren't allowed to stay out by yourself, are you ? "

" I *have* to stay out," replied the shepherd. " I would like to go home."

" You'd like to go home ? Funny ! Why, I'd

give anything to be allowed to sit on that silvery frost! Have you been playing with those nice woolly sheep for long? What pretty bells they've got! And wherever did you get that splendid crook'd staff? I'd like to have one just like that."

"Sire," broke in the tall man with a low bow, "we must return home. His Excellency, your Tutor-in-Chief, said that only one hour could be spared from your Majesty's studies to-day."

Olaf the Fair stamped his foot.

"Oh, bother!" he cried. "I can't bear to go in to yawny lessons! I want to stay out in the shinyness. I say, Boy, when have you got to go home and do lessons?"

"Don't do any lessons," grunted Olaf the Dark.

"You don't do any lessons?" exclaimed Olaf the Fair. "Oh, you *are* a lucky one! How long will you stay out?"

"Till it gets dark."

"Till it gets dark? Oo-oo-oo-ee! Lovely! I've never been out in the night. I would like to see how the stars get there. Have you ever seen one just pricking through the blackness? But, where's your coat?"

"Don't have a coat."

"Don't you wear anything but just that one dead sheep? It must be beautifully comfortable. My clothes are so hot and heavy," said the king.

"Sire!" pleaded the attendant.

"All right, I'm coming," said Olaf the Fair, and reluctantly mounting his palfrey, he turned its arched neck towards the distant palace. "Good-bye, boy."

Deep in thought, his forgotten flute on the grass, the shepherd boy sat on. Hours passed. The sun sank in flaming glories of orange and gold. Dusk thickened into darkness, and heavy drops of rain fell coldly on his bare head. Still pondering, Olaf the Dark at last rose and wearily drove his drowsy sheep towards home.

He sat down to his supper. Silently he spooned his burnt porridge, and gnawed at his crust of black bread.

"What's come to thee, son ?" asked his mother. "I miss the gabble of thy tongue."

"I've seen the king, mother," said Olaf.

"Seen his small majesty, have you ? To think of it ! Born the very same day as you, he was. Be you two boys much of a size ?"

"Yes, he's no taller nor I, and I guess I'm the stronger. But oh, mother, the lovely horse he was riding, and the clothes he had on him, and the glittering crown on his head ! 'Twas as though he had caught rays from the sun itself ! Oh, mother, I'd like to be a king the same as him, and ride around in coloured clothes, nor need to mind no silly sheep."

"Is it wanting to be a king you are, Olaf ?" laughed his mother. "Sure, there's no contentment under the sun. But I'm thinking a good shepherd's better nor a bad king, and they're saying to be a good king's no easy calling—subjects being more unaccountable troublesome than sheep themselves. Anyways, you two lads have the same God to serve, and sure you can serve Him from a cottage just as easy as from a palace. To be a good shepherd's a proud thing, I'm thinking, and as for the rheumatics, they enters the joints be you high or be you low."

But Olaf the Dark was not to be consoled. For the first time he noticed the shabbiness of his sheepskin suit, and the smallness of the cottage.

"What would the king's palace be like?" he asked.

"Oh!" said his mother. "They do say it be all marble and gold, with thousands of lights a-twinkling from the ceiling, and I've heard as the wee king sleeps in a bed that's bigger nor this room, and the roof of it's of gold, and there be curtains to it."

Olaf the Dark blinked and drew in a deep breath.

"Oo-oo-oo-ee!" he sighed, as though sucking the sweetest of sweets. "Oo-oo-oo-ee!"

Now that same evening, when bedtime came, Olaf the Fair pressed his face against the cold bars of the window and stared wistfully at the spangled blue-blackness outside. He thought with envy of the shepherd-boy out there all alone on the hidden hill. For the little king yearned to go out while darkness was spread over the earth. How mysterious the world looked! What, he wondered, happened to all the ordinary daylight things during the night?

After he had climbed into his soft, golden bed, the queen came in to say good-night.

"Oh, mother!" he said, snuggling into her white arms, "I've done such a dreadful, dreadful lot of lessons to-day."

"Poor little Olaf!" said the queen, kissing her son.

"Oh, mother," the little king continued, "I saw such a nice boy to-day out on the hill. And isn't he lucky? He doesn't do any lessons at all, and he's allowed to stay out by himself with nothing but a lot of sheep. Mayn't I have some nice woolly sheep to play with, mother?"

"Sheep aren't toys, Olaf. They're duties, like lessons."

"Duties, are they, mother? Then I'd much rather do sheep than do lessons. But was he a real shepherd, that boy? Why, he's only my age! Oh, mother, can't I be a shepherd?"

"You are a sort of shepherd, Olaf. But you've got human beings to look after instead of animals. I want you to be so good a king that I shall be proud that you were my baby."

"I do try, mother. But I wish I was a proper out-of-doors shepherd. And please, mother, must

I always wear my crown ? It is so heavy, and it bites my forehead."

"Yes, darling. I am afraid you must. Your crown is to remaind you that you are a king and not your own master. Now go to sleep, and dream that you are a shepherd, and have to shiver out of doors in all the cold and wet. You'd soon be glad to wake up in your own bed."

But Olaf the Fair was not to be persuaded.

" I'd love to be out in the rain ! " he explained. "I hate indoors."

Days, weeks, months passed away, and Olaf the Fair and Olaf the Dark still continued to think of one another. More and more did the little king weary of the long lessons which kept him indoors, and of all the solemn attendants who surrounded him. More and more did he pine to be free and wander at will over the hillside. Above all he yearned to go out into the night and feel the darkness. When he looked up at the sad, solemn moon, he would thrill with a strange, unaccountable excitement. The moon ! She flooded the earth with a queer, transforming light that drew him out of all sleepiness and made his soul shiver till his body became too excited to lie still. Passionately he envied the shepherd-boy out there in the darkness, playing his flute beneath the pine trees. One night the longing grew too strong, and, as he tossed on his golden bed, it flashed into his memory that the bars of the window in the great hall were wide enough apart to allow his body to squeeze through them. (This was long before even kings had glass in their windows.)

He sat upright. The leaves of the trees just outside rustled mysteriously, and tiny twigs tapped against the bars, beckoning him out of bed. Yes, his mind was made up. He was going to escape and run out into the strange, silvery light that the moon was making. With hammering heart he slid from his high bed and tiptoed towards the door. There was a low growl, and the mastiff raised his huge head. Oh, heavens, if he were to bark, or follow, he would surely arouse the man who slept just outside across the door! But, fortunately, Olaf remembered the bone he was to give his dog next morning, and in a moment busy sounds of scrunching filled the room.

One danger passed. But now Olaf must step across the body of the man who, with a dagger in his mouth, guarded his royal master's door. Supposing the man were awake. Then the adventure would become impossible, and Olaf would have to return to the dreariness of trying to go to sleep. Trembling, he turned the handle and pulled the door towards him. Regular breathing reassured him. The man was fast asleep.

A little scared, Olaf slipped down the wide, shallow steps of the huge staircase. Now he was in the great hall. The night wind blew in, and the tapestries trembled on the walls. Olaf shivered with something that was more than cold. High up in the sky a pale moon raced through trailing clouds.

He reached the window, and seized the bars. Oh, heavens, what was this? Consternation crushed into his heart, for criss-cross along the iron bars there now ran new horizontal ones. Alas! alas! he had adventured too late. Impossible now to squeeze through to liberty. His palace was a prison. In vain he tugged at the cruel bars. They could not even be shaken. He stamped his foot. Strong sobs shook his small body.

But what was this he saw through the dancing blur of his tears? Exactly opposite, a face stared through at him! The moon had raced behind a cloud, and her light was dim. Was he looking into a mirror instead of out of doors? No, this pale face was surrounded with dark hair, and now his fingers felt the touch of other warm fingers. Yes, other hands were clasping the forbidding bars, and sobs that were not his own fell on his ear. The moon again sailed forth into the open sky, and clearly Olaf the Fair recognized the face of the shepherd-boy.

The one craning in, the other craning out, the two boys stared at one another.

"Why are you crying, Boy?" asked Olaf the Fair.

"Because I can't get in," sobbed the little shepherd. "Why are you crying?"

" Because I can't get out," sobbed the little king.

" Funny ! " they both said, and their next sobs rode up on the top of two little laughs, and their tears fell into the cracks made by their smiles.

" Why ever do you want to get in here ? " asked the king.

" Because it looks so lovely—all gorgeous and glowing. I want to know what it feels like inside. I'm so cold—I'm quite blue, and I mustn't go home till morning breaks. I thought I'd squeeze through the bars and ' catch warm,' and then go back to my sheep. There they are. Do you hear their bells ? But why ever do you want to get out ? "

" Because I hate the palace. Ugh ! It's a great big prison. Besides, I want to feel the moonlight, dance in it, alone and free, and I want to be cold."

" Wish I were you ! " said both boys at once, smiling as they sighed.

" Where's your golden crown ? " asked Olaf the Dark. " Don't you always wear it ? "

" Oh, no. I don't sleep in it. I hang it on its peg. I hate it ! "

" Oh, I did want to try it on."

" You wouldn't like it. It makes my head ache, it's so heavy. I'd much rather have a staff like that crooked one of yours."

" It's awfully heavy," sighed the shepherd.

" Heavy ? " exclaimed Olaf the Fair. " I don't see how a heavy thing in your hand could matter. Push it through. I want to hold it."

" Fetch me your crown, then, and we'll exchange."

" All right, I'll fetch it," he said, and tiptoed up the stairs. Stealthily he stepped across the sleeping man, and the dog, recognizing his master's scent, made no sound. Olaf seized the crown, and hastened back to the moon-flooded window.

" Here it is," he said, pushing the crown through the bars that were just wide enough to let it through. " Try it on, and give me your staff."

" It isn't a bit heavy ! I can't feel it ! " they both exclaimed.

Then for a few minutes they chattered, comparing one another's days : the little king complaining of confinement and of being always in a crowd, the little shepherd complaining of having to stay out of doors and be all alone.

" Mother says I am the servant of my subjects," said the king. " And oh, I've got such an awful lot of them ! I'd far rather be the master of sheep, as you are."

" I'm not their master," replied the shepherd. " I'm no better than their slave. Father says so. Besides, they're really yours. They've all got little crowns stamped on their backs."

" Have they ? That's funny ! Why, my sceptre's the shape of a shepherd's crook."

As they talked, Olaf the Dark felt the crown beginning to eat into his forehead. Heavier and heavier it grew until his brows ached and his head drooped. Meanwhile, in Olaf the Fair's hand the staff which had seemed so light grew heavier and heavier. Surely it must be made of lead, he thought, and at last with a sigh he changed it into his other arm. At the same moment, with a groan, the shepherd tore the crown from his head.

"Phew! it *is* a weight! How can you wear it all day?" he said, pushing it back through the bars.

"Phew! it *is* a weight!" said the king, poking the staff through the bars. "I can't think how you can carry it all day."

"Funny!" they both said, and they laughed quite loud; the king feeling proud of his head that could carry so heavy a weight, and the shepherd feeling proud of his right arm, grown strong from carrying so heavy a staff.

"The dawn breaks," he said. "I must return to my sheep."

"Come again," cried the king. "Come again and talk to me."

So once in every year the little shepherd returned to the palace walls, and through the bars the boys talked long and eagerly. The king always told the shepherd how stuffy it was within, and the shepherd always told the king how cold it was outside, and during the rest of the year, whenever the king's discontentment grew, he remembered the weeping boy who had tried so hard to get *in*. And whenever the shepherd wearied of his lot, he remembered the boy who wept because he could not get *out*.

These two boys grew into men. Sorrows they had—as all men have, yet to each was given much happiness, for the one was a good king, and the other a good shepherd. Far and wide Olaf the Fair was famed as the " Shepherd of all his People," and Olaf the Dark, who guarded the royal sheep, was called the " King of all Shepherds."

THE MANNIKINS AND THE GREEN PEAS

By Rhoda Power

Once upon a time there was a German village which always seemed to have good luck. The people who lived in it always looked rosy and well fed. They had nice clothes to wear, enough to eat and to drink, just enough money in their purses to make them feel contented, and plenty of wood to burn on their fires when it was cold. The farmer had cows in the barn and sheep in the fields. The baker had plenty of good flour to make cakes and loaves. The schoolmaster had plenty of little boys and girls to teach, and when they were good, they were as good as gold, and when they were bad, they weren't *too* bad ; they were just full of fun, that's all ! There was enough milk for the cats, and there were enough bones for the dogs, and there was quite enough happiness to go round, and I think you will agree with me, that *that* was the most important thing of all.

People from other places sometimes went to see that village, to try to find out what it *was* that made everybody so contented. But they couldn't see anything, and when they asked the villagers, the answer was always the same. " Ah ! The mannikins live here." " But what are they like ? " asked the other people. Always the same answer came, " We don't know ! We've never seen them." And the strangers went away very much puzzled. Are you feeling puzzled too ? Have you ever seen the mannikins ? No ? Neither have I. But I can tell you what they were like. They were little tiny men, no bigger than forks. They dressed in green—green caps, green jackets, green leggings, and little green boots with long, pointed toes. Wherever they were, they brought good luck, for they were fairies.

They didn't live outside in the woods and the trees. They lived in people's houses. Yet nobody ever saw them. You see they used to go to sleep in the day-time—hidden away somewhere—up in the chimney, curled up at the back of the plates on the dresser, behind the coal-scuttle, in the wood-shed, in any place where they knew they wouldn't be disturbed. And then, when all the people in the house had gone upstairs to bed, and were snugly tucked up and fast asleep, out came the little green mannikins from their hiding-places, and played about like a lot of jolly children.

You can't imagine the fun they had. They simply squeaked with laughter, and they didn't care what they did. They filled the sink with water and had baths. They turned the blind-cord into swings. They put butter all up the legs of the kitchen table, then tried to climb up and, of course, slithered about all over the place. They rode on the cat's back round the room, and when pussy jumped they all fell off in a heap

with their legs in the air. They put the bread knife on to the milk jug, and made it into a see-saw. They played ball with the lumps of sugar, and turned the plates into hoops. In fact they had a splendid time, just like a party.

But, you know, they were good little fellows, these mannikins. They didn't play about in people's houses and do nothing in return. Oh no, they were very honest. If they had had a good time, they were willing to pay for it. At twelve o'clock at night all the fun stopped, and the mannikins began to pay for their good time. And how do you suppose they did that? By work. They simply rolled up their little green sleeves and began to do the work of the house. And if you had lived in a house where there were mannikins, and put your ear to the keyhole, you would have heard them buzzing about like bees, and bless me! how they chattered.

Brush the floor, brothers, take away the dust.
Polish all that ought to shine! Rub away the rust.
Wash each plate and dish and cup,
The mess you've made you must clear up!
Patch the clothes, brothers, don't you leave a hole,
Scour the sink, chop the wood! Go and fetch the coal.
Lay the table, black the shoes,
Clean the grate and brush the flues!
Do the work, brothers, get the whole thing done!
The mannikins say "Thank you," now they've had their fun!

That's why the villagers always looked happy and contented. They left the mannikins in peace, and so the mannikins helped them. Why, do you know, they even made butter for the dairy-maid and bread for the baker? But the person whom they loved most of all was the tailor. They were *very* fond of him. Every night, before he went up to bed, he put out sugar and biscuits and any tasty little tit-bit which he thought the mannikins would like, and of course they were grateful, and at night they did half his sewing for him, and at last he grew so rich that he was able to marry.

But I'm afraid he didn't choose his wife very wisely. It was a great pity that he didn't choose a wife from his own village. No, he went outside to a town quite far away, and he brought back a fashionable lady. She didn't wear wool or cotton. She wore silk and satin. She didn't wear her hair in two nice fat plaits like the village girls. She had it all curled and frizzled by the barber. She didn't wash her face in cold water till her cheeks glowed. *She* used warm milk to keep her skin white. She didn't cook the dinner and make the beds, but she had a little rosy-cheeked servant girl to come and do it for her. But the worst of it all was, she wanted to see the mannikins! She used to look up the chimney and in the roof, and was always trying to find them, and at last her husband grew quite cross with her for being so inquisitive.

"You know quite well," he said, "that if once we set eyes on the mannikins they'll go away from the village and nobody will ever be lucky again."

"B-but I w-want to see them!" wept the spoilt little wife.

"Then want must be your master," said the tailor.

"I *will* see them!" said the wife, and stamped

her foot. " I'll sit up all night and peep through the keyhole."

" That you won't!" said the tailor, and at bedtime he picked her up and carried her upstairs and locked the door.

The next day he thought she had forgotten all about it because she said nothing. He really thought she had turned over a new leaf, because she spent all day shelling peas in the kitchen. And when she went upstairs to bed she never said a word about the mannikins.

Poor tailor! Can you guess what that naughty little bride of his had done? She had filled her pockets with peas, and when her husband had lighted her to bed, holding the candle as he went upstairs, she followed a little way behind, dropping peas all over the kitchen floor and the stairs.

Then she went to bed, thinking to herself, " Ha ha! Now the mannikins will fall over the peas and hurt themselves, and I shall find them in the morning."

And she went to sleep, feeling quite pleased with herself. That night the tailor heard a queer sound down in the kitchen and up the stairs—a sound like a swarm of angry bees.

Leave the floor, brothers, never mind the dust,
Never mind the polishing, never mind the rust!
Leave each plate and dish and cup,
The peas she dropped she must clear up!
Leave the work, brothers, leave it all undone!
When peas are dropped to hurt us, we can't have any fun!

The next day the tailor found that all his stitches had been unpicked, the house was dirty and the chimney full of soot.

And as for the mannikins, they never came back, and that poor little German village lost all its luck.

ANN'S BATH

By Elizabeth Godley

Ann is having her bath. Both the taps are dripping. Or so you think. Really they are having a talk.

The Hot Tap.	Flippety Flop I drip and I drop.
The Cold Tap.	Don't.
Hot.	I drip and I sing "One day I'll be king."
Cold.	Won't.
Hot.	Why don't you say Something clever and gay?
Cold.	Can't.
Hot.	Flippety Flop Then I wish you would stop.
Cold.	Shan't.

[*Ann turns on the Hot Tap.*]

Hot. A sudden sort of feeling of a rushing and a gushing has come over me and made me unexpectedly uproarious——

You're looking very small and silly now, my dear old Cold-as-Ice, while I am boiling hot and belching steam—it's simply glorious!

Oh, don't pretend you haven't heard. . . .

I'm filling up the bath so full that Ann has lost Jemima Soap—I see her skulking near the flannel——

And I am steaming, spouting, bubbling—I

can do all three at once—I am a hot Niagara *besides* a boiling English Channel. . . .

Cold. Sot !

Hot. My poor old silly, you can't talk except in monosyllables, while I can say a thousand things polite or otherwise to you——

But just to show you what the really *clever* sort, like me, you know, can do with monosyllables— Here's one for you, old fellow : BOO !

I love this sudden rushing gushing splashing splishing sploshing splushing—such a comfort after saying merely " Flip " or " Flop "——

Cisterns alive ! Ann's getting up—I think she's going to turn me off. Oh, Nuts and Spanners ! Ann ! Oh, don't ! I never, *never* want to stop. . . .

[*Ann turns off the Hot Tap*.]

Cold. Flip
Hot. Flop
Cold. Splosher.
Hot. Somebody
Cold. said
Hot. new washer.

ON the edge of the Black Forest there grew a little fir tree. She was so young that her skirts still brushed the ground. She was glad of this when the woodcutter came with his sharp axe, for then many trees were felled and lay stiff and awkward—trees which had been mighty kings of the forest, and gracious queens, before.

When Christmas-time drew near, however, and each tree wore a hood of snow, it was on a different errand that the woodman came. This time the trees were not left to lie on the ground after they were felled, but were carried away, upright, in a cart—each one to be a Christmas tree.

Then the little fir tree thought to herself, How lovely to be a Christmas tree! To be hung with tinsel and shining balls, lit by soft candle-light, and be the centre of a dancing ring of children! But the woodman passed by without so much as a glance in her direction: she was so small.

Christmas-time came. Christmas-time, when every housewife hangs garlands in her hall, and fills her basket at the shops with grapes, apples, and oranges—all the bright show that makes the house look gay. But in the Orphanage that stood on the hill no festive differences were made.

Over the portraits of the benefactors that lined the walls no evergreens were hung. There were no little tables piled high with presents, such as all lucky German children love to have. No music of carolling was to be heard: only the tramp, tramp, tramp of heavy little feet moving along the narrow corridors and up and down the stone staircases.

At ten o'clock all the orphans, in their stiffly-buttoned-up cloaks and hard-peaked hats, were lined up by the Beadle, ready to go to church.

The church was down in the valley. As they moved towards it, its square end seemed like a bottle, the straight tower making the bottle neck, and there was a small round dome on top which the orphans thought looked like the cork.

They all trotted along, making an enormous jointed centipede—the Beadle and the tallest orphans were the head, and the five littl'st orphans of all made its wriggling tail.

As they walked they talked to each other, rather low, in case the Beadle should ask them what they were saying. Sometimes he did, quite suddenly. And it might be you had said: "Beadle's nose is very red this morning," or "Beadle's arms seem to sway about like spiders' legs," which made it very awkward to know what to answer.

"It's Christmas Day," said the first of the five.

"That's why there's lace at the edge of the gutter," said the second.

"And such a blue sky for us," said the third.

"Rich people get more than that," thought the fourth one; but here they reached the church door. The church was very cold, and there seemed a thick fog inside.

The orphans did exactly as the Beadle did, for then they knew that they could not go wrong. When he sat down, then they sat down; and when he stood up, they stood up, too—while the five smallest orphans stumbled off their seats, for their legs were rather short.

He sang very loud and clear, as though he were singing for the whole hundred of them.

Coming back through the valley they skirted the edge of the wood. The five littl'st orphans were walking hand in hand in a long chain, and were getting left behind, for the frost had stiffened their heavy boots, and that made their chilblains sore. They went down a little grassy path,

thinking it to be the right one. The trees on either side made it dark, although they were white as ghosts in their snow cloaks, when the path led into an open glade, and there, full in the sunlight, was the little fir tree! hung with frosted tinsel and tinkling icicles, and edged with pale-blue frozen drops. Changed by the sunshine into a dazzling, glittering, diamond thing!

"See!" said the very smallest of the five small orphans, "it's like a little frost tree on a window-pane."

Forgetting cold and chilblains, they cast aside their little stiff hats, freed their arms from the close-buttoned cloaks, and danced round, and round, and round the little fir tree.

A robin came to see what all the noise was about, and planted himself to sing on the topmost point, by way of another piece of Christmas decoration.

Feet capering, eyes shining, stiffly-cut locks caught and made wild by the winter air, and singing:

"Deedle deedle deedle,
Beadle beadle beadle,"

the five littl'st orphans of all danced their

MERRY CHRISTMAS.

THE LITTLE WEE HAIRY MAN

By Charles M. Campbell

I'M not sure when it was that the wee hairy man came down the shepherd's chimney, but it was a long, long time ago, many years before you or I were born or even thought of.

The shepherd lived in a little cottage in a lonely glen among the blue mountains, with his wife and his three sons. The two elder were really stepsons, for the shepherd, whose wife had died long before, had married a widow with two sons. Why the stepmother could not have loved the shepherd's little son as much as her own I do not know, but she was unkind to the boy in all sorts of little ways, and often made him very unhappy. He was always the one who had to go into the dark pine wood near the cottage to collect wood for the fire, or down the steep path to the stream to draw water in a heavy bucket. And many a time, in the cold winter, when the pines were weighted down with the snow on their branches, and birds sang no longer in the wood, the little boy would have to take a stone and smash the ice before he could get to the water.

The family was poor, and had very little to spare to buy dainties or fine clothes. But if there was anything nicer than usual to eat, or any new thing to wear, it was always for the woman's two sons and never for the youngest, if she could avoid it. And, not content with that, she would often sneer at the boy for being a little idle dreamer, and tell him that it wasn't by wandering about and watching beasts and birds that he would ever get on in life. And then the two other sons, in all sorts of ways that I would not like to tell about, teased and tormented him, so that he was often very sad.

One winter night the little boy was seated alone by the fireside, watching the flames dancing and the long shadows leaping on the walls of the kitchen, and thinking his own thoughts. The shepherd had gone away to a distant market, and the woman and her two sons were away to the town for a day's holiday. The little boy was eating some dry bread the woman had left for his supper.

The only sound in the house was the " tick-tock, tick-tock " of the clock, and sometimes a falling cinder. Outside the house the world lay silent and still in the grip of a hard frost, and the moon shining on the snow made everything look as if it were made of silver. Suddenly the little boy heard a " fustle-fustle " in the chimney, as if a little bird were fluttering there. Some soot came dropping down, and a moment later, to his great astonishment, a pair of little hairy legs came dangling, and finally a little hairy man dropped down and sat looking at the boy with wee bright eyes as round as buttons. And you may be sure the little boy's eyes were round too, for he had never heard of such a thing before. The wee man was only about twelve inches high, and he had a little clay-pipe in his mouth.

"Who are you, please ?" asked the little boy politely. He was really a little bit scared, although the little visitor had quite a kind, comical expression on his wee hairy face.

"Och, I'm just a little wee hairy man that's come down the chimney to light his pipe at your fire," said the wee man, and picked a live coal out with his fingers, and held it to his pipe, and puffed hard until it was smoking like a little chimney.

"Don't you burn yourself when you pick up red-hot cinders, sir ?" asked the little boy.

"What would I be burning myself for ?" replied the little man. "I've been picking up red-hot cinders for about two thousand years now, so I ought to know how to do it."

"Are you as old as that ?" asked the little boy in astonishment.

"I am that," said the little man, puffing away at his pipe, and winking his beady eyes ; "I'll be two thousand and nineteen on the first Tuesday of next month."

"It's a cold night," he went on, "for a wee

hairy man that's got nothing to eat and nothing to wear."

"Oh, poor wee man!" said the boy, who was growing quite accustomed to him. "I've only

got dry bread, for the jam's locked up, but I'll share it with you, if you don't mind dry bread. And I could give you a little green jersey, although it's a bit ragged."

The little man thanked him, and took the bread and the jersey. He was very pleased when he put the jersey on, even although it came right down to his heels like a long nighty. The boy noticed for the first time that the wee hairy man was carrying a sack on his back. After the wee man had finished off his bread, he said, " One good turn deserves another. Now watch me do a funny thing."

He undid the string that his sack was tied with, and opened it up. Then he took out of the sack a tiny table and cloth, and two chairs. They looked just as if they had been taken from some doll's house. The table and chairs were no sooner set on the ground than they began to grow to ordinary size ; then the little man started to pull out of the sack plates of chocolate biscuits, iced cakes, coloured jellies, apples, nuts, caramels, and I forget how much more. Anyway, there was enough there to make any one ill five times over if it had been ordinary food. But, of course, with fairy food it's quite different. You can eat as much as you like without ever feeling ill, as you will know if you are ever lucky enough to taste any.

The little boy, dumb with wonder, sat down to table with the little man, and ate his fill. Just as they had finished, they heard footsteps and voices outside. " Oh," said the little boy, " here's my stepmother and brothers ! Whatever shall we do ? "

The little man put his fingers to his lips, and said, " Not a word about me to anybody. I'm off!" Before the little boy had time to bid him "Good-bye," the table and chairs had shrunk to toy size again, and were pushed back into the sack. The little man popped it on to his back, and vanished up the chimney just as the door opened.

"Well, good-for-nothing, you aren't in bed yet?" said the stepmother sharply, as soon as she saw him. The boy rose to his feet, and there on the stool beside him lay a red-and-gold fairy apple. The elder brother saw it, and snatched at it, saying, "Where did you get this, eh?" But as he grabbed it, the apple shrivelled up and vanished away. The boy gazed at his empty hand, and said, "I was certain there was an apple there. It must have been the firelight!" The little boy smiled to himself, and went off to his bed.

The next evening the two brothers were seated at the fire, eating bread and strawberry jam and fresh butter. The little boy was out in the dark wood, gathering sticks for the fire, and the mother was in the cowshed milking.

Suddenly the boys heard a scraping little noise in the chimney, and the little man dropped down once more, with his wee clay-pipe in his mouth. The boys gazed at him open-mouthed, and got white in the face with fear, for they weren't very brave.

The little man said, "What harm would I be

doing to ye? I'm just a little wee hairy man that's come down your chimney to light his pipe."

When they knew he wasn't going to hurt them, the boys started to laugh at his funny appearance, and say impudent things about him that aren't worth repeating. The wee man lit his pipe with a live coal as he had done before, and said, "That's a fine piece ye have for your supper. An' it's a cold night for a wee hairy man that's got nothing to eat and nothing to wear."

"Yes," said the elder, "too fine a piece to give any to a funny little man that comes from nobody knows where."

"And as for having nothing to wear," said the younger, "anybody that's all covered with hair like a puggy—and if ye don't know what a puggy is, well, it's a monkey—doesn't need any clothes."

They both thought what they had said was so smart and funny that they shrieked with laughter. The wee man looked at them for a long time without speaking, then vanished up the chimney again.

If the boys had not been very stupid, they might have guessed that it was some kind of fairy they had been so rude and cruel to, and that the last thing any sensible person would wish to do was to give offence to any of the Little People if they should chance to come his way. However, it never occurred to them that there was anything unusual about the little man. If it had, they would have known who to blame for all the things that began to happen to them. They just seemed to go from one bit of bad luck to another. As they were sitting at the fire, a red-hot cinder suddenly popped out of the fire and burned the younger brother's toe. And, a minute later, the kettle boiled over, and the hot water spattered against the elder one's legs and blistered them. And when they went up the stairs to bed one tripped over a worn bit in the carpet and fell and skinned his knee, and the other walked against the door in the darkness and bumped his nose.

Next day things grew worse and worse. One was bitten by the old sheep-dog, the other was scratched by his cat. Both of them were chased by a turkey-cock, and had their calves nipped. Hens pecked at them, cows chased them and tried to toss them, and as for nettles and brambles, why, you would have thought they almost came out of the ground to sting them and scratch them as they passed.

If they touched pins they pricked themselves, if they handled knives they cut themselves, if they went near the fire they burned themselves, and if they climbed a tree they tumbled down and hurt themselves.

To make things even worse for them, the more bad luck they had, the more good luck their little brother had. He whistled, and sang, and was as happy as the day is long, and bustled about doing all sorts of things for his stepmother, until at last she would say, "I don't know what's come over you clumsy good-for-nothings. If you would try to be bright and helpful like your little brother, it would be the better for you."

But the worst was yet to come. The three boys had to go and help at the harvest at a farm over the hills, and they took a short cut over a bog. The youngest boy crossed safely, but the others stuck, and began to sink. The youngest did his best to help them out, but was not strong enough. They all shouted for help, and suddenly the wee hairy man appeared before them, and in a twinkling had them all out safe and sound.

"Now," he said sternly to the two elder brothers, "let the bad luck of the last few days be a lesson to you. Ye little knew it was the King of the Little People himself that ye were so cruel to, and if it hadn't been for your little brother there, who was so kind to me, it might have gone worse with ye. For it's ill work angering the Little People!"

From that day the two boys treated their little brother kindly, until it became a habit with them to be kind always. Their mother changed too, and in a short time the household was as bright and cheery a little corner as any one could wish to live in. The old shepherd used to sit in the chimney-corner and smoke his pipe, and say, " I don't know what's come over this house, it's so cheery now ! " All the three boys knew who was at the bottom of it all, but they never said a word.

THE FAIRY HOUSE

By Rose Fyleman

I found it in the forest
  Upon a grassy mound ;
The elder trees and hazels
  Stood very closely round.
There were little curtained windows,
  And one was open wide—
I climbed the little hillock
  And knelt, and peeped inside.

Teeny, weeny carpets
  On shiny polished floors ;
Teeny, weeny handles
  On little painted doors ;

A teeny, weeny table
All delicately spread,
And a teeny, weeny bedroom
With a teeny, weeny bed.

But no one trod the carpets,
Nor danced upon the floors ;
No one turned the handles
Of the charming little doors.
No one sat at table,
No one cut the bread,
And nobody was sleeping
Upon the little bed.

I waited until sunset,
As quiet as a mouse ;
I almost cried to leave it—
My darling fairy house.
But when I reached the meadows,
Behind me, in the dark,
I saw a lighted window
That glimmered like a spark.

THE THREE STONES

By M. Braidwood

Early one morning, while the dew still hung on the brambles, a ploughboy set out with his team of horses to the fields.

" If you want to go to the fair to-morrow," said the farmer, " you must finish ploughing the field to-day."

" I'll do it," resolved the ploughboy. He wanted very much to go to the fair.

As they went up the lane, a hare ran across the fields, but he would not stop to watch it ; while he was putting his horses to the plough, a dormouse slipped out of the hedge almost at his feet, but he would not follow it ; he had made up his mind that nothing should hinder him from finishing the ploughing of the field by sundown.

Up the field and down the field he went, whistling to his horses as he steered the plough. In the middle of the field was a hollow, and in the bottom were three big stones just where the plough must go. There was nothing for it but to move them, and pulling up his horses, he went to shift the first of the stones.

He strained and tugged, and at last up it came. Out from under it sprang an elf, as brown as a clod and as nimble as a squirrel. Off he went, hoppity-skippity, across the furrows, and slid into the hedge like a stoat.

" Well, *he's* glad to be free, such a fine day and all," thought the ploughboy, as he carried the stone to the side of the field. " He might have stayed to give me a wish for lifting the stone off him. I'd have wished for a bag of money to spend at the fair. I've no time to run after him, for I must hurry or I shall not be done by sunset."

He ploughed a furrow and a half, and then he came to the second stone. He tugged, and strained, and pulled, and at last up it came. Out from under it sprang another elf, as brown as a beech leaf in autumn, and off he went, hoppity-skippity, across the furrows, till he reached the end of the wood and scuttled into it like a rabbit.

" There's another who's glad to be loose," said the ploughboy, dropping the second stone by the hedge. " And *he* never offered me a wish either. I'd have asked him for a new hat to wear at the fair. Well, I dare not stop to follow him, or I shall never be done in time." And back he went to the plough.

Another furrow and a half brought him to the third stone. He tugged, and strained, and pulled, and panted, for it was buried very deep. At last he got it up. Out from under it jumped a third elf, as brown as a wren, and off he went, hoppity-skippity, across the furrows, till he reached the ditch and slipped into it like a mouse.

"There goes another off to enjoy himself," sighed the ploughboy as he trudged to the hedge

with the last stone. "It would be no good now if he *had* given me a wish, for moving those stones has taken so long that I shall never get to the fair at all."

It was past noon, so he sat down under an oak

to eat his dinner. He was tired with his work, the sun was warm, and a soft breeze stirred in the leaves overhead. In a minute or two he was fast asleep.

He did not wake till the sun was half below the hill, and the rooks were flying home.

" Mercy me ! " he exclaimed, rubbing his eyes, " it's sunset, and the field not half done. Here have I been asleep all this time, and dreaming that the three elves were doing the ploughing for me. One led each of my horses, and one sat astride the ploughshare, and up and down the field they went."

Then he jumped up and rubbed his eyes harder than ever, for beside him stood his team with the plough, and the whole field was ploughed, furrow beyond furrow, from end to end. And on one hilt of the plough hung a bag of silver money, and on the other a new hat with ribbons for the fair.

THE BOY IN THE WILDERNESS

By Samuel Taylor Coleridge

Encinctured with a twine of leaves,
That leafy twine his only dress—
A lovely boy was plucking fruits,
By moonlight, in a wilderness.
The moon was bright, the air was free,
And fruits and flowers together grew
On many a shrub and many a tree ;
And all put on a gentle hue,
Hanging in the shadowy air
Like a picture rich and rare !
It was a climate where, they say,
The night is more beloved than day.
But who that beauteous boy beguiled,
That beauteous boy, to linger here,
Alone by night, a little child,
In place so silent and so wild ?
Has he no friend, no loving mother near ?

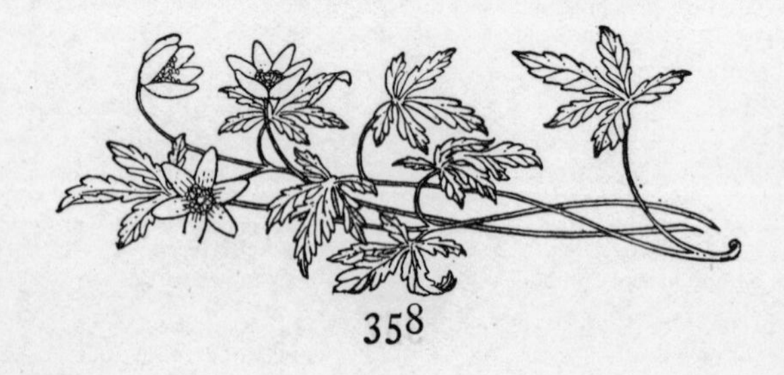

THE PRINCESS LINDENGOLD

By Zacharias Topelias

Translated by C. W. Foss

I

PURER THAN CRYSTAL

And now let us hasten on the wings of the wind to the land of the lily and the rose, where sweet little Fairies build their airy castles in the glow of the dawn, and Black Gnomes fly about in the midnight darkness ; where the sun glows like a ball of fire over the mountains of Ginnistan ; where the water-lilies mirror themselves in the deep and quiet lakes, and where the eyes of the fierce tiger glow among reeds along the river banks ; and where the people, sunburnt and dark-eyed, burn with love or glow with hate.

We hasten to Persia.

There was once a King of Persia named Nadir Shah. He was immensely rich. Under his sceptre were many wide and beautiful lands, and millions of people. He had large chambers filled with gold and precious stones. His ships, laden with the spices of India, sailed over every sea. When he appeared in public there stood about him a bodyguard of a hundred thousand men with silver armour glowing like fire in the rays of the sun, and fifty thousand knights mounted on the finest steeds, with bridles of gold and saddles studded with jewels—all ready at the King's signal to go forth to the conquest of the world.

But the powerful Nadir Shah was old, and had no longer any desire for war and conquests. He had won many victories in his day. Hostile cities had been consumed by his fire, and armies cut down by his sword when his arm was young and strong. But now he was old and feeble, and spent most of his time resting upon the soft divans within his beautiful palace.

Only at times, when in the spring the gold-bordered clouds hid Persia's burning sun from view, and a delightful coolness streamed down from the Zagros Mountains, old Nadir Shah, seated upon a golden palanquin, borne by eight black slaves all dressed in silver robes, would come forth to review his army, or witness the fights of wild beasts.

Nadir Shah had many wives, as is the custom in the East, and he had a large number of sons. But his sons were little joy to him, for they were greedy and ungrateful. They thought that their father lived too long, and they plotted against his life and his crown.

He, therefore, sent his sons away from his Court to distant provinces, which they were to rule as his lieutenants. He kept with him his only daughter, the Princess Lindengold, for her he loved more than anything else on earth, yes, more than all his treasures and his whole Kingdom.

Now, it is true that such a name as Lindengold had never before been heard in Persia. Lindengold's mother had come from the distant north. In her girlhood she had been carried off by African pirates. Because of her rare beauty, she had been sold to the King of Persia, who had made her his Sultana, and loved her more than all his other wives.

This beautiful Sultana was now dead. She had called her little daughter Lindengold, hoping that the child would become as beautiful and pure as the golden sunshine playing among the lindens in her mother's native northland.

And it is true that no sweeter and purer being could be found on this stained earth. Lindengold had the kingly bearing of her father, but her features and her heart were her mother's. Her complexion was as pure as snow, and her eyes as mild as stars in August when no moon appears. Her heart was noble, tender, and good. There was no one in all the Kingdom who did not love the Princess Lindengold, for the fame of her beauty and goodness had spread throughout all Persia.

This the old King knew very well, and his

proud heart became soft as wax whenever he looked upon his kind and lovely child. She was the delight of his eyes, of his thoughts by day and his dreams by night. One word from her disarmed his keenest wrath. No prayer of hers for some unfortunate prisoner could the King ever refuse. And when he thought of his wicked sons, he made up his mind to choose for his daughter some worthy husband and give the whole kingdom to them and their descendants.

Indeed, Nadir Shah loved his daughter so much that he cared more for her than for all his million subjects. He loved her even more than his God. He adored her as no mortal should ever adore another.

One could have no lovelier home than had Princess Lindengold. In the cool park, beneath the lofty palms, surrounded by the murmur of a hundred fountains, and enveloped in the fragrance of a thousand flowers, stood her beautiful marble palace. The sun's rays were reflected by crystal windows. On soft silken pillows she rested by night. But by day, sitting with her maids, she embroidered beautiful designs, or listened to the song of birds and the sweet strains of the cithern, or strolled in the garden and park. She played like a child with golden butterflies and roses. For the Princess Lindengold was not more than twelve years old. But twelve years in the East is as old as sixteen in the North.

The Princess Lindengold was sad. She did not know why, but the flutter of the butterflies, the fragrance of the flowers, the murmur of the fountains, and the tones of the cithern amused her no more. Her heart felt empty, and she was often ready to cry. This she could not understand.

She did not know, the little Lindengold, that no earthly picture is truly light and beautiful unless sorrow and trouble stand as a frame around it, setting off the lights in greater splendour. It was even so with her life. She had to pass through sorrow in order to enjoy happiness more fully.

At last the Princess thought that she had found the reason of this sadness. It must be because she was so closely shut up in her palace. She wanted, for once, to see and enjoy the great crowds of the people in mighty Ispahan. And the next time her father came to visit her, she asked him to let her see the fight between the wild beasts, which was soon to be held in honour of the King's sixtieth birthday. And as the King could never deny his daughter anything, he gave his permission, although, for the first time, he did it unwillingly.

II

THE GIANT BOM BALI

NADIR SHAH was a mighty King, whom one half of Asia obeyed. Now, such men have many enemies. One of them, Nadir Shah so thoroughly despised that he shaved off his beard and let him go. This enemy was the King of the Giants of Turan, the great country of mountains and deserts north of Persia. This Giant King's name was Bom Bali.

In one of his raids in the far North, Giant Bom Bali had captured a Lapland Wizard named Hirmu, who at will could change himself into any kind of animal and back to a man. When Giant Bom Bali, through his spies, had learned that there was to be a great fight of wild beasts at Ispahan, he summoned Hirmu, the Wizard, and said :

" Dog, wouldst thou live ? "

And Hirmu answered, " My Lord, may thy shadow never grow less. Thou knowest that thy dog desireth to live."

And Bom Bali said, " The first day of the month there will be a great celebration at Ispahan. Nadir Shah has sent out his huntsmen to our mountains to capture wild animals. Change thyself into a tiger, and allow them to capture thee. Seek a chance to carry off Lindengold, who is the pride of Nadir Shah and of all Persia."

" Thy dog will do as thou sayest," replied the Wizard.

The first day of the month was at last come. All was ready for the great show. Some of the fiercest animals of India, Arabia, Turan, and even of the Sahara, had been captured and were kept in cages and closets along the sides of the arena. Seats were arranged in tiers to hold sixty thousand people. For the safety of the people, the arena, upon which the beasts were to fight, was surrounded by a strong and high iron fence.

Early in the morning, the city was in motion. Lindengold was as happy as a child. She was to fly like a captive bird from her cage. She was to see a real show, where the actors were real lions and tigers.

The people had all assembled and were only waiting for Nadir Shah. Finally he came, accompanied by his splendid bodyguard and his beautiful daughter, the Princess Lindengold. She was closely veiled. Accompanied by her maids, she rode upon the prettiest little striped zebra you ever saw, which arched its neck in pride at carrying such a beautiful burden.

And though the people could not see Lindengold's face, they had all heard of her wonderful beauty and goodness. They knew that by her prayers she had saved many a poor captive's life, and that every day she sent out her maids with medicine and food to the poor of Ispahan. Therefore, when the Princess now, for the first time, showed herself in public, there arose such a shout of joy from the sixty thousand throats, as had not been heard in Persia since the day that Nadir Shah had returned from one of his victorious campaigns with twenty captive kings in his train.

The Princess took her seat beside the King upon one of the richly embroidered pillows that lay upon the royal rug. And then the fight began.

First there was a cock-fight. The poor fowls picked off each other's feathers, while the people roared with laughter. Some thought it was rare sport, but Lindengold did not enjoy it at all.

Then followed a fight between a wild cat and an eagle.

Then two immense crocodiles were brought in a large vat filled with water. Between them was thrown a dead pig. The crocodiles discovered the dead pig, and both rushed toward it. There was a terrible fight over it. The sharp teeth of neither crocodile could penetrate through the hard shell of the other. The fight might have lasted until now, if one of them had not tumbled on its back, while the other swallowed the pig and thus won the prize.

The next was a fight between six large Arabian dogs and the same number of jackals from the deserts of Turan. The six jackals tried hard to escape, but failed, and were compelled to fight. And what a fight there was! At last five of the dogs lay dead on the arena, while only one of the jackals had fallen. Then was heard a quick, sharp whistle. It was the brave Saracen, Prince Abderraman, encouraging his favourite dog, Valledivan. The dog knew his master's voice, fought harder, and finally felled the five remaining jackals. With a tremendous shout the people declared Abderraman's dog a hero.

A fight between hyenas and wolves was followed by one between a leopard and a panther, in which the panther came out victorious.

At last a large elephant from India, bearing a little tower on its back, was led in. Four archers were seated in the tower. They were to fight a large and beautiful royal tiger. At the tiger the archers pointed their arrows, but he sat crouching and did not seem to wish to fight. At last, however, he was wounded in the nose by a flying arrow. He uttered a tremendous roar, made a spring, and lighted upon the trunk of the elephant. The elephant in turn roared with pain, and raising its mighty trunk flung the tiger to the ground with such force that for a moment he seemed dead.

After the royal tiger had been allowed a few moments' rest, there was led into the arena a majestic lion. Then ensued the most terrible fight of the day. The country around for miles re-echoed with the roar of the infuriated beasts. The sand of the arena was tossed high in the air. The spectators were breathless with fear and awe. At last the tiger, wounded and exhausted, sank lifeless to the ground. The lion was led away in triumph.

Lindengold was curious to see the wild beasts

at closer range. She, who hitherto had seen nothing but flowers and singing birds, had no idea how these fearful beasts looked. She, therefore, went down to the arena accompanied by her maids and a guard, while slaves spread gold-embroidered rugs before her lest she might soil her feet on the gory sand.

What should she fear? All the living beasts were shut up, and the one most dreaded, the royal tiger, lay dead upon the arena. She went up to the fallen tiger to admire his beautiful colour. She decided to ask her father for the tiger's skin as a mat for her marble palace.

But suddenly the fallen tiger sprang to his feet, caught the Princess Lindengold between his horrible jaws, and ran off with lightning speed.

A cry of horror went up from thousands of throats. But no one had the courage to pursue the tiger, except the brave Prince Abderraman. With great courage he threw himself in the path of the flying beast. A desperate struggle ensued. The tiger triumphed. The brave Prince lay helpless and bleeding, without his right arm. The tiger made off with Lindengold.

Great was the sorrow of the aged Nadir Shah, and great was the sorrow of Ispahan and all Persia. The King's guard and his fifty thousand knights rushed forth to seek the Princess. They searched every bush, every cave in the wastes of Turan where the tiger had been captured. Hundreds of tigers fell victims to their shafts, but all in vain. Nothing could be seen of Lindengold.

Nadir Shah tore his grey hair and cursed his sixtieth birthday, which had cost him his dearest treasure on earth, his Lindengold. He ordered all the people to put on mourning for her as over the death of a Sultana.

He further issued a proclamation, that whosoever should restore to him his daughter alive should receive the hand of the Princess and the crown of Persia. He who brought her back dead, should receive as a reward sixty donkeys laden with gold and precious things.

The hope of such a reward induced many noble Princes to attempt the search. But sooner or later they all returned empty-handed—all but the brave Prince Abderraman. He made a solemn vow to keep up the search for fifteen years, and to rescue Lindengold with his left arm, or to die in the attempt.

III

TIGER-WIZARD

If Lindengold had been carried off by a real tiger our story would no doubt end here, for to a royal tiger nothing is sacred, not even the most beautiful

Princess in the world. But it was not so. The Wizard Hirmu had changed himself into *that tiger*, had allowed himself to be caught, had played dead upon the arena, and had made the chance to carry off the Princess. But, instead of taking her to King Bom Bali in Turan, he decided to keep Lindengold himself, and so carried her off to his own home in distant Lapland.

It was the fall of the year, and there was darkness in Lapland. The old Lapp Woman Pimpedora sat in her tent stirring a kettle of mush over the fire. Her son, Pimpepanturi, sat patiently waiting for the mush, staring at his rough reindeer-skin boots. Pimpepanturi was a good-natured lad, but a little stupid, and not a little lazy into the bargain. His father, Hirmu, had tried to make a Wizard of him, but had failed, for Pimpepanturi liked better to eat and sleep than to learn anything.

The old Lapp Woman now turned to the boy, and said :

" Do you hear a noise ? "

" I hear the fire crackle, and the mush sputter in the kettle," replied Pimpepanturi with a yawn.

" Do you not hear a roaring in the distance ? " asked she again.

" Yes," said Pimpepanturi, " it is the wolf catching one of our reindeer."

" No," returned the woman, " it is Father coming home. He has been away four winters. But I hear him coming like a wild beast. He must be in a hurry to come home now."

Just then Hirmu entered in the shape of a tiger, with Lindengold in his mouth. He laid down his burden on the soft moss of the tent floor, became a man again, and said :

" What have you to eat, Mother ? I have run a great distance."

The poor Lapp Woman came near falling into the kettle from fright, but she saw it was her husband. She promised him a good supper if he would tell her where he had been these four winters, and what this fine doll was that he had brought home with him.

" It is too long to tell," returned the Wizard. " Attend to this doll. Give her some reindeer milk that she may revive. She is a Princess from Persia, and will bring us good luck."

The Princess Lindengold was not dead, not

even hurt. She had only fainted from fear. When she came to herself she lay, in her fine robes of silk and pearls and silver, on a reindeer skin spread upon moss in the tent. It was dark and cold. The glare of the fire lighted up the old tent and the Lapp Woman, who was giving her reindeer milk to drink. Lindengold thought herself in the abodes of the dead, and wept bitterly to be snatched away so young from Persia's sun and Ispahan's beautiful rose gardens.

The Wizard had, in the meantime, made up a cunning plan to win Persia's wealth, and said to Lindengold :

" Don't cry, beautiful Princess, you are not dead. You have only been carried away by a fierce tiger. My son, the brave Knight, Morus Pandorus von Pikkulukulikuckulu, has rescued you at much danger to his own precious life. We will be your slaves, and serve you with great zeal, until we have the chance of returning you to Persia."

" Why do you lie so, Hirmu ? " exclaimed the honest old Lapp Woman in her own language.

" My wife says," continued the Wizard to Lindengold, " that if you will marry our son, the incomparably handsome and brave Knight, Morus Pandorus von Pikkulukulikuckulu, we will take you to Persia at once."

Pimpepanturi did not understand the Persian language, but his eyes grew big when his father led him before the Princess and made him bend his awkward back into something like a bow.

Lindengold would not have been a Princess and the daughter of the proud Nadir Shah if she had not felt insulted by such presumption. She looked at the Wizard, she looked at his awkward son—no, she did not *look*, she fairly shot fire from her eyes at them until both were terribly frightened.

"No!" muttered the Wizard. "This will not do, she must be tamed first."

The Wizard had curtained off a little corner of his tent, and into this he put Lindengold, and gave her a tiny piece of reindeer cheese and a cup of snow-water each day. Here she was left alone and in darkness, for at this time of the year in Lapland the sun never rises. The Northern Lights could shine in only through an opening in the tent.

Poor Lindengold! she had shot fire like lightning from her eyes, but after the lightning comes the rain. And Lindengold wept. She wept as only one can weep who is twelve years old, and has been a Princess in Persia, and lived in rose gardens and beautiful marble palaces, and has been waited on by friendly little maids; and then is suddenly transported to a Lapland winter and left cold and hungry, frightened and alone, to pine in darkness. She wept as the dew does of evenings in the gardens of Ispahan. She wept until she fell asleep.

And then there stood at her side the good old friend, the Sleep Man, whom the Finns call Nukku Matti. He took her in his arms and carried her softly to Dreamland's shores, and laid her upon a bed of fragrant flowers. All was so peaceful and calm. The soft moonlight spread over the date-palms and myrtle groves, just as in Persia's loveliest spring. Little dream maidens danced up to her in their silken shoes over velvet carpets, and led her back to her home, to her father, the aged Nadir Shah, to her kind little maids, and to every dear place of her childhood. And thus passed that winter night.

Thus passed many, many weeks and months. And Lindengold was patient, she wept no more. The little dream maidens had told her to wait, and her deliverer would come.

But who was to rescue her ? Who could find the way across the dreary wastes of snow and ice in Lapland ? The Lapp Woman wanted to rescue Lindengold, but she feared her husband. Pimpepanturi had thought of rescuing her, but for this he was too lazy.

And the winter passed, the sun began to shine, the snow melted, and the mosquitoes danced. Then thought the Wizard :

" Now she must be tame."

He went to Lindengold and asked her if she would go to Persia. All she needed to do was to take the brave and handsome Knight, Morus

Pandorus von Pikkulukulikuckulu, for a husband, and the reindeer were ready to take her and her bridegroom to the south.

Lindengold did not shoot fire from her eyes any more. She thought only of the young Prince Abderraman who had bled on the sands of Ispahan for her sake. She hid her face and made no reply.

The Wizard grew very angry. There was a high mountain, and in the mountain a deep cave. In this cave he now shut up Lindengold, and said to her :

" The cloudberries will soon be ripe, now count the days well. The first day I will give you thirty berries to eat and thirty dewdrops to drink, the next day twenty-nine berries and twenty-nine dewdrops, and so on, one less for each day. On the last day I shall demand your answer."

And Lindengold sat there, shut up in the cave for thirty days and nights. It is true that there was no dark night now in Lapland, but it was always dark in the cave. And the berries and the dewdrops became fewer and fewer, but the Princess did not grow thinner or paler, for what she missed during the day the Sleep Man and the dreams made up for during the nights. They lifted the top of the cave with their wonderful power, and she could see the glowing Midnight Sun, and hear the murmur of the mountain

stream. There rained into the cave a sweet honey dew to refresh her. She thought of Prince Abderraman, and sang Eastern songs, and listened with delight to their echoes which the cave repeated after her.

On the thirtieth day, the Wizard brought her the last berry and the last dewdrop in a leaf of Lapland birch.

"Now, then," said he, "have you decided?"

Lindengold only covered her face and made no reply.

"I will grant you one more day," said the Wizard, "and now I will give you a great company."

So saying he opened the door of the cave, and

in rushed a dark cloud of Lapland mosquitoes —thousands, and thousands, and again thousands, till the cave was filled as with a thick smoke.

"I wish you much joy from your new acquaintances," said the Wizard, and slammed the cave door shut after him.

Lindengold did not understand what he meant, for she knew as little of Lapland's mosquitoes as of Persia's fireflies. She had always had a maid stand by her with a fan to keep off all the pests of the air, whether she was awake or asleep. She was saved even now from feeling their stings, for as the door was shut, a light veil, such as the Fairies weave, fell over her. The mosquitoes could not pass through it, and after trying and trying again, they finally settled like spider webs along every crack and corner of the cave.

About midnight the door was softly opened, and the Lapp Woman entered with a bucket in her hand, and after her came Pimpepanturi with a burning pine knot.

"Poor child!" said the good old woman, "I feel sorry for you. But I dare not let you out, for my Husband would change me into a mouse. But I have brought you a little pine turpentine. Rub it all over your body, it is the best thing to keep off mosquitoes."

"And I have brought you a smoked reindeer shoulder," said Pimpepanturi in a generous tone, "so that you may not starve to death. It is a little gnawed at the end, for I got terribly hungry on the way, but there is still some meat upon it. I took the key to the cave while Father slept. But I dare not let you out, for Father would change me into a wolverine. But you need not take me as a husband, for I'll wager you could not make me a good blood dumpling."

"No, that I couldn't," replied Lindengold, and thanked them for their kindness, but declared that she was neither hungry nor bitten by mosquitoes.

"Just keep the turpentine anyhow, for safety's sake," said the woman.

"Yes, keep the reindeer shoulder too," added Pimpepanturi.

"Many, many thanks," said Lindengold.

The next morning came, and with it the Wizard. He expected now to find Lindengold as tame as any person can be who is half dead with mosquito bites. But when he saw her as well as ever, and when she again covered her face and made no reply, his anger knew no bounds.

"Come out," roared he.

IV

THE ENCHANTED HEATH-FLOWER

AND Lindengold came forth into the bright sunshine, as light and sweet as a Fairy in a moonbeam.

"I could take you to the Giant, Bom Bali," said the Wizard. "He would give six donkey-loads of gold to have you in his possession, if only for a day. But hear my plan. You are to be a heath-flower on this Lapland heath, and live as long as a heath-flower lives. Watch the sun. It is low in the heavens. In two weeks and a day the first polar frost will come. Then the heath-flowers die. I will ask you again the day before the frost."

He remained silent for a few moments as if he even now expected her reply. But when Lindengold again covered her face and said nothing, he exclaimed in great anger:

"*Adóma donaï marrabataësan!*" which means "*O human life, sink into a flower.*"

The Wizard had learned these words one autumn afternoon, when the south wind came from the deserts of Africa and lay down to rest in the mountains of Lapland. The wind knows all languages, as all languages are spoken in the wind.

At these terrible words it seemed to Lindengold as if all the flowers of the heath suddenly changed into tall trees above her head. But it was she herself who sank into the earth. In another moment no human eye could know her from the thousand and thousand other pale heath blossoms that lived and died on the wastes of Lapland.

"In two weeks from to-day," muttered the Wizard, and returned to the tent.

While all this happened, Prince Abderraman was travelling over the world with his sword at his side and a staff in his left hand. There was no mountain in Asia which he did not ascend, no desert in Africa which he did not cross, no city or town in Europe which he did not visit. In vain he searched. With sorrowful steps he was making his way toward Persia, when one day his faithful dog, Valledivan, pursued a wild duck and brought it alive to his master. When the Prince was just about to kill it, the duck quacked :

"Grant me my life, and I will tell you something."

"Strange bird," said he, "I will give you your life. What do you have to tell me ?"

"Go to Lapland," quacked the duck as it flew away.

Lapland ! Never had the Prince heard of such a country. He inquired about Lapland, and was told to go north, always toward the north, and never to stop until all roads came to an end, the woods came to an end, and where he no longer found houses with fireplaces in them.

"Strange !" thought the Prince ; but he followed the directions and rode northward, always northward, and did not stop till all roads came to an end, and the woods came to an end, and he found no other houses than movable tents. This was the last day of August. The sun still shone, the wastes were still green, but the sky had a greenish tint, and the wind blew cool from the north. Should the wind go down, the frost would come !

The Prince had travelled several days without seeing a trace of human life, when he suddenly noticed a tent of reindeer skins near the foot of a mountain. He rode toward it to inquire his way.

As he rode along he saw a word written on the side of the mountain which he started to spell out. To his great surprise he spelled out the name *Lindengold*. The Wizard had written this word over the cave where he kept the Princess, in order to be able to find the place when he moved his tent.

The Prince drew his sword and was about to enter the tent, when the Wizard Hirmu rushed out from it on his way to the heath.

" Give me back the Princess Lindengold, or I'll send you to Death's kingdom ! " exclaimed the Prince.

The Wizard was a shrewd man, who had saved himself by his cunning in many a tight place, but now he seemed to have lost his cunning. He quickly changed himself into a fox, and thought that in this shape he could easily escape the sword of the Prince, but he forgot *the dog*.

No sooner did Valledivan see the fox start off than he began the pursuit. The fox leaped nimbly from cliff to cliff, but the dog was swifter, and caught him at last on the top of the mountain, and tore him to pieces. Thus perished the wicked Wizard Hirmu.

The dog returned bloodstained, and the Prince knew that it was all over with the Wizard. But where was Lindengold ?

The Prince entered the tent. The Lapp Woman, Pimpedora, was boiling reindeer meat, and her son, Pimpepanturi, was sleeping on the soft moss in the tent while waiting for his dinner.

" Woman," said the Prince, " your old man is dead ! Give me back the Princess Lindengold, and no harm shall come to you."

" Alas ! and is he dead ? " said the woman, without showing any signs of real sorrow. " Well, what else could one expect from his wicked tricks ? But the Princess Lindengold you must seek among the heath-flowers. My old man turned her into a heath-flower just like the thousand others that you see. To-night the frost will come, and that will be the end of her."

" My dearest Lindengold, must you die to-night and I be unable to find even the stem on which you have withered ? " exclaimed the Prince, and in despair threw himself upon the heath, where thousands of pale flowers were awaiting their doom that night.

" Wait a moment," said the woman. " I remember now the words he used in changing her into a flower. I felt sorry for the child, and so I crept up behind a rock to see what would become of her. Then I heard him say: *Adóma donaï Marrabataësan.*"

"But what good are those words when we do not know the charm that will restore her?" groaned the Prince.

Pimpepanturi felt that he had waited altogether too long, and came out of the tent to seek his mother. When he heard the Prince's wail he said:

"Father always reversed the words when he wanted to break a spell."

"Yes, that is so," said the Lapp Woman.

The Prince grasped at this straw, climbed upon a rock, and cried as loud as he could over the boundless heath:

"*Marrabataësan donaï Adóma!*"

The sound died away without effect, the sun sank lower, and the wind was almost gone.

The Prince was frightened, but he kept on repeating the words over and over again in different order. But all in vain. Only once did it seem to him as if the heath-flowers in the distance bent to listen to him. But they fell back again into the dead silence of the endless waste.

"The sun is setting," cried the Lapp Woman. "Unless you find the right words soon, the frost will come, and then all will be over!"

And the red disc of the sun rolled to the horizon. All Nature was still. A cold evening mist, foreboding the frost, sank down like a veil over the plains and hills. The plants which had dared for a short time to blossom in Lapland were now about to die.

The Prince was white with fear. His voice began to fail him. It was with great difficulty that he uttered the magic words in a new order :

" *Marraba donaï Adóma taësan !* "

And, behold ! on a hill not far away a little flower raised its head. It grew as rapidly as when the Fairies of Ginnistan touch the mountains with their wands and make sweet lilies arise in the morning light. The mist lay about the hill. Out of the mist a slender form arose. And when the Prince in breathless haste reached the hill, Lindengold herself came forward to meet him. She was as pale as those are who have already felt the first chill of death.

Prince Abderraman carried the pale Princess to the tent. Her strength gradually came back under the kindly care of the Lapp Woman. Pimpedora was happy. Pimpepanturi forgot, in his glee, his long-looked-for dinner, which was scorched in the kettle. Abderraman did something which heroes seldom do—he fainted for joy. When he came to himself, he asked Lindengold how it felt to be changed into a flower.

" As when you sink back into your childhood's cradle, and know nothing of the world, but to drink and sleep and be happy in God's love," replied Lindengold.

" And how did it seem to be restored to life ? "

" As when you awake on a clear morning after a sweet sleep."

" To-morrow we return to Persia," said Prince Abderraman.

" Yes," answered Lindengold. " But this good woman and her son have been kind to me in my distress. We will take them with us, and they shall live in a Palace at Ispahan."

" No, no ! thank you ! " exclaimed Pimpedora. " I like my reindeer tent in Lapland better."

" Do you have snow and reindeer in Persia ? " asked Pimpepanturi.

" Snow we have only on the highest mountains, and in place of reindeer we have antelopes, deer, and gazelles," replied the Princess.

" Then I will stay here," said Pimpepanturi, " and you may go to Persia and marry whom you please. There is no land to me like Lapland."

There was no use in discussing this matter. The Prince and Princess set out the following day for Persia, after having given their rich apparel—gold, silver, and jewels—to the Lapp Woman and her son. From them they secured Lapland costumes instead.

The Lapp Woman put away in a birch-bark box all the treasures she had received. She rejoiced to know that for it she could buy a whole tent full of flour.

V

FROM LAPLAND TO THE GOLDEN PALACE

NADIR SHAH sat alone and weeping in his Golden Palace in Ispahan. He could not forget his lost daughter, Lindengold. His ungrateful sons had raised a rebellion against him, and were marching with a large army to drive their father from his throne.

Just then the Grand Vizier announced that two savages, a man and a girl, dressed in skins, and accompanied by a dog, were standing at the gate, desiring to throw themselves at the King's feet. The King never refused admission to strangers. Perhaps they might know something of his lost daughter, his dear Lindengold.

The two savages were brought into his presence. The man prostrated himself at the King's feet, but the girl threw her arms about the King's neck, giving the Grand Vizier such a shock that his beard turned green. But the King recognized, even in this odd disguise, his loved and lost daughter.

" Allah ! " he cried, " now I am ready to die ! "

" No, my Lord King," said the Prince, " now you must live to rejoice with us and to win back your Kingdom."

When the King heard how his daughter had been carried away, and how she had been rescued by the faithful Prince, he at once declared Prince Abderraman his heir to the throne, and promised him the Princess Lindengold in marriage. Then he sent Prince Abderraman at the head of his fifty thousand knights, mounted on horses with golden bridles and silver saddles, against the rebel army. It was not long before the brave Prince, with his valiant left hand, gained a complete victory, took captive the rebellious sons, and returned in triumph to the jubilant Ispahan.

Then was celebrated the wedding of Abderraman and Lindengold with great rejoicing—but without any animal contests or fights. Long and happy did they live.

Nadir Shah reigned to a good old age, and often enjoyed his little grandchildren's prattle. His wicked sons ended their lives as swineherds for the wicked Giant Bom Bali. The dog, Valledivan, lived to the remarkable age of thirty years, and finally died of the toothache. His skin was stuffed, and thus his memory was preserved.

As to Pimpedora, and Pimpepanturi, who had once been honoured with the proud name of Morus Pandorus von Pikkulukulikuckulu, no news of them has ever reached Persia. They have never found, most probably, a better country than Lapland.

The FIRE ENGINE

By S. G. Hulme Beaman

Illustrated by the Author

"I've just thought of something!" cried the Mayor of Toytown one morning.

"How clever you are!" said his secretary. "You're always thinking of something."

"Ah, but this is something very important," the mayor pointed out. "Something I've never thought of before. Do you know," he whispered, "that we haven't a fire engine in Toytown? What a terrible thing it would be if one of the houses caught fire! Particularly if it were *my* house."

The secretary looked quite frightened. "I never thought of that," he said.

"You never think of anything," cried the mayor. "You leave everything to me. I must go and see the inventor, and arrange for a fire engine at once." And putting on his hat and his gold chain, the mayor set out for the inventor's house.

The inventor was very busy with a lot of cog-wheels and pieces of string and wire, but when he saw the mayor he asked politely what he could do for him.

" I've decided we must have a fire engine in Toytown," the mayor said. " Now, what do you suggest ? "

" Well, of course, I could make you a fire engine," replied the inventor thoughtfully. " Or I could make you a nice state coach, if you prefer it. Wouldn't you sooner have a state coach ; it would be much easier to make ? "

" But you can't put a fire out with a state coach ! " cried the mayor.

" And you can't go for a ride on a fire engine," the inventor pointed out. " It wouldn't look dignified. Of course, if you'd sooner have a fire engine, I could make you one. You'd want a lot of brass helmets to go with it ? "

" I want a proper fire engine, all complete," the mayor ordered.

" You leave it to me," said the inventor. So the mayor left it to him, and went home to dinner.

Some time afterwards the mayor was sitting in the town hall when he heard a lot of cheering and a jingling of bells. Then the inventor came hurrying in, looking very pleased with himself.

"It's finished!" he cried. "The fire engine is outside!"

"Splendid!" said the mayor; and he jumped up and followed the inventor into the square. And there, surrounded by a crowd of people, stood a very curious-looking thing.

"What's that?" asked the mayor, staring in amazement.

"That's the fire engine," the inventor said proudly. "You'll notice that I've made it so that you can use it as a state coach if you want to."

"But it's not *like* a fire engine," the mayor exclaimed. "I've never seen a fire engine like that before."

"Ah, but it's a special sort of fire engine," the inventor pointed out. "You see, if you want a ride, you just get inside. And if you want a fire engine, the coachman and the footman put on brass helmets and light a fire in the boiler, and there you are. And you'll notice that it has a nice long ladder so that persons in burning houses can climb out."

"But how does it put a fire out?" the mayor asked.

"Well, I don't know that it would actually put a fire *out*," the inventor admitted. "But, you see, there is a long piece of hose which you can fix on to the nearest tap, and plenty of buckets to fill with water. Of course we could easily test it by setting fire to your house."

"No, not at all," cried the mayor hastily. "I'm quite sure it will be excellent. It's not *quite* what I expected, but still——! We'd better keep it in my stable."

The people of Toytown were very proud of their new fire engine, and whenever the mayor went for a ride in it crowds stood about the streets and cheered. But no houses caught fire, and every one felt disappointed because no opportunity arose of finding out how the fire engine worked.

One afternoon the town policeman was standing outside the inventor's house when he noticed a wisp of smoke coming from an upper window. "At last!" he said to himself. "Now we shall be able to try the new engine!" And he began to run towards the mayor's house, shouting "Fire!" as he did so.

"Fire! Fire!" he cried, banging on the mayor's front door until it was opened by the secretary. "Fire!" shouted the policeman. "Turn out the engine quickly before it burns out."

"Well, it's rather awkward," said the secretary. "You see the mayor has gone for a ride, and I don't know how long he may be. He has gone to the castle."

"Oh dear!" said the policeman, mopping his face. "I shall have to go after him. And it's such a hot day." And turning away, he began to run along the road towards the castle. Fortunately he had not to go very far, for he soon met the mayor driving towards home.

" Fire ! " shouted the policeman, waving his arms. " The inventor's house is on fire ! "

The mayor jumped out and began to shout orders. Immediately the coachman and the footman scrambled down and pulled their helmets out from under the carriage seat, while the policeman (after a lot of trouble) lit the fire under the boiler. " Jump up ! " cried the mayor ; and the engine dashed away towards the inventor's house.

When they got there the policeman was surprised to find the same thin wisp of smoke coming from the window, instead of a roar of flames, as he had expected. A crowd of people had collected in the street, and cheers went up as the engine dashed round the corner and the mayor, the policeman, and the two helmeted servants jumped down. Then all was bustle and confusion.

" What tap shall we fix the hose to ? " asked the policeman.

" The inventor's tap, of course," replied the mayor. " It's his house which is on fire ; use his tap."

So the policeman beat in the door with a hatchet and disappeared into the house, dragging one end of the hose behind him. In a few minutes the hose began to spurt water, and everybody gave a fresh cheer.

Then the coachman planted the ladder against the side of the house, and the policeman, taking the hatchet in his hand, climbed towards the window from which the smoke was coming, while the footman took up the nozzle of the hose and commenced to squirt water over the house front and every one near him. The crowd ceased to cheer and drew farther back.

Crash! The policeman dashed in the glass of the window, and a stream of water squirted in from the footman's hose. But, to the surprise of every one, instead of flames coming from the window, there appeared a lot of pretty coloured stars. Then the inventor appeared, wiping the water from his face with a large handkerchief.

"Don't do that," cried the inventor. "You've made all my fireworks wet!"

"But isn't the house on fire?" asked the policeman.

"Of course not," said the inventor. "I was just inventing some new fireworks, and now you've spoilt them. Go away!"

So the policeman climbed slowly down the ladder, and the crowd, feeling most disappointed, went home. But the mayor was very angry.

"Fancy all that trouble for nothing!" he cried. "I don't see the use of having a fire engine if we can never use it!" And *he* went home.

The next day the mayor called in a workman, and they set to work on the fire engine. They took off the buckets, pulled the hose away into the garden to water the garden, and dragged the boiler into the bathroom. Then they chopped up the ladder for firewood.

"There!" cried the mayor. "Now it's just

an ordinary coach; that will be much more useful."

So now they have no fire engine in Toytown, and if ever one of the houses does catch fire, they will probably put it out with a bucket of water.

THE UNAMIABLE CHILD

By Christopher Morley

Budget, the teddy bear, had been left out in the rain ; and you know how wet a large, fat, fleecy, stomachy bear can get. So he was pinned up on the clothes-line to dry.

The easiest way to fasten a teddy bear to a clothes-line is to pin him by his ears. So there he hung, with the forked pegs tightly pinched on his two tender flaps of ear. He was surprisingly patient. His yellow glass eyes looked a bit wild, and his mouth, sewn in black wool, drooped in a mournful curve, and the palms of his muddy paws hung soggy, but for a long while he was silent. Then he could endure it no more, and the animals in the Grape Arbour Tea Room heard him utter a scream of bad temper.

" You make me sad ! You make me terribly sad ! " he yelled (it was a phrase he had caught from four-year-old Blythe). " I hope you'll all go to Bide-a-Wee ! You sit there telling stories, and I'm pinned up by my ears and can't hear a word ! "

The animals gazed in astonishment. They had been so busy enjoying their tea and talk it had never occurred to them that Budget might like to hear what was going on. They had never taken Budget very seriously, or regarded him as a real animal. Now they gathered under the clothes-line and looked up in concern.

Budget, after suffering so long in silence, was in a fierce tantrum. He hung there trembling with rage. He had caught a cold from getting so wet—the kind of cold that is always referred to as "nasty," and that also added to his irritation. Now he kept shouting out all the rude words he could remember from listening to croquet games. He shouted very loud, too ; louder than he realized, for with his ears pinned up he could not hear himself.

" Dumb-bells ! " he screamed. " Big simps ! Boobs ! Poor fish ! Haven't you any manners for other people's feelings ? My gracious ! You just sit there and have a good time and never think about me. Rough-necks ! You better go to Bide-a-Wee, bettn't you ! "

They were all scandalized by this outburst. Donny and Fritz tried to jump up to reach his feet, but the line had been put high on purpose. It was the squirrels who saved the day. Two of them ran out on the rope, one from each end. With their clever little paws they unfastened the clothes-pins from his ears. He dropped on to Donny's broad back, and they carried him over to the grape arbour and propped him in a comfortable chair. A cup of hot cambric tea made him feel better, though his ears were still sore. It was agreed that as he had been so ill-treated, a story should be told for his special benefit.

" What kind of story would you like ? " asked Escargot, the wise snail who always acted as host at these meetings.

" A story in which children get the worst of it," he said peevishly. " I shall never forget their carelessness in leaving me out in the rain. I do think, after all I've done for them, they might be more thoughtful. Four children have used me to go to bed with, one after the other, all these years. Every night of my life, as soon as they're comfortably asleep, I get crowded out of bed. I'm all bruises from falling on the floor. I hope they'll get punished some day. I hope—gosh, I hope they'll all grow up and marry people who kick in their sleep. Yes, tell me a story in which children get the worst of it."

The animals looked at each other in some embarrassment. They could think of a number of stories of that sort, but it is dangerous to repeat them. For they had all been carefully trained to idealize children, to say of them " they are just little animals." But they knew well enough that children are powerful enough and uncertain, and that no animal is as full of dangerous energy as a child.

The big grey squirrel who had unpinned Budget's left ear volunteered to tell the story.

Squirrels are reckless, because they are so agile, and live safely in trees. This one took up a comfortable position on top of the grape arbour, shifted the nuts out of his mouth, and looked sharply round to make sure that no outsiders could overhear.

This isn't really a Roslyn Fairy Tale, he said. It happened in the city. Nothing so scandalous could happen out here. My cousin told it to me; he is one of the squirrels in Riverside Park.

There was once a very small boy called Philip, who used to go walking in the park with his nurse. And like all proper boys, he always took along a bag of peanuts to feed the squirrels.

I think that in the beginning the trouble was more the nurse's fault than Philip's. Her father had been in the circus business, and perhaps for that reason she had a strong passion for peanuts. As they walked along the streets on the way to Riverside Drive she could not resist eating them, and, just to be fair, she allowed Philip to have some too. The five-cent bag of peanuts, as every squirrel knows, does not hold nearly as many as it used to in the good old days; and sometimes by the time they got to the park there were hardly any nuts left for the squirrels.

That, of course, was regrettable; but it could be forgiven. Any squirrel can understand other people, too, having a weakness for peanuts. What was really unfair was that Philip learned that the squirrels were easily fooled by empty shells. It

was quite easy to hold out the end of a shell in such a way that it looked like an unopened nut. The hopeful animals would come scampering, and this mischievous boy would lure them on until they even climbed up his legs and clustered about his hands. Then they would discover it was only a trick. They would look at him reproachfully with their bright eyes, and he would shout with laughter at their disappointment.

If his nurse had been the right sort she would soon have taught him not to do this sort of thing. She might have reminded Philip, my cousin said, that in Riverside Park there is the famous little memorial of the Amiable Child, which so many visitors to New York have seen. This very small tomb of a peaceful child, right next to the huge tomb of a very warlike man, General Grant, should have suggested to her that the Riverside children ought all to be Amiable. But she was sitting on a bench reading one of those small newspapers that are so popular in the park. My cousin used to wonder what there can be in those papers that is so nourishing? Evidently they have the same attraction for nursemaids that peanuts have for squirrels. Anyhow, this shabby behaviour of Philip's went on until all the squirrels knew him by sight. Then he could not hoax them any more. When they saw him holding out peanut shells and calling to them, they paid no attention.

All this did not matter much in summer, when peanuts are plentiful. In summer the city squirrels get probably more nuts than are good for them. That little groaning you sometimes hear in the trees along Riverside Drive at night comes from some young squirrels with stomach-ache, due to an excess of rich diet. But winter came, when peanuts mean much to the New York squirrels. For they have been so spoiled by having food scattered about for them, my cousin says, that they have lost their thrifty habit of storing up a supply for the barren season. And then, when Philip and his nurse still continued to eat most of the peanuts before they got to the park, and still amused themselves by offering the empty husks, it was determined to do something.

The boy and his companion did not notice, as they walked home one snowy dusk, that two watchful grey squirrels were following. Up the steep hill from the Drive, hiding now and then behind the piles of snow along the kerb, hurrying into doorways to avoid being seen, darting briskly across streets when the traffic was halted, these two trailed Philip and the nurse. In their handsome grey fur they looked like two small busy postmen delivering letters. In that December season the streets are full of all sorts of cheerful doings, and even if the two squirrels were noticed, they were merely supposed to be hurrying on Christmas errands. Their sharp little faces were full of purpose, and they followed the unsuspecting pair until they reached the big apartment house on West End Avenue, where Philip lived. Even then their task was not finished. They ran up to the top of a tree in front of the building. Swaying about in the bare branches, and arguing briskly together, they waited a long time. They kept careful watch on all the windows of the apartment house. Then they saw Philip's face appear at one of those windows. He saw them too, and was pleased, for, he thought, here were two squirrels who had not yet been fooled. He threw down some empty peanut shells that had remained in his overcoat pocket. The squirrels disregarded this unmannerly gesture, and hurried back to the park.

A few days later it was Christmas Eve. It

seemed to Philip that an afternoon had never gone so slowly. Along Broadway the shops were bright with toys and pretty things ; as he walked with his nurse he wondered impatiently what surprises he was going to get the next day. He had heard the papery rustle of wrappings in his mother's room, the constant buzz of the door-bell as mysterious bundles were delivered at the apartment. He had no brothers and sisters, so he had no one's pleasure to consider but his own. The nurse kept him out late, so that he would be sleepy, and then, after a light supper, he was put to bed. When he was sound asleep his father and mother began setting up the Tree.

Meanwhile, down in Riverside Park, a remarkable thing was happening. From every corner of the grounds squirrels were assembling at the appointed meeting-place—the little rocky hill near 84th Street which is where they hold their parliament. It was an extraordinary gathering. The biggest, strongest, most active squirrels had been chosen. There must have been nearly a hundred of them ; they covered the outcrop of rock, and all chattered together. On any other evening such a crowd would have been noticed, but on Christmas Eve every one was busy with his own concerns. Windows hung with wreaths shone in the tall

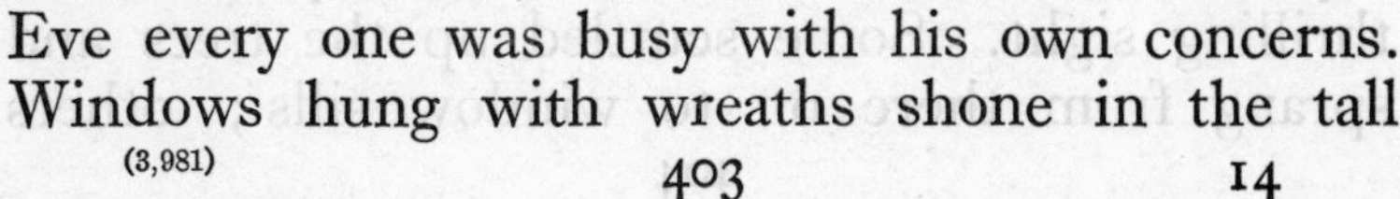

cliffs of building along the Drive, the buses were full of people carrying parcels wrapped in red ribbon, the sky was clear, and dark, and frosty, all the gaiety of that tender evening sparkled in the air.

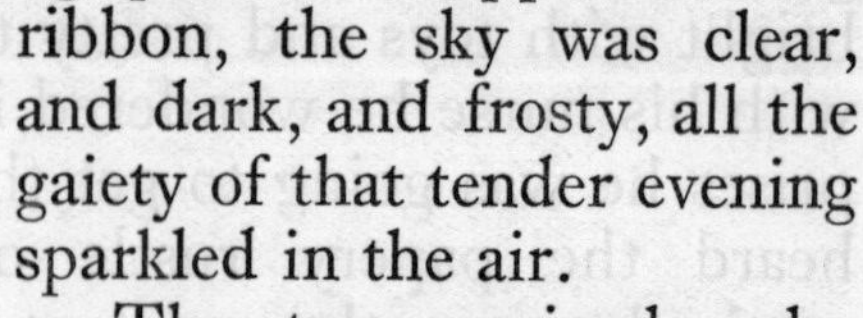

The two squirrels who knew the way acted as leaders. At their command all conversation ceased; with well-drilled swiftness the furry regiment set off in column of twos. Their plumy tails flirted with nervous excitement as they advanced, in short quick scampers, along the wall that bounds the Drive. The policeman at the crossing was startled when they approached, but he knew that on Christmas Eve you must not be surprised at anything. He saluted them, and held up the buses while they crossed in an orderly rush. They ran swiftly up to West End Avenue. There, in front of the apartment house, they paused in a long line while the leaders pointed out Philip's window. It was open, as healthy bedroom windows ought to be at night. There was a sharp squeak of command, and the army of squirrels charged upon the tall building.

No one but squirrels could have done it! My cousin, who was one of them, says it was a thrilling sight. Some scuttled up the trees and sprang from there on to window sills; others scaled straight up the front of the wall. They darted in quick zigzags up the face of the cliff, their strong toes took advantage of every little ornament and roughness in the stone. The sills were slippery and required careful going, but these were the picked athletes of all the Riverside squirrels, and they were lean and agile with winter hunger. Before you could have guessed what was happening, the whole pack had swarmed up to the twelfth floor and entered through Philip's window.

There lay the Unamiable Child, fast asleep; and there in the next room was the beautiful Christmas Tree. Parents and nurse had trimmed it well, and gone to bed exhausted. From every fragrant bough hung tinsel ornaments, peppermint canes, cornucopias, coloured bulbs, popcorn strings, shining trinkets. It is sad to have to tell it, but the angry squirrels made short work of that Tree. The Star at the top they did not touch, for squirrels respect the Christmas Star as much as any one; and the glass and tinsel decorations didn't interest them; but everything else they raided to their hearts' content. They stripped the tree of everything eatable, they hung the popcorn strings out of the window to make a rope by which they could get down again. Imagine their

pleasure when they found a large box of peanut brittle underneath the tree. Among so many sharp teeth it did not last long. They did not care much for the sweet part, but they carefully ate out every peanut embedded in the candy, and left the box a mass of sticky crumbs.

They worked quietly and fast. If any one heard the rustle of their movements he would have thought it only the secret wrappings of packages. They did not bother the presents piled beside the Tree, for they did not want to spoil Philip's Christmas altogether, merely to give him a hint. Then each squirrel hooked a tiny peppermint cane round his neck. They gave a satisfied look at the devastated tree, then they were out of the window and ran nimbly down the long chains of pink and white popcorn.

There was a silence when the squirrel finished this story. The animals looked at each other rather doubtfully. Only the indignant Budget, still remembering his woes, seemed entirely pleased.

"That's fine, that's fine!" he exclaimed. "An excellent story. I think they let him off very easily. He ought to have been hung up by his ears. That story ought to be printed where people could read it."

But Donny was shocked. " Rubbish ! " he growled. " It's a terrible story. It could never be published."

The squirrel twitched his tail anxiously as he looked down on his troubled audience. " I don't know whether it's part of the story or not," he said, " but my cousin added that the squirrels ate the peppermint canes for Christmas dinner, and felt very poorly afterward."

It was left to Escargot, the French snail, who was always tactful, to turn their thoughts into a happier mood.

" The French word for peanuts," he said solemnly, " is *cacahuètes*. Very few Americans know that."

They all burst into a laugh. " *Cacawate, cacawate !* " they shouted, imitating his delicate pronunciation. And the big grey squirrel is nicknamed Cacahuète to this day.

THE PAPER HOOP

By Hugh Chesterman

Mr. Brewster was a Circus dog. His mother had been a Circus dog, and his grandmother and his great-grandmother. Mr. Brewster was very proud of his family, and when he was a puppy he would never tire of hearing his mother boast that she had once performed before the King and Queen. That had happened a long time ago; and his mother was dead now.

Mr. Brewster was not the only dog in the Circus. There were four others: Fangs, the wolf-hound; Snuffle and Sniff, who helped Mr. Brewster pull the cart in which Fangs, dressed like the Lord Mayor's coachman, used to drive round the ring; and lastly Freda, the dachshund, who wore a soldier's coat and fired a cannon by pulling the string with her mouth.

During business hours they sat waiting their turn in a corner of the tent where the bags of sawdust and paper hoops, and all the other things that belonged to the Circus, were kept, and where Panlo the clown used to come to practise his somersaults and dress himself up for the show.

Besides Panlo, there was William Jasper, the Circus owner (Mr. Brewster did not like him very much), and Mrs. Jasper, who was certainly kind when she remembered to be, but usually she was too busy with the affairs of the Circus to pay much attention to the dogs. Then there was Max, the acrobat, and old George Dangar, who took the money at the doors, packed up the wagons when the Circus moved from town to town, cooked dinner for the troupe, understudied most of them, and could be just as funny as Panlo and just as clever as Max. It was George who fed the dogs. He certainly gave them plenty to eat—when business was good ; but when the Circus fell on bad days, he was not so generous.

Mr. Brewster was not a very happy little dog. There were times when he grew very tired of the Circus, and of doing the same tricks night after night. He could not help envying the other dogs that he used to see as he trotted along under the last wagon when the Circus was on the move. He thought it would be nice to be like them. They were free to go where they liked, and they didn't have to wear a ridiculous uniform, and walk on their hind legs, and dance to a band.

He had thought sometimes about running away, but, somehow, the chance never came. His masters took care of that. For Mr. Brewster was a dog of many accomplishments. He could beg and turn somersaults, and sham death, and pull a handkerchief from the Clown's pocket without the Clown ever knowing (at least he pretended not to, because that was part of the trick). And in addition to this, he could do all Freda's tricks better than Freda herself.

All, that is, except *one.*

He could not jump through the Paper Hoop. Ever since he was a puppy he had steadily refused to do that. Old George had tried coaxing and bribery, and Mr. Jasper had tried thrashing and starvation. But it was all no good. The sight of that hoop was the signal for Mr. Brewster to droop his stumpy little tail and slink away. Fangs and Freda and the two terriers always went through their hoops without hesitation. But Mr. Brewster stolidly refused to. It made his masters very angry.

Nevertheless the day came when he did jump through, and you shall hear how it happened.

The Circus was performing in a small country town, and it was the last day of the visit. It had been a very tiring one for Mr. Brewster. All that afternoon, and again in the evening, he had worn his uniform, turned somersaults, fired the cannon, marched up and down in time to the band, balanced things on his nose, and done it all again and again because the audience liked it and kept on calling for more. But at last the hot, wearisome evening came to an end, and nothing remained but the Hoop Trick. Freda and the terriers had already leaped through theirs with a crackling of paper and a shout of delight from the audience, and it only remained for Fangs to follow suit to bring the performance to a close. Panlo held up the Hoop. It was the biggest one of all. Fangs was standing some yards away, waiting for the signal to jump.

Quite suddenly, while Panlo was still waiting for Fangs, Mr. Brewster was possessed by a great longing to see what lay on the other side of the Hoop. That great, round, dazzling disc seemed to him to be a door that might lead—he knew not where. Without a note of warning he made a dash for the Hoop, and, shutting his eyes, leaped high in the air and crashed through the paper.

. . . .

When Mr. Brewster opened his eyes again he was puzzled at first to know where he was. The Circus had gone. Of Panlo, and the audience, and Mr. Jasper and the others there was no sign. He found himself standing in a green field through which ran a shallow stream, and he noticed that he was not alone, for in the field were many other dogs. Some were basking in the morning sun which shone brightly, but not too fiercely, upon them. Others were swimming in the stream, while others again were rushing wildly here and there after rabbits, which kept popping up out of the grass and disappearing again as quickly. On the bank of the river he saw another curious sight. Hanging from a low branch were dozens and dozens of bones of every shape and size.

GERVIS

Every now and again a dog would run up to this branch and pull away one of the bones. And the most curious part about it was that every time a bone was pulled away another came in its place. So there was always a good supply. A little farther on he saw a large white notice board which said, " BURYING-PLACE FOR BONES," and quite a score of happy dogs were busy here. With a yelp of joy he rushed to meet them.

. . . .

Mr. Jasper, and Panlo, and Max, and old George Dangar are still looking for Mr. Brewster. I expect they are wondering why he doesn't come back—but that would never do. And if ever their Circus comes to your town, you must be sure not to tell them about the other side of the Hoop, because Mr. Brewster is much too happy where he is.

By Rosalind Vallance

If you want to be gay
There's no place like the South,
Where melons lie ready
To melt in your mouth ;
Where the sea's as blue
As a pictured sea,
And the water's as warm
As you'd wish it to be ;
And the people who live
In this flowery land
Build their houses in trees
That grow in the sand ;
With a leafy roof,
And a creaky floor,
And a big front window,
And no front door,
And a venturesome ladder
To get them upstairs.

Would you change your own house
For one of theirs ?

IF YOU WANT TO BE GAY

Would you like a brown skin
And fuzzy hair,
And a raffia skirt ?
Then be born out there.

Would you lie in the shade
Of an afternoon,
Listening while Father
Pipes a tune
On a wooden whistle,
And Mother sings
To her sleepy brown babe
In his cradle of strings ?

Would you leave this England—
The song of the thrush
On the rain-sweet briar
In the evening hush :
The frosty morning
(Blood beating high),
The sun a red ball
In the daffodil sky ;
To swim and dive
With the folk of the Isles,
White teeth flashing
In berry-brown smiles ?

Would you sleep in the day,
And wake at night,
And run barefoot
In the dawning light ?

Or wouldn't you rather
Just be you,
With Londony things
To see and do ?
With London river,
A London park,
And the street lamps glinting
In the early dark ?
And Londony shops,
And a house with a door,
And a cloth on the table,
And rugs on the floor,
And muffins for tea
By a roasting fire ?

Which is the land
Of your desire ?

THE STOLEN TURNIPS, THE MAGIC TABLECLOTH, THE SNEEZING GOAT AND THE WOODEN WHISTLE

By ARTHUR RANSOME

THIS is the story which old Peter used to tell whenever either Vanya or Maroosia was cross. This did not often happen ; but it would be no use to pretend that it never happened at all. Sometimes it was Vanya who scolded Maroosia, and sometimes it was Maroosia who scolded Vanya. Sometimes there were two scoldings going on at once. And old Peter did not like crossness in the hut, whoever did the scolding. He said it spoilt his tobacco, and put a sour taste in the tea. And, of course, when the children remembered that they were spoiling their grandfather's tea and tobacco, they stopped just as quickly as they could, unless their tongues had run right away with them —which happens sometimes, you know, even to grown-up people. This story used to be told in two ways. It was either the tale of an old man who was bothered by a cross old woman, or the tale of an old woman who was bothered by a cross old man. And the moment old Peter began the story both children would ask at once, " Which is the cross one ? "—for then they would know which of them old Peter thought was in the wrong.

" This time it's the old woman," said their grandfather ; " but, as like as not, it will be the old man next."

And then any quarrelling there was came to an end, and was forgotten before the end of the story. This is the story.

An old man and an old woman lived in a little wooden house. All round the house there was a garden, crammed with flowers, and potatoes, and beetroots, and cabbages. And in one corner of the house there was a narrow wooden stairway which went up and up, twisting and twisting, into a high tower. In the top of the tower was a dovecot, and on the top of the dovecot was a flat roof.

Now, the old woman was never content with the doings of the old man. She scolded all day, and she scolded all night. If there was too much rain, it was the old man's fault ; and if there was a drought, and all green things were parched for lack of water, well, the old man was to blame for not altering the weather. And though he was old and tired, it was all the same to her how much work she put on his shoulders. The garden was full. There was no room in it at all, not even for a single pea. And all of a sudden the old woman sets her heart on growing turnips.

" But there is no room in the garden," says the old man.

" Sow them on the top of the dovecot," says the old woman.

" But there is no earth there."

" Carry earth up and put it there," says she.

So the old man laboured up and down with his tired old bones, and covered the top of the dovecot with good black earth. He could only take up a very little at a time, because he was old and weak, and because the stairs were so narrow and dangerous that he had to hold on with both hands and carry the earth in a bag which he held in his teeth. His teeth were strong enough, because he had been biting crusts all his life. The old woman left him nothing else, for she took all the crumb for herself. The old man did his best, and by evening the top of the dovecot was covered with earth, and he had sown it with turnip seed.

Next day, and the day after that, and every day, the old woman scolded the old man till he went up to the dovecot to see how those turnip seeds were getting on.

" Are they ready to eat yet ? "

" They are not ready to eat."

" Is the green sprouting ? "

" The green is sprouting."

And at last there came a day when the old man came down from the dovecot and said: " The turnips are doing finely—quite big they are getting ; but all the best ones have been stolen away."

" Stolen away ? " cried the old woman, shaking with rage. " And have you lived all these years and not learned how to keep thieves from a turnip-bed, on the top of a dovecot, on the top of a tower, on the top of a house ? Out with you, and don't you dare to come back till you have caught the thieves."

The old man did not dare to tell her that the door had been bolted, although he knew it had, because he had bolted it himself. He hurried away out of the house, more because he wanted to get out of earshot of her scolding than because he had any hope of finding the thieves. " They may be birds," thinks he, " or the little brown squirrels. Who else could climb so high without using the stairs ? And how is an old man like me to get hold of them, flying through the tops of the high trees and running up and down the branches ? "

And so he wandered away without his dinner into the deep forest.

But God is good to old men. Hasn't He given me two little pigeons, who nearly always are as merry as all little pigeons should be ? And God led the old man through the forest, though the old man thought he was just wandering on, trying to lose himself and forget the scolding voice of the old woman.

And after he had walked a long way through the dark green forest, he saw a little hut standing

under the pine trees. There was no smoke coming from the chimney, but there was such a chattering in the hut you could hear it far away. It was like coming near a rookery at evening, or disturbing a lot of starlings. And as the old man came slowly nearer to the hut, he thought he saw little faces looking at him through the window and peeping through the door. He could not be sure, because they were gone so quickly. And all the time the chattering went on louder and louder, till the old man nearly put his hands to his ears.

And then suddenly the chattering stopped. There was not a sound—no noise at all. The old man stood still. A squirrel dropped a fir cone close by, and the old man was startled by the fall of it, because everything else was so quiet.

"Whatever there is in the hut, it won't be worse than the old woman," says the old man to himself. So he makes the sign of the holy Cross, and steps up to the little hut and takes a look through the door.

There was no one to be seen. You would have thought the hut was empty.

The old man took a step inside, bending under the little low door. Still he could see nobody, only a great heap of rags and blankets on the sleeping-place on the top of the stove. The hut was as clean as if it had only that minute been swept by Maroosia herself. But in the middle of the floor there was a scrap of green leaf lying, and the old man knew in a moment that it was a scrap of green leaf from the top of a young turnip.

And while the old man looked at it, the heap of blankets and rugs on the stove moved, first in one place and then in another. Then there was a little laugh. Then another. And suddenly there was a great stir in the blankets, and they were all thrown back helter-skelter, and there were dozens and dozens of little queer children, laughing and laughing and laughing, and looking at the old man. And every child had a little turnip, and showed it to the old man and laughed.

Just then the door of the stove flew open, and

out tumbled more of the little queer children—dozens and dozens of them. The more they came tumbling out into the hut, the more there seemed to be chattering in the stove and squeezing to get out, one over the top of another. The noise of chattering and laughing would have made your head spin. And every one of the children out of the stove had a little turnip like the others, and waved it about and showed it to the old man, and laughed like anything.

"Ho," says the old man, "so you are the thieves who have stolen the turnips from the top of the dovecot?"

"Yes," cried the children; and the chatter rattled as fast as hailstones on the roof. "Yes! yes! yes! *We* stole the turnips."

"How did you get on to the top of the dovecot when the door into the house was bolted and fast?"

At that the children all burst out laughing, and did not answer a word.

" Laugh you may," said the old man ; " but it is I who get the scolding when the turnips fly away in the night."

" Never mind ! never mind ! " cried the children. " We'll pay for the turnips."

" How can you pay for them ? " asks the old man. " You have got nothing to pay with."

All the children chattered together, and looked at the old man and smiled. Then one of them said to the old man, " Are you hungry, grandfather ? "

" Hungry ! " says the old man. " Why, yes, of course I am, my dear. I've been looking for you all day, and I had to start without my dinner."

" If you are hungry, open the cupboard behind you."

The old man opened the cupboard.

" Take out the tablecloth."

The old man took out the tablecloth.

" Spread it on the table."

The old man spread the tablecloth on the table.

" Now ! " shouted the children, chattering like a thousand nests full of young birds, " we'll all sit down and have dinner."

They pulled out the benches and gave the old man a chair at one end, and all crowded round the table ready to begin.

" But there's no food," said the old man.

How they laughed!

" Grandfather," one of them sings out from the other end of the table, " you just tell the tablecloth to turn inside out."

" How ? " says he.

" Tell the tablecloth to turn inside out. That's easy enough."

" There's no harm in doing that," thinks the old man ; so he says to the tablecloth as firmly as he could, " Now then you, tablecloth, turn inside out ! "

The tablecloth hove itself up into the air, and rolled itself this way and that as if it were in a whirlwind, and then suddenly laid itself flat on the table again. And somehow or other it had covered itself with dishes and plates and wooden spoons with pictures on them, and bowls of soup and mushrooms and kasha, and meat and cakes and fish and ducks, and everything else you could think of, ready for the best dinner in the world.

The chattering and laughing stopped, and the old man and those dozens and dozens of little queer children set to work and ate everything on the table.

" Which of you washes the dishes ? " asked the old man, when they had all done.

The children laughed.

" Tell the tablecloth to turn outside in."

" Tablecloth," says the old man, " turn outside in."

Up jumped the tablecloth with all the empty dishes and dirty plates and spoons, whirled itself this way and that in the air, and suddenly spread itself out flat again on the table, as clean and white as when it was taken out of the cupboard. There was not a dish or a bowl, or a spoon or a plate, or a knife to be seen ; no, not even a crumb.

" That's a good tablecloth," says the old man.

" See here, grandfather," shouted the children : " you take the tablecloth along with you, and say no more about those turnips."

" Well, I'm content with that," says the old man. And he folded up the tablecloth very carefully and put it away inside his shirt, and said he must be going.

" Good-bye," says he, " and thank you for the dinner and the tablecloth."

" Good-bye," say they, " and thank you for the turnips."

The old man made his way home, singing through the forest in his creaky old voice until he came near the little wooden house where he lived with the old woman. As soon as he came near there he slipped along like any mouse. And as soon as he put his head inside the door the old woman began :

" Have you found the thieves, you old fool ? "

" I found the thieves."

" Who were they ? "

"They were a whole crowd of little queer children."

"Have you given them a beating they'll remember?"

"No, I have not."

"What? Bring them to me, and I'll teach them to steal my turnips!"

"I haven't got them."

"What have you done with them?"

"I had dinner with them."

Well, at that the old woman flew into such a rage she could hardly speak. But speak she did—yes, and shout too and scream—and it was all the old man could do not to run away out of the cottage. But he stood still and listened, and thought of something else; and when she had done he said, "They paid for the turnips."

"Paid for the turnips!" scolded the old woman. "A lot of children! What did they give you? Mushrooms? We can get them without losing our turnips."

"They gave me a tablecloth," said the old man; "it's a very good tablecloth."

He pulled it out of his shirt and spread it on the table; and as quickly as he could, before she began again, he said, "Tablecloth, turn inside out!"

The old woman stopped short, just when she was taking breath to scold with, when the tablecloth jumped up and danced in the air and settled on the table again, covered with things to eat and to drink. She smelt the meat, took a spoonful of the soup, and tried all the other dishes.

" Look at all the washing-up it will mean," says she.

" Tablecloth, turn outside in !" says the old man ; and there was a whirl of white cloth and dishes and everything else, and then the tablecloth spread itself out on the table as clean as ever you could wish.

" That's not a bad tablecloth," says the old woman ; " but, of course, they owed me something for stealing all those turnips."

The old man said nothing. He was very tired, and he just laid down and went to sleep.

As soon as he was asleep the old woman took the tablecloth and hid it away in an iron chest, and put a tablecloth of her own in its place. " They were my turnips," says she, " and I don't see why he should have a share in the tablecloth. He's had a meal from it once at my expense, and once is enough." Then she lay down and went to sleep, grumbling to herself even in her dreams.

Early in the morning the old woman woke the old man and told him to go up to the dovecot and see how those turnips were getting on.

He got up and rubbed his eyes. When he saw the tablecloth on the table, the wish came to him to have a bite of food to begin the day with. So he stopped in the middle of putting on his shirt, and called to the tablecloth, " Tablecloth, turn inside out ! "

Nothing happened. Why should anything happen ? It was not the same tablecloth.

The old man told the old woman. " You should have made a good feast yesterday," says he, " for the tablecloth is no good any more. That is, it's no good that way ; it's like any ordinary tablecloth."

" Most tablecloths are," says the old woman. " But what are you dawdling about ? Up you go and have a look at those turnips."

The old man went climbing up the narrow twisting stairs. He held on with both hands for fear of falling, because they were so steep. He climbed to the top of the house, to the top of the tower, to the top of the dovecot, and looked at the turnips. He looked at the turnips, and he counted the turnips, and then he came slowly down the stairs again, wondering what the old woman would say to him.

" Well," says the old woman in her sharp voice, " are they doing nicely ? Because if not, I know whose fault it is."

" They are doing finely," said the old man ; " but some of them have gone. Indeed, quite a lot of them have been stolen away."

" Stolen away ! " screamed the old woman. " How dare you stand there and tell me that ? Didn't you find the thieves yesterday ? Go and find those children again, and take a stick with you, and don't show yourself here till you can tell me that they won't steal again in a hurry."

" Let me have a bite to eat," begs the old man. " It's a long way to go on an empty stomach."

" Not a mouthful ! " yells the old woman. " Off with you. Letting my turnips be stolen every night, and then talking to me about bites of food ! "

So the old man went off again without his dinner, and hobbled away into the forest as quickly as he could to get out of earshot of the old woman's scolding tongue.

As soon as he was out of sight the old woman stopped screaming after him, and went into the house and opened the iron chest and took out the tablecloth the children had given the old man, and laid it on the table instead of her own. She told it to turn inside out, and up it flew and whirled about and flopped down flat again, all covered with good things. She ate as much as she could hold. Then she told the tablecloth to turn outside in, and folded it up and hid it away again in the iron chest.

Meanwhile the old man tightened his belt, because he was so hungry. He hobbled along through the green forest till he came to the little hut standing under the pine trees. There was no smoke coming from the chimney, but there was

such a chattering you would have thought that all the Vanyas and Maroosias in Holy Russia were talking to each other inside.

He had no sooner come in sight of the hut than the dozens and dozens of little queer children came pouring out of the door to meet him. And every single one of them had a turnip, and showed it to the old man, and laughed and laughed as if it were the best joke in the world.

" I knew it was you," said the old man.

" Of course it was us," cried the children. " *We* stole the turnips."

" But how did you get to the top of the dovecot when the door into the house was bolted and fast ? "

The children laughed and laughed, and did not answer a word.

" Laugh you may," says the old man ; " but it is I who get the scolding when the turnips fly away in the night."

" Never mind, never mind ! " cried the children. " We'll pay for the turnips."

" All very well," says the old man ; " but that tablecloth of yours—it was fine yesterday, but this morning it would not give me even a glass of tea and a hunk of black bread."

At that the faces of the little queer children were troubled and grave. For a moment or two they all chattered together, and took no notice of the old man. Then one of them said:

"Well, this time we'll give you something better. We'll give you a goat."

"A goat?" says the old man.

"A goat with a cold in its head," said the children; and they crowded round him and took him behind the hut where there was a grey goat with a long beard cropping the short grass.

"It's a good enough goat," says the old man; "I don't see anything wrong with him."

"It's better than that," cried the children. "You tell it to sneeze."

The old man thought the children might be laughing at him, but he did not care, and he remembered the tablecloth. So he took off his hat and bowed to the goat. "Sneeze, goat," says he.

And instantly the goat started sneezing as if it would shake itself to pieces. And as it sneezed, good gold pieces flew from it in all directions, till the ground was thick with them.

"That's enough," said the children hurriedly; "tell him to stop, for all this gold is no use to us, and it's such a bother having to sweep it away."

"Stop sneezing, goat," says the old man; and the goat stopped sneezing, and stood there panting and out of breath in the middle of the sea of gold pieces.

The children began kicking the gold pieces about, spreading them by walking through them as if they were dead leaves. My old father used to say that those gold pieces are lying about still for anybody to pick up; but I doubt if he knew just where to look for them, or he would have had better clothes on his back and a little more food on the table. But who knows? Some day we may come upon that little hut somewhere in the forest, and then we shall know what to look for.

The children laughed and chattered and kicked the gold pieces this way and that into the green bushes. Then they brought the old man into the hut and gave him a bowl of kasha to eat, because he had had no dinner. There was no magic about the kasha; but it was good enough kasha for all that, and hunger made it better. When the old man had finished the kasha and drunk a glass of tea and smoked a little pipe, he got up and made a low bow and thanked the children. And the children tied a rope to the goat and sent the old man home with it. He hobbled away through the forest, and as he went he looked back, and there were the little queer children all dancing together, and he heard them chattering and shouting: "Who stole the turnips? *We* stole the turnips. Who paid for the turnips? *We* paid for the turnips. Who stole the tablecloth ? Who will pay for the tablecloth ? Who will steal turnips again ? *We* will steal turnips again."

But the old man was too pleased with the goat to give much heed to what they said ; and he hobbled home through the green forest as fast as he could, with the goat trotting and walking behind him, pulling leaves off the bushes to chew as they hurried along.

The old woman was waiting in the doorway of the house. She was still as angry as ever.

"Have you beaten the children ?" she screamed. "Have you beaten the children for stealing my good turnips ?"

"No," said the old man ; "they paid for the turnips."

"What did they pay ?"

"They gave me this goat."

"That skinny old goat ! I have three already, and the worst of them is better than that."

"It has a cold in the head," says the old man.

"Worse than ever !" screams the old woman.

"Wait a minute," says the old man as quickly as he could, to stop her scolding.—"Sneeze, goat."

And the goat began to shake itself almost to bits, sneezing and sneezing and sneezing. The good gold pieces flew all ways at once. And the old woman threw herself after the gold pieces, picking them up like an old hen picking up corn. As fast as she picked them up more gold pieces

GERVIS.

came showering down on her like heavy gold hail, beating her on her head and her hands as she grubbed after those that had fallen already.

" Stop sneezing, goat," says the old man ; and the goat stood there tired and panting, trying to get its breath. But the old woman did not look up till she had gathered every one of the gold pieces. When she did look up, she said :

" There's no supper for you. I've had supper already."

The old man said nothing. He tied up the goat to the doorpost of the house, where it could eat the green grass. Then he went into the house and lay down, and fell asleep at once, because he was an old man and had done a lot of walking.

As soon as he was asleep the old woman untied the goat and took it away and hid it in the bushes, and tied up one of her own goats instead. " They were my turnips," says she to herself, " and I don't see why he should have a share in the gold." Then she went in, and lay down grumbling to herself.

Early in the morning she woke the old man.

" Get up, you lazy fellow," says she ; " you would lie all day and let all the thieves in the world come in and steal my turnips. Up with you to the dovecot and see how my turnips are getting on."

The old man got up and rubbed his eyes, and climbed up the rickety stairs, creak, creak, creak, holding on with both hands, till he came to the top of the house, to the top of the tower, to the top of the dovecot, and looked at the turnips.

He was afraid to come down, for there were hardly any turnips left at all.

And when he did come down, the scolding the old woman gave him was worse than the other two scoldings rolled into one. She was so angry that she shook like a rag in the high wind, and the old man put both hands to his ears and hobbled away into the forest.

He hobbled along as fast as he could hobble, until he came to the hut under the pine trees. This time the little queer children were not hiding under the blankets or in the stove, or chattering in the hut. They were all over the roof of the hut, dancing and crawling about. Some of them were even sitting on the chimney. And every one of the little queer children was playing with a turnip. As soon as they saw the old man they all came tumbling off the roof, one after another, head over heels, like a lot of peas rolling off a shovel.

" *We* stole the turnips ! " they shouted, before the old man could say anything at all.

" I know you did," says the old man ; " but that does not make it any better for me. And it is I who get the scolding when the turnips fly away in the night."

" Never again ! " shouted the children.

" I'm glad to hear that," says the old man. " And we'll pay for the turnips."

" Thank you kindly," says the old man. He hadn't the heart to be angry with those little queer children.

Three or four of them ran into the hut and came out again with a wooden whistle, a regular whistle-pipe, such as shepherds use. They gave it to the old man.

"I can never play that," says the old man. " I don't know one tune from another ; and if I did, my old fingers are as stiff as oak twigs."

" Blow in it," cried the children ; and all the others came crowding round, laughing and chattering and whispering to each other. " Is he going to blow in it ? " they asked. " He *is* going to blow in it." How they laughed !

The old man took the whistle, and gathered his breath and puffed out his cheeks, and blew in the whistle-pipe as hard as he could. And before he could take the whistle from his lips, three lively whips had slipped out of it, and were beating him as hard as they could go, although there was nobody to hold them. Phew ! phew ! phew ! The three whips came down on him one after the other.

" Blow again ! " the children shouted, laughing as if they were mad. " Blow again—quick, quick, quick !—and tell the whips to get into the whistle."

The old man did not wait to be told twice. He

blew for all he was worth, and instantly the three whips stopped beating him. " Into the whistle ! " he cried ; and the three lively whips shot up into the whistle, like three snakes going into a hole. He could hardly have believed they had been out at all if it had not been for the soreness of his back.

" You take that home," cried the children. " That'll pay for the turnips, and put everything right."

" Who knows ? " said the old man ; and he thanked the children, and set off home through the green forest.

" Good-bye," cried the little queer children. But as soon as he had started they forgot all about him. When he looked round to wave his hand to them, not one of them was thinking of him. They were up again on the roof of the hut, jumping over each other and dancing and crawling about, and rolling each other down the roof and climbing up again, as if they had been doing nothing else all day, and were going to do nothing else till the end of the world.

The old man hobbled home through the green forest with the whistle stuck safely away into his shirt. As soon as he came to the door of the hut, the old woman, who was sitting inside counting the gold pieces, jumped up and started her scolding.

" What have the children tricked you with this time ? " she screamed at him.

"They gave me a whistle-pipe," says the old man, "and they are not going to steal the turnips any more."

"A whistle-pipe!" she screamed. "What's the good of that? It's worse than the tablecloth and the skinny old goat."

The old man said nothing.

"Give it to me!" screamed the old woman. "They were my turnips, so it is my whistle-pipe."

"Well, whatever you do, don't blow in it," says the old man, and he hands over the whistle-pipe."

She wouldn't listen to him.

"What?" says she; "I must not blow my own whistle-pipe?"

And with that she put the whistle-pipe to her lips and blew.

Out jumped the three lively whips, flew up in the air, and began to beat her—phew! phew! phew!—one after another. If they made the old man sore, it was nothing to what they did to the cross old woman.

"Stop them! Stop them!" she screamed, running this way and that in the hut, with the whips flying after her, beating her all the time. "I'll never scold again. I am to blame. I stole the magic tablecloth, and put an old one instead of it. I hid it in the iron chest." She ran to the iron chest and opened it, and pulled out the tablecloth. "Stop them! Stop them!" she screamed, while the whips laid it on hard and fast, one after the other. " I am to blame. The goat that sneezes gold pieces is hidden in the bushes. The goat by the door is one of the old ones. I wanted all the gold for myself."

All this time the old man was trying to get hold of the whistle-pipe. But the old woman was running about the hut so fast, with the whips flying after her and beating her, that he could not get it out of her hands. At last he grabbed it. " Into the whistle," says he, and put it to his lips and blew.

In a moment the three lively whips had hidden themselves in the whistle. And there was the cross old woman, kissing his hand and promising never to scold any more.

"That's all right," says the old man ; and he fetched the sneezing goat out of the bushes and made it sneeze a little gold, just to be sure that it was that goat and no other. Then he laid the tablecloth on the table and told it to turn inside out. Up it flew, and came down again with the best dinner that ever was cooked, only waiting to be eaten. And the old man and the old woman sat down and ate till they could eat no more. The old woman rubbed herself now and again. And the old man rubbed himself too. But there was never a cross word between them, and they went to bed singing like nightingales.

"Is that the end ?" Maroosia always asked.

" Is that all ? " asked Vanya, though he knew it was not.

" Not quite," said old Peter ; " but the tale won't go any quicker than my old tongue."

In the morning the old woman had forgotten about her promise. And, just from habit, she set about scolding the old man as if the whips had never jumped out of the whistle. She scolded him for sleeping too long, sent him upstairs, with a lot of cross words after him, to go to the top of the dovecot to see how those turnips were getting on.

After a little the old man came down.

" The turnips are coming on grandly," says he, " and not a single one has gone in the night. I told you the children said they would not steal any more."

" I don't believe you," said the old woman. " I'll see for myself. And if any are gone, you shall pay for it, and pay for it well."

Up she jumped, and tried to climb the stairs. But the stairs were narrow and steep and twisting.

She tried and tried, and could not get up at all. So she gets angrier than ever, and starts scolding the old man again.

" You must carry me up," says she.

" I have to hold on with both hands, or I couldn't get up myself," says the old man.

" I'll get in the flour sack, and you must carry me up with your teeth," says she ; " they're strong enough."

And the old woman got into the flour sack.

" Don't ask me any questions," says the old man ; and he took the sack in his teeth and began slowly climbing up the stairs, holding on with both hands.

He climbed and climbed, but he did not climb fast enough for the old woman.

" Are we at the top ? " says she.

The old man said nothing, but went on, climbing up and up, nearly dead with the weight of the old woman in the sack which he was holding in his teeth.

He climbed a little farther, and the old woman screamed out :

" Are we at the top now ? We must be at the top. Let me out, you old fool ! "

The old man said nothing ; he climbed on and on.

The old woman raged in the flour sack. She jumped about in the sack, and screamed at the old man :

"Are we near the top now? Answer me, can't you! Answer me at once, or you'll pay for it later. Are we near the top?"

"Very near," said the old man.

And as he opened his mouth to say that the sack slipped from between his teeth, and bump, bump, bumpety bump, the old woman in the sack fell all the way to the very bottom, bumping on every step. That was the end of her.

After that the old man lived alone in the hut. When he wanted tobacco or clothes or a new axe, he made the goat sneeze some gold pieces, and off he went to the town with plenty of money in his pocket. When he wanted his dinner he had only to lay the tablecloth. He never had any washing-up to do, because the tablecloth did it for him. When he wanted to get rid of troublesome guests, he gave them the whistle to blow. And when he was lonely and wanted company, he went to the little hut under the pine trees and played with the little queer children.

THE LORDS OF THE WHITE AND GREY CASTLES

By Frances Browne

Once upon a time there lived two noble lords in the east country. Their lands lay between a broad river and an old oak forest, whose size was so great that no man knew it. In the midst of his land each lord had a stately castle ; one was built of the white freestone, the other of the grey granite. So the one was called Lord of the White Castle, and the other Lord of the Grey.

There were no lords like them in all the east country for nobleness and bounty. Their tenants lived in peace and plenty ; all strangers were hospitably entertained at their castles ; and every autumn they sent men with axes into the forest to hew down the great trees, and chop them up into firewood for the poor. Neither hedge nor ditch divided their lands, but these lords never disputed. They had been friends from their youth. Their ladies had died long ago, but the Lord of the Grey Castle had a little son, and the Lord of the White a little daughter ; and when they feasted in each other's halls it was their custom to say, " When our children grow up they will marry, and have our castles and our lands, and keep our friendship in memory."

So the lords and their little children, and tenants, lived happily till one Michaelmas night ; as they were all feasting in the hall of the White Castle, there came a traveller to the gate, who was welcomed and feasted as usual. He had seen many strange sights and countries, and, like most people, he liked to tell his travels. The lords were delighted with his tales, as they sat round the fire drinking wine after supper, and at length the Lord of the White Castle, who was very curious, said :

" Good stranger, what was the greatest wonder you ever saw in all your travels ? "

" The most wonderful sight that ever I saw,"

replied the traveller, " was at the end of yonder forest, where in an ancient wooden house there sits an old woman weaving her own hair into grey cloth on an old crazy loom. When she wants more yarn she cuts off her own grey hair, and it grows so quickly that though I saw it cut in the morning, it was out of the door before noon. She told me it was her purpose to sell the cloth, but none of all who came that way had yet bought any, she asked so great a price ; and, only the way is so long and dangerous through that wide forest full of boars and wolves, some rich lord like you might buy it for a mantle."

All who heard this story were astonished ; but when the traveller had gone on his way the Lord of the White Castle could neither eat nor sleep for wishing to see the old woman that wove her own hair. At length he made up his mind to explore the forest in search of her ancient house, and told the Lord of the Grey Castle his intention. Being a prudent man, this lord replied that travellers' tales were not always to be trusted, and earnestly advised him against undertaking such a long and dangerous journey, for few that went far into that forest ever returned. However, when the curious lord would go in spite of all, he vowed to bear him company for friendship's sake, and they agreed to set out privately, lest the other lords of the land might laugh at them. The Lord of the White Castle had a steward who had served him many years, and his name was Reckoning Robin. To him he said :

" I am going on a long journey with my friend. Be careful of my goods, deal justly with my tenants, and, above all things, be kind to my little daughter Loveleaves till my return."

And the steward answered :

" Be sure, my lord, I will."

The Lord of the Grey Castle also had a steward who had served him many years, and his name was Wary Will. To him he said :

" I am going on a journey with my friend. Be careful of my goods, deal justly with my tenants, and, above all things, be kind to my little son Woodwender till my return."

And his steward answered him :

" Be sure, my lord, I will."

So these lords kissed their children while they slept, and set out each with his staff and mantle before sunrise through the old oak forest. The children missed their fathers, the tenants missed their lords. None but the stewards could tell what had become of them ; but seven months wore away, and they did not come back. The lords had thought their stewards faithful, because they served so well under their eyes ; but instead of that both were proud and crafty, and thinking that some evil had happened to their masters, they set themselves to be lords in their room.

Reckoning Robin had a son called Hardhold, and Wary Will a daughter called Drypenny. There was not a sulkier girl or boy in the country, but their fathers resolved to make a young lord and lady of them; so they took the silk clothes which Woodwender and Loveleaves used to wear to dress them, clothing the lords' children in frieze and canvas. Their garden flowers and ivory toys were given to Hardhold and Drypenny; and at last the stewards' children sat at the chief tables and slept in the best chambers, while Woodwender and Loveleaves were sent to herd the swine and sleep on straw in the granary.

The poor children had no one to take their part. Every morning at sunrise they were sent out—each with a barley loaf and a bottle of sour milk, which was to serve them for breakfast, dinner, and supper—to watch a great herd of swine on a wide, unfenced pasture hard by the forest. The grass was scanty, and the swine were continually straying into the wood in search of acorns; the children knew that if they were lost the wicked stewards would punish them, and between gathering and keeping their herds in order, they were readier to sleep on the granary straw at night than ever they had been within their own silken curtains. Still Woodwender and Loveleaves helped and

comforted each other, saying their fathers would come back, or God would send them some friends: so, in spite of swine-herding and hard living, they looked blithe and handsome as ever; while Hardhold and Drypenny grew crosser and uglier every day, notwithstanding their fine clothes and the best of all things.

The crafty stewards did not like this. They thought their children ought to look genteel, and Woodwender and Loveleaves like young swineherds; so they sent them to a wilder pasture, still nearer the forest, and gave them two great black hogs, more unruly than all the rest, to keep. One of these hogs belonged to Hardhold, and the other to Drypenny. Every evening when they came home the stewards' children used to come down and feed them, and it was their delight to reckon up what price they would bring when properly fattened.

One sultry day, about midsummer, Woodwender and Loveleaves sat down in the shadow of a mossy rock: the swine grazed about them more quietly than usual, and they plaited rushes and talked to each other, till, as the sun was sloping down the sky, Woodwender saw that the two great hogs were missing. Thinking they must have gone to the forest, the poor children ran to search for them. They heard the thrush singing and the wood-doves calling; they saw the squirrels leaping from bough to bough, and the great deer bounding by; but though they searched for hours, no trace of the favourite hogs could be seen. Loveleaves and Woodwender durst not go home without them. Deeper and deeper they ran into the forest, searching and calling, but all in vain; and when the woods began to darken with the fall of evening, the children feared they had lost their way.

It was known that they never feared the forest, nor all the boars and wolves that were in it; but being weary, they wished for some place of shelter, and took a green path through the trees, thinking it might lead to the dwelling of some hermit or forester. A fairer way Woodwender and Loveleaves had never walked. The grass was soft and mossy, a hedge of wild roses and honeysuckle grew on either side, and the red light of sunset streamed through the tall trees above. On they went, and it led them straight to a great open dell, covered with the loveliest flowers, bordered with banks of wild strawberries, and all overshadowed by one enormous oak, whose like had never been seen in grove or forest. Its branches were as large as full-grown trees. Its trunk was wider than a country church, and its height like that of a castle. There were mossy seats at its great root, and when the tired children had gathered as many strawberries as they cared for, they sat down on one, hard by a small spring that bubbled up as clear as crystal. The huge oak was covered with thick ivy, in which thousands of birds had their nests. Woodwender and Loveleaves watched them flying home from all parts of the forest, and at last they saw a lady coming by the same path which led them to the dell. She wore a gown of russet colour; her yellow hair was braided and bound with a crimson fillet. In her right hand she carried a holly branch; but the most remarkable part of her attire was a pair of long sleeves, as green as the very grass.

"Who are you?" she said, "that sit so late beside my well?" and the children told her their story, how they had first lost the hogs, then their way, and were afraid to go home to the wicked stewards.

"Well," said the lady, "ye are the fairest swineherds that ever came this way. Choose whether ye will go home and keep hogs for Hardhold and Drypenny, or live in the free forest with me."

"We will stay with you," said the children, "for we like not keeping swine. Besides, our fathers went through this forest, and we may meet them some day coming home."

While they spoke, the lady slipped her holly branch through the ivy, as if it had been a key—presently a door opened in the oak, and there was a fair house. The windows were of rock crystal, but they could not be seen from without. The walls and floor were covered with thick green moss, as soft as velvet. There were low seats and a round table, vessels of carved wood, a hearth inlaid with curious stones, an oven, and a store chamber for provisions against the winter. When they stepped in, the lady said :

"A hundred years have I lived here, and my name is Lady Greensleeves. No friend or servant have I had except my dwarf, Corner, who comes to me at the end of harvest with his handmill, his pannier, and his axe : with these he grinds the nuts, and gathers the berries, and cleaves the firewood, and blithely we live all the winter. But Corner loves the frost and fears the sun, and when the topmost boughs begin to bud, he returns to his country far in the north, so I am lonely in the summer-time."

By this discourse the children saw how welcome they were. Lady Greensleeves gave them deers' milk and cakes of nut-flour, and soft green moss to sleep on ; and they forgot all their troubles, the wicked stewards, and the straying swine. Early in the morning a troop of does came to be milked, fairies brought flowers, and birds brought berries, to show Lady Greensleeves what had bloomed and ripened. She taught the children to make cheese of the does' milk, and wine of the wood-berries. She showed them the stores of honey which wild bees had made and left in hollow trees, the rarest plants of the forest, and the herbs that made all its creatures tame.

All that summer Woodwender and Loveleaves lived with her in the great oak tree, free from toil and care ; and the children would have been happy, but they could hear no tidings of their fathers. At last the leaves began to fade, and the flowers to fall ; Lady Greensleeves said that Corner was coming ; and one moonlight night she heaped sticks on the fire, and set her door open, when Woodwender and Loveleaves were going to sleep, saying she expected some old friends to tell her the news of the forest.

Loveleaves was not quite so curious as her father, the Lord of the White Castle : but she kept awake to see what would happen, and terribly frightened the little girl was when in walked a great brown bear.

" Good-evening, lady," said the bear.

" Good-evening, bear," said Lady Greensleeves. " What is the news in your neighbourhood ? "

" Not much," said the bear ; " only the fawns

are growing very cunning—one can't catch above three in a day."

"That's bad news," said Lady Greensleeves; and immediately in walked a great wild-cat.

"Good-evening, lady," said the cat.

"Good-evening, cat," said Lady Greensleeves. "What is the news in your neighbourhood?"

"Not much," said the cat; "only the birds are growing very plentiful—it is not worth one's while to catch them."

"That's good news," said Lady Greensleeves; and in flew a great black raven.

"Good-evening, lady," said the raven.

"Good-evening, raven," said Lady Greensleeves. "What is the news in your neighbourhood?"

"Not much," said the raven; "only in a hundred years or so we shall be very genteel and private—the trees will be so thick."

"How is that?" said Lady Greensleeves.

"Oh!" said the raven, "have you not heard how the king of the forest fairies laid a spell on two noble lords who were travelling through his dominions to see the old woman who weaves her own hair? They had thinned his oaks every year, cutting firewood for the poor: so the king met them in the likeness of a hunter, and asked them to drink out of his oaken goblet, because the day was warm; and when the two lords drank, they forgot their lands and their tenants, their castles and their children, and minded nothing in all this world but the planting of acorns, which they do day and night, by the power of the spell, in the heart of the forest, and will never cease till some one makes them pause in their work before the sun sets, and then the spell will be broken."

"Ah!" said Lady Greensleeves, "he is a great prince, that king of the forest fairies; and there is worse work in the world than planting acorns."

Soon after, the bear, the cat, and the raven bade Lady Greensleeves good-night. She closed the door, put out the light, and went to sleep on the soft moss as usual.

In the morning Loveleaves told Woodwender what she had heard, and they went to Lady Greensleeves, where she milked the does, and said:

"We heard what the ravens told last night, and we know the two lords are our fathers: tell us how the spell may be broken!"

"I fear the king of the forest fairies," said Lady Greensleeves, "because I live here alone, and have no friend but my dwarf, Corner; but I will tell you what you may do. At the end of the path which leads from this dell turn your faces to the north, and you will find a narrow way sprinkled over with black feathers—keep that path, no matter how it winds, and it will lead you straight to the ravens' neighbourhood, where you will find your fathers planting acorns under the forest trees. Watch till the sun is near setting, and tell them the most wonderful things you know to make them forget their work ; but be sure to tell nothing but truth, and drink nothing but running water, or you will fall into the power of the fairy king."

The children thanked her for this good counsel. She packed up cakes and cheese for them in a bag of woven grass, and they soon found the narrow way sprinkled over with black feathers. It was very long, and wound through the thick trees in so many circles that the children were often weary and sat down to rest. When the night came, they found a mossy hollow in the trunk of an old tree, where they laid themselves down and slept all the summer night—for Woodwender and Loveleaves never feared the forest. So they went, eating their cakes and cheese when they were hungry, drinking from the running stream, and sleeping in the hollow trees, till on the evening of the seventh day they came into the ravens' neighbourhood. The tall trees were laden with nests and black with ravens. There was nothing to be heard but continual cawing ; and in a great opening, where the oaks grew thinnest, the children saw their own fathers busy planting acorns. Each lord had on the velvet mantle in which he left his castle, but it was worn to rags with rough work in the forest. Their hair and beards had grown long ; their hands were soiled with earth ; each had an old wooden spade, and on all sides lay heaps of acorns. The children called them by their names, and ran to kiss them, each saying, " Dear father, come back to your castle and your people ! " but the lords replied :

" We know of no castles and no people. There is nothing in all this world but oak trees and acorns."

Woodwender and Loveleaves told them of all their former state in vain—nothing would make them pause for a minute : so the poor children first sat down and cried, and then slept on the cold grass, for the sun set, and the lords worked on. When they awoke it was broad day ; Woodwender

cheered up his friend, saying, " We are hungry, and there are still two cakes in the bag, let us share one of them—who knows but something may happen ? "

So they divided the cake, and ran to the lords, saying : " Dear fathers, eat with us."

But the lords said :

" There is no use for meat or drink. Let us plant our acorns."

Loveleaves and Woodwender sat down and ate that cake in great sorrow. When they had finished, both went to a stream hard by and began to drink the clear water with a large acorn shell ; and as they drank there came through the oaks a gay young hunter ; his mantle was green as the grass ; about his neck there hung a crystal bugle, and in his hand he carried a huge oaken goblet, carved with flowers and leaves, and rimmed with crystal. Up to the brim it was filled with milk, on which the rich cream floated ; and as the hunter came near, he said : " Fair children, leave that muddy water, and come and drink with me."

But Woodwender and Loveleaves answered :

" Thanks, good hunter, but we have promised to drink nothing but running water."

Still the hunter came nearer with his goblet, saying :

" The water is foul ; it may do for swineherds and woodcutters, but not for such fair children as you. Tell me, are you not the children of mighty kings? Were you not reared in palaces?"

But the boy and girl answered him:

"No; we were reared in castles, and are the children of yonder lords; tell us how the spell that is upon them may be broken!" and immediately the hunter turned from them with an angry look, poured out the milk upon the ground, and went away with his empty goblet.

Loveleaves and Woodwender were sorry to see the rich cream spilled, but they remembered Lady Greensleeves' warning, and seeing they could do no better, each got a withered branch and began to help the lords, scratching up the ground with the sharp end, and planting acorns; but their fathers took no notice of them, nor all that they could say; and when the sun grew warm at noon, they went again to drink at the running stream. Then there came through the oaks another hunter, older than the first, and clothed in yellow: about his neck there hung a silver bugle, and in his hand he carried an oaken goblet, carved with leaves and fruit, rimmed with silver, and filled with mead to the brim. This hunter also asked them to drink, told them the stream was full of frogs, and asked them if they were not a young prince and princess dwelling in the woods for their pleasure? But when Woodwender and Loveleaves answered as before, "We have promised to drink only running water, and are the children of yonder lords: tell us how the spell may be broken!" he turned from them with an angry look, poured out the mead, and went his way.

All that afternoon the children worked beside their fathers, planting acorns; but the lords would mind neither them nor their words. And when the evening drew near they were very hungry; so the children divided their last cake, and when no persuasion would make the lords eat with them, they went to the banks of the stream and began to eat and drink, though their hearts were heavy.

The sun was getting low, and the ravens were coming home to their nests in the high trees; but

one, that seemed old and weary, alighted near them to drink at the stream. As they ate the raven lingered, and picked up the small crumbs that fell.

" Woodwender," said Loveleaves, " this raven is surely hungry ; let us give it a little bit, though it is our last cake."

Woodwender agreed, and each gave a bit to the raven ; but its great bill finished the morsels in a moment, and hopping nearer, it looked them in the face by turns.

" The poor raven is still hungry," said Woodwender, and he gave it another bit. When that was gobbled, it came to Loveleaves, who gave it a bit too, and so on till the raven had eaten the whole of their last cake.

" Well," said Woodwender, " at least we can have a drink." But as they stooped to the water, there came through the oaks another hunter, older than the last, and clothed in scarlet ; about his neck there hung a golden bugle, and in his hand he carried a huge oaken goblet, carved with ears of corn and clusters of grapes, rimmed with gold, and filled to the brim with wine. He also said :

" Leave this muddy water and drink with me. It is full of toads, and not fit for such fair children. Surely ye are from fairyland, and were reared in its queen's palace ! "

But the children said :

" We will drink nothing but this water, and

yonder lords are our fathers ; tell us how the spell may be broken ! " And the hunter turned from them with an angry look, poured out the wine on the grass, and went his way. When he was gone, the old raven looked up into their faces, and said :

" I have eaten your last cake, and I will tell you how the spell may be broken. Yonder is the sun, going down behind yon western trees. Before it sets, go to the lords, and tell them how their stewards used you, and made you herd hogs for Hardhold and Drypenny. When you see them listening, catch up their wooden spades, and keep them if you can till the sun goes down."

Woodwender and Loveleaves thanked the raven, and where it flew they never stopped to see, but running to the lords began to tell as they were bidden. At first the lords would not listen, but as the children related how they had been made to sleep on straw, how they had been sent to herd hogs in the wild pasture, and what trouble they had with the unruly swine, the acorn planting grew slower, and at last they dropped their spades. Then Woodwender, catching up his father's spade, ran to the stream and threw it in. Loveleaves did the same for the Lord of the White Castle. That moment the sun disappeared behind the western oaks, and the lords stood up, looking, like men just awoke, on the forest, on the sky, and on their children.

So this strange story has ended, for Woodwender and Loveleaves went home rejoicing with their fathers. Each lord returned to his castle, and all their tenants made merry. The fine toys and the silk clothes, the flower gardens and the best chambers were taken from Hardhold and Drypenny, for the lords' children got them again ; and the wicked stewards, with their cross boy and girl, were sent to herd swine, and live in huts in the wild pasture, which everybody said became them better. The Lord of the White Castle never again wished to see the old woman that wove her own hair, and the Lord of the Grey Castle continued to be his friend. As for Woodwender and Loveleaves, they met with no more misfortunes, but grew up, and were married, and inherited the two castles and the broad lands of their fathers. Nor did they forget the lonely Lady Greensleeves, for it was known in the east country that she and her dwarf, Corner, always came to feast with them in the Christmas-time, and at midsummer they always went to live with her in the great oak in the forest.

THE ARTIST

By Eleanor Farjeon

The artist sitting in the street
  Chalks loaves of bread he cannot eat,
And purple hills, and emerald vales,
  And salmon, and the Prince of Wales.
Give him a penny now and then ;
  He wants real bread like other men.

HIS MAJESTY COMES OVER ALL HANDY-MAN

By Norman Hunter

The Queen of Quella-Quarmia gave a little shriek of delight as three footmen carried in a large parcel for her.

" Oo-oo ! " she exclaimed, " a present for me. Whoever can it be from, and whatever can it be ? Lend me your knife, quick," turning to the King, " so that I can cut the string and unwrap it."

" No, no, not at all, my dear," said the King ; " I can untie the knots, and we can save the string. You have always said you liked string saved, you know you have," which, of course, was quite true, for the Queen made everybody save all the string and brown paper that came into the palace, until they had enough to have covered the kingdom, if it had been all spread out—which it wasn't. But this time Her Majesty was so frantically eager to open the parcel that she simply couldn't wait to have the string saved.

But she jolly well had to wait all the same, for the King was very busily and patiently untying the many sorts of complicated knots with which the parcel was tied, saying, " Never waste a piece of string ; you may be glad of it one day when you haven't got a piece of string," and, "Waste not, want not," and things like that; while the Queen began to get so absolutely hopelessly excited to get the present unwrapped that she began to hop up and down on one foot, and made the footmen go quite dizzy watching her.

At last the parcel was undone, and there was the present. A beautiful table with carved legs, and a ticket attached:

" To Queenie, with love from Uncle Ned."

· · · · · ·

" There now," said the Queen, drawing up a chair and sitting at the table to see how it seemed. " How nice it is to have Uncles."

" Yes," said the King, who was winding up a long piece of string and not thinking it was lovely to have Uncles at all, because there were about twenty-seven young nieces and nephews that he was Uncle to. And he had to keep giving them presents, and take them on roundabouts, and buy them sweets, because, being a King as well as an Uncle, he was expected to be a simply double-barrelled gold-mounted special kind of Uncle.

" It's ever so lovely," said the Queen, putting her hands on the table, " but just a weeny bit too high. Get the carpenter to cut a bit off the legs for me."

" Yes, my dear," said the King, and feeling slightly pleased that he wasn't the carpenter's Uncle, and needn't give him anything but orders, he went away to find him. But the carpenter was away on his holidays.

"Oh, well," said the King to himself, "I'm pretty handy with a hammer and saw. I daresay I can do a simple little thing like cutting a bit off the legs of a table myself."

. . . . . .

So His Majesty went cheerfully away to find a saw. But, bother it all, the carpenter had locked all the tools up, because he rather fancied that perhaps the Queen might go borrowing his chisels to open boxes with, or using his saws to dig plants up with, or making do with his carefully sharpened drills to knock into the walls to hold clothes-lines. All of which Her Majesty was all too probably likely to have done any time she felt a bit handy about the house.

"Has anybody seen a saw?" cried the King, rummaging about in the kitchen cupboards, and under the larder shelves, and behind the gas cooker, and on top of the meat safe, and anywhere else where he thought an odd saw might be, even though it almost certainly wasn't.

"I saw a saw," said the Cook, bustling about with a hearty cabbage, "but I haven't seen it since I saw it last."

"Er—thank you," said the King, peeping under a pile of old newspapers, which immediately slithered over and went slump, flomp on top of him and all over the floor in a cloud of dust, out-of-date news, and ancient competitions. "I'm sure I saw a saw somewhere, but I can't see where I saw it."

"See-saw, Marjorie Daw," squawked the Cook's parrot.

"Pah," snorted the King. He started to stamp out of the kitchen, tripped over the old newspapers, and found himself under the sink.

"Ha!" he exclaimed. For wedged behind the waste-pipe was a saw. A very old saw. A positively rusty, slightly buckled, definitely damaged and frightfully incapable-looking saw. But still a saw.

"I'll show carpenters if they can stop Kings cutting pieces off Queen's tables while they're on holiday," said the King, as he carried off the saw. But he found he could do nothing of the kind, because the saw was so desperately disused that its teeth wouldn't cut.

"This won't do," said the King, after sawing away for half an hour and only just making a slight scratch on the table leg. "I shall have to get a file sort of thing and sharpen the saw."

"Fetch me a file," he called. And more hunting about sort of bother started. The Queen offered him her nail file as long as he didn't use it much; but it was far too weeny to use at all. The Lord Chamberlain brought him a file of letters and bills, which was all nonsense, even though the bills had all been paid, which was probably nice for the people they had been paid to, but didn't help the King to sharpen his saw. The guards marched past in single file, which looked rather smart but got nobody anywhere, except themselves, and it only got them to the places they had to guard, and they'd rather have been somewhere else where they could have a nice quiet read. The Court Doctor came in with a phial of medicine guaranteed to make you grind your teeth if you took it, but not in any way likely to sharpen a saw's teeth whatever you did with it.

" Well, I shall have to buy a file, that's all," said the King. So he climbed carefully on his horse with the help of two soldiers and a pair of steps, and rode cautiously to the shops, hoping he wouldn't fall off on anywhere hard, and managed to slide off eventually on something definitely soft, which turned out to be a hiking sort of some one having a slight sleep.

" Oh dear, dear, tut-tut, bless me now and bother it all, I do declare ! " he cried. For it was early-closing day, and nowhere open except a penny-in-the-slot chocolate machine, a pedlar kind of person selling coloured bootlaces, and the mouth of the hiking person who hadn't troubled to wake up when the King got off his horse on to him, as he wasn't expecting Royalty to call.

Worst of all, there were no soldiers and no suitable steps for getting on to horses by, so His

Majesty had to walk back to the Palace, was late for tea, and the Queen had eaten the last chocolate éclair.

" I'm beginning to wish your Uncle Ned somewhere," he grumbled, munching bread and butter dismally, with everything cleared off the tea-table except his plate and cup and saucer, which made it a most uncomfortable and temporary sort of tea.

" He's probably there already," said the Queen, whisking the tablecloth off with a terrifically sharp flick, which left the King's plate and cup and saucer still on the table, even if it did land most of his tea in the saucer.

" Pah," snorted the King again.

Next day he set off for the shops, accompanied by an entire regiment of soldiers carrying five pairs of steps, and a mattress to fall off on in case of need.

" I want a file sort of thing to sharpen a saw," he said, walking into an Ironmongery kind of shop.

" Yes, Majesty; but pardon, Majesty, if I may make a suggestion, Majesty," said the Ironmonger gentleman, going down on one knee after every word, and getting tremendously tangled in plentiful pennyworths of wire. " Sharpening saws, Majesty, is difficult work, Majesty. Respectfully beg, Majesty, that Majesty brings saw here for us to sharpen, Majesty."

"Well, why didn't you say so before?" snorted the King, thinking it wasn't such a bad idea all the same. So back they all went, and brought the positively rusty, slightly buckled, and frightfully incapable-looking saw along to the shop to be sharpened. And this time the King rode into the shop, still on his horse, to save all the bother of getting off and on again, which was all right for him, but scared a small boy who was buying a pennyworth of mixed nails, and wanted mostly big ones.

"Ha—hum—er—ah—oo," said the Ironmonger gentleman, looking at the saw out of one eye, possibly because it only looked half as damaged and disused as when looked at with both eyes. "If I may suggest, Majesty," he said, going up and down on one knee again and bonking his head slightly on a half-crown kettle reduced to one-and-eleven, which was hanging by the counter, "it would be better, Majesty, for Majesty to have a new saw, Majesty. This saw is—er—that is to say, Majesty, it will not, or rather, Majesty, I fear, Majesty will find . . ."

"Give me a new saw, for goodness' sake," squealed the King, who was getting so impatient he felt he would burst, but that was only because his belt was rather tightish after rather much dinner.

The Ironmonger gentleman shuffled off, still on one knee, and brought ten saws of different sizes and sorts, and began explaining no end of complicated and ironmonger sorts of things about them. But the King didn't wait to hear them. He leaned over, snatched up the nearest saw and stuck it in his belt so vigorously that it sawed his belt in two, and his robes started to come apart all over the place, which would have been awful only the assistant Ironmonger, who wasn't so worried about Kings as the chief Ironmonger, came to the rescue with sash cord, and picture chain, and galvanized wire, and, between them, they managed to get the King all fastened up.

"Well, well, what a business this is, to be sure," said His Majesty, when at last he was back at the Palace with a new belt on, and the Queen's too high table in front of him, and the new saw beside him. "Bother it all, I might just as well have taken the table along to a shop and had it cut down while I was about it. However, it's no use crying over spilt milk: something attempted, nothing done; a bird in the hand's worth something or other—I forget which." And so, mumbling old saws, and wielding a definitely new one, the King set to work and soon had a nice little piece sawn off each of the legs to make the table lower. But when he stood it up it wobbled slightly, because he'd cut a little bit more off some legs than others.

"Tut, tut!" he said to himself, "I'd better

cut just a weeny bit more off to make it stand steady."

But alas! When His Majesty had cut a little bit more off, the table was rather more wobbly than before, because, through trying to cut a little bit more off the legs he hadn't cut enough off, and not quite so much off the legs he'd cut too much off, he got kind of muddled, and cut too much off the ones there was too much off already.

"Oh, bother!" said the King, starting all over again. "Why must Uncles send Queens tables that are too high when carpenters are away on holiday?" He couldn't think of the answer to that question himself, and, anyway, he was soon far too worried to think of one, because, ever so much more, alas ! he found he'd now made the table so wobbly that it would hardly stand up.

"Heavens ! " exclaimed His Majesty, taking his crown off in order to clap his hand to his forehead. "The table is still unsteady, and much too low now. I shall have to fetch the carpenter back from his holiday."

He had just gone away to call him back when in came the Prime Minister, who also had an Uncle, and his Uncle had just given him a new box of tools.

" Aha ! " he said when he saw the table. " What this needs is a little bit off some legs and not off the others," and very soon he, too, was sawing away at the Queen's table.

But alas and alack, all over again ! After three attempts the Prime Minister had only succeeded in making the table about as high as a chair, and just as wobbly as ever. He was just going to burst into tears when in came the Prince's tutor, who knew all about multiplication tables but very little about ordinary tables, but that wasn't going to stop him having a shot at getting the Queen's table steady. And when he and the Lord Chief Justice, and the Lord Chancellor, and the assistant butler had all finished having a go at it, the table was about two inches high and still wobbly.

Just then in came the Queen, and they all

stood in a row looking very sheepish at the little two-inches-high table on the floor, wondering what on earth to do or say, except the assistant butler, who pretended to be frightfully busy polishing one of the cushions.

"My lovely new table!" gasped the Queen, her eyes opening so wide that she didn't recognize her own reflection in the mirror.

Then in came the King with the carpenter, whom he had fetched back from his holiday because he wasn't very far away. When he saw what had happened he tried to turn round and rush out again, but the Queen stopped him, and they all stood waiting with frightfully bated breath to see whose heads were going to be ordered off.

But suddenly the Queen clapped her hands. "Ah!" she cried, "that will make a simply lovely pastry-board now, and I did so want a nice big pastry-board, and I really didn't want another table."

"Especially one that was too high," said the King hurriedly, grasping what he thought was a good opportunity.

"And all wobbly," said the others, eagerly leaning forward.

So the Queen got the carpenter to turn the too low, wobbly table into a pastry-board, and none of the tarts she made on it would stand steady without wobbling, but that didn't matter.

Then the King, who believed in making the best of a bad job, collected up all the little pieces of table leg that had been cut off and gave them to one of his nephews, who was just going to have a birthday, as a box of bricks.

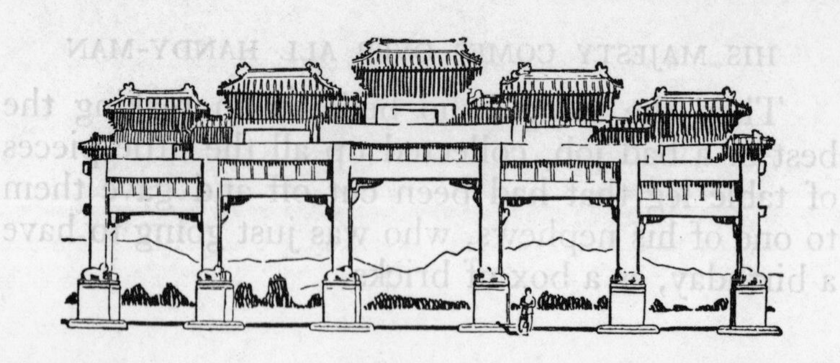

THE FOOLING OF KING ALEXANDER

By Mervyn Skipper

Alexander was a very great king. The Kings of Persia, Media, India, and Brunei are all descended from him. He conquered Stamboul, Mesopotamia, Bombay, and Singapore, and when he had conquered all these he thought he had conquered all the world ; but one day he met an old woman washing rice in a river, and he spoke to her about it.

" No," said the old woman, " there is still one country left to conquer. You have not conquered China."

" Where is this China ? " asked Alexander.

" It lies beyond the great snow mountains, the deserts of sliding sands, the land of two-headed men, beyond the jungle of knives and scissors, the land where geese grow on trees, the land of legless people who go about on wheels, the country of tongueless women, and the ocean of flying whales."

" And how far away is that ? " asked Alexander.

" Just how far that is, my lord," said the old woman, " nobody knows."

" However far away it is," said Alexander, " I will conquer it." And he ordered all his army to be got together, his hundreds of elephants, his thousands of camels, his tens of thousands of horses, and of foot-soldiers and their wives and children, thousands without number ; and at the head of these he set out to conquer China. Such was the size of his army that the jungle of knives and scissors was trampled flat, the snow mountains nodded their heads till their snow caps fell off and ran down into the valleys, the sliding sands rose in clouds and obscured the sun and made the day so dark that if it had not been for the glittering of the swords and shields, and the crowns of the rajas, nobody would have been able to see his way. When it thundered, the thunder could not be heard for the shouting of the foot-soldiers, the neighing of the horses, and the trumpeting of the elephants ; and the very swiftest camels were required if one wished to go from the head of the army to the tail of it between breakfast time and dinner.

It was a very great army.

For many days King Alexander marched, and at last he came to Temasek, which is not very far from China. Now, when the Emperor of China heard that King Alexander was coming to take his country from him with this great army, he was

frightened, and his liver turned to water. Calling all his wisest men together, he asked them what was the best thing to be done. Some said one thing and some said another, and they all talked at once and made a great noise; but none of them could tell the Emperor how he could stop King

Alexander and his soldiers from taking China. At last, when they had all got tired of talking, the little boy who carried the Emperor's snuff-box stood out and said he knew a way to stop King Alexander. The wise men laughed, but the Emperor said : " Let the boy speak ! A small stone can sometimes break a large jar ! "

So the little boy asked the Emperor to give him the oldest, leakiest, rottenest, and most ill-found junk that he had in his navy ; and he had it filled right up to the decks with small and rusty needles. Then he took a kesma tree and a jujube tree that were in fruit and planted them in tubs on the deck. Then he asked the Emperor to give him for his crew six old men whose teeth had all dropped out, and six old women whose backs were bent like water-wheels, to keep them company. So the Emperor sent his messengers out to find six old men whose teeth had all dropped out, and six old women whose backs were bent like water-wheels, and when they were found they were put on board the junk, the small boy took the tiller, and the junk set sail towards Temasek.

The wise men laughed when they saw the junk go ; but the Emperor said, " Wait and see : beards sometimes grow before eyebrows."

After a few days the junk came to Temasek, and when King Alexander's people saw it they ran to the king, crying that a junk had arrived that had come from China.

"Go, fools," said King Alexander, "and ask the crew of the junk how they have come and how far it is to China."

"Alas," said the crew of the junk, "the day that we set sail from China we were all young men and beautiful women, twelve years was the age of the oldest of us. These bearing trees, we planted them as seeds. Now, alas! we are old, and our teeth have fallen out, and our backs have become bent like water-wheels, and the seeds have grown into great trees, and at last we have come to this place."

And they showed their cargo of needles to King Alexander's people, and said, "As big round as our arms were these bars of iron when we left China; see how they have rusted to the size of needles; that is how long our journey has been so that we forget the number of the years of it; and if the small boy who steers had not been born to us ten years ago there would have been none left strong enough to sail the vessel."

So King Alexander's people went to King Alexander and told him all that the crew of the junk had told them.

"If, as these Chinese say, this country of China is so far away that boys grow into old men on the journey, how should I ever be able to reach it since I am already an old man?" said King Alexander.

"True, O King!" cried all his people. "Let

us return ! " And so King Alexander and all his army returned to their own country. And when they came to the river from whence they had started, the old woman was still washing rice in it.

THE PORCELAIN STOVE

By "Ouida"

Augustus lived in a little town in Germany. He was a small boy nine years old, with rosy cheeks, big hazel eyes, and clusters of curls the brown of ripe nuts. His mother was dead, his father was poor, and there were ten children's mouths to feed at home, beginning with Dorothy, a sweet dark-haired girl of seventeen, who kept house for them all : down to the three-year-old baby, with eyes like forget-me-nots. The children were always clean and happy, and the table was seldom without its big pot of soup once a day. Still, very poor they were ; and their father's debts were many for flour, and meat, and clothing.

When indoors the children spent most of their time in a large room with a red brick floor that was bare and uneven. It had a wooden cupboard, a big deal table, and several stools for furniture. But at the top of the room, sending out warmth and colour together as the lamp shed its rays upon it, was a tower of porcelain china shining with all the hues of a king's peacock and a queen's jewels. On the top were armed figures, and shields, and flowers, with a great golden crown above all. There were also letters, H. R. H., which showed it had been made by a great potter many, many years before, and no doubt it had once stood in the palace of some prince, and had warmed the silk stockings of kings and queens.

But of its past history nothing was known, except that Augustus's grandfather, who had been a mason, had dug it up out of some ruins where he was building, and finding it quite whole, had taken it home. That was now sixty years ago, and ever since the stove had stood in the big empty room, warming the children who clustered round it.

How the children loved the porcelain stove! In summer they laid a mat of fresh roses all round it, and dressed it up with green boughs and the beautiful wild flowers of the countryside. And in winter they would sit close beside it, and cry, "Tell us a story, Augustus;" and the boy, looking up at the ardent glow of its noble tower, with all its pictures, and flowers, and crowns, would imagine the many adventures of the people who were pictured on its shining sides. Augustus had never seen a story-book in his life, but he loved inventing stories, and the children never tired of listening to their brother's tales.

One cold winter's night, just a week before Christmas, in the midst of the children's chatter and laughter, the door opened and let in a blast of frozen air as their father entered. Very weary he was, and Dorothy soon took the little ones to bed, while Augustus curled himself up in front of the warm stove, and lay silent so as not to disturb his tired father.

The cuckoo clock in the corner struck eight as Dorothy came downstairs, and the room was strangely quiet. Suddenly the father struck his hand on the table, and said in a husky, dogged voice, "I have sold the stove to a dealer for two hundred florins. He saw it this morning when you were all out, and to-morrow he comes to pack it and take it away."

Dorothy gave a low shrill cry; and Augustus sprang to his feet, crying, "Oh, father, it is not true; say it is not true! You are jesting, father!"

But the father only gave a dreary laugh. "I owe money everywhere; we must have bread to eat. The stove is much too grand for a poor room like this; it is a stove for a museum, the dealer said, and to a museum it will now go."

Augustus threw himself at his father's feet, and clasped his knees. "Oh, father, dear father, you cannot mean what you say! To us it is not just a stove, as you say it is: it is a living thing—it is our fire-king. It loves us though we are only poor little children, and we love it with all our hearts. Give the florins back to the man. Oh, father, do hear me for pity's sake!"

"You are a foolish boy," said the father; "get up and go to bed. The stove is sold. There is no more to be said. The old black stove in the kitchen will warm you all quite as well as this painted thing. Go to bed, I say." Then he took the oil-lamp that stood at his elbow and went upstairs to his room.

Augustus lay beside the stove he loved so dearly, covering it with kisses, and sobbing as though his heart would break. What could he do? Nothing, nothing, nothing.

"Come to bed, dear," whispered Dorothy. "Oh! Augustus, do not cry like that, you frighten me; do come to bed."

"No; I shall stay here all night," he answered; "they might come to take it away." And alone he stayed through the long dark hours. The lamp went out, rats came and ran across the floor, the fire in the stove slowly died, and the room grew cold as ice, but Augustus never moved.

There the children found him when they came downstairs in the morning, and roughly his father thrust him out into the back court when men came with straw and ropes to pack up and carry away the beloved stove.

Into the court an old neighbour hobbled to fetch water, and seeing the boy lying with his face hidden in the ground, he said, "Child, is it true your father is selling the big painted stove?" Augustus nodded his head, then burst into passionate tears.

"Well, for sure he is a foolish man," said the

neighbour. " It was worth a mint of money, for I do remember, in your grandfather's time, that a stranger gentleman saw it, and said that it would bring its weight in gold."

" I do not care what its value was," sobbed Augustus ; " I loved it, loved it, loved it ! "

" Well, if I were you," said the old man kindly, " I would do better than cry, I would go after it. The world is a small place, after all, and your stove will be safe enough whoever gets it. When you are big you can follow it, and see your stove again." And the old man hobbled away.

The boy's heart gave a leap of hope. Yes ; he would go after it. At once he hid himself in a doorway, and watched till he saw the straw-covered bundle carefully carried out by four men and laid on a wagon. Then, unseen by Dorothy or his father, he followed it.

At the railway station Augustus heard the dealer arrange that the stove should be sent on a goods train that was due in half an hour, and he at once made up his mind that where his fire-king went he would go too. How he managed it he never clearly knew, but certain it is that when the goods train left the station Augustus was hidden behind the stove, in the great covered truck.

It was very dark and very crowded, and the truck smelt strongly of the hams and hides that were packed in it. But Augustus was not frightened. He was close to his fire-king, and presently he would be closer still, for he meant to do nothing less than get inside it.

He had bought some bread and sausage at the station, and this he ate in the darkness, in spite of the lumbering, pounding, thundering noise of the train, which made him giddy, for he had never before been in any kind of train.

After he had eaten, he set to work like a little mouse to make a hole in the bands of straw that were wrapped round the stove. He gnawed and nibbled, and pulled and pushed, just as a mouse would have done, making his hole where he guessed the door of the stove would be. And get through them at last he did.

He slipped through the door into the inside of the stove, as he had often done at home for fun, and curled himself up to see if he could really hide there for many hours. He found he could, as plenty of air came in through the brass fretwork of the door.

He leaned out and drew the hay and straw together, so that no one could have dreamed that even a little mouse had been at them. Then he curled himself up again, and, being safe inside his dear fire-king, he fell fast asleep, as if he were in his own bed at home.

For many a weary hour the train rolled on in its heavy, slow fashion : it took all the long day, and all the long night, and half of the next day before their station was reached.

Then Augustus felt the stove lifted out of the truck, and very carefully it was laid on a wagon, which drove to a shop. The stove was then gently lifted down, and set upright on its four gilded feet in a small room.

"I shall not unpack it to-night," he heard a voice say ; then a key was turned in the lock, and there was silence.

After some time Augustus ventured to peep through the straw and hay which wrapped the stove, and what he saw was a room filled with many curious things. There were pictures and carvings, old blue jugs, armour, daggers, china, and many other wonderful bits of furniture, all very old. But oh ! there was not a drop of water, and Augustus was so thirsty.

There was a small window, and on the broad ledge outside he saw snow lying. Quickly he darted out of his hiding-place, raised the window, and crammed his mouth full of snow, broke off some icicles, then flew back to the stove, drew the hay and straw over the hole, and shut the door again.

It was not very cold in this lumber-room, and soon he slept again, and forgot how hungry and how tired he was. Midnight was chiming from all the clocks of the city when he awoke, and the room seemed strangely light. Everything was quiet, so he ventured to put his head out to see why such a bright light was shining, and what he saw did not frighten or amaze him as I think it would have alarmed you or me.

All the things in the room were alive and moving about! A big jug was dancing a polka with a fat blue jar. The tall clock was bowing to an old chair with spindle legs. A broken violin was playing to itself, and a queer little tune came from a piano covered with painted roses. Meanwhile, the bright light which filled the room shone from three silver candlesticks that had no candles in them. Strange to say, Augustus somehow did not feel at all surprised; all he longed for was to creep out and dance too!

Just then a lovely little china lady, dressed in pink and gold and white, tripped up to him and invited him to dance with her, and in a minute the little country lad, in his thick shoes and shabby jacket, was dancing round the room with the dainty china lady on his arm.

"I am a princess," she said to him when the dance was over. And he took courage to say to her, "Madam, my princess, could you tell me kindly why some of the things dance and speak, and some stand still and silent like lumber? Is it rude to ask?"

"My dear child," said the princess, "is it possible you do not know the reason? Why, these silent, dull things are imitation!"

"Imitation," repeated Augustus timidly, for he did not understand.

"Of course," said the princess. "They only pretend to be what we are. They are copies, so

they never wake up. How could they? No imitation ever had any soul in it."

"Oh!" said Augustus humbly, not sure that he understood yet, and he looked at his dear fire-king: surely it had a royal soul within it; would it not wake up and speak? Oh dear! how he longed to hear its voice!

"What will you be when you are a man?" asked the princess suddenly.

"I wish—I hope," said Augustus, stammering, "to be a painter, such as the master who painted yonder stove."

"Bravo!" cried all the real things in the room, for they all knew the name of the great artist who had made the fire-king. But the stove remained silent, and then a sickening fear shot through Augustus's heart.

Could it be that his beloved fire-king was only an imitation? "No, no, no," he said to himself stoutly; "that I will never believe," and he said it so loudly and sharply that the china princess looked at him in surprise.

"Ah! if we could only all go back to our masters," sighed the china princess; and somehow they all grew sad as they thought of the men who had made them and loved them so well.

Then from where the great stove stood there came a solemn voice. All eyes turned towards it, and Augustus's heart gave a great leap of joy.

"My friends," said the voice, "I have listened to all you have said. For over two hundred years I have not spoken, and I only speak now because I see amidst you a little human child who loves me, and I want him ever to remember this night and these words.

"I want him to remember that we are what we are because of these beloved masters who created us many, many years ago. They are all dead, these masters, but we live on—we, the things that they made and loved. And so through us do they yet speak and live."

Then the voice sank away in silence. The light in the candlesticks faded and went out. The clocks of the city struck six, and Augustus awoke with a start to find himself lying on the bare brick floor of the room, while everything in it was still and silent.

Tramp, tramp, came heavy steps up the stairs. Augustus crept into the stove as the door opened. The dealer entered, and began to wrap up the stove again in its straw and hay, and presently it was carried by six porters back to the railway station. There the precious bundle was hoisted into a great van, but this time the dealer and the porters stayed beside it.

The train rolled on with all its fuss and roar of steam, and in about an hour it stopped, and once more the stove was tenderly lifted out. It was now nearly ten o'clock, the sun had come out, and Augustus could see through the fretwork of the brass door that a large lake lay before them.

Soon the stove was gently placed in a boat, and the rowers pulled steadily for the other side of the lake. Presently they reached a pier. "Now, men, for a stout mile and a half," said the dealer to the porters, and the precious bundle was gently carried along a road heavy with snow.

It seemed a very long time to Augustus till they entered a house, and he knew by their movements that they were going upstairs. Warm air was about him, and there was a delicious fragrance of flowers. The stove was set down, all its wrappings were removed, and then the dealer and the porters left.

Presently Augustus heard a step beside him, and a low voice said, "Oh, how exceedingly beautiful. No; it is not an imitation, it is indeed the work of the great master."

Then the hand of the speaker turned the handle of the brass door, and some one looked in. "What is this in it? A live child!" he heard the voice exclaim.

Augustus sprang out of the stove and fell at the feet of the speaker. "Oh! let me stay, let me stay; I love it. I have come all the way," he sobbed.

Some gentlemen seized him, not gently, and a voice whispered, "Be quiet, it is the King." They were about to drag him away, but the King said: "Poor little child, he is very young, leave him alone, let him speak to me."

The men let Augustus go, and looking up he saw a young man with a beautiful dark face and eyes full of dreams, and this young man said to him: "My child, how came you here, hidden in the stove ? Be not afraid, tell me the truth ; I am the King."

"Oh, dear King," said Augustus, with trembling entreaty in his faint little voice, "the fire-king was ours, and we have loved it all our lives : and father sold it. I have come all the way inside it, and last night it spoke and said beautiful things.

"And I do pray you to let me live beside it, and I will go out every morning and cut wood for it, if only you will let me stay with it, for I love it so." And as he lifted his little eager face to the young King's, great tears were falling down his cheeks.

"Who bought the stove from your father, and what did they pay him ? " asked the King.

"Two hundred florins," said Augustus with a sob. "It was so much money, and we were so poor, and there were so many of us."

The dealer who had bought the stove was waiting downstairs, and the King sent for him. "How much did the gentleman who bought this stove for me give you for it ? " he asked. "Two thousand sovereigns, your Majesty," said the man.

The King then said, "You will give at once to this boy's father the two thousand sovereigns you received, less the two hundred silver florins you paid him. You are a great rogue ; begone, and be thankful you are not punished."

Augustus listened, but he understood little of

what the King said. " Oh ! do, please do let me stay," he murmured when the King stood silent, and clasping his little brown hands together he knelt before the young King.

" Rise up, child," he said in a kind voice. " Yes, you shall stay, and you shall live here and be taught at my own school. And if, when you are twenty-one years old, you have done well and bravely, I will give you your own stove back again."

He smiled and stretched out his hand, but Augustus threw his two arms about the King's knees and kissed his feet. Then he lost all sense of where he was, and fainted from hunger, and tiredness, and great joy.

OVERHEARD ON A SALT-MARSH

By Harold Monro

Nymph, Nymph, what are your beads?

Green glass, Goblin. Why do you stare at them?

Give them me.

No.

Give them me. Give them me.

No.

Then I will howl all night in the reeds,
Lie in the mud and howl for them.

Goblin, why do you love them so?

They are better than stars or water,
Better than voices of winds that sing,
Better than any man's fair daughter,
Your green glass beads on a silver ring.

Hush, I stole them out of the moon.

Give me your beads, I want them.

No.

I will howl in a deep lagoon
For your green glass beads. I love them so.
Give them me. Give them.

No.

THE SNOW QUEEN

By Hans Andersen

PART I

Once upon a time there was a little boy called Kay. And there was a little girl. Her name was Gerda.

They were not brother and sister, this little boy and girl, but they lived in tiny attics next door to one another.

When they were not playing together, Gerda spent her time peeping at Kay, through one of the little panes in her window. And Kay peeped back at Gerda.

Outside each attic was a tiny balcony, just big enough to hold two little stools and a window-box. Often Gerda would step out of her attic window into the balcony, carrying with her a three-legged wooden stool. Then she would climb over the low wall that separated her from Kay.

And there in Kay's balcony the two children would sit and play together, or tell fairy tales, or tend the flowers that bloomed so gaily in the window-box.

At other times it was Kay who would bound over the low wall into Gerda's balcony, and there, too, the little boy and girl were as happy as though they had been in fairyland.

In each little window-box grew a rose-bush, and the bloom and the scent of the red roses they bore gave Kay and Gerda more delight than you can imagine ; and all her life long a red rose remained little Gerda's favourite flower.

But it was not always summer-time, and when cold, frosty winter came, and the Snow Queen sailed down on the large white snowflakes from a grey sky, then no flowers bloomed in the window-boxes. And the balcony was so slippery that the children dared not venture to step out of their attic windows, but had to run down one long flight of stairs and up another to be able to play together.

Sometimes, however, Kay stayed in his own little room and Gerda stayed in hers, gazing and gazing at the lovely pictures of castles, and mountains, and sea, and flowers that the Snow Queen had drawn on the window-panes as she passed.

But now that the little panes of glass were covered with pictures, how could Kay and Gerda peep at each other from the attic windows ?

Ah, they had a plan, and a very good plan too. Kay would heat a penny on the stove, and then press it against the window-pane, and so make little round peep-holes. Then he would put his eye to one of these little rounds and—what did he see? A bright black eye peeping from Gerda's attic, for she too had heated a penny and made peep-holes in her window.

It was in winter, too, when the children could not play together on the balcony, that Gerda's grandmother told them stories of the Snow Queen.

One night, as Kay was undressing to go to bed, he climbed on a chair and peeped out of one of his little round holes, and there, on the edge of the window-box, were a few big snowflakes. And as the little boy watched them, the biggest grew bigger and bigger, until it grew into a white lady of glittering, dazzling ice. Her eyes shone like two bright stars.

"It must be the Snow Queen," thought Kay, and at that moment the white lady nodded to him, and waved her hand, and as he jumped from his chair, he fancied she flew past the window. "It must be the Snow Queen." Would he ever see her again?

At last the white winter melted away and green spring burst upon the earth. Then once more summer—warm, bright, beautiful summer.

It was at five o'clock, one sunny afternoon, that Kay and Gerda sat together on their little stools in the balcony, looking at a picture-book.

"Oh!" cried Kay suddenly, "oh, there is something sharp in my eye, and I have such a pain in my heart."

Gerda put her arms round Kay's neck and looked into his eye.

"I can see nothing, Kay dear."

"Oh! it is gone now," said the boy, and they turned again to the picture-book.

But something had flown into Kay's eye, and it was not gone; a little bit had reached his heart, and it was still there. Listen, and I will tell you what had happened.

There was about this time a most marvellous mirror in the world. It belonged to the worst hobgoblin that ever lived, and had been made by his wicked little demons.

Those who looked into this mirror saw reflected there all the mean and ugly people and things in the world, and not one beautiful sight could they see. And the thoughts of those who looked into this mirror became as mean and ugly as the people and things they saw.

This delighted the hobgoblin, who ordered his little demons to carry the mirror all over the world and to do as much mischief with it as they could.

But one day, when they had travelled far, the mirror slipped from the hands of the little imps, and fell to earth, shivered into hundreds of thousands of millions of bits. Then it did more harm than ever, for the tiny pieces, some no bigger than a grain of sand, were blown all over the world, and often flew in people's eyes, and sometimes even found their way into their hearts.

And when a big person or a child had a little bit of this magic mirror in his eye, he saw only what was mean and ugly ; and if the tiniest grain of the glass reached the heart, alas ! alas ! it froze all the kindness and gentleness and love that was there, and the heart became like a lump of ice.

This is what had happened to poor little Kay. One tiny bit of the magic mirror had flown into his eye ; another had entered his heart.

" How horrid you look, Gerda. Why are you crying ? And oh, see the worm in that rose. Roses are ugly, and so are window-boxes." And Kay kicked the window-box, and knocked two roses from the rose-bush.

" Kay dear, what is the matter ? " asked Gerda.

The little boy did not answer, but broke off another rose, and then, without saying good-bye, stepped in at his own window, leaving Gerda alone.

The next time the little girl brought out the picture-book, Kay tore the leaves, and when the grandmother told them a story, he interrupted her and made ugly faces. And he would tread on Gerda's toes and pull her hair, and make faces at her too.

" How cruel little Kay grows," said his friends, for he mocked the old people and ill-treated those who were weak. And all through the blue summer and the yellow autumn Kay teased little Gerda, or left her that he might play with the bigger children in the town.

But it was when winter came, and the big white snowflakes once more fell from a grey sky, that Gerda felt loneliest, for Kay now drew on his thick gloves, slung his little sledge across his back, and marched off alone. " I am going to ride in the square," he shouted in her ear as he passed. But Gerda could not answer ; she could only think of the winters that had gone, when she and Kay always sat side by side in that same little sledge. How happy they had been! Oh, why, why had he not taken her with him?

Kay walked briskly to the square, and there he watched the bolder of the boys tie their sledges to the farmers' carts. With what glee they felt themselves being drawn over the snow-covered ground! When they reached the town gates they would jump out, unfasten their sledges, and return to the square to begin the fun all over again.

Kay was thinking how much he would like to tie his little sledge behind a cart, when a big sledge, painted white, drove by. In it sat some one muffled in a white fur coat and cap. Twice the sledge drove round the square.

As it passed Kay the second time, he quickly fastened on his little sledge behind, and in a moment found himself flying through the streets. What fun! On and on through snowdrifts, bounding over ditches, rushing down hills, faster and faster they flew.

Little Kay grew frightened. Twice he tried to unfasten the string that tied his sledge to the other, but both times the white driver turned round and nodded to him to sit still. At last they had driven through the town gates. The snow fell so heavily that it blinded him. Now he could not see where they were going, and Kay grew more frightened still. He tried to say his prayers, but could only remember the multiplication table.

Bigger and bigger grew the snowflakes, till they seemed like large white birds. Then, suddenly, the sledge stopped. The driver stood up. She was a tall lady, dazzlingly white. Her eyes shone like two stars. She was the Snow Queen.

"It is cold," said the white lady; "come into my sledge. Now, creep inside my furs."

Kay did as he was told, but he felt as if he had fallen into a snowdrift.

"You are still cold," said the Snow Queen, and she kissed his forehead. Her lips were like ice, and Kay shivered and felt the old pain at his heart. But only for a minute, for the Snow Queen kissed him again, and then he forgot the pain and he forgot Gerda, and he forgot his grandmother and his old home, and had not a thought for anything or any one but the Snow Queen.

He had no fear of her now, no, not although they flew up and up on a dark cloud, away over woods and lakes, over rivers, islands, and seas. No, he was not afraid, although the cold wind whistled around them, and beneath the wild wolves howled. Kay did not care.

Above them the moon shone bright and clear. All night long the boy would gaze at it and the twinkling stars, but by day he slept at the feet of the Snow Queen.

PART II

But what of little Gerda ?

Poor child, she watched and she waited and she wondered, but Kay did not come, and nobody could tell her where he was. The boys had seen him drive out of the town gates behind a big sledge painted white. But no one had heard of him since.

Little Gerda cried bitterly. Perhaps Kay was drowned in the river. Oh, what a long, cold winter that was! But spring came at last—bright spring with its golden sunshine and its singing birds.

" Kay is dead," said Gerda.

" Kay dead ? It is not true," said the sunshine.

" Kay dead ? We do not believe it," twittered the swallows.

And neither did little Gerda really believe it.

"I will put on my new red shoes," said the child one morning, "and go to the river and ask it about Kay." So she put on her little red shoes, and kissed her old grandmother who was still asleep, and wandered alone, out beyond the town gates, and down to the river bank.

"Have you taken my little playfellow?" she asked. "I will give you these if you will bring him back to me," and she flung her little shoes into the river.

They fell close to the bank and the little waves tossed them back on to the dry pebbles at her feet. "We do not want you, we will keep Kay," they seemed to say.

"Perhaps I did not throw them far enough," thought Gerda, and, stepping into a boat that lay among the rushes, she flung the red shoes with all her might into the middle of the river.

But the boat was not fastened, and it glided

out from among the rushes. Soon it was drifting faster and faster down the river. The little shoes floated behind.

" Perhaps I am going to little Kay," thought Gerda, as she was carried farther and farther down the river.

How pretty it was ! Trees waved and flowers nodded on its banks. Sheep grazed and cattle browsed, but not one person, big or little, was to be seen.

After a long time Gerda came to a cherry garden which stretched down to the river-bank. At the end of this garden stood a tiny cottage with a thatched roof, and with red, blue, and yellow glass windows.

On either side of the door stood a wooden soldier. Gerda thought the soldiers were alive, and shouted to them.

The wooden soldiers, of course, did not hear, but an old, old woman who lived in the tiny house wondered who it could be that called. She hobbled out, leaning on her hooked stick. On her head she wore a big sun-hat, and on it were painted beautiful flowers.

" You poor child," said the old, old woman, walking straight into the river and catching hold of the boat with her hooked stick, " you poor dear ! " And she pulled the boat ashore and lifted out little Gerda on to the green grass.

Gerda was delighted to be on dry land again,

but she was a little bit afraid of the old, old woman, who now asked her who she was and where she came from.

"I am looking for Kay, little Kay. Have you seen him?" began Gerda, and she went on to tell the old, old woman the whole story of her playmate and his strange disappearance. When she had finished, she asked again, "Have you seen him?"

"No," said the old, old woman, "but I expect him. Come in," and she took little Gerda by the hand. "Come to my house and taste my cherries." And when they had gone into the cottage, the old, old woman locked the door. Then she gave Gerda a plate of the most delicious cherries, and while the little girl ate them, the old, old woman combed her hair with a golden comb.

Now this old, old woman was a witch, and the comb was a magic comb, for as soon as it touched her hair, Gerda forgot all about Kay. And this was just what the witch wished, for she was a lonely old woman, and would have liked Gerda to become her own little girl and stay with her always.

Gerda did enjoy the red cherries, and while she was still eating them, the old, old woman stole out to the garden and waved her hooked stick over the rose-bushes and they quickly sank beneath the brown earth. For Gerda had told her how fond Kay had once been of their little rose-bushes in the balcony, and the witch was afraid the sight of roses would remind the little girl of her lost playmate. But now that the roses had vanished, Gerda might come into the garden.

How the child danced for joy past the lilies and bluebells, how she suddenly fell on her knees to smell the pinks and mignonette, and then danced off again, in and out among the sunflowers and hollyhocks !

Gerda was perfectly happy now, and played among the flowers until the sun sank behind the cherry trees. Then the old, old woman again took her by the hand, and led her to the little house. And she undressed her and put her into a little bed of white violets, and there the little girl dreamed sweet dreams.

The next day and the next again and for many more Gerda played among the flowers in the garden.

One morning, as the old, old woman sat near, Gerda looked at her hat with the wonderful painted flowers. Prettiest of all was a rose.

" A rose ! Why, surely I have seen none in the garden," thought Gerda, and she danced off in search.

But she could find none, and in her disappointment hot tears fell. And they fell on the very spot where the roses had grown, and as soon as the warm drops moistened the earth, the rose-bushes sprang up.

" You are beautiful, beautiful," she said ; but

in a moment the tears fell again, for she thought of the rose-bushes in the balcony, and she remembered Kay.

" Oh, Kay, dear, dear Kay, is he dead ? " she asked the roses.

" No, he is not dead," they answered, " for we have been beneath the brown earth, and he is not there."

" Then where, oh, where is he ? " and she went from flower to flower whispering, " Have you seen little Kay ? "

But the flowers stood in the sunshine, dreaming their own dreams, and these they told the little maiden gladly, but of Kay they could not tell her, for they knew nothing.

Then the little girl ran down the garden path until she came to the garden gate. She pressed the rusty latch. The gate flew open, and Gerda ran out on her little bare feet into the green fields. And she ran, and she ran, until she could run no longer. Then she sat down on a big stone to rest.

" Why, it must be autumn," she said sorrowfully, as she looked around. And little Gerda felt sorry that she had stayed so long in the magic garden, where it was always summer.

" Why have I not been seeking little Kay ? " she asked herself, and she jumped up and trudged along, on and on, out into the great wide world.

At last the cold white winter came again, and

still little Gerda was wandering alone through the wide world, for she had not found little Kay.

" Caw, caw," said a big raven that hopped on the stone in front of her. " Caw, caw."

" Have you seen little Kay ? " asked Gerda, and she told the bird her sad story.

" It may have been Kay," said the raven, " I cannot tell. But if it was, he will have forgotten you now that he lives with the Princess."

" Does he live with a Princess ? " asked Gerda.

" Yes, he does. If you care to listen, I will tell you how it came about. In this kingdom lives a Princess so clever that she has read all the newspapers in the world, and forgotten them again. Last winter she made up her mind to marry. Her husband, she said, must speak well. He must know the proper thing to say, and say it prettily. Otherwise she would not marry. I assure you what I say is perfectly true, for I have a tame sweetheart who lives at Court, and she told me the whole story.

" One day it was pub-

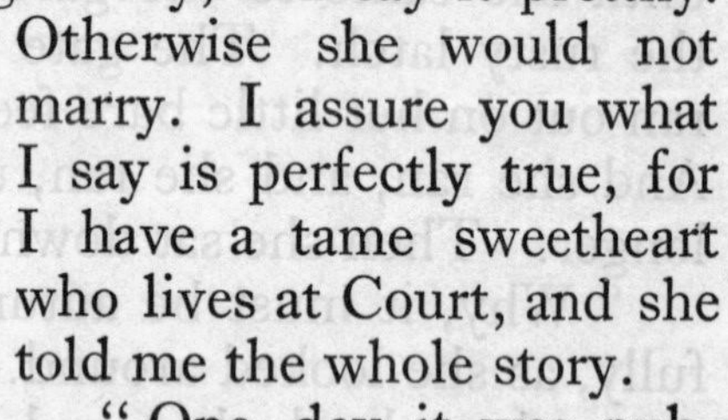

lished in the newspapers that any handsome young man might go to the palace to speak to the Princess. The one who spoke most prettily and answered most wisely should be chosen as her husband. What a stir there was! Young men flocked to the palace in crowds, chattering as they came. But when they saw the great staircase, and the soldiers in their silver uniform, and the grand ladies in velvet and lace, they could only talk in whispers. And when they were led before the beautiful Princess, who was seated on a pearl as big as a spinning-wheel, they were silent. She spoke to them, but they could think of nothing to say, so they repeated her last words over and over again. The Princess did not like that, and she——"

"But Kay, little Kay, did he come?" interrupted Gerda.

"You are in too great a hurry," said the raven, "I am just coming to that. On the third day came a boy with sparkling eyes and golden hair, but his clothes were shabby. He——"

"Oh, that would be Kay. Dear, dear Kay, I have found him at last."

"He had a knapsack on his back, and——"

"No, it must have been a sledge," again interrupted Gerda.

"I said he had a knapsack on his back, and he wore boots that creaked, but——"

"Oh, then it must be Kay, for he had new boots. I heard them creak through our attic wall when——"

"Little girl, do not interrupt, but listen to me. He wore boots that creaked, but even that did not frighten him. He creaked up the great staircase, he passed the soldiers in silver uniform, he bowed to the ladies in velvet and lace, and still he was quite at his ease. And when he was led before the beautiful Princess who was seated on a pearl as big as a spinning-wheel, he answered so prettily and spoke so wisely that she chose him as her husband."

"Indeed, indeed it was Kay," said little Gerda. "He was so clever. He could do arithmetic up to long division. Oh, take me to him."

"I will see what can be done," said the raven. "I will talk about it to my tame sweetheart. She will certainly be able to advise us. Wait here by the stile," and the raven wagged his head and flew off.

It was growing dark before he returned. "Here is a roll my tame sweetheart sent you. 'The little maiden must be hungry,' she said. As for your going to the palace with those bare feet—the thing is impossible. The soldiers in silver uniform would not let you go up the great stair. But do not cry. My sweetheart knows a little back staircase. She will take you to the Prince and Princess. Follow me."

On tiptoe little Gerda followed the raven, as he hopped across the snow-covered field and up the long avenue that led to the palace garden. And in the garden they waited silently until the last light had gone out. Then they turned along the bare walk that led to the back door. It stood wide open.

Oh, how little Gerda's heart beat, as on the

tips of her little bare toes she followed the raven up the dimly-lighted back staircase !

On the landing at the top burned a small lamp. Beside it stood the tame sweetheart.

Gerda curtsied as her grandmother had taught her.

" He," said the tame sweetheart, nodding to the raven of the field, " he has told me your story. It has made me sad. But if you carry the lamp, I will lead the way, and then we shall see——"

" We shall see little Kay," murmured Gerda.

" Hush ! we shall see what we shall see," said the tame sweetheart.

Through room after room Gerda followed her strange guide, her heart thumping and thumping so loudly that she was afraid some one in the palace would hear it and wake.

At last they came to a room in which stood two little beds, one white and one red. The tame sweetheart nodded to the little girl.

Poor Gerda ! she was trembling all over as she peeped at the little head that rested on the pillow of the white bed.

Oh ! that was the Princess.

Gerda turned to the little red bed. The Prince was lying on his face, but the hair, surely it was Kay's hair ! She drew down the little red coverlet until she saw a brown neck. Yes ! it was Kay's neck, she felt sure.

" Kay, Kay, it is I, little Gerda ! Wake ! wake ! "

And the Prince awoke. He turned his head. He opened his eyes, and—alas ! alas ! it was not little Kay.

Then Gerda cried and cried as if her heart would break. She cried until she awoke the Princess, who started up bewildered.

" Who are you, little girl, and where do you come from, and what do you want ? "

" Oh, I want Kay, little Kay. Do you know where he is ? " And Gerda told the Princess all her story, and of what the ravens had done to help her.

"Poor little child," said the Princess, "how sad you must feel."

"And how tired," said the Prince, and he jumped out of his little red bed, and made Gerda lie down.

The little girl was grateful indeed. She folded her hands and was soon fast asleep.

And Gerda dreamed of Kay. She saw him

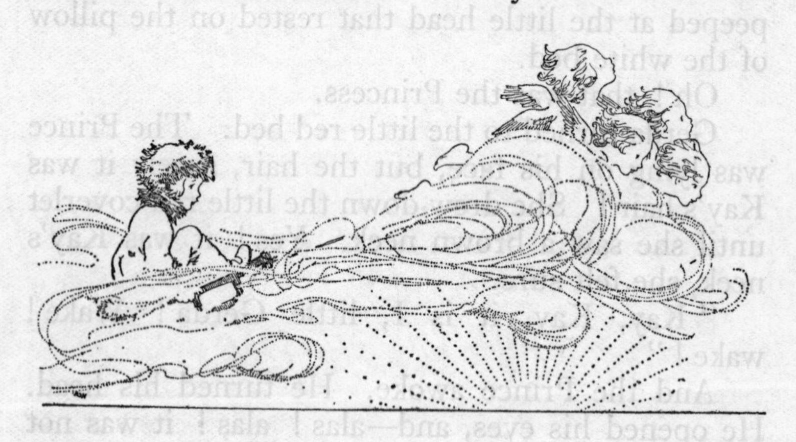

sitting in his little sledge, and it was dragged by angels. But it was only a dream, and when she awoke, her little playmate was as far away as ever.

The ravens were now very happy, for the Princess said that, although they must never again lead any one to the palace by the back staircase, this time they should be rewarded. They should for the rest of their lives live together in the palace garden, and be known as the Court Ravens, and be fed from the royal kitchen.

When little Gerda awoke from her dreams she saw the sunbeams stealing across her bed. It was time to get up.

The Court ladies dressed the little girl in silk and velvet, and the Prince and Princess asked her to stay with them at the palace. But Gerda begged for a little carriage, and a horse, and a pair of boots, that she might again go out into the great wide world to seek little Kay.

So they gave her a pair of boots and a muff, and when she was dressed, there before the door stood a carriage of pure gold. The Prince himself helped Gerda to step in, and the Princess waved to her as she drove off.

But although Gerda was now a grand little girl, she was very lonely. The coachman and footmen in the scarlet and gold livery did not speak a word. She was glad when the field raven flew to the carriage and perched by her side. He explained that his wife—for he was now married—would have come also, but she had eaten too much breakfast and was not well. But at the end of three miles the raven said good-bye, and, flapping his shiny black wings, flew into an elm. There he watched the golden carriage till it could no longer be seen.

Poor Gerda was lonely as ever! There were ginger-nuts and sugar-biscuits and fruit in the carriage, but these could not comfort the little girl. When would she find Kay?

PART III

In a dark forest lived a band of wild robbers. Among them was an old robber-woman, with shaggy eyebrows and no teeth. She had one little daughter.

"Look! look! what is that?" cried the little robber-girl one afternoon, as something like a moving torch gleamed through the forest.

It was Gerda's golden carriage. The robbers rushed towards it, pulled the door open, and dragged out the little girl.

"How plump she is! You will taste nice, my dear," the old woman said to Gerda, as she drew out her long, sharp knife. It glittered horribly. "Now, just stand still, so, and—oh! stop, I say, stop," screamed the old woman, for at that moment her daughter sprang upon her back and bit her ear. And there she hung like some savage little animal. "Oh, my ear, my ear, you bad, wicked child!" But the woman did not now try to kill Gerda.

Then the robber-child said, "Little girl, I want you myself, and I want to ride beside you." So together they stepped into the golden carriage and drove deep into the wood. "No one will hurt you now, unless I get angry with you," said the robber-girl, putting her arm round Gerda. "Are you a Princess?"

" No," said Gerda, and she told the robber-girl all her story. " Have you seen little Kay ? " she ended.

" Never," said the robber-girl, " never." Then she looked at Gerda and added, " No one shall kill you even if I am angry with you. I shall do it myself." And she dried Gerda's eyes. " Now this is nice," and she lay back, her red hands in Gerda's warm, soft muff.

At last the carriage stopped at a robber's castle. It was a ruin. The robber-girl led Gerda into a large old hall and gave her a basin of hot soup. " You shall sleep there to-night," she said, " with me and my pets."

Gerda looked where the robber-girl pointed, and saw that in one corner of the room straw was scattered on the stone floor.

" Yes, you shall see my pets. Come, lie down now."

And little Gerda and the robber-girl lay down together on their straw bed. Above, perched on poles, were doves.

" Mine, all mine," said the little robber-girl. Jumping up, she seized the dove nearest her by the feet and shook it till its wings flapped. Then she slung it against Gerda's face. " Kiss it," she said. " Yes, all mine ; and look," she went on, " he is mine too," and she caught by the horn a reindeer that was tied to the wall. He had a bright brass collar round his neck. " We have to keep him tied, or he would run away. I tickle him every night with my sharp knife, and then he is afraid," and the girl drew from a hole in the wall a long knife, and gently ran it across the reindeer's neck. The poor animal kicked, but the little robber-girl laughed, and then again lay down on her bed of straw.

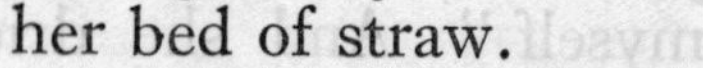

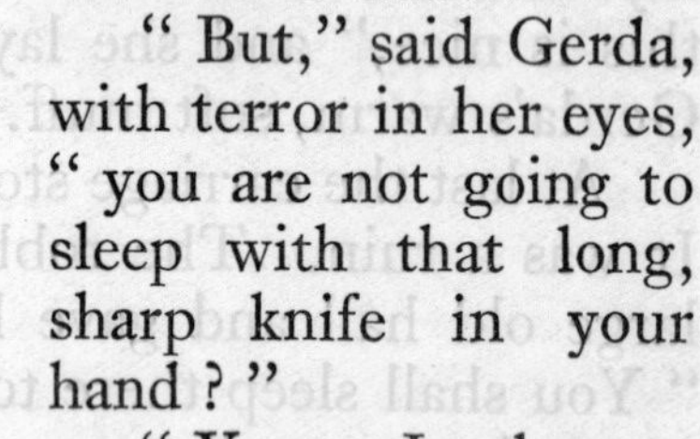

" But," said Gerda, with terror in her eyes, " you are not going to sleep with that long, sharp knife in your hand ? "

" Yes. I always do," replied the robber-girl—" one never knows what may happen. But tell me again all about Kay, and about your journey through the wide world."

And Gerda told all her story over again. Then the little robber-girl put one arm round Gerda's neck, and with her long knife in the other, she fell sound asleep.

But Gerda could not sleep. How could she, with that sharp knife close beside her ? She would try not to think of it. She would listen to the doves. " Coo, coo," they said. Then they came nearer.

"We have seen little Kay," they whispered. "He floated by above our nest in the Snow Queen's sledge. She blew upon us as she passed, and her icy breath killed many of us."

"But where was little Kay going? Where does the Snow Queen live?" asked Gerda.

"The reindeer can tell you everything," said the doves.

"Yes," said the reindeer, "I can tell you.

Little Kay was going to the Snow Queen's palace, a splendid palace of glittering ice, away in Lapland."

"Oh, Kay, little Kay," sighed Gerda.

"Lie still, or I shall stick my knife into you," said the little robber-girl.

And little Gerda lay still, but she did not sleep. In the morning she told the robber-girl what the doves and the reindeer had said.

The little robber-girl looked very solemn and

thoughtful. Then she nodded her head importantly. At last she spoke, not to Gerda, but to the reindeer.

" I should like to keep you here always, tied by your brass collar to that wall. Then I should still tickle you with my knife, and have the fun of seeing you kick and struggle. But never mind. Do you know where Lapland is ? "

Lapland ! Of course the reindeer knew. Had he not been born there ? Had he not played in its snow-covered fields ? As the reindeer thought of his happy childhood, his eyes danced.

" Would you like to go back to your old home ? " asked the robber-girl.

The reindeer leapt into the air for joy.

" Very well, I will soon untie your chain. Mother is still asleep. Come along, Gerda. Now, I am going to put this little girl on your back, and you are to carry her safely to the Snow Queen's palace. She must find her little playfellow." And the robber-girl lifted Gerda up and tied her on the reindeer's back, having first put a little cushion beneath her. " I must keep your muff, Gerda, but you can have mother's big black mittens. Come, put your hands in. Oh ! they do look ugly."

" I am going to Kay, little Kay," and Gerda cried for joy.

" There is nothing to whimper about," said the robber-girl. " Look ! here are two loaves and a ham." Then she opened wide the door, loosened the reindeer's chain, and said, "Now run."

And the reindeer darted through the open door, Gerda waving her black-mittened hands, and the little robber-girl calling after the reindeer, "Take care of my little girl."

On and on they sped, over briers and bushes, through fields and forests and swamps. The wolves howled and the ravens screamed. But Gerda was happy. She was going to Kay.

PART IV

The loaves and the ham were finished, and Gerda and the reindeer were in Lapland.

They stopped in front of a little hut. Its roof sloped down almost to the ground, and the door was so low that to get into the hut one had to creep on hands and knees. How the reindeer squeezed through I cannot tell, but there he was in the little hut, telling an old Lapp woman who was frying fish over a lamp, first his own story, and then the sad story of Gerda and little Kay.

"Oh, you poor creatures," said the Lapp woman, "the Snow Queen is not in Lapland at present. She is hundreds of miles away at her palace in Finland. But I will give you a note to a Finn woman, and she will direct you better than I can." And the Lapp woman wrote a letter on a dried fish, as she had no paper.

Then, when Gerda had warmed herself by the lamp, the Lapp woman tied her on to the reindeer again, and they squeezed through the little door and were once more out in the wide world.

On and on they sped through the long night, while the blue northern lights flickered in the sky overhead, and the crisp snow crackled beneath their feet.

At last they reached Finland and knocked on

the Finn woman's chimney, for she had no door at all. Then they squeezed down the chimney, and found themselves in a very hot little room.

The old woman at once loosened Gerda's things, and took off her mittens and boots. Then she put ice on the reindeer's head. Now that her visitors were more comfortable she could look at the letter they brought. She read it three times, and then put it in the fish-pot, for this old woman never wasted anything.

There was silence for five minutes, and then the reindeer again told his story first, and afterwards the sad story of Gerda and little Kay.

Once more there was silence for five minutes, and then the Finn woman whispered to the reindeer. This is what she whispered : "Yes, little Kay is with the Snow Queen, and thinks himself the happiest boy in the world. But that is because a little bit of the magic mirror is still in his eye, and another tiny grain remains in his heart. Until they come out, he can never be the old Kay. As long as they are there, the Snow Queen will have him in her power."

"But cannot you give Gerda power to overcome the Snow Queen ? " whispered the reindeer.

"I cannot give her greater power than she has already. Her own loving heart has won the help of bird and beast and robber-girl, and it is that loving heart that will conquer the Snow Queen. But this you can do. Carry little Gerda to the palace garden. It is only two miles from here. You will see a bush covered with red berries. Leave Gerda there, and hurry back to me."

Off sped the reindeer.

"Oh, my boots and my mittens!" cried Gerda.

But the reindeer would not stop. On he rushed through the snow until he came to the bush with the red berries. There he put Gerda down and kissed her, while tears trickled down his face. Then off he bounded, leaving the little girl standing barefoot on the crisp snow.

Gerda stepped forward. Huge snowflakes were coming to meet her. They did not fall from the sky. No, they were marching along the ground. And what strange shapes they took! Some looked like white hedgehogs, some like Polar bears. They were the Snow Queen's soldiers.

Gerda grew frightened. But she did not run away. She folded her hands and closed her eyes. "Our Father which art in Heaven," she began, but she could get no further. The cold was so great that she could not go on. She opened her eyes, and there, surrounding her, was a legion of bright little angels. They had been formed from her breath, as she prayed, "Our Father which art in Heaven." And the bright little angels shivered into a hundred pieces the snowflake army, and Gerda walked on fearlessly towards the palace of the Snow Queen.

Little Kay sits alone in the great ice hall. He

does not know that he is blue with cold, for the Snow Queen has kissed away the icy shiverings and left his heart with no more feeling than a lump of ice.

And this morning she has flown off to visit the

countries of the south, where the grapes and the lemons grow.

" It is all so blue there," she had said, " I must go and cast my veil of white across their hills and meadows." And away she flew.

So Kay sits in the great ice hall alone. Chips of ice are his only playthings, and now he leaves them on the ice floor and goes to the window to gaze at the snowdrifts in the palace garden. Great gusts of wind swirl the snow past the windows. Kay can see nothing. He turns again to his ice toys.

Outside, little Gerda struggles through the biting wind, then, saying her morning prayer, she enters the vast hall. At a glance she sees the

lonely boy. In a twinkling she knows it is Kay. Her little bare feet carry her like wings across the ice floor. Her arms are round his neck.

"Kay, dear, dear Kay!"

But Kay does not move. He is still and cold as the palace walls.

Little Gerda bursts into tears, hot, scalding tears. Her arms are yet round Kay's neck, and her tears fall upon his heart of ice. They thaw it. They reach the grain of glass, and it melts away.

And now Kay's tears fall hot and fast, and as they pour, the tiny bit of glass passes out of his eye, and he sees—he knows—his long-lost playmate.

"Little Gerda, little Gerda!" he cries, "where have you been, where have you been, where are we now?" and he shivers as he looks round the vast cold hall.

But Gerda kisses his white cheeks, and they grow rosy; she kisses his eyes, and they shine like stars; she kisses his hands and feet, and he is strong and glad.

Hand in hand they wander out of the ice palace. The winds hush, the sun bursts forth. They talk of their grandmother, of their rose trees.

The reindeer has come back, and with him there waits another reindeer. They stand by the bush with the red berries.

The children bound on to their backs, and are carried first to the hut of the Finn woman, and then on to Lapland. The Lapp woman has new clothes ready for them, and brings out her sledge. Once more Kay and Gerda are sitting side by side. The Lapp woman drives, and the two reindeer follow. On and on they speed through the white-robed land. But now they leave it behind. The earth wears her mantle of green.

" Good-bye," they say to the kind Lapp woman, " good-bye," to the gentle reindeer.

Together the children enter a forest. How strange and how sweet the song of the birds !

A young girl on horseback comes galloping towards them. She wears a scarlet cap, and has pistols in her belt. It is the robber-girl.

" So you have found little Kay."

Gerda smiles, and asks for the Prince and Princess.

" They are travelling far away."

" And the raven ? "

" Oh, the raven is dead. But tell me what you have been doing, and where you found little Kay."

The three children sit down under a fir tree, and Gerda tells of her journeys, and how at last she had found little Kay in the palace of the Snow Queen.

" Snip, snap, snorra ! " shouts the robber-girl, which is her way of saying " Hurrah ! " Then, promising that if ever she is near their town she will pay them a visit, off she gallops into the wide world.

On wander the two children, on and on. At last they see the tall towers of the old town where they had lived together. Soon they come to the narrow street they remember so well. They climb the long, long stair, and burst into the little attic.

The rose-bush is in bloom, and the sun pours in upon the old grandmother, who reads her Bible by the open window.

Kay and Gerda take their two little stools and sit down one on either side of her, and listen to the words from the Good Book. As they listen, a great peace steals into their souls.

And outside it is summer—warm, bright, beautiful summer.

THE THRUSH'S SONG

By Marjorie Christmas

Come and kiss me! Come and kiss me!
    Dō it! Dō it!
    Sēe to it! Sēe to it!
Nor rūe it—rūe it!

Sūch a pretty Dick!
    Pretty Dick! Pretty Dick!
    Pretty! Pretty! Pretty!
Be quick! Be quick!

Churl! Churl! Churl! Churl!
  Tschurl!!!—not to dō it!—
  Pōōr-y Dick! Pōōr-y Dick!
    Dō-oo-ōō it!

Kiss me! Kiss me! Kiss me! Kiss me!
    Dō it! Dō it!
    Sweet! Sweet! Sweet! Sweet!
You're thrōugh it—thrōugh it!

Pretty! Pretty! Pretty!
    Be quick! Be quick!
    Sūch a pretty Dick!
Pretty Dick! Pretty Dick!

Luck! Luck! Luck! Luck!
Luck that you dō it!
Sweet! Sweet! Sweet of you!
Swēēt it is to dō it!

Tell me that you'll marry me!
Dō it! Dō it!
Sweet! Sweet! Sweet! Sweet!
I knēw it—knēw it!

Sūch a pretty Dick!
Pretty Dick! Pretty Dick!
Pretty! Pretty! Pretty!
Be quick! Be quick!

Chuck! Chuck! Chuck! Chuck!
Chuck! Let us dō it!
Mārry me! Mārry me!
Pretty girl! Do it!

CONRAD OF THE RED TOWN

By Mrs. Alfred Baldwin

Once upon a time in a fair valley there was a town enclosed by red walls crowned by red towers. The red houses in the streets had high red-tiled roofs. The Schloss, the churches, the Rathhouse in the market-place, were built of red brick ; the fountain with the statue of the huntsman holding the red deer by the horns was carved in red stone ; and, because everything in the town was red, what better name could it have than the Red Town ?

The Red Town was in a fruitful country, watered by a broad stream, in summer drought dwindling to a silver thread that lost its way wandering in the dried-up bed of the river. Orchards and vineyards came so close to the town that the children playing on the ramparts gathered red apples from the boughs through the loopholes in the walls. They looked down on the slow oxen drawing the loaded wain from the vineyard, and saw the grapes crushed till the red juice poured out and became bright red wine. The very cows in the fields were red. The cock that crowed in the morn had a red eye and a fierce red wattle, and the good people had red cheeks, and some of them red hair, and all were proud that they were born and lived in the Red Town.

The Red Town was known by its colour from afar. Many a traveller riding up the valley after a stormy night has caught sight of the rain-washed walls shining crimson in the sunrise ; and in the evening light the Red Town glowed among the meadows like a ruby set in green enamel, so that the wayfaring stranger thought that he beheld a fairy vision and no real abode of living men.

Two gates there were to the Red Town : one in the tower to the east overlooking the cornfields, and called the Breadgate ; the other in the tower on the south overlooking the vineyards, and called the Winegate. Both gates were shut and barred at night, and the dwellers in the town slept in safety. There had been no war for some years to desolate the country, and children were growing up to the blessed heritage of peace that their fathers had fought and died to secure. Among these was young Conrad, whose father had been killed fighting on the walls of the Red Town longer ago than the boy could remember. Conrad's mother was left in poverty ; but she was young, strong, and industrious, and kept herself and her child by spinning. Her old father, a cobbler, lived with them, and between the two they earned enough money to supply the simple needs of a household that had few wants and no fancies to gratify.

They dwelt in a small red house built high on the town wall near the Winegate. The front of the house was reached by a long, straggling flight of steps, and the back had no outlet. From the leaded casements you saw the wide valley bounded by blue hills, or you could lean out of the window and look straight down the face of the red wall and the rock it was built on, to sunny vineyards below. A rusty weather-vane on the gable of the attic where Conrad slept creaked and groaned for a drop of oil that could only be taken to it by means of a long ladder, which the boy was too young and the grandfather too old to climb.

Conrad began betimes to help his mother, and when he was ten years old a farmer hired him to take care of his geese. He was a strong, merry boy, red-cheeked, blue-eyed, and sunburnt, with a thatch of yellow hair. Early every morning he drove his cackling flock before him with a willow-wand tufted with leaves to switch over them when they were silly and obstinate. On through the town he led them, out by the Winegate where old Ulrica the applewoman sat under the arch at her fruit-stall.

Conrad easily carried his light dinner in his pocket, and he stopped on his way to add to it a handful of cherries. The boy was a great favourite with the old woman, who had known him all his life, and if she could have afforded it she would never have taken money from him for anything. But she always gave him more cherries for a groschen than to any one else, and good words into the bargain. She would push the curls back from his brow, and say, "You have elf-locks, my child. Your hair grows as the fairies love it to grow. They have set their mark upon you; take care, or they will steal you away. Remember, you are only safe so long as you neither eat nor drink anything they offer you. If you eat a morsel of their food or drink a drop of their wine you give yourself to the fairies, and they will take you away."

The boy laughed and shook his yellow locks, and said, "How can I eat their food or drink their wine, grandmother, when I have never even seen a fairy?" and he switched his roving geese into a flock before him, cackling like the women at their cottage doors on a summer evening when the day's work is done.

Conrad was a clever little gooseherd. He knew where to find sweet, short grass, or the clean water for his birds to drink, and in autumn he led them to the stubble-fields. He took great pride in his work, and wore a long white goose-quill in his cap that every one might see he was a gooseherd.

Neither Conrad, his mother, nor his grandfather could read. The only book they had seen was the big Bible chained to the desk, that the priest read from in the church. They were obliged to remember what they had heard, and their minds were stored with tales and legends and wise sayings handed down from generation to generation.

One winter evening, while the widow was spinning busily, and Conrad was preparing goose-feathers for the arrow makers, and the cat sat thrumming a song of her own invention, the grandfather told them wonderful stories as he mended a huntsman's boot. Old Ulrica was with them, seated in the most comfortable chair, sharing the warmth and candlelight, and without asking their leave she threw fresh logs on the fire, which she was loath to do in her own hut. Now, the applewoman could tell even stranger and

longer stories than the cobbler, and she was a very impatient listener. So, when he came to that part of his story where the Prince smites off the dragon's head, and red roses sprang up wherever a drop of the dragon's blood fell, she said, " Yes, yes, that is all very well ; but now I want you to listen to a true story. And true I know it is, because I had it from my great-grandmother, and she had it from her great-grandmother."

" And she had it from the father of lies ! " shouted the cobbler, for nothing made him so angry as to be interrupted by the applewoman.

When peace was restored the grandfather began his story over again from the beginning. After he had finished the old woman had her turn, and if the cobbler interrupted her she too went back to the beginning of all things, so that Conrad learned many wonderful tales by heart. The grandfather's stories were about witches and dragons, war and pestilence, and Conrad liked them be cause they made him shudder. The

old applewoman's stories were of fairies and elves that danced in rings by summer moonlight on the grass, of changelings and dwarfs, of weird and pretty things that graved themselves deep in the boy's mind.

One story of old Ulrica's annoyed the grandfather exceedingly, and he bet a pound of cobbler's wax it wasn't true. Neither did it please Conrad's mother ; but that was because it frightened her. She thought it might really have happened. The applewoman said that two hundred years ago, here in the Red Town, the fairies had stolen a beautiful boy of Conrad's age, and carried him away. They offered the child fairy-food to eat, and no sooner had he swallowed it than he forgot home and parents, and followed the Little People out of the Winegate into the country to a green hill where the fairies danced by moonlight. The boy joined in the dance, and when the moon had set and all was dark, just before dawn the hillside opened, and there came out sweet music and a brilliant light. The dancers trooped into the opening, the hillside closed upon them, and neither boy nor fairies were ever seen again. The green hill stood to this day to witness whether or not her story was true. But the worst of it was that the applewoman said that the Little People stole a child out of the Red Town every two hundred years. Let Conrad be on his guard, for his hair grew in elf-locks such as the fairies loved. They must never say she had not warned them.

Winter wore itself away, and bright spring came at last. Conrad was up at break of day to drive his cackling long-necked flock through the Winegate into the country. With his dinner in his pocket, and the white goose-quill stuck in his cap, he sang and whistled gaily as he led his birds to find the short grass and to drink from the clear pool. But wherever he went he looked for traces of the Little People ; nor was it long before he found what he sought. One day when he had driven his geese hissing and stumbling farther than usual, they all fell asleep in the hot sunshine, with their heads tucked under their white wings. Conrad left them for a little, while he wandered about the fields gathering wild flowers. To his surprise, he came upon a large circle of grass of darker green than the rest of the meadow, and he

knew it for one of the " fairy rings " Ulrica had told him about. It marked the spot where the fairies danced by moonlight, and he might hope soon to see the fairies themselves.

That night, when the geese were safe in the farmer's barn, Conrad's mother and grandfather asleep in their beds, and the gates of the Red Town shut and bolted, the boy let himself down with a rope from his attic window. He alighted in the boughs of an apple tree, and was soon on the ground, where he took to his heels across the open country. Conrad had never before been out so late, and he was astonished to find how many creatures were awake in the dead of night. The air was full of the buzz of busy insects : a little rabbit with long ears and white scut bounded across the path, wood-pigeons cooed softly, grass-hoppers chirped and leapt, the nightingale poured out her song, and the owl cried *tewit*, *tewoo*.

When Conrad reached the meadow where the fairy rings grew, the silvery moon shone bright as day. He hid himself in a great wild rose bush, and, peeping out from the thorny, sweet-smelling branches, beheld the very sight he longed to see. On the green turf a great circle of tiny creatures were dancing hand in hand, swaying to and fro with shrill laughter, capering and throwing up their heels to the sound of merry music that came from an invisible source. The tallest of the Little People did not come up to Conrad's knee. They were perfectly formed little men ; there was not a woman elf among them. They were inexpressibly nimble and neat in their close-fitting garments, and each wore on his head a little peaked cap with a feather in it. Their small faces between lank locks of dark hair looked old and cunning, their voices were high and thin, and they spoke in rhyme instead of prose. All that Ulrica had told Conrad was true. Without doubt these were the Little People.

Conrad was not afraid, but overawed, so that he neither moved nor spoke. His eyes were fixed on the antic dancers ; he followed their every movement with breathless attention. Just then a thin cloud veiled the moon, and he no longer saw clearly light, capering heels and nodding peaked caps ; and one of the elves sang shrilly :

> " Brother, brother, much I fear,
> Mortal eyes are peeping here ! "

And another answered him :

"Twice a hundred years have passed
Since mortal eye beheld us last!"

Then a clear, sweet sound was heard from far away, and all the little dancers sang:

"Oh, these are elfin horns that blow,
And when they call us hence we go!
When elfin horns blow clear and sweet
We must haste with nimble feet."

Moonlight once more flooded the meadow, but it shone only on grass and wild flowers; the Little People were gone. Conrad sprang from the wild rose bush into the open field, where a moment before the merry elves had danced, and he was the only living creature there. Back to the Red Town he ran, climbed into the apple tree, up the rope to his attic window, and was soon asleep, dreaming he heard the blowing of elfin horns from over the hills and far away.

Night after night, when the moon shone, Conrad went secretly to watch the Little People dance, till he grew pale for want of sleep, and his mother thought that he was ill. He was late in driving the geese out in the morning, and the farmer complained that he was getting lazy, and threatened if he did not mend his ways to put another gooseherd in his place. But neither tears nor threats availed. Conrad grew more and more dreamy. He heard the horns of elfland blowing night and day, and cared for nothing but to watch the tiny dancers circling hand in hand over the fields in the pale moonlight.

The Little People were uneasily conscious that mortal eyes were fixed upon them in their wild gambols. One night when they were merrier than ever, Conrad laughed outright at their antics, and they saw his pale face peering from behind the trunk of an oak. Instantly each tiny elf dropped his brother's hand. The great ring broke up into a scattered throng of shrill-tongued mites that swarmed about him thick as bees. Conrad tried to run away, but his feet were rooted to the ground. He tried to speak, but he could not, for his mouth was dry. The crowd of elves seethed round him, filling the air with the thin clamour of their voices. One of their number pointed at Conrad with a lean yellow finger, and said :

" Tell us, mortal, by what right
You have watched us dance to-night ? "

And Conrad confessed that he had no right to be there. Curiosity had brought him, and he begged forgiveness if he had unwittingly offended.

The elf replied :

" We do not forgive so fast,
Nor do we overlook the past ;
Those who pry and those who prowl
Must be beaten till they howl."

And hundreds of tiny hands dealt Conrad stinging

blows about his feet and legs till he cried out with pain, and the Little People laughed with glee.

Then the elf said :

> " By elfin law you ought to die,
> Thus we punish those who pry.
> Death is certainly your due ;
> But, as mortal days are few,
> Live your life out to its span,
> From boy to youth, from youth to man.
> And remember to the end,
> Never, never more offend !
> Since by stealth you've seen the elves,
> We must mark you for ourselves ! "

Instantly a nimble little man ran like a cat up Conrad's side and perched on his shoulder. He seized a lock of the boy's yellow hair, and ran a tight knot in it that neither tooth nor nail could undo. A shrill laugh rose from the Little People ; the elf climbed down from Conrad's shoulder as nimbly as he had mounted, and they seemed to forget all about him.

Once more they joined hand in hand and spun round in giddy rings upon the grass, casting wild shadows in the moonlight as they danced, singing :

> " Before the acorn held the oak
> We fairies were an ancient folk.
> Before the hills and forests grew
> We danced on grass and quaffed the dew.
> Before the hare fled from the hound
> The meadow was our dancing-ground.
> Before the hunter led the chase
> The fairies were an ancient race."

Then the elf who was spokesman for them pointed at the moon, and said :

> " Brothers, hasten ; we must fly !
> The moon is sinking in the sky !
> Here we may no longer wait.
> Conrad follows soon or late."

And the elves were gone. The boy rubbed his eyes, but could not see how they had gone.

When Conrad ran back to the Red Town, and clambered up into his room, he tried hard to undo the knot the elves had tied in his hair. The more he pulled it the tighter it became. Nothing would stir it. It was on the side of his head where his cap would not hide it, and even the boy saw that it gave him an uncanny look. His mother and grandfather cried out at his pale face with dark rings round his eyes, and wild, knotted hair, and tried to comb it out, but in vain.

They sent for the old applewoman to give her opinion, for they were aware that this was no ordinary case. When she saw Conrad's hair she struck her hands together in dismay. " These be elf-locks as sure as my name's Ulrica and I sell apples eight for a groschen under the Winegate. Boy, what have you done that the elves have set their mark upon you ? Quick, give me the scissors ! I will cut out the knot, breathe on it three times, and cast it over my left shoulder into the fire before any evil happens to the child."

But the scissors were powerless. Snip and snap as the old woman would, she could not cut Conrad's hair. His mother tried with no more effect ; and, lastly, the grandfather brought the sharp shears that he cut shoe-leather with, and said, " I warrant these will cut off little boys' hair and their naughty little heads too ! " But

Conrad's yellow hair was like wire. It turned the edge of the shears, and that was all that happened ; the knot was firmer than ever. Then Conrad's mother began to abuse old Ulrica, and said all the trouble came of the silly tales about fairies and elves she had told the boy. Ulrica scolded back again, and the grandfather railed at both ; and while the three squabbled, the cause of the dispute slipped unnoticed out of the house.

Conrad soon discovered that the elf-knot tied in his yellow locks was no badge of disgrace, but a mark of favour. The Little People often met him now by daylight without waiting for the moon to shine, and helped him in his work. When his geese were troublesome and took to wandering, the elves ran after them, and mounting on their backs, brought them to him again in a flock. And one windy night, when Conrad could not sleep for the groaning and creaking of the rusty weather-vane above his attic window, he saw in the moonlight a tiny man dressed all in green astride the gilded arrow. When a gust of wind twirled it round with a harsh noise, the elf dropped oil on the rusty iron till it worked silently and smoothly, and coughed a little thin cough at his own cleverness.

When Conrad slept late in the morning, tired with watching the moonlight dancing, the elves sent his cackling flock in time to meet him at the Winegate, so that he might not get into trouble with his master. The Little People showed their goodwill in many ways, and they once brought fairy fruit to refresh him when he was hot and weary. But luckily he remembered Ulrica's warning, and though he was much tempted, he refused to eat.

One bright summer's day a wonderful thing happened in the Red Town. A shining youth clad in white-and-gold, riding a white horse richly caparisoned, and carrying a silver trumpet in his hand, rode slowly under the Breadgate, through the Schloss Street into the market-place. All who saw the glorious stranger felt compelled to follow him in the hope of learning who he was and what was his business in the Red Town. Men, women, and children gathered about him; and aged folk and cripples joined the increasing throng that filled the streets. They moved in silence, overawed by the brilliant stranger, who neither spoke nor looked to right or left. When he reached the market-place he drew up his white horse before the Town Hall, facing the coppersmiths' and potters' booths, put his silver trumpet to his lips, and sounded three blasts.

It was a wonderful trumpet: not very loud, yet it was heard in every corner of the town, and rang through every street and house. It woke from sleep every sick person and little child, and thrilled the ears of the deaf. When they heard it the whole town felt that something wonderful was about to happen, and the market-place was soon thronged from end to end. Then the magnificent trumpeter spoke, and each listened as though his life depended on what he heard. These were his words:

"Good people of the Red Town! I have come from afar to tell you that early to-morrow morning a great and wonderful procession will pass through your streets, entering the town by the Breadgate, and leaving it by the Winegate. In the market-place there will be seats where you will sit to watch your uninvited guests pass by. It will be useless to ask whence they come or whither they go. Enough that you will witness a pageant such as you have never seen before, and will never again see in the Red Town."

The trumpeter turned his white horse about, and walking at a foot's pace through the silent, wondering crowd, left the town by the gate opposite to that by which he entered. Beyond the Winegate all trace of the beautiful stranger was lost. If all had not either seen or heard the mysterious trumpeter, they would have thought both visit and proclamation a dream; and a great clack of tongues rose in the crowd after the unaccountable silence that had restrained them in his presence.

When Conrad came home in the evening his mother and grandfather told him all that had happened while he was abroad with his geese. The old applewoman, too, had seen the wonderful stranger, and did not hesitate to say that he had come from the Fairy Court.

This, however, the grandfather would not allow, and for this reason: they knew very well that the Grand Duke of Schwartwurst had long had a grudge against their town, and it was evident that he had laid a trap to cast ridicule upon it by trying to bring a gaping crowd together to make fools of them all. The Duke's trumpeter no doubt was a splendid youth royally clad ; but fine feathers make fine birds. And as to seats in the market-place, who was going to put them up ? he should like to know. It was some scandalous hoax of the Duke's, and they ought not to have let the trumpeter go away unquestioned. The old man forgot that he had been one of the crowd, and was as unable to speak as the rest. "No fooling shall take me abroad to-morrow, early or late," said he. "You can go if you like, and get laughed at for your pains. I shall stick to my last !"

Conrad could not sleep for thinking of the strange trumpeter, and wondering what the morrow would bring forth. He would have been surprised had he known that he was the only human creature awake that night. For deep sleep had fallen on the inhabitants of the Red Town. From the Burgomaster himself to the blind beggar in the front of the church, from the wearied old man to the teething baby, all slept as quietly in their beds as their forefathers in their graves. But when Conrad in his restlessness looked out of a front window of the house, the narrow street below was thronged with the Little People hurrying to and fro ; and a sound of hammering came from the market-place as of many carpenters hard at work. Though Conrad was the only person awake to feel it, there was an indescribable sense of stir and expectancy in the air. At last he, too, fell asleep, with his head resting on his arm on the window-sill.

Very early in the morning Conrad and every other sleeper in the Red Town were waked by the ringing and pealing of bells. The bells of the Town Hall, the bells of the Schloss Tower, and the church bells were clanging, tolling, and chiming ; nor could they tell who rang them, for no order had been given that the town should be waked in this way. Conrad looked out of the casement, his mother and grandfather looked out of theirs, and as far as he could see down the street, night-capped heads were stretched out of every window. The morning sun shone from a cloudless sky ; birds flew to and fro, scared by the clamour of the bells ; banners floated on the high houses, and the road was covered with freshly mown grass. A great deal of work had been done during the night, and preparations made for a grand pageant.

Conrad's grandfather was as much excited as any one else. He forgot all that he had been so sure about the day before, and in a few minutes he and his daughter and grandson were hastening with crowds of fellow townsmen to the market-place. And what a sight met their eyes ! The whole wide place decorated with green boughs and banners ; seats rising one above another half-way up the houses, ready to be filled with spectators ;

and the open spaces grass-strewn and kept clear for the procession. None knew by whose hands the town had been transformed in the short summer night. The people were sure that the strange words of the trumpeter were about to come true, and they were too much bent on seeing the great sight to stop to ask questions that no one was able to answer.

Soon every seat in the stands, gay with fir branches and flowers, was filled, and the footpaths thronged with sightseers, while the bells overhead still chimed and tolled. Conrad, his mother and his grandfather, and the old applewoman, stood on the kerbstone dumb with amazement at the changed aspect of the market-place. The old cobbler put on his spectacles, for, though he said there would be nothing to see, he was determined to see it, and be able to contradict any foolish stories that might be told about it afterwards.

Every dweller in the Red Town not bedridden was now in the streets. Mothers carried their babies in their arms, and fathers held their little ones on their shoulders so that they might look over the heads of the crowd. No one was left behind, no one stayed indoors even to kindle the morning fire, and no cheerful smoke rose from the red chimneys. All eyes were turned towards the Breadgate. A tall stranger clad in green drew back the bolts and opened the wide doors to the east, and the sunshine streamed through the great arch under the tower on the grass-strewn way.

The trumpeter of yesterday, in gold-and-white, was the first to enter the Red Town. Behind him on the winding road, far as the eye could reach, stretched a glittering procession of glorious beings —some walking, some riding, and all in shining raiment. He sounded a fanfare on his silver trumpet that mingled with the tolling and chiming of bells. By his side, holding his stirrup, ran a little withered goblin chuckling to himself with silent glee. After him followed groups of maidens wreathed with flowers, singing sweetly in a foreign tongue, and no man knew the words they sang. Behind them, in a silver car, came Oberon and Titania, King and Queen of the Fairies, and Titania's veil fell about her clear and bright as moonbeams. Sprightly Ariel floated lightly by them, and merry Puck flung up his heels in the fresh-strewn grass underfoot. Sprites and elves and fairies innumerable followed the King and Queen, some riding on hedgehogs and squirrels, some in tiny cars drawn by fluttering doves.

Not far behind the brilliant group a distinguished figure was seen and greeted with delighted recognition by old and young, and cries of "Puss in Boots!" rent the air. A magnificent tortoise-shell cat majestically walking on his hind legs, with tail waving courteously, advanced, hat in hand, bowing acknowledgments to right and left.

The Marquis of Carabas accompanied him, and Dick Whittington followed, carrying his favourite cat in his arms. But none of them attracted so much attention as gallant Puss in Boots, who looked and behaved as if the whole pageant had been devised in his honour.

Presently Hänsel and Grethel drew all eyes towards them. They were crumbling their bread and dropping it as they walked, for a clue to lead them through the forest home again. Behind them toddled the Babes in the Wood hand in hand, and beside them hopped pious Robin Redbreasts who were soon to bury them under the fallen leaves. At sight of the little wanderers, and thinking of the wicked uncle of the pretty Babes, the women in the crowd

cried and held their children closer. But before their tears were dry they were laughing at the pious Robins pecking and eating up the guiding crumbs as fast as Hänsel and Grethel dropped them.

Next came Cinderella, bright and beautiful, the Prince carrying the glass slipper ; and her Stepsisters, ugly as they were bad-tempered, stalked after her. Then followed, for contrast, the sweet little sisters, Snow-White and Rose-Red, dancing along, each clinging to the furry arm of the kind and smiling Bear. Behind them hastened along the old Witch clutching the cage with Jorindel in it, whom she had by her evil art changed into a bird. She was closely

pressed by Jorind, who sought to disenchant his love and restore her to her natural form. The Witch was hissed by the crowd, and stones were thrown. Red Riding-Hood then came tripping along with the fierce-eyed Wolf that pretended to be her Grandmother, and cries were heard of "Oh, the cruel brute!"

Storms of cheers burst forth when Beauty and the excellent Beast walked past together. Then followed the Dwarf Brothers with Snow-White in her glass coffin, to whom the wicked Stepmother gave the poisoned apple. The Sleeping Beauty was then borne past, and after her came Rapunzel with her wonderful hair hanging down and carried behind her like a train by a couple of pages. Then followed a homely group that was greeted with broad smiles, Little Rumpelstiltskin stamping with rage because they had guessed his name; and the King and Queen and fat nurse carrying the royal baby, all laughing at the dwarf's impotent rage.

Next came Tom Thumb riding gallantly on mouseback, and every one said how lucky it was the cats went first in the procession, where they could neither see nor smell the saddled and bridled mouse. Towering above Tom Thumb followed Jack, bearing a branch of the Beanstalk taller than himself, and close to him the fair Sister with the Enchanted Brothers. Next after them came singing past a delightful company of lucky younger sons, light of heart and light of purse, with a heritage of courage and good humour that overcame ill-fortune everywhere. After them came stupid and sullen giants of many lands—Cornish, Welsh, and German, walking heavily, and shaking the ground as they trod.

All, all were there : fairies, dwarfs, elves, and sprites, heroes and heroines of the wondrous tales handed down from generation to generation! Old men and women felt themselves once more little children at their mothers' knees as they saw their earliest friends troop past them, and they searched with dim eyes to find their young parents among the motley throng.

None noted how time was passing. The sun was high in the heavens, and still the enchanting procession went on its way with floating banners and silvery clash of music. Conrad's mother was crying, and said, as she grasped her boy's hand, "Ah, what a world is this! To think that I should see Cinderella alive and well, while my sweet young mother who first told me of her lies in the churchyard!"

"Hey! what is that you say?" said the old cobbler. "What are you grumbling about? Haven't you got me? Haven't you got an old father alive?" And he took off his spectacles and rubbed them bright on his leather apron.

Conrad had watched the marvellous sight with breathless interest. Several times, without knowing what he was doing, he had leapt on the grass-strewn road as though he were about to join the procession, and had been pulled back again to the kerbstone by his mother and the applewoman. Some of the Little People, as they passed by, pointed at the knot in his yellow locks, and threw in his face handfuls of rose leaves, which faded to nothing as they touched his cheek. Among the elves he recognized many whom he had seen dancing in the meadows in rings by moonlight, and they nodded and beckoned and called him by his name.

Just then a beautiful Fairy Prince, on a milk-white horse and clad in silver armour, rode in among the elves, carrying in his hand a golden dish of ripe, many-coloured fruit. He looked at Conrad, who was hot and thirsty with standing in the sunshine, and threw him a juicy red strawberry. The boy caught it and ate it greedily. The instant he tasted it he forgot his mother, his grandfather, his home, his flock of geese, and, drawn by a power he could not resist, shook himself free and rushed into the procession among the elves. They laughed shrilly. The Fairy Prince leaned down towards Conrad, took him by the hand, bade him mount by his foot, and in a moment had him before him on his horse.

The boy's mother and the old applewoman shrieked, and the grandfather called, "Conrad! Conrad!" But he never turned his head. He neither knew nor heeded their voices. The pageant was now at an end, and the long procession swept through the Winegate into the country. Elfin horns began to blow, and Conrad's heart answered to the sound as an elf's heart answers. For human love was dead in him, and he did not know his own home when he rode past with the Fairy Prince, eating fairy fruit from his golden dish.

A great crowd out of the Red Town followed, shouting and crying, " Stop ! stop ! Give us back Conrad ! Give us back Conrad, the poor widow's son ! " But ever swifter rode the Fairy Prince towards the green hill whence elfin horns rang loud and clear. They could not overtake him, and stopped, panting and crying, on the road, Conrad's mother among them distraught with grief.

Then they saw from afar the green hill open wide, and a bright light stream forth, and into it the glittering procession trooped to a sound of wild music. The last sight they beheld was Conrad standing high on the Fairy Prince's saddle-bow waving his arms above his head. Then the light went out, the music ceased, the hill closed its green gates upon them all, and Conrad was lost for ever.

THE STOLEN CHILD

By W. B. Yeats

Where dips the rocky highland
Of Sleuth Wood in the lake,
There lies a leafy island
Where flapping herons wake
The drowsy water-rats ;
There we've hid our faery vats,
Full of berries,
And of reddest stolen cherries.
Come away, O human child !
To the waters and the wild
With a faery, hand in hand,
For the world's more full of weeping than you can understand.

Where the wave of moonlight glosses
The dim grey sands with light,
Far off by farthest Rosses
We foot it all the night,
Weaving olden dances,
Mingling hands and mingling glances
Till the moon has taken flight ;
To and fro we leap
And chase the frothy bubbles,
While the world is full of troubles
And is anxious in its sleep.

Come away, O human child !
To the waters and the wild
With a faery, hand in hand,
For the world's more full of weeping than you can
understand.

Where the wandering water gushes
From the hills above Glen-Car,
In pools among the rushes
That scarce could bathe a star,
We seek for slumbering trout,
And whispering in their ears
Give them unquiet dreams ;
Leaning softly out
From ferns that drop their tears
Over the young streams.
Come away, O human child !
To the waters and the wild
With a faery, hand in hand,
For the world's more full of weeping than you can
understand.

Away with us he's going,
The solemn-eyed :
He'll hear no more the lowing
Of the calves on the warm hillside ;
Or the kettle on the hob
Sing peace into his breast,
Or see the brown mice bob
Round and round the oatmeal-chest.

For he comes, the human child,
To the waters and the wild
With a faery, hand in hand,
From a world more full of weeping than he can
understand.

ON THE LAWN

By Hugh Chesterman

The play takes place on a lawn in front of a castle, seven hundred years ago. The carpet will serve for a lawn, and the castle can be cut out of paper and pinned on a blue " back cloth " stretched on string across the stage.

The players are Alys, Giles, and Joan, four Crusaders—Sir Rollo, Sir Tabarie, Sir Duffy, Sir Dinadan, and four Turks—Harum, Scarum, Higgledi, Piggledi. When the curtain goes up, Alys and Giles are playing cat's cradle, and Joan is reading. The children are any age you please, but certainly not older than ten.

Alys. Twist and turn, turn and twist,
Spread your fingers, and bend your wrist ;
Why, every time we play, I vow
I have to stop and show you how.

Giles. I'm tired of this, a stupid game,
Whatever you do, it comes the same.

Joan. What are we going to do instead ?
It's an hour before we go to bed ;
Think of something really exciting,
Like ghosts, or magic, or

Giles. Battles and fighting,
Proud princesses, and conquering kings.

Alys. Nice little girls don't do such things.

Giles. You a princess, and I a knight
On a prancing steed with a helmet bright.

Alys. From dawn to dusk we'd ride together,
We wouldn't be stopped by wind or weather.

Giles. We'd gallop for miles, and miles, and miles,
And visit the far-away sunset isles.

Alys. The Lady Alys

Giles. And fair Sir Giles,
Spelt with a very big capital " G."

Joan. Sh ! Somebody's coming, now who can it be ?

[*Enter Four Crusaders. They have white surcoats, helmets, and swords, and ride hobby-horses. The last one carries a drum instead of a sword, and as they march round the stage he beats a steady rat-a-plan in time to their step. After marching twice round the stage, they line up at the back. As each Crusader says his lines, the drummer continues to beat on his drum.*]

Alys. Oh, please, kind stranger, stop your drum,
And tell us your names, and why you've come.

Sir Duffy. I'm a Crusader, the gay Sir Duffy,
Spick and span ;
I'm a terrible fellow when I get huffy.
Rat-a-plan, rat-a-plan.

Sir Rollo. I am Sir Rollo, a rollicking rover
Since Time began ;

I go crusading all the world over.
Rat-a-plan, rat-a-plan.

Sir Tabarie. I am Sir Tabarie, born and bred
Of a fighting clan;
If any one's rude to me—off goes his head.
Rat-a-plan, rat-a-plan.

Alys. You all look very pretty, and I like your rat-a-plan,
But oh, where are you going, pray tell us if you can?

Song of the Crusaders

Alys. Oh, where are you going, Sir Rollo and Sir Tabarie,

Sir Duffy and Sir Dinadan ?
You four proud men,

Giles. With your battle-cries and banners,
And your high and mighty manners,
Pray tell me, tell me, tell me, will you ride this way again ?

Sir Tabarie and Sir Rollo. We are going far away, said Tabarie and Rollo,
To the dry and dreary deserts
And the pestilential plain ;

Sir Duffy and Sir Dinadan. We're off to kill the Turcoman,
Said Duffy and Sir Dinadan,
So follow, follow, follow, for we'll soon be back again.

Alys and Giles. No, I will never follow you,
Sir Rollo and Sir Tabarie,
Sir Duffy and Sir Dinadan,
You four fond men.
For the desert will dismay you,
And the Turcoman will slay you,
And it's never, never, never that you'll ride this way again.

[*When the song is over, the Four Crusaders gallop round the stage again, and then ride away. The children watch them till they are out of sight.*]

Alys. Oh, how their swords and helmets shone.
There they go riding, on and on !

Giles. Oh dear, I rather wish we'd gone.

[*When the last hoof-beat has died away they*

return rather sadly to their cat's cradle. They have hardly begun their game when a new sound of galloping is heard. The children drop their string and stand together in a corner of the stage as the Four Turks enter. The Turks wear baggy trousers and turbans. They carry long spears, and ride "hobby-horse" camels.]

Alys. Why, goodness me, here come some more.
Look, these are Turks ; one, two, three, four.

[*The Turks ride round the stage, and then line up at the back, in the same way as the Crusaders did. They introduce themselves*.]

Higgledi. *My* name is Higgledi, a sleek and swarthy Saracen,
This is my camel, a beast beyond comparison.

Piggledi. *My* name is Piggledi, I'm polished and I'm proud,

The tallest of the spearmen in all the Paynim crowd.

Harum. I'm known as Harum, if you cross me you'll regret it.

Scarum. And *my* name is Scarum—and please don't forget it !

Desert Song of the Saracens

Higgledi. Over the desert sands we ride,
Follow my leader, or side by side ;
We take no notice of time or tide,
Clippety, clippety, clopp.

Piggledi. We gallop all day, o'er vale and hill,
Up or down, whichever you will ;
When the sun goes down we're galloping still,
Clippety, clippety, clopp.

Harum. And should we meet crusading men,
It's ten to one—or one to ten,
That we shall harry those gentlemen,
Clippety, clippety, clopp.

Scarum. Our camels are swift and their legs are strong,
And we turn them round when they go wrong ;
And we always sing as we gallop along,
Clippety, clippety, clopp.

[*When the song is over the Four Turks stand quite still. Giles goes up and prods each of them with his finger. As he does so, each Turk answers by striking a grotesque and fantastic attitude.*]

Alys. Oh, aren't they fun ! I do like Turks,
Giles. You press the knob and the figure works ;
But where, good sirs, are you off to, pray ?
Tell us what brings you here to-day.
Higgledi. We're on the track of some proud Crusaders,
Piggledi. Pigs and pirates,
Harum. Rogues and
Scarum. Raiders.
Higgledi. We heard they'd passed this way just now,
And we want to know why, and when, and how.
No fibs, please. That we can't allow.
Alys. Of course you can't, now, let me see ;
Four Crusaders [or was it three ?]
Passed this way before you came in,
With rattle and bang, and dust and din.
They didn't stop long, a minute, not more,
And that's the way they went, I'm sure.
[*Pointing in the opposite direction.*]
Higgledi. We'll follow them hard with bit and spur ;
Thank you, lady, and thank you, sir.
[*The Turks ride away.*]
Giles. Surely, Alys, the way you showed
The Turks just now was a different road ?
Why did you send them out that way ?
Poor little Turks, they're all astray.
Alys. I liked those gay crusading men,
They looked so pretty and sang so sweet.

I'd hate to think [and so would you]
Of what might happen if they should meet.
If stupid people *must* fall out,
And go to war with each other, for shame,
When neither side know what it's all about,
Cat's cradle's a much more sensible game.

[*Alys picks up the string and begins to twist it round her fingers.*]

CURTAIN

THE JELLY-FISH TAKES A JOURNEY

A Japanese Fairy Tale

By Grace James

Once upon a time the jelly-fish was a very handsome fellow. His form was beautiful, and round as the full moon. He had glittering scales and fins and a tail as other fishes have, but he had more than these. He had little feet as well, so that he could walk upon the land as well as swim in the sea. He was merry and he was gay, he was beloved and trusted of the Dragon King. In spite of all this, his grandmother always said he would come to a bad end, because he would not mind his books at school. She was right. It all came about in this wise.

The Dragon King was but lately wed when the young Lady Dragon, his wife, fell very sick. She took to her bed and stayed there, and wise folk in Dragonland shook their heads and said her last day was at hand. Doctors came from far and near, and they dosed her and they bled her, but no good at all could they do her, the poor young thing, nor recover her of her sickness.

The Dragon King was beside himself.

" Heart's Desire," he said to his pale bride, " I would give my life for you."

"Little good would it do me," she answered. "Howbeit, if you will fetch me a monkey's liver, I will eat it and live."

"A monkey's liver!" cried the Dragon King. "A monkey's liver! You talk wildly, O light of mine eyes. How shall I find a monkey's liver? Know you not, sweet one, that monkeys dwell in the trees of the forest, whilst we are in the deep sea?"

Tears ran down the Dragon Queen's lovely countenance.

"If I do not have the monkey's liver, I shall die," she said.

Then the Dragon went forth and called to him the jelly-fish.

"The Queen must have a monkey's liver," he said, "to cure her of her sickness."

"What will she do with the monkey's liver?" asked the jelly-fish.

"Why, she will eat it," said the Dragon King.

"Oh!" said the jelly-fish.

"Now," said the King, "you must go and fetch me a live monkey. I have heard that they dwell in the tall trees of the forest. Therefore swim quickly, O jelly-fish, and bring a monkey with you back again."

"How will I get the monkey to come back with me?" said the jelly-fish.

"Tell him of all the beauties and pleasures of Dragonland. Tell him he will be happy here, and that he may play with mermaids all the day long."

"Well," said the jelly-fish, "I'll tell him that."

Off set the jelly-fish; and he swam and he swam, till at last he reached the shore where grew the tall trees of the forest. And, sure enough, there was a monkey sitting in the branches of a persimmon tree, eating persimmons.

"The very thing," said the jelly-fish to himself; "I'm in luck."

"Noble monkey," he said, "will you come to Dragonland with me?"

"How should I get there?" said the monkey.

"Only sit on my back," said the jelly-fish, "and I'll take you there; you'll have no trouble at all."

"Why should I go there, after all?" said the monkey. "I am very well off as I am."

"Ah," said the jelly-fish, "it's plain that you know little of all the beauties and pleasures of Dragonland. There you will be happy as the day is long. You will win great riches and honour. Besides, you may play with the mermaids from morn till eve."

"I'll come," said the monkey.

And he slipped down from the persimmon tree and jumped on the jelly-fish's back.

When the two of them were about half-way over to Dragonland, the jelly-fish laughed.

"Now, jelly-fish, why do you laugh?"

"I laugh for joy," said the jelly-fish. "When you come to Dragonland, my master, the Dragon King, will get your liver, and give it to my mistress, the Dragon Queen, to eat, and then she will recover from her sickness."

"My liver?" said the monkey.

"Why, of course," said the jelly-fish.

"Alas and alack," cried the monkey, "I'm grieved indeed, but if it's my liver you're wanting I haven't it with me. To tell you the truth, it weighs pretty heavy, so I just took it out and hung it upon a branch of that persimmon tree where you found me. Quick, quick, let's go back for it."

Back they went, and the monkey was up in the persimmon tree in a twinkling.

"Mercy me, I don't see it at all," he said.

" Where can I have mislaid it ? I should not be surprised if some rascal has stolen it," he said.

Now if the jelly-fish had minded his books at school, would he have been hoodwinked by the monkey ? You may believe not. But his grandmother always said he would come to a bad end.

" I shall be some time finding it," said the monkey. " You'd best be getting home to Dragonland. The King would be loath for you to be out after dark. You can call for me another day. *Sayonara.*"

The monkey and the jelly-fish parted on the best of terms.

The minute the Dragon King set eyes on the jelly-fish, " Where's the monkey ? " he said.

" I'm to call for him another day," said the jelly-fish. And he told all the tale.

The Dragon King flew into a towering rage. He called his executioners and bid them beat the jelly-fish.

" Break every bone in his body," he cried ; " beat him to a jelly."

Alas for the sad fate of the jelly-fish ! Jelly he remains to this very day.

As for the young Dragon Queen, she was fain to laugh when she heard the story.

" If I can't have a monkey's liver I must needs do without it," she said. " Give me my best brocade gown and I will get up, for I feel a good deal better."

THE MAGIC ROOM

By Irene Thompson

There's a room at the top of our
house,
But it isn't a room to me;
It's an island surrounded with
palms
And a whispering sea.

There's a room at the top of our
house,
But it isn't a room to me;
It's a palace where I live alone,
With a magical key.

There's a room at the top of our house,
But it isn't a room at all;
It's a cavern where treasures are kept
In a wonderful wall.

There's a room at the top of our house,
But it isn't really a room;
It's a castle built on a rock
Where the billows boom.

There's a room at the top of our
house,
But it isn't a room
to me;
It is just whatever I
choose.
So it's magic, you
see.

THE LADY OF THE PYRAMIDS

By E. D. Hancock

I

Once upon a time there lived in Egypt a beautiful lady who wore a pair of jewelled sandals. Red rubies were set in the heels of the sandals, and little blue stones shone at the edge of the soft leather soles.

The pointed toes were spangled with all the colours of the rainbow, and diamonds sparkled in the fine straps that fastened them.

No one else in all Egypt had such brightly jewelled sandals; and the lady often wore them as she walked through the garden of the palace in which she lived.

Rhodopis was this lady's name, and many people had heard of her; for it was said that not only did she wear jewelled sandals, but she was the most beautiful lady in Egypt. And yet few people had seen her, for she lived in a palace that was hidden behind a high stone wall.

Rhodopis, though rich and beautiful, was very shy, and she disliked to feel that strangers in the street were staring at her lovely face. She seldom left her palace, and only walked in the palace garden in the early morning and in the evening time, when no passers-by were standing at the gateway, staring into the garden.

The people outside the palace could only listen to what the slave girls had to tell; for they looked in vain through the gates, and no one could see over the high walls.

The slave girls said that Rhodopis was always beautiful, but that she looked loveliest in the early morning. Every morning, as the sun was rising, Rhodopis went into her garden to bathe in a pool of crystal water. She wore her jewelled sandals then, and she gathered flowers as she walked, so that she might scatter their petals on the water.

II

One morning Rhodopis went as usual to bathe in her garden pool. The sunlight was spreading across the sky, and in every corner of the garden birds were singing happily.

When Rhodopis came to the edge of the water, it looked so cool that she slipped her feet from her pretty sandals and stepped down into the pool.

But whilst she was in the water the birds changed their pretty songs to little frightened calls. Then they were quiet, and a shadow passed over the garden. In the sky overhead a great eagle was flying.

The beat of its long heavy wings sounded in the morning stillness, and when the huge bird hovered in the air without moving, there was a strange and sudden silence in the garden.

The eagle was looking for food, and the birds were almost dead with fright, lest the eagle should spy their bright feathers and snatch them from their hiding. The eagle spread its strong wings and rested in the air, looking sharply to the ground.

Suddenly it caught sight of the bright, jewelled sandals, and swooped down over the garden. It snatched at the jewels, and flew up into the air again, carrying one of the sandals in its great claws.

Higher and higher the eagle flew until it could no longer be seen, and Rhodopis had lost one of her beautiful shoes.

The eagle flew swiftly, and was soon a long distance away from the garden of Rhodopis, but still it carried the bright sandal in its claws. It flew over desert sand, and over the blue water of the river Nile, until it reached a great city.

This was the city of Memphis, where Pharaoh,

the King of Egypt, held his court; and when he judged his people he sat on a throne in a great open space, so that crowds might gather round to listen to his commands.

By this time the eagle had found out that the brightest things are not always best to eat, and it dropped the sandal, which fell away through the air, the bird knew not, and cared not, where.

III

Pharaoh was speaking in his court one day. He was sitting on his throne, and all the people who stood near were looking towards the king and listening. No one saw a great bird fly overhead.

Suddenly something fell through the air into Pharaoh's lap. The king's eyes opened wide with surprise, for on his lap lay a jewelled sandal. He picked it up, and looked at it closely.

There were rubies in the heel, and blue stones shone at the edge of the leather sole. The toe was spangled with all the colours of the rainbow, and diamonds sparkled in the fine leather strap, which was unfastened.

Pharaoh turned the sandal in his hand and looked at all the bright gems. He thought how beautiful it was; and he wondered if the lady who had worn it was beautiful too. He wanted to know to whom it belonged.

Then Pharaoh spoke again. He stood in front of his throne, holding the sandal in his hand.

" The lady who wore this sandal shall be found,

and he who finds her shall be given a rich reward. Search the cities of Egypt until a lady is found who can show you another sandal such as this, and whose foot is small enough to wear it. Great honour shall be paid to her if she will come to Memphis."

IV

Pharaoh's messengers went out to all the cities of the Nile. They carried the sparkling sandal, and they read the king's message so that all might hear.

Many beautiful Egyptian ladies came to claim the pretty thing, and some, who had heard what it was like, tried to bring another to match it.

But when they were asked to try on the shoe that the messengers carried, they were sent away; for the sandal always proved to be too small.

At last the messengers arrived at the city called Naukratis, where Rhodopis lived in the palace hidden behind a high stone wall. They read Pharaoh's message, but it seemed as though there was no lady in this city who could wear the sandal.

But soon an old woman, wrinkled and bent, came to the chief of the king's messengers. He laughed when he saw this old woman making her way through the rich ladies who had been trying to push the sandal on to their slender feet. He thought she had come to try the sandal on her own foot.

"Ha! Ha! Is the foot of an old woman likely to fit this pretty thing?" he said. And the people round laughed too.

"It is not to try on the sandal that I have come," said the old woman, "but to ask for the king's reward."

"Why! This old woman thinks she knows where we must search for the lady who wears the sandal," laughed the messengers.

"Do not laugh at an old woman's wisdom," she said, "but go to the house of the lady Rhodopis and ask her to try it on."

"The lady Rhodopis! Who is she?" asked the messengers.

"She is the most beautiful lady in Egypt," said the old woman, "but few have ever seen her beauty, for she seldom leaves the palace where she lives."

"Where does she live?" said the chief messenger. "Tell us, that we may go to her at once."

"Her palace is hidden by a high stone wall, and stands alone on the river bank on the north side of the town."

V

The messengers hurried through the town. They found a high stone wall, and through the gateway they caught sight of a beautiful garden. But the gate was fastened, and the king's messengers had to wait until the servants of this beautiful lady would come to answer their call.

"Is this the palace of the lady Rhodopis?" they called.

A servant came quietly to the gateway.

"My mistress is the beautiful lady Rhodopis," said the servant, "but no visitors are allowed to enter her palace unless she has invited them to come."

"Tell her," said the messengers, "that we are come from Pharaoh."

The servant bowed and went to seek his mistress.

Rhodopis was more than a little surprised to hear that Pharaoh's messengers were standing at her palace gateway.

"What can the mighty Pharaoh want with me?" she said. "Would that I dared to send his messengers away! But since I dare not do that, they must come before me and deliver their message."

So the royal messengers were allowed to enter the palace of Rhodopis, and they bowed before her, and waited until she spoke.

"My servant tells me that you bring word to me from the mighty Pharaoh. What message can the great ruler have for me?"

For answer, the chief messenger read Pharaoh's promise that he would for ever honour the lady whose foot would fit the jewelled sandal that was being carried through all the cities of Egypt.

When the messenger had finished reading he showed Rhodopis a glittering sandal, and she smiled, a beautiful, happy smile. The messenger knelt before Rhodopis, and begged that she would try on the sandal. She took the jewelled shoe from his hand, and bending down, she slipped it on to her foot. It fitted perfectly and exactly. It was not too small, and the strap fastened round her ankle. The messenger cried with delight: "It fits! See, the jewelled sandal fits. Our search is ended."

Then Rhodopis turned to a small chest, and from it she took another sandal which she put on her other foot. The messengers were amazed and

delighted; for this was the companion to the sandal they had carried through Egypt at the command of Pharaoh, in their search for the lady to whom it belonged.

Then the chief messenger spoke again to Rhodopis, saying, "It is the wish of the great Pharaoh that the lady who wears the jewelled sandals shall return with us to the royal city."

And Rhodopis, shy and beautiful, answered, "The word of Pharaoh must be obeyed."

So the next day Rhodopis left her palace and travelled to Memphis, and when she reached the royal city she wore her jewelled sandals.

Pharaoh looked from her twinkling shoes to her lovely face, and he loved the lady Rhodopis for her beauty. He made her his queen, so that she might live always in the royal city ; and when a bent old woman travelled to Memphis to claim a reward from Pharaoh, she was given a bag of gold, enough to make her rich for the rest of her life.

Pharaoh had promised great honour to the lady of the jewelled sandals, and to Rhodopis he gave all that a queen could desire.

As long as she lived, Rhodopis was beautiful, and when she died she was carried into the silence of one of the great pyramids.

Pharaoh had ordered his slaves to build this great tomb for his queen who wore jewelled sandals, and who was the loveliest lady in the land of Egypt.

MEG MERRILIES

By John Keats

Old Meg she was a gipsy,
  And lived upon the moors;
Her bed it was the brown heath turf,
  And her house was out of doors.
Her apples were swart blackberries,
  Her currants pods o' broom;
Her wine was dew of the wild white rose,
  Her book a churchyard tomb.

Her brothers were the craggy hills,
  Her sisters larchen trees;

Alone with her great family
  She lived as she did please.
No breakfast had she many a morn,
  No dinner many a noon,
And, 'stead of supper she would stare
  Full hard against the moon.

But every morn of woodbine fresh
  She made her garlanding,
And every night the dark glen yew
  She wove, and she would sing.
And with her fingers old and brown
  She plaited mats of rushes,
And gave them to the cottagers
  She met among the bushes.

Old Meg was brave as Margaret Queen,
  And tall as Amazon,
An old red blanket cloak she wore,
  A chip-hat had she on;
God rest her aged bones somewhere!
  She died full long agone.

STORIES OF ST. FRANCIS

By A. M. Ramsay and M. R. Keary

I

Of the Early Life of St. Francis, and how he left it

In the land of Italy there stands a little town on the top of a steep hill, called the town of Assisi. In this little town, seven hundred years ago, there lived a well-to-do cloth merchant who had a son named Francis—a handsome, dark-haired, dark-eyed boy, very full of gaiety and high spirit, yet very loving and gentle, not only to his father and mother and his little sisters and brothers, but also to all birds and animals. Everybody liked him for his bright face and merry ways, and the good temper and politeness he always showed. He was very fond of singing, too, and the neighbours used to hear him, and say, "There goes that boy of the cloth merchant's, bless him! He sings as sweetly as an angel."

He was just the same when he grew up to be a young man—merry and gay, full of laughter, delighting in fun, but always good tempered and kind, and as fond of singing as ever. In the earlier part of the day he used to help his father in the shop, but in the evenings, when the stalls in the market-place were closed, Francis could go and amuse himself as he liked.

Although he was so gay, Francis never joined in anything bad, or harmed any one. If at any time one of the others proposed anything that he thought was wrong, he did not " preach " about it, but would just say, " Oh no, don't let us do that," or, " I don't think that would really be very good fun," and as he was the leader the rest did just what he suggested. What they liked best was to go and have their supper together somewhere, and then, if it was a fine night (and most nights were fine in Italy), go out and wander about through the town, singing songs. They used to make a great many of these songs themselves, both words and tunes, but none of them could do this so well as Francis.

Well, this was the sort of life Francis used to lead until he was grown up, and then he fell ill. It was a very bad illness, and lasted a long, long time ; and even when it was over, poor Francis was so weak that he could not go about with his friends as he used to, nor even help his father in the shop, but had to keep still, lying on his bed in the house or sitting outside in the sunshine. He had nothing to do, and in those days there were hardly any books to be had. And it was very,

very dull. " Oh, how miserable it is to be ill ! " he said to himself, " and not to be able to go about and do things and enjoy yourself any more ! "

Now one day, when Francis was well enough to walk about just a little, his father had helped him along to the market-place, where there were many people going about, and it was not so dull as sitting at home alone, and Francis was sitting there in a comfortable seat in front of the stall where his father's goods were laid out for sale, and watching the people go to and fro, when he saw an ugly old beggar-man go past. This beggar-man was not only old and ugly and dirty, and dressed in miserable rags, but he was also a cripple, and could only just drag himself along on crutches, very slowly. Francis had always been sorry for beggars before, but now, quite suddenly, the thought came into his mind, " If it is so wretched to be weak and ill for a few weeks, how perfectly dreadful it must be to be a poor cripple like that always ! " And he said to himself, " I never really thought about it before, but now, when I get well again, I will try to do something for other people who are sick and in misery."

Time passed on, and Francis grew well and strong again. His friends were all delighted, and began planning all sorts of gaiety and fun. Every day they had something new to suggest, and the time was so full that Francis forgot about the resolve he had made the day he saw the poor cripple. So he lived the old life again, just as before he was ill, except that now he did not really enjoy it so much as he used to ; for often and often it would come into his mind, " How many poor people there are, who are ill and sick now, as I was ! " And the thought of them spoiled his pleasure. But he laughed and talked more, and sang louder, and spent more money on fine clothes, and tried to make himself think that he was enjoying it all as much as ever.

At last there came a day of days, when some of the others had planned a very special party, to which, of course, Francis must go, for was he not the chief of them all ? First of all they had a particularly fine supper. The room was lit up with many bright lights, and the dishes on the table were of silver, and there was red wine and yellow wine sparkling and foaming in the silver cups. Francis was made to sit in a special chair at the end of the table, and they crowned him king of the feast with a crown of red roses. And they ate and drank, and laughed and talked and sang songs till it was late in the evening and most people had gone to bed. And Francis and his friends were just thinking it was time they went home to bed too, when one of them, who had gone to the window to look out, said, " Comrades, the night is fine and not dark, for though there is no moon the stars are very bright. Let us take a walk before we go home."

On this they all tumbled down the stairs anyhow, laughing and shouting, into the narrow, dark street. One of them struck up a merry song, and the others joined in, and they set off down the street, singing at the top of their voices.

But one of them did not go with the others. Francis had clattered down the stair as noisily as any of them, but when he came out from the hot, brightly-lit room into the cool, fresh air and the quiet night, he suddenly stopped short. His friends, not seeing in the dark that he was not with them, went on down the street and left him alone. Francis stood where they had left him, silent ; he looked up to the sky above the tall black houses, and there was no moon there, but the sky was the very darkest blue, almost black, and thousands and thousands of stars were looking down at him with their bright eyes. There was not a sound anywhere except the singing of his friends, growing fainter in the distance ; the very houses around seemed asleep. And Francis looked up at the stars, and the stars seemed to say to him, " Francis, Francis, have you forgotten all the poor people who are sick and in misery, while you are living in luxury, wearing fine clothes, while they are in rags, and spending your money on gorgeous feasts, while they have hardly enough to buy a crust of bread ? "

So Francis stood in silence, while the silent stars above seemed to speak to him. How long he stood there he did not know. But after a while he heard the noise of feet on the stones, and the voices of his friends—they had found he was not among them and had come back to look for him. " Where are you, Francis ? " they called to him. " Come, king of the feast, why are you standing there ? Are you dreaming ? We can't do without you ! "

Francis, indeed, both looked and felt as if he were dreaming, and the voices of his comrades had just wakened him. He could not go with them and join in their merry singing—he wanted to get away by himself and think. " I am very sorry," he said, " but I do not think I can come any farther to-night. Do you others go on, and I will go home quietly. And here I resign my crown as king of the feast," and he took off the crown of red roses with which they had crowned him king, and put it on the head of one of his friends. They could not quite make out what was the matter with him. So they went with him to the door of his father's house, and said good-night to him, and then went off to their own homes, for they did not care to go singing through the town without him. And this was the last supper that Francis and his friends had together.

II

How Francis met with the Leper

From that night when the stars spoke to him, Francis was quite changed from what he had been. He worked much harder to help his father than before, and was as kind and gentle as ever; but he who had been so merry and light-hearted, singing gaily wherever he went, now became sad and silent.

He gave up going to parties, or out for rides with his friends, and when he went out he would go long walks by himself. And all the time he was alone he would be praying to God silently in his heart to help him to do what was right; or thinking of Jesus Christ, how when He was on earth He healed the sick, and cared for the poor, and had told those who followed Him to do the same. And the more Francis thought about it, the more wonderful it seemed to him that Jesus should have been filled with such pity and gentleness and love for all poor suffering people, and the more he longed to help them, as Jesus had done, and to be like Him. So, instead of spending his money on fine clothes or parties, Francis began to give it all away to beggars and poor folk, or to people who were ill and had no one to look after them.

In those days there was a very dreadful disease which used to attack many people, called leprosy. Those who took it hardly ever recovered; but it was a slow, wasting disease, that did not kill them quickly, but often allowed them to live for many years, growing more and more ill and miserable. One of the worst things about this terrible disease was that it made people most hideous and loathsome to look at, and, moreover, it was infectious. So nobody would go near any one who had it, but the lepers, as they were called, were driven away even by their own relations, and hated and shunned. They sometimes wandered about the country, finding shelter wherever they could, in ruined and deserted buildings, or in woods or caves, and keeping alive with difficulty on berries and roots, and on what they could get by begging. And sometimes they were put, a great many of them together, into places called leper-houses, or lazar-houses.

Now, when Francis began to visit the sick, while he was kind to all others and generous in giving to them, he could not bear to go near the lepers. They were so hideous to look upon, and their disease was so loathsome, that the very thought of them made him shudder; and he felt that if his very life depended upon it he could not touch or even speak to one of them.

Meanwhile, he still continued to work and help his father, the cloth merchant. Now one day his father had some business to be done with a man who lived in another little town, on a hill at the other side of the valley, and thinking that it would do Francis good to have a ride, he asked him to go across to this town and do the business for him. Francis was quite willing to go ; he rode away down the street and out through the gate of Assisi, and down the steep stony road that led down to the valley ; and he rode across the valley on a level road between pleasant green fields, away to the other town, where he did his father's business. When that was over, he started to come home again.

He was riding along the level part of the road enjoying the sunshine and the green of the grass and the shade of the trees, and listening to the birds singing, and feeling not quite so unhappy as usual, when he heard a miserable voice crying out, " Sir, sir ! " Francis looked, and there, by the roadside, he saw a wretched leper, hideous to see, and clad in filthy rags, who was stretching out his hand and begging for money, saying he had had nothing to eat since two days before, and had not a farthing to buy food. Francis was filled with horror at the sight of him, and almost put spurs to his horse to ride on quickly and leave him. Then he thought how cruel that would be, and he took his purse from his pocket and was going to fling some money to the beggar without going near him ; but even as he put his hand into the purse to take the money out, the thought came into his mind: "Is not this poor wretch my brother? Certainly it is not because I am such a very good man that I am well and sound, while he is a leper. Why, then, should I shudder at him because he has suffered such a cruel misfortune? I ought rather to pity him the more." And he remembered, too, how it is told in the Bible that Jesus did not shrink from the lepers when He met them, but healed them and made them well. And when Francis remembered that, he said to himself, "If I wish to be truly a follower of Jesus Christ, I must first overcome myself." So he dismounted from his horse, and with his own hand put the money into the hand of the leper, saying, "Here, brother, take this." And he kissed the beggar's hand as he placed the money in it. Then he mounted his horse and rode on again; but before he had gone far he looked back, and lo! the beggar was nowhere to be seen! There was the long, white, dusty road stretching across the valley, and the green fields on either side, and nowhere where the beggar could possibly have hidden himself. Yet the road and the fields were empty—the beggar was gone! And suddenly all the unhappiness left Francis, and he was filled with wonder and joy and peace, for he knew that the leper was no leper, but that Christ Himself had come in the shape of the leper to beg from him by the roadside.

So Francis left Assisi, and began to go about through all the countryside, to preach the peace of God among men. Everywhere he went on foot, taking no money with him, nor any provision for the journey. He wore the simplest dress—just a plain greyish-brown gown, with a hood, and a rough cord round his waist, and his feet were bare. So sweet and kind was his face, and so gentle his words, that no one could see and speak to him without becoming his friend, and wherever he went people welcomed him. His fame spread abroad through the whole of Italy, and people began to call him "Saint Francis."

III

How St. Francis loved all Living Creatures, and how he tamed a Fierce Wolf

Now you have heard already that Francis, from the time he was a little boy, was very fond of all

animals and birds ; and after he had left his father's house and begun to wander about, he grew to love them still more, and he used to call them his little brothers and sisters. And he had a wonderful power over them all, as people sometimes have who love animals very much, for the animals seem to know it, and trust them. So the wild rabbits, who are so frightened of people and dart away whenever they see them, were not a bit afraid of Francis, but would scamper round him, and even let him stroke them. And when he whistled to the birds on the trees they would fly down to him and sit on his finger or his shoulder, and eat crumbs out of his hand. And no dog, however bad-tempered and fierce, was ever known to snap at him.

It was not only gentle creatures, like the birds, that loved and obeyed St. Francis, but fierce, wild, cruel beasts also. You must know that at that time in Italy, especially among the hills and in lonely places, there were terrible wolves, that used to come down from their haunts and terrify people, and carry off sheep, and do dreadful damage. And it happened that at one time, while St. Francis was staying for a while in a certain town, just such a wolf appeared in the neighbourhood. He was of enormous size, and the fiercest and boldest wolf that had ever been known there; for not only did he attack the farms and carry off lambs and sheep, to devour them in his den, but he even came quite close to the walls of the town, and fell upon travellers and slew them. And as for children, if any of them strayed away a little from their homes to play in the fields or pick flowers or wild berries, they never came back again, for the terrible wolf was always on the watch to seize and devour them. Not even a grown-up strong man could defend himself against the wolf if he was alone. They got up parties to go and hunt him with dogs, but the fierce wolf made them flee in terror, and slew many, both of the dogs and of the huntsmen. At last things had come to such a pass that the people scarcely dared to stir beyond the gates of the city, and if any one had to go outside, he would get a number of others to keep him company, and they went armed with swords and knives and spears, as if they were soldiers going to fight a battle.

Now, St. Francis thought to himself, "I cannot remain quiet and let this dreadful beast terrify every one, and carry off and devour the lambs and the children as he chooses." And he said to the people, "I will go out against this beast, and try to subdue him." At this they all cried out that it was impossible, he must not go, for the wolf was afraid of nothing, and even St. Francis could not subdue him, but would be slain and devoured. But at last, when they saw his mind was made up, they began to think, "The saint is so holy and wise that perhaps he will be able to drive the wolf away, or, at any rate, the wolf will not harm him, for all animals love him." So St. Francis started out, with a great crowd accompanying him as far as the gates of the town; there the people stopped, but stood at the gate and round about it to watch him, praying that he might come back again in safety.

The wolf had his den some distance away from the town, in a thick wood, and the saint took his way towards this place. A few men, braver than the rest, had come with him from the town ; but when they drew near the wood, even their courage failed them, and they hung back, and St. Francis went on alone. Presently he saw the wolf slinking

along among the trees, and soon he came out into the open. He was a huge beast, as big as a small pony, with a thick, shaggy grey coat, and glaring red bloodshot eyes. He had his mouth open, so that Francis could see his fierce white teeth, like a dog's, but much longer and sharper. And he licked his jaws with his long red tongue, as he thought of the feast he expected to have ; for he was even fiercer and hungrier than usual, because the people had of late kept themselves and their sheep and cattle so carefully shut up that he had not been able to get as much food as he wanted.

He came trotting smoothly and easily towards the saint, his soft paws, like a dog's, making no noise on the ground, intending to get quite near and then make a sudden swift leap upon his prey. And he looked so cruel and wicked that Francis could not help shrinking a little ; but he said to himself, " Are not all living creatures my brothers and sisters ? I love them all, and would not harm them, and why should they wish to harm me ? God will take care of me and protect me against this wolf if he tries to hurt me." And he walked on steadily. At this the wolf was much surprised, for he was accustomed to seeing people turn and fly whenever he came in sight, and he did not know what to make of this man, who came quietly to meet him instead of running away. And he stopped, and looked sideways at Francis. Then Francis called to him gently, " Brother wolf, I have not come to hurt you, but to speak with you quietly." And his voice was so kind and friendly that the wolf came a little nearer, and let Francis come close up to him, and stroke his head and scratch his ears ; and then, quite suddenly, the great wolf lay down on the ground, and rolled over on his side, just as a dog might do, and, stretching out his head, began to lick the saint's foot with his hot, red tongue.

Francis stooped down and patted him again, and said, " Ah, brother wolf, you have done much harm and evil here. You deserve to be hanged as a robber and a wicked murderer, and all the country folk hate you and cry out against you. But I wish, brother wolf, to make peace between you and them; so if you will not do them any more harm, they will forgive the evil you have done, and not hate you any longer or try to kill you."

Then the wolf stood up and wagged his tail, and rubbed his head against Francis's knee, to show he understood, and his eyes were not fierce and bloodshot any longer, but gentle and kind, like a dog's. And Francis said, "Brother wolf, since you are willing to agree to this peace, and keep it, I promise you I will see to it that the people of the town shall always give you food, for I know it was through hunger that you did so much wickedness. But if I gain this favour for you, you must promise me that you will never again harm either man or beast."

The wolf wagged his tail again, and rubbed his head against Francis as before.

"Now, brother wolf," said Francis, "give me a sign that you will keep this promise." And as he held out his right hand to the wolf, the wolf lifted up his right fore-paw and put it in Francis's hand, thus giving the best sign of good faith that he was able. Then said the saint, "Brother wolf, I bid you now, in the name of Jesus Christ, come back to the town with me, fearing nothing, and we will make this peace with the people."

Francis's companions had been watching all this from a distance, scarcely able to believe their eyes. And when they all got back to the town, with the fierce wolf trotting quietly along beside Francis like a big dog, the townspeople could hardly speak for wonder and admiration. The news spread through the town in no time, and all the people—men, women, and children, rushed to the market-place to see St. Francis and the wolf. And Francis stood up in the midst of them, with his hand on the head of the wolf, and said, " Listen to me, my brothers: brother wolf, who stands here before you, has promised me faithfully that he will make peace with you, and never do you any harm, if you will promise to give him food every day. And I will be surety for him that he will keep this promise he has made." Then all the people together cried out that they would give the wolf food every day.

Then said St. Francis to the wolf before them all, " And you, brother wolf, will you promise me to keep this peace, and do no harm to man or beast or any living creature?" And, as before, the wolf wagged his tail and rubbed his head against Francis's knee. "Now, brother wolf," said Francis, "I wish you now to give me a sign that you will keep this promise, here before all the people, as you gave it to me outside the town." And when he had said that, the wolf immediately lifted his right fore-paw and placed it in Francis's hand.

Then all the people, who were watching in amazement, shouted aloud, thanking Francis and giving praise to God, who had sent the saint to save them from the jaws of the cruel beast. And after that the wolf lived until his death in the town, and went about like a dog, from door to door, and in and out of the houses, never doing any harm to any one. The people fed him gladly and kindly, and the children played with him and rode on his back, and all the dogs knew him and never barked at him. And when at last he died of old age, all the people grieved for him for a long time.

The taming of this fierce wolf was only one of many wonderful things that St. Francis did. For many years he went about in Italy, teaching the people everywhere to be good and gentle, and to care nothing for riches or power or great possessions, but only to love God and help and be kind to one another. And he set them the example, so that his name and his goodness have always been remembered ever since.

THE PEDLAR'S CARAVAN

By W. B. Rands

I wish I lived in a caravan,
With a horse to drive, like a pedlar-man!
Where he comes from nobody knows,
Or where he goes to, but on he goes!

His caravan has windows two,
And a chimney of tin, that the smoke comes
through;
He has a wife, with a baby brown,
And they go riding from town to town.

Chairs to mend, and delf to sell !
He clashes the basins like a bell ;
Tea-trays, baskets ranged in order,
Plates, with alphabets round the border !

The roads are brown, and the sea is green,
But his house is like a bathing-machine ;
The world is round, and he can ride,
Rumble and slash, to the other side !

With the pedlar-man I should like to roam,
And write a book when I came home ;
All the people would read my book,
Just like the Travels of Captain Cook !

THINGS I'D LIKE TO DO

By Enid Blyton

I'd like to drive an omnibus,
And be conductor too;
I'd like to feed the elephants
That live up at the Zoo.

I'd like to keep a grocer's shop,
It has such lovely smells;
I'd like to go to early church
And help to ring the bells.

I'd like to use the garden hose
And wash the garage down;
I'd like a circus for my own,
I'd *love* a funny clown.

I'd like to be a policeman and
Make all the traffic stop;
I'd like to press the fuchsia buds,
And make them all go pop!

I'd go on wanting all these things
Till I'm grown up like you;
And then when I do what I like
I'll make them all come true!

By Hans Andersen

No one in the whole world knows so many stories as Ole Luk-Oie; yes, he is a master in story-telling.

As soon as it begins to grow dark and the children are sitting quietly in their little chairs, Ole Luk-Oie comes.

He comes up the stairs without the slightest noise, for he walks in his stockings only; gently he opens the door, and throws sand into the children's eyes. It is fine, fine sand, and there is so much of it that they can keep their eyes open no longer, and therefore they cannot see him. He steals close behind them, and as soon as his warm breath touches the backs of their necks their heads become heavy and sink forward.

But it does not hurt them—oh no!—for the good Ole Luk-Oie only plays that joke upon them for their good.

He only wishes them to be quiet, and it is best for them to be taken to bed. He wants them to be silent in order to tell them stories in peace as he sits on their beds after they are asleep.

Ole Luk-Oie's dress is very strange. His coat, rather like a loose tunic, is of a rich silk ; but no one can say what colour it is, for it is green, red, or blue, according to the way the gentleman turns.

He carries two umbrellas, one under each arm. One of these umbrellas is lined with the most beautiful pictures, and this he holds over the good children, so that during the whole night they dream the most delightful stories. In the other there is nothing whatever to be seen, and that he opens over the thoughtless children who do not deserve to be told pleasant stories.

Now we shall see how Ole Luk-Oie, during six nights, all in one week, came to a little Danish boy whose name was Hjalmar, which you must sound like Yalmar ; and you shall hear also what he told him.

Monday

" Now, pay attention," Ole Luk-Oie said at night, after he had covered Hjalmar up warm in his soft bed, " for I will show you something worth looking at."

Suddenly all the little plants in the china flower-pots grew to large trees, which spread out their long branches across the walls of the room, forming a leafy dome at the top, so that it looked like a beautiful greenhouse.

The branches were thickly covered with flowers and buds, and each of the thousands of flowers was more beautiful and sweeter than a rose. The fruits themselves shone like pure gold, and altogether it was a scene of great splendour.

Nor was there any want of the most delicious cakes and tartlets, so full of jam that they could scarcely contain it. But at that moment there arose a dreadful moaning in the table-drawer where Hjalmar's school-books were kept.

"What can that be?" said Ole Luk-Oie, going up to the noisy table and pulling out the creaking drawer. The moaning came from a slate, set in a wooden frame, with metal corners, for a wrong figure had got into the sum, which was just about to fall to pieces.

The hopping and jumping of the slate-pencil, fastened with a piece of string to the frame, were truly deafening. You see it was trying with all its might to correct the mistake in the sum.

Then Hjalmar's copy-book began to complain so bitterly that it was quite painful to listen to it. At the beginning of each line, all the way down the leaves, was written a capital letter of the alphabet, and a small letter next to it.

After these came some strange scratches, which Hjalmar had thought were copies of the other letters. They were all falling, head first, over the lines, which were meant for them to stand upon.

"Look, this is the way you should hold your-

selves," the good letters cried. "Look here, in this manner, with a graceful bend to one side."

"We would like to do so," Hjalmar's letters said; "but we cannot, we are so badly made."

"You must feel the edge of the knife then," said Ole Luk-Oie, holding up his finger.

"Oh no!" they cried; and they stood upon the line so straight that it was now quite a pleasure to look at them.

"There will be no stories to-night," said Ole Luk-Oie, "for I must drill these crazy letters. One, two!" and he drilled them until they stood as well as only the best writing-master could make them. But when he had gone, and Hjalmar looked at them in the morning, they were as bad as ever. Oh dear me!

Tuesday

As soon as Hjalmar was in bed Ole Luk-Oie touched the pieces of furniture, and all began to chatter, each about itself.

Over the chest of drawers there hung a large painting in a gilt frame. It showed high old trees, flowers in the grass, and a large river, which wound round the wood, past several castles, till it was lost in the wild, raging sea.

Ole Luk-Oie only gently touched the picture, and the birds in it began to sing ; the branches of the trees moved, set in motion by the wind ; and the flight of the clouds was seen, for their shadows could be seen gliding across the ground.

Ole Luk-Oie now held Hjalmar up towards the frame. Hjalmar put out one leg into the painting, right into the grass, and there he stood.

The sun shone through the fresh green leaves, as if smiling upon him. He ran down to the water, and seated himself in a little red-and-white boat which lay there as if waiting for him.

The sails shone like silver, and six swans, each with a gold crown on its neck, and a bright blue star on its head, drew the boat past the green forests.

The most beautiful fish, with scales like gold and silver, swam after the boat. Now and again one would jump into the air, and then go splash into the water again. Birds, blue and red, large and small, followed in two long rows.

That was indeed a joyous trip along the flowing stream. At one time the forests were thick and dark, then bright with sunshine and flowers, and to the right and left were palaces of glass and marble.

Lovely princesses leaned over the gilt railings

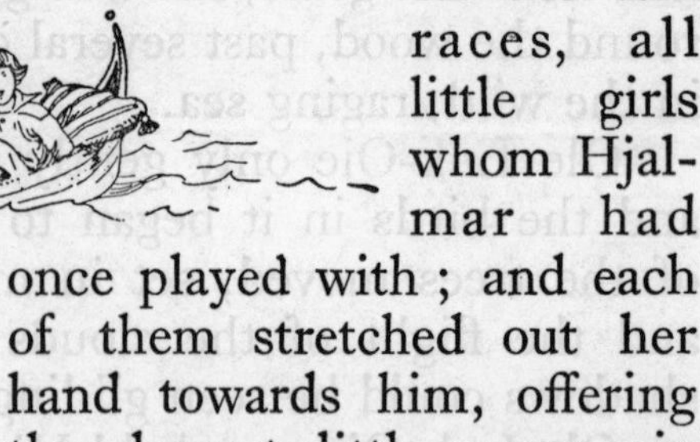

on the terraces, all little girls whom Hjalmar had once played with ; and each of them stretched out her hand towards him, offering the dearest little sugar pig that any confectioner ever sold.

As he sailed past, Hjalmar would lay hold of one end of a pig, whilst the princess held tight hold of the other, so that when it broke each had a piece ; but Hjalmar had the larger.

By the side of each palace little princes kept watch with gold swords, and threw down showers of figs and tin soldiers.

Now he passed through forests, and then, as it were, through large rooms of royal cities, till he came to the village where his kind nurse lived. She nodded and sang to him ; and all the birds sang too, the flowers nodded on their stalks, and the old trees nodded, as if Ole Luk-Oie had been telling them these stories.

Wednesday

The rain came down heavily just as Hjalmar was falling to sleep. Then it seemed as if the whole town was one big lake, and when Ole Luk-Oie opened the window a fine ship lay close to the house where the little boy's parents lived.

"Will you sail with me, little Hjalmar?" Ole Luk-Oie asked. "You can visit far distant lands during this night, and be back in time for school to-morrow morning."

All at once Hjalmar stood upon the deck of the vessel, the rain left off, and the sky became clear. Quickly they sped on, through straight and crooked streets, and turned round to the left of the church. Then there was nothing to be seen but the wild sea, with waves and foam.

They had long lost sight of land, when they saw above them, in the air, a body of long-legged storks, who came from their distant home, bound for a warmer country.

One stork flew after the other, in a close line, and one of them was now so tired that his wings could scarcely carry him any farther.

He was last in the row, and he fell farther and farther behind, at the same time sinking lower and lower. At last his feet touched the ropes of the ship, and, shaking with fear, he slid down the sail, till, plump, he stood upon the deck.

He was caught by the ship-boy, who put him into the chicken-house with the chickens, geese, and ducks. The poor stork did not know how he ought to behave, and the other birds left him neither peace nor time to make up his mind.

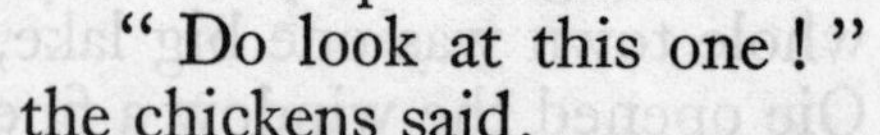

"Do look at this one!" the chickens said.

The proud cock, making himself as tall as he could, like a policeman, asked the new-comer who and what he really was. The ducks waddled backwards and, knocking against each other, cried, "Be quick! be quick! will you?"

Then the stork told them about hot Africa, and of the ostrich that races across the desert like a wild horse; but the ducks did not know what he said, and cried, "We are all agreed that the new-comer is stupid."

"Yes, he is stupid—as stupid as an owl!" the cock cried in his shrill voice. "Stupid, stupid, stupid!"

Then the stork was quite silent and thought of his dear Africa.

"What thin legs you have!" cackled a fat goose; "how much are they a yard?"

"Quack! quack! quack!" cried the ducks.

But the stork pretended not to hear.

"You may as well laugh with the rest, Mister Longleg," the goose said, "for that was a very good joke; but perhaps it was too low for such a high gentleman! Cackle! cackle! cackle!" and the ducks joined in, "Quack! quack! quack!"

But Hjalmar, who liked the stork, made an attack upon the chicken-house and set it free.

The stork, hearing himself called by name, hopped joyfully on to the deck, spread out his wings, and flew away, nodding to his little friend, as if to thank him for his help.

He flew off to a warmer country, where he, no doubt, hoped shortly to be married to a young lady of the same old noble race.

The ducks continued to "quack," the geese to "cackle," and the cock crowed so loudly that his comb was as red as fire.

"To-morrow we will make soup of you, you stupid birds!" Hjalmar said, and spoke so loudly that his own voice awoke him. Only half awake, he rubbed his eyes as he lay in his soft, warm bed, when the church clock struck seven: and at eight o'clock exactly he had to be in school, so he had not much time to waste.

It was certainly a wonderful voyage Ole Luk-Oie had taken him that night. Hjalmar wished he could go again on such a journey. But Ole Luk-Oie never tells the same story twice. He always has something quite new to tell the children. Perhaps you have noticed this for yourselves.

Thursday

" Do you know what is here ? " said Ole Luk-Oie ; " but do not be afraid, you shall now see a little mouse."

He stretched out his hand, in which he held the pretty creature, towards the boy, who was smiling in his sleep.

" The little mouse has come to invite you to a wedding," he said, " for two little mice are going to be married to-night."

" But how shall I get through the little mouse's hole in the floor ? " Hjalmar asked in alarm.

" Leave that to me," said Ole Luk-Oie. " I will make you small enough." Then he touched Hjalmar, who became smaller and smaller till he was not quite as big as a man's finger.

" You can now borrow the tin soldier's clothes, which, I think, will just fit you, for it always looks well to wear uniform in the company of ladies."

" That is true," Hjalmar said ; and the same moment he was dressed in the clothes of the smartest of the tin soldiers in the nursery box.

" Will you have the goodness to seat yourself in your mother's thimble ? " the pretty little mouse said in its little voice, " and then I shall have the honour to drag you."

" I am quite ashamed that you should have that trouble," Hjalmar said, with a graceful bow ; but, seating himself, was dragged off to the wedding.

The first part of their way lay through a very narrow passage under the floor, which was lit up by the light from dried herrings' heads instead of torches.

" Does it not smell lovely here ? " the little mouse squeaked. " The passage has been rubbed

with lard from top to bottom. What can be nicer ? "

They stopped at the entrance to a very pretty room. To the right, inside the room, stood the most lovely little lady-mice, giggling and whispering in each other's ears ; to the left stood the gentlemen-mice, stroking their chins.

In the middle, seated side by side, in a piece of rind of cheese, were the bride and bridegroom.

More and more guests came in, till the crowd grew so great that they almost squeezed each other to death. And now the bride and bridegroom took their place right in the centre of the door. The whole room was well smeared with the fat of bacon, and that was all the refreshment they got. But ought they not to have been satisfied with smelling that ?

For dessert, however, a pea was shown them, on which a mouse had nibbled the names—that is, the first letters of the names—of the newly married couple. That was something very wonderful.

All the mice said that they had never seen so splendid a wedding ! Then Hjalmar awoke.

Friday

" How are we to pass this night ? " Hjalmar asked Ole Luk-Oie, for he was no longer afraid of his old friend.

" Well, I scarcely know whether you would like to come to another wedding, though it will be quite a different one from that of last night," said Ole Luk-Oie. " Your sister's big doll, which looks like a man, and is called Hermann, is going to marry the doll Bertha ; and as it is Bertha's birthday there will be plenty of presents."

" Yes, I know that," Hjalmar said, " for when

the dolls want new clothes, my sister makes them keep their birthday, or marries them. That has happened at least a hundred times."

"Yes; but to-night will be the hundred-and-first time," Ole Luk-Oie broke in: "and when the hundred-and-first time is over, all is over, and therefore this gala will be more splendid than any. Just look."

Hjalmar looked towards the table to which Ole Luk-Oie pointed. There stood the pretty little cardboard house, with all the windows lighted up, and in front of the house the tin soldiers presented arms.

Hermann and Bertha sat on the floor, leaning against one of the legs of the table and looking down upon the ground. Ole Luk-Oie married them as well as he could. Then all the furniture joined in a pretty song written by the slate-pencil.

"Shall we take lodgings somewhere in the country here, my dear Bertha?" the bridegroom asked; "or shall we travel far away?"

Bertha did not seem to know which she would prefer, so they asked the swallow, which had travelled far, and the old hen in the yard, which had five times reared a brood of chicks.

The swallow told of the warm lands where the grapes are beautiful and large, and where the air is soft and warm.

"But they have not got our green cabbage,

which is not good till there has been a sharp frost," the hen said. "I was in the country one summer with all my little chicks, where there was a sand-pit in which we could scratch to our hearts' content, and we had the right to go into a garden of green cabbages—oh! how green they were."

"But one cabbage is always like the other," the swallow said; "and then there is very bad weather here sometimes."

"But we are used to that," the hen said.

"And, besides, it is cold here; it snows, it freezes."

"Oh, that, as I have said, does the cabbage good," the hen said; "and besides, we sometimes have it warm enough. Had we not a summer four years ago which lasted quite five weeks? And it was so hot, so hot, that one could scarcely breathe."

And the good, honest hen cried as she added, "I have travelled too, and have something to say about it. Shut up in a coop with my dear little ones, I was carried above thirty miles, and know that travelling is anything but pleasant."

"Oh, the hen is a wise woman," the doll Bertha said. "I vote for the sand-pit and the cabbage-garden, where we can wander about in peace."

And thus it was settled, for Hermann said nothing at all.

Saturday

" Am I now to hear more stories ? " asked little Hjalmar, as soon as Ole Luk-Oie had put him quietly to sleep.

" To-night we have no time for that," he answered, opening his most beautiful umbrella over the boy. " Look at these Chinese."

When Hjalmar looked the umbrella seemed to be a large Chinese plate, with blue trees, pointed bridges, and Chinese men and women, who stood there nodding their heads.

" Before to-morrow the whole world must be put in order," Ole Luk-Oie said, " for to-morrow is a holy day. First I must go into the church steeples to see whether the little church-elves have made the bells shine, that their sound may be clear.

" I must go out into the fields to see whether the winds have blown the dust off the grass and leaves; and, the most important of all, I must quickly fetch down all the stars in order to polish them.

" I carry them in my apron, but they have all to be numbered first, as well as the holes in which they are fixed up there, so that they may be put back in their proper places. If not, they might not fit tightly, and we should have too many falling stars."

" Listen to me, I pray, Mr. Ole Luk-Oie," said an old portrait which hung in the room. " I am Hjalmar's great-grandfather—do you know that ?

"Now, I am very much obliged to you for telling the boy stories, but you must not fill his head with such wrong ideas. The stars cannot be taken down and polished, for they are round bodies, like our earth."

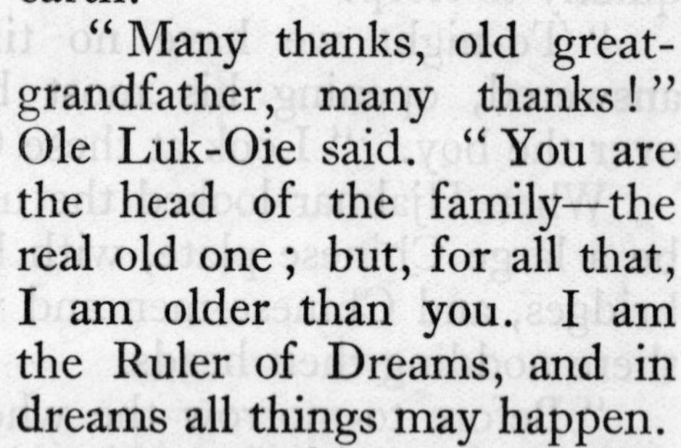

"Many thanks, old great-grandfather, many thanks!" Ole Luk-Oie said. "You are the head of the family—the real old one; but, for all that, I am older than you. I am the Ruler of Dreams, and in dreams all things may happen.

"I know how to manage big and small—indeed, I am suited to all. But now you can help me for once in a way, and amuse the little sleeper with merry tales."

But the portrait had no merry tales to tell, and the boy awoke out of his sweet sleep.

He looked up at the portrait, and then he thought of Ole Luk-Oie's kind, merry face. And you know quite well which one he loved to recall.

WHEN YOU WALK

By James Stephens

When you walk in a field,
Look down
Lest you tramp
On a daisy's crown !

But in a city
Look always high,
And watch
The beautiful clouds go by !

THE WHY OF THE WEATHER

By MARGARET BAKER

HAVE you ever heard of the Clerk of the Weather? Perhaps you know him better as the Man in the Moon, for that is where he lives. The moon is much bigger than it looks; there are two or three very comfortable rooms in it, and a fine big workshop where the weather is kept in store. The rain is in a large tank over which hangs a row of watering-cans and squirts of various sizes; the ice and snow are in a refrigerator, the sunshine is stored in large brass bottles with screw-tops, and there is an enormous pair of bellows to make the winds. The clouds are folded up neatly like sheets, and kept in a chest of drawers; when one is wanted it is shaken open and thrown out of the window. Thunder and lightning, which look exactly like fifth of November fireworks, are kept in an iron box on the top shelf, because they are not often wanted.

The Clerk of the Weather is a well-meaning man and very good-natured; he is never so happy as when he is pleasing people, and so it used to distress him very much to hear grumbles about the wind, or the rain, or the temperature he had chosen for any particular day.

" I'm sure I only want to be obliging," said he ; " if I knew the kind of weather people wanted I'd be very glad to supply it."

One day he got up feeling very cheerful and happy, and he opened a large bottle of sunshine. " That will please every one," he chuckled ; " they all like sun ! "

But his satisfaction did not last long.

" This sunshine is too hot for words ! " grumbled a man who was sawing logs. " Why can't we have a breath of wind to keep us cool ? "

" Wind ! " said the Clerk of the Weather. " If that's all you want I can soon make you happy." And he began to work the bellows.

" It's dreadfully treacherous weather ! " sighed a little old lady who had just sat down to rest in the park. " A nasty little wind like this, creeping unexpectedly round corners, is enough to give any one her death of cold on such a warm day. I wish, if it is going to be windy, that it would blow hard and then we should know what was happening and could stay indoors."

" Anything to suit you, ma'am," said the Clerk of the Weather, and pumped the bellows with a will ; the wind raced over the country, roaring round chimney-pots, and whistling under doors, and driving everything before it.

" Hurrah ! Hurrah ! " shouted all the little boys who had kites ; but the people who were

walking along the road sighed, " Just look at the dust ! What we want is rain."

" I'm glad you've had enough wind," panted the Clerk of the Weather, quite out of breath with his exertions, and he took down the medium-sized watering-can.

But were people satisfied when he began to sprinkle them with rain ? Not a bit of it. They all began to grumble because they had left home that morning without umbrellas, or they had just hung out the washing, or were afraid of getting their feet wet. " Why ever should it rain now ? " they cried. " It's ridiculous to have such changeable weather ! "

" It's ridiculous to have such changeable

minds ! " cried the Clerk of the Weather, and he lit the smudge fire and made a good black fog. " That ought to keep them quiet while I think ! " said he.

He thought and thought, and nothing happened but a headache. " I'll never be able to satisfy them all," he sighed ; " they all want different things."

Then he had a brilliant idea ! " I'll serve the weather out in little pieces ! " he cried. " Every one shall have his own bit—they won't be able to grumble then ! "

He jumped up, took off his coat and hung it behind the door, rolled up his sleeves, and set to work.

Farmer Fuddle wanted wind to dry the hay, Gardener Grubbins wanted rain for his seedlings, Mrs. Muffin wanted it cool because it was ironing day, Miss Miffin wanted it warm because she wished to wear her new thin summer dress ; Tommy Todd wanted to play snowballs, and his little sister Tilly wanted sunshine so that she could sit on the grass and pick daisies ; and lazy Larry Littlewits thought a thunderstorm would be nice, because it would give him an excuse not to go to school. The Clerk of the Weather bustled round and round his room, sprinkling a little rain here, letting out a few rays of sunshine there, taking a turn at the bellows every now and again, opening the ice-chest to get a lump of snow, hunting through the clouds for the various sizes needed, stretching up to the top shelf for a thunder-and-lightning firework, backwards and forwards, hither and thither, attending to the wishes as fast as he could. He grew hotter and hotter, and more and more out of breath. "It's dreadfully hard work," he panted; "but if the new arrangement pleases people, I don't mind. But I'm afraid they'll have to have fog every other day—I must get a little rest!"

At first every one was delighted to find he had exactly the weather he wanted—all but Lazy Larry, who grew tired of his thunderstorm in a very short time; and as long as people stayed far enough from each other it was all right. But when Miss Miffin, walking happily along in her own patch of sunshine, stopped at the gate of the hayfield to talk to Farmer Fuddle, working with his collar turned up in his own patch of wind, the two weathers got all mixed at the edges; Miss Miffin began to shiver, and Farmer Fuddle began to mop his brow, and instead of remarking, as they intended to do, "Delightful weather, isn't it?" they both exclaimed, "Dreadfully changeable! There's no telling what's going to happen in the next five minutes!"

It was worse even than that when Mrs. Todd told Tommy to mind his little sister for the afternoon: *her* sunshine melted *his* snow, and *his* snow shrivelled *her* daisies, and they did nothing but quarrel ; and when Lazy Larry, thunderstorm and all, ran up to play with them, such queer things happened as the three weathers mixed that the children ran home crying and frightened.

" What *can* you make of a day like this ? " exclaimed everybody. " The weather used to be changeable before, but now it alters every time you meet any one else. Whatever is the Clerk of the Weather doing ? "

" Doing ? " panted the poor Clerk. " I'm trying to be obliging, and this is all the thanks I get ! If *I* choose the weather it's wrong, and if I let people choose it for themselves it's worse ; there's nothing for it but to shut my eyes every morning, turn round three times, and take the weather I touch first ! "

So that is how the weather is chosen nowadays ; if you do not like it you had better think of a better way of doing things ; no doubt the Clerk of the Weather will be very glad to give it a trial.

THE TRAVELLING MAN

A Miracle Play

By Lady Gregory

PERSONS

A Mother.
A Child.
A Travelling Man.

SCENE.—*A cottage kitchen. A woman setting out a bowl and jug and board on the table for bread-making.*

Child. What is it you are going to make, mother?

Mother. I am going to make a grand cake with white flour. Seeds I will put in it. Maybe I'll make a little cake for yourself too. You can be baking it in the little pot while the big one will be baking in the big pot.

Child. It is a pity Daddy to be away at the fair on a Samhain night.

Mother. I must make my feast all the same, for Samhain night is more to me than to any other one. It was on this night seven years I first came into this house.

Child. You will be taking down those plates

from the dresser so, those plates with flowers on them, and be putting them on the table.

Mother. I will. I will set out the house today, and bring down the best delf, and put whatever thing is best on the table, because of the great thing that happened me seven years ago.

Child. What great thing was that?

Mother. I was after being driven out of the house where I was a serving girl. . . .

Child. Where was that house? Tell me about it.

Mother [*sitting down and pointing southward*]. It is over there I was living, in a farmer's house up on Slieve Echtge, near to Slieve na n-Or, the Golden Mountain.

Child. The Golden Mountain! That must be a grand place.

Mother. Not very grand indeed, but bare and cold enough at that time of the year. Anyway, I was driven out a Samhain day like this, because of some things that were said against me.

Child. What did you do then?

Mother. What had I to do but to go walking the bare bog road through the rough hills where there was no shelter to find, and the sharp wind going through me, and the red mud heavy on my shoes. I came to Kilbecanty. . . .

Child. I know Kilbecanty. That is where the woman in the shop gave me sweets out of a bottle.

Mother. So she might now, but that night her

door was shut and all the doors were shut ; and I saw through the windows the boys and the girls sitting round the hearth and playing their games, and I had no courage to ask for shelter. In dread I was they might think some shameful thing of me, and I going the road alone in the night-time.

Child. Did you come here after that ?

Mother. I went on down the hill in the darkness, and with the dint of my trouble and the length of the road my strength failed me, and I had like to fall. So I did fall at the last, meeting with a heap of broken stones by the roadside.

Child. I hurt my knee one time I fell on the stones.

Mother. It was then the great thing happened. I saw a stranger coming towards me, a very tall man, the best I ever saw, bright and shining that you could see him through the darkness ; and I knew him to be no common man.

Child. Who was he ?

Mother. It is what I thought, that he was the King of the World.

Child. Had he a crown like a King ?

Mother. If he had, it was made of the twigs of a bare blackthorn ; but in his hand he had a green branch, that never grew on a tree of this world. He took me by the hand, and he led me over the stepping-stones outside to this door, and he bade me to go in and I would find good shelter. I was kneeling down to thank him, but he raised me up and he said, " I will come to see you some other time. And do not shut up your heart in the things I give you," he said, " but have a welcome before me."

Child. Did he go away then ?

Mother. I saw him no more after that, but I did as he bade me. [*She stands up and goes to the door*.] I came in like this, and your father was sitting there by the hearth, a lonely man that was after losing his wife. He was alone and I was alone, and we married one another; and I never wanted since for shelter or safety. And a good wife I made him, and a good housekeeper.

Child. Will the King come again to the house ?

Mother. I have his word for it he will come, but he did not come yet ; it is often your father and myself look out the door of a Samhain night, thinking to see him.

Child. I hope he won't come in the night-time, and I asleep.

Mother. It is of him I do be thinking every year, and I setting out the house, and making a cake for the supper.

Child. What will he do when he comes in ?

Mother. He will sit over there in the chair, and maybe he will taste a bit of the cake. I will call in all the neighbours ; I will tell them he is here. They will not be keeping it in their mind against me then that I brought nothing, coming to the house. They will know I am before any of them, the time they know who it is has come to visit me. They will all kneel down and ask for his blessing. But the best blessing will be on the house he came to of himself.

Child. And are you going to make the cake now ?

Mother. I must make it now indeed, or I will be late with it. I am late as it is ; I was expecting one of the neighbours to bring me white flour from the town. I'll wait no longer, I'll go borrow it in some place. There will be a wedding in the stone-cutter's house Thursday, it's likely there will be flour in the house.

Child. Let me go along with you.

Mother. It is best for you to stop here. Be a good child now, and don't be meddling with the things on the table. Sit down there by the hearth and break up those little sticks I am after bringing in. Make a little heap of them now before me, and we will make a good fire to bake the cake. See now how many will you break. Don't go out the door while I'm away, I would be in dread of you going near the river and it in flood. Behave yourself well now. Be counting the sticks as you break them. [*She goes out.*]

Child [*sitting down and breaking sticks across his knee*]. One—and two—oh, I can break this one into a great many—one, two, three, four. This one is wet—I don't like a wet one—five, six—that is a great heap. Let me try that great big one. That is too hard. I don't think mother could break that one. Daddy could break it.

[*Half-door is opened and a travelling man comes in. He wears a ragged white flannel shirt, and mud-stained trousers. He is bareheaded and barefooted, and carries a little branch in his hand.*]

Travelling Man [*stooping over the child and taking the stick*]. Give it here to me and hold this.

[*He puts the branch in the child's hand, while he takes the stick and breaks it.*]

Child. That is a good branch, apples on it and flowers. The tree at the mill has apples yet, but all the flowers are gone. Where did you get this branch ?

Travelling Man. I got it in a garden a long way off.

Child. Where is the garden ? Where do you come from ?

Travelling Man [*pointing southward*]. I have come from beyond those hills.

Child. Is it from the Golden Mountain you are come ? From Slieve na n-Or ?

Travelling Man. That is where I come from surely, from the Golden Mountain. I would like to sit down and rest for a while.

Child. Sit down here beside me. We must not go near the table or touch anything, or mother will be angry. Mother is going to make a beautiful cake, a cake that will be fit for a King that might be coming in to our supper.

Travelling Man. I will sit here with you on the floor. [*Sits down*.]

Child. Tell me now about the Golden Mountain.

Travelling Man. There is a garden in it, and there is a tree in the garden that has fruit and flowers at the one time.

Child. Like this branch ?

Travelling Man. Just like that little branch.

Child. What other things are in the garden ?

Travelling Man. There are birds of all colours that sing at every hour, the way the people will come to their prayers. And there is a high wall about the garden.

Child. What way can the people get through the wall ?

Travelling Man. There are four gates in the wall : a gate of gold, and a gate of silver, and a gate of crystal, and a gate of white brass.

Child [*taking up the sticks*]. I will make a garden. I will make a wall with these sticks.

Travelling Man. This big stick will make the first wall. [*They build a square wall with sticks*.]

Child [*taking up branch*]. I will put this in the middle. This is the tree. I will get something to make it stand up. [*Gets up and looks at dresser*.] I can't reach it. Get up and give me that shining jug.

[*Travelling Man gets up and gives him the jug*.]

Travelling Man. Here it is for you.

Child [*puts it within the walls, and sets the branch in it*]. Tell me something else that is in the garden.

Travelling Man. There are four wells of water in it, that are as clear as glass.

Child. Get me down those cups, those flowery cups, we will put them for wells. [*He hands them down.*] Now I will make the gates. Give me those plates for gates—not those ugly ones, those nice ones at the top.

[*He takes them down, and they put them on the four sides for gates. The Child gets up and looks at it.*]

Travelling Man. There now, it is finished.

Child. Is it as good as the other garden ? How can we go to the Golden Mountain to see the other garden ?

Travelling Man. We can ride to it.

Child. But we have no horse.

Travelling Man. This form will be our horse. [*He draws a form out of the corner, and sits down astride on it, putting the child before him.*] Now, off we go ! [*Sings, the Child repeating the refrain*]—

Come ride and ride to the garden,
Come ride and ride with a will :
For the flower comes with the fruit there
Beyond a hill and a hill.

Refrain

Come ride and ride to the garden,
  Come ride like the March wind ;
There's barley there, and water there,
  And stabling to your mind.

Travelling Man. How did you like that ride, little horseman ?

Child. Go on again ! I want another ride !

Travelling Man [*sings*]—

The Archangels stand in a row there
  And all the garden bless,
The Archangel Axel, Victor the angel
  Work at the cider press.

Refrain

Come ride and ride to the garden, etc.

Child. We will soon be at the Golden Mountain now. Ride again. Sing another song.

Travelling Man [*sings*]—

Oh, scent of the broken apples !
  Oh, shuffling of holy shoes !
Beyond a hill and a hill there
  In the land that no one knows.

Refrain

Come ride and ride to the garden, etc.

Child. Now another ride.

Travelling Man. This will be the last. It will be a good ride.

[*The Mother comes in. She stares for a second, then throws down her basket and snatches up the Child.*]

Mother. Did ever any one see the like of that! A common beggar, a travelling man off the roads, to be holding the child! To be leaving his ragged arms about him as if he was of his own sort! Get out of that, whoever you are, and quit this house, or I'll call to some that will make you quit it.

Child. Do not send him out! He is not a bad man; he is a good man; he was playing horses with me. He has grand songs.

Mother. Let him get away out of this now, himself and his share of songs. Look at the way he has your bib destroyed that I was after washing in the morning!

Child. He was holding me on the horse. We were riding; I might have fallen. He held me.

Mother. I give you my word you are done now with riding horses. Let him go on his road. I have no time to be cleaning the place after the like of him.

Child. He is tired. Let him stop here till evening.

Travelling Man. Let me rest here for a while. I have been travelling a long way.

Mother. Where did you come from to-day?

Travelling Man. I came over Slieve Echtge from Slieve na n-Or. I had no house to stop in. I walked the long bog road, the wind was going through me, there was no shelter to be got, the red mud of the road was heavy on my feet. I got no welcome in the villages, and so I came on to this place, to the rising of the river at Ballylee.

Mother. It is best for you to go on to the town. It is not far for you to go. We will maybe have company coming in here.

[*She pours out flour into a bowl*, *and begins mixing*.]

Travelling Man. Will you give me a bit of that dough to bring with me ? I have gone a long time fasting.

Mother. It is not often in the year I make bread like this. There are a few cold potatoes on the dresser, are they not good enough for you ? There is many a one would be glad to get them.

Travelling Man. Whatever you will give me, I will take it.

Mother [*going to the dresser for the potatoes*, *and looking at the shelves*]. What in the earthly world has happened all the delf ? Where are the jugs gone, and the plates ? They were all in it when I went out a while ago.

Child [*hanging his head*]. We were making a garden with them. We were making that garden there in the corner.

Mother. Is that what you were doing after I

bidding you to sit still and to keep yourself quiet? It is to tie you in the chair I will another time! My grand jugs! [*She picks them up and wipes them.*] My plates that I bought the first time I ever went marketing into Gort. The best in the shop they were. [*One slips from her hand and breaks.*] Look at that now, look what you are after doing. [*She gives a slap at the child.*]

Travelling Man. Do not blame the child. It was I myself took them down from the dresser.

Mother [*turning on him*]. It was you took them! What business had you doing that? It's the last time a tramp or a tinker or a rogue of the roads will have a chance of laying his hand on anything in this house. It is jailed you should be! What did you want touching the dresser at all? Is it looking you were for what you could bring away?

Travelling Man [*taking the Child's hands*]. I would not refuse these hands that were held out for them. If it was for the four winds of the world he had asked, I would have put their bridles into these innocent hands.

Mother [*taking up the jug and throwing the branch on the floor*]. Get out of this! Get out of this I tell you! There is no shelter here for the like of you! Look at that mud on the floor! You are not fit to come into the house of any decent respectable person!

[*The room begins to darken.*]

Travelling Man. Indeed, I am more used to

the roads than to the shelter of houses. It is often I have spent the night on the bare hills.

Mother. No wonder in that! [*She begins to sweep floor*.] Go out of this now to whatever company you are best used to, whatever they are. The worst of people it is likely they are, thieves and drunkards and shameless women.

Travelling Man. Maybe so. Drunkards and thieves and shameless women, stones that have fallen, that are trodden under foot, bodies that are spoiled with sores, bodies that are worn with fasting, minds that are broken with much sinning, the poor, the mad, the bad. . . .

Mother. Get out with you! Go back to your friends, I say!

Travelling Man. I will go. I will go back to the highroad that is walked by the bare feet of the poor, by the innocent bare feet of children. I will go back to the rocks and the wind, to the cries of the trees in the storm! [*He goes out*.]

Child. He has forgotten his branch!

[*Takes it*, *and follows him*.]

Mother [*still sweeping*]. My good plates from the dresser, and dirty red mud on the floor, and the sticks all scattered in every place. [*Stoops to pick them up*.] Where is the child gone? [*Goes to door*.] I don't see him—he couldn't have gone to the river—it is getting dark—the bank is slippy. Come back! Come back! Where are you?

[*Child runs in*.]

Mother. Oh, where were you ? I was in dread it was to the river you were gone, or into the river.

Child. I went after him. He is gone over the river.

Mother. He couldn't do that. He couldn't go through the flood.

Child. He did go over it. He was as if walking on the water. There was a light before his feet.

Mother. That could not be so. What put that thought in your mind ?

Child. I called to him to come back for the branch, and he turned where he was in the river, and he bade me to bring it back, and to show it to yourself.

Mother [*taking the branch*]. There are fruit and

flowers on it. It is a branch that is not of any earthly tree. [*Falls on her knees.*] He is gone, he is gone, and I never knew him ! He was that stranger that gave me all ! He is the King of the World !

THE BOUNCIBLE BALL

By E. Nesbit

It is very hard, when you have been accustomed to go to the seaside every summer ever since you were quite little, to be made to stay in London just because an aunt and an uncle choose to want to come and stay at your house to see the Royal Academy and go to the summer sales.

Selim and Thomasina felt that it was very hard indeed. And aunt and uncle were not the nice kind either. If it had been Aunt Emma, who dressed dolls and told fairy-tales—or Uncle Reggie, who took you to the Crystal Palace, and gave you five bob at a time, and never even asked what you spent it on, it would have been different. But it was Uncle Thomas and Aunt Selina.

Aunt Selina was all beady, and sat bolt upright, and told you to mind what you were told, and Selim had been named after her—as near as they could get. And Uncle Thomas was the one Thomasina had been named after: he was deaf, and he always told you what the moral of everything was, and the housemaid said he was "near."

"I know he is, worse luck," said Thomasina.

"I mean, miss," explained the housemaid, "he's none too free with his chink."

Selim groaned. "He never gave me but a

shilling in his life," said he, " and that turned out to be bad when I tried to change it at the ginger-beer shop."

The children could not understand why this aunt and uncle were allowed to interfere with everything as they did : and they quite made up their minds that when they were grown up they would never allow an aunt or an uncle to cross their doorsteps. They never thought—poor, dear little things—that some day they would grow up to be aunts and uncles in their turn, or, at least, one of each.

It was very hot in London that year : the pavement was like hot pie, and the asphalt was like hot pudding, and there was a curious wind that collected dust and straw and dirty paper, and then got tired of its collection, and threw it away in respectable people's areas and front gardens. The blind in the nursery had never been fixed up since the day when the children took it down to make a drop-scene for a play they were going to write and never did. So the hot after-noon sun came burning in through the window, and the children got hotter and hotter, and crosser and crosser, till at last Selim slapped Thomasina's arms till she cried, and Thomasina kicked Selim's legs till he screamed.

Then they sat down in different corners of the nursery and cried, and called each other names, and said they wished they were dead. This is very naughty indeed, as, of course, you know ; but you must remember how hot it was.

When they had called each other all the names they could think of, Thomasina said suddenly, " All right, Silly " (that was Selim's pet name), " cheer up."

" It's too hot to cheer up," said Selim gloomily.

" We've been very naughty," said Thomasina, rubbing her eyes with the paint rag, " but it's all the heat. I heard Aunt Selina telling mother the weather wore her nerves to fiddle-strings. That just meant she was cross."

" Then it's not *our* fault," said Selim. " People say be good and you'll be happy. Uncle Reggy says, ' Be happy, and perhaps you'll be good.' *I* could be good if I was happy."

" So could I," said Thomasina.

" What *would* make you happy ? " said a thick, wheezy voice from the toy cupboard, and out rolled the big green and red india-rubber ball that Aunt Emma had sent them last week. They had not played with it much, because the garden was so hot and sunny—and when they wanted to play with it in the street, on the shady side, Aunt Selina had said it was not like respectable children, so they weren't allowed.

Now the Ball rolled out very slowly—and the bright light on its new paint seemed to make it wink at them. You will think that they were surprised to hear a ball speak. Not at all. As you grow up, and more and more strange things happen to you, you will find that the more astonishing a thing is the less it surprises you. (I wonder why this is. Think it over, and write and tell me what you think.)

Selim stood up and said, " Hallo," but that was only out of politeness. Thomasina answered the Ball's question.

" We want to be at the seaside—and no aunts—and none of the things we don't like—and no uncles, of course," she said.

" Well," said the Ball, " if you think you can be good, why not set me bouncing ? "

" We're not allowed in here," said Thomasina, " because of the crinkly ornaments people give me on my birthdays."

" Well, the street then," said the Ball ; " the nice shady side."

" It's not like respectable children," said Selim sadly.

The Ball laughed. If you have never heard an india-rubber ball laugh you won't understand. It's the sort of quicker, quicker, quicker, softer, softer, softer chuckle of a bounce that it gives when it's settling down when you're tired of bouncing it.

" The garden, then," it said.

" I don't mind, if you'll go on talking," said Selim kindly.

So they took the Ball down into the garden and began to bounce it in the sun, on the dry, yellowy grass of the lawn.

" Come on," said the Ball. " You do like me ! "

" What ? " said the children.

" Why, do like I do—bounce !" said the Ball. " That's right—higher, higher, higher !"

For then and there the two children had begun bouncing as if their feet were india-rubber balls, and you have no idea what a delicious sensation that gives you.

"Higher, higher," cried the green and red ball, bouncing excitedly. "Now, follow me —higher, higher." And off it bounced down the blackened gravel of the path, and the children bounced after it, shrieking with delight at the new feeling. They bounced over the wall—all three of them—and the children looked back just in time to see Uncle Thomas tapping at the window, and saying, "Don't."

You have not the least idea how glorious it is to feel full of bouncibleness ; so that, instead of dragging one foot after the other, as you do when you feel tired or naughty, you bounce along, and every time your feet touch the ground you bounce higher, and all without taking any trouble or tiring yourself. You have, perhaps, heard of the Greek gentleman who got new strength every time he fell down. His name was Antæus, and I believe he was an india-rubber ball, green on one side where he touched the earth, and red on the other where he felt the sun. But enough of classical research.

Thomasina and Selim bounced away, following the Bouncible Ball. They went over fences and walls, and through parched, dry gardens and burning-hot streets ; they passed the region where fields of cabbages and rows of yellow brick cottages mark the division between London and the suburbs. They bounced through the suburbs, dusty and neat, with geraniums in the front gardens, and all the blinds pulled half-way down; and then the lamp-posts in the road got fewer and fewer, and the fields got greener and the hedges thicker—it was real, true country—with lanes instead of roads; and down the lanes the green and red Ball went bouncing, bouncing, bouncing, and the children after it. Thomasina, in her white, starched frock, very prickly round the neck, and Selim, in his everyday sailor suit, a little tight under the arms. His Sunday one was a size larger. No one seemed to notice them, but they noticed and pitied the children who were being "taken for a walk" in the gritty suburban roads.

"Where are we going?" they asked the Ball, and it answered, with a sparkling green and red smile:

"To the most delightful place in the world."

"What's it called?" asked Selim.

"It's called Whereyouwantogoto," the Ball answered, and on they went. It was a wonderful journey—up and down, looking through the hedges and over them, looking in at the doors of cottages, and then in at the top windows, up and down—bounce—bounce—bounce.

And at last they came to the sea. And the Bouncing Ball said, "Here you are! Now be good, for there's nothing here but the things that make people happy." And with that he curled himself up like a ball in the shadow of a wet seaweedy rock, and went to sleep, for he was tired out with his long journey. The children stopped bouncing, and looked about them.

" O Tommy ! " said Selim.

" O Silly ! " said Thomasina. And well they might ! In the place to which the Ball had brought them was all that your fancy can possibly paint, and a great deal more beside.

The children felt exactly as you do when you've had the long, hot, dirty train journey—and every one has been so cross about the boxes, and the little brown portmanteau that was left behind at the junction—and then when you get to your lodgings you are told that you may run down and have a look at the sea if you're back by tea-time, and mother and nurse will unpack.

Only Thomasina and her brother had not had a tiresome journey—and there were no nasty, stuffy lodgings for them, and no tea with oily butter and a new pot of marmalade.

" There's silver sand," said she—" miles of it."

" And rocks," said he.

" And cliffs."

" And caves in the cliffs."

" And how cool it is," said Thomasina.

" And yet it's nice and warm too," said Selim.

" And what shells ! "

" And seaweed."

" And the Downs behind ! "

" And trees in the distance ! "

" And here's a dog to go after sticks. Here, Rover, Rover."

A big black dog answered at once to the name, because he was a retriever, and they are all called Rover.

" And spades ! " said the girl.

" And pails ! " said the boy.

" And what pretty sea-poppies," said the girl.

" And a basket—and grub in it ! " said the boy. So they sat down and had lunch.

It was a lovely lunch. Lobsters and ice-creams (strawberry and pine-apple), and toffee and hot buttered toast and ginger-beer. They ate and ate, and thought of the aunt and uncle at home, and the minced veal and sago pudding, and they were very happy indeed.

Just as they were finishing their lunch they saw a swirling, swishing, splashing commotion in the green sea a little way off, and they tore off their clothes and rushed into the water to see what it was. It was a seal. He was very kind and convenient. He showed them how to swim and dive.

"But won't it make us ill to bathe so soon after meals ? Isn't it wrong ? " asked Thomasina.

"Not at all," said the seal. "Nothing is wrong here—as long as you're good. Let me teach you water-leapfrog—a most glorious game —so cool, yet so exciting. You try it."

At last the seal said: " I suppose you wear man-clothes. They're very inconvenient. My two eldest have just outgrown their coats. If you'll accept them——"

And it dived, and came up with two golden sealskin coats over its arm, and the children put them on.

" Thank you very much," they said. " You *are* kind."

I am almost sure that it has never been your luck to wear a fur coat that fitted you like a skin, and that could not be spoiled with sand or water, or jam, or bread and milk, or any of the things with which you mess up the nice new clothes your kind relations buy for you. But if you like, you may try to imagine how jolly the little coats were.

Thomasina and Selim played all day on the

beach, and when they were tired they went into a cave, and found supper—salmon and cucumber, and welsh-rabbit and lemonade—and then they went to bed in a great heap of straw and grass and fern and dead leaves, and all the delightful things you have often wished to sleep in. Only you have never been allowed to.

In the morning there were plum-pudding for breakfast, and roast duck and lemon jelly, and the day passed like a happy dream, only broken by surprising and delightful meals. The Ball woke up and showed them how to play water polo; and they bounced him on the sand, with shrieks of joy and pleasure. You know, a Ball likes to be bounced by people he is fond of—it is like slapping a friend on the shoulder.

There were no houses in "Whereyouwantogoto," and no bathing machines or bands, no nursemaids or policemen, or aunts or uncles. You could do exactly what you liked as long as you were good.

"What will happen if we're naughty?" Selim asked. The Ball looked very grave, and answered:

"I must not tell you; and I very strongly advise you not to try to find out."

"We won't—indeed, we won't," said they, and went off to play rounders with the rabbits on the Downs—who were friendly fellows, and very keen on the game.

On the third evening Thomasina was rather silent, and the Ball said, " What's the matter, girl-bouncer? Out with it."

So she said, " I was wondering how mother is, and whether she has one of her bad headaches."

The Ball said, " Good little girl! Come with me and I'll show you something."

He bounced away, and they followed him, and he flopped into a rocky pool, frightening the limpets and sea-anemones dreadfully, though he did not mean to.

" Now look," he called from under the water, and the children looked, and the pool was like a looking-glass, only it was not their own faces they saw in it.

They saw the drawing-room at home, and father and mother, who were both quite well, only they looked tired—and the aunt and uncle were there—and Uncle Thomas was saying, " What a blessing those children are away."

" Then they know where we are?" said Selim to the Ball.

" They think they know," said the Ball, " or you think they think they know. Anyway, they're happy enough. Good-night."

And he curled himself up like a ball in his favourite sleeping-place. The two children crept into their pleasant, soft, sweet nest of straw and leaves and fern and grass, and went to sleep. But Selim was vexed with Thomasina because she had thought of mother before he had, and he said she had taken all the fern—and they went to sleep rather cross. They woke crosser. So far they had both helped to make the bed every morning, but to-day neither wanted to.

"I don't see why I should make the beds," said he ; " it's a girl's work, not a boy's."

"I don't see why I should do it," said Thomasina ; " it's a servant's place, not a young lady's."

And then a very strange and terrible thing happened. Quite suddenly, out of nothing and out of nowhere, appeared a housemaid—large and stern and very neat indeed, and she said :

"You are quite right, miss ; it is my place to make the beds. And I am instructed to see that you are both in bed by seven."

Think how dreadful this must have been to children who had been going to bed just when they felt inclined. They went out on to the beach.

"You see what comes of being naughty," said Thomasina ; and Selim said, "Oh, shut up, do ! "

They cheered up towards dinner-time—it was roast pigeons that day and bread sauce, and white-bait and sillabubs—and for the rest of the day they were as good as gold, and very polite to the Ball. Selim told it all about the dreadful apparition of the housemaid, and it shook its head (I know *you've* never seen a ball do that, and very likely you never will) and said :

" My Bouncible Boy, you may be happy here for ever and ever if you're contented and good. Otherwise—well, it's a quarter to seven—you've got to go."

And, sure enough, they had to. And the housemaid put them to bed, and washed them with yellow soap, and some of it got in their eyes. And she lit a night-light, and sat with them till they went to sleep, so that they couldn't talk, and were ever so much longer getting to sleep than they would have been if she had not been there. And the beds were iron, with mattresses and hot, stuffy fluffy sheets and many more new blankets than they wanted.

The next day they got out as early as they could, and played water football with the seal and the Bouncible Ball, and when dinner-time came it was lobster and ices. But Thomasina was in a bad temper. She said, " I wish it was duck." And before the words had left her lips it was cold mutton and rice pudding, and they had to sit up to table and eat it properly too, and the housemaid came round to see that they didn't leave any bits on the edges of their plates, or talk with their mouths full.

There were no more really nice meals after that, only the sort of things you get at home. But it is possible to be happy even without really nice meals. But you have to be very careful. The days went by pleasantly enough. All the sea and land creatures were most kind and attentive. The seal taught them all it knew, and was always ready to play with them. The star-fish taught them astronomy, and the jelly-fish taught them fancy cooking. The limpets taught them dancing as well as they could for their lameness. The sea-birds taught them to make nests—a knowledge they have never needed to apply—and if the oysters did not teach them anything it was only because oysters are so very stupid, and not from any lack of friendly feeling.

The children bathed every day in the sea, and if they had only been content with this all would have been well. But they weren't.

" Let's dig a bath," said Selim, " and the sea will come in and fill it, and then we can bathe in it."

So they fetched their spades and dug—and there was no harm in that, as you very properly remark.

But when the hole was finished, and the sea came creep, creep, creeping up—and at last a big wave thundered up the sand and swirled into the hole, Thomasina and Selim were struggling on the edge, fighting which should go in first, and the wave drew sandily back into the sea, and neither of them had bathed in the new bath. And now it was all wet and sandy, and its nice sharp edges rounded off, and much shallower. And as they looked at it angrily, the sandy bottom of the bath stirred and shifted and rose up, as if some great sea-beast were heaving underneath with his broad back. The wet sand slipped back in slabs at each side, and a long pointed thing like a thin cow's back came slowly up. It showed broader and broader, and presently the flakes of wet sand were dropping heavily off the top of a brand-new bathing machine that stood on the sand over where their bath had been.

"Well," said Selim, "we've done it this time."

They certainly had, for on the door of the bathing machine was painted: "You must not bathe any more except through me."

So there was no more running into the sea just when and how they liked. They had to use the bathing machine, and it smelt of stale salt water and other people's wet towels.

After this the children did not seem to care so much about the seaside, and they played more on the Downs, where the rabbits were very kind and hospitable, and in the woods, where all sorts of beautiful flowers grew wild—and there was nobody to say "Don't" when you picked them. The children thought of what Uncle Thomas would have said if he had been there, and they were very, very happy.

But one day Thomasina had pulled a lot of white convolvulus and some pink geraniums and calceolarias—the kind you are never allowed to pick at home—and she had made a wreath of them and put it on her head.

Then Selim said, " You *are* silly ! You look like a Bank Holiday."

And his sister said, " I can't help it. They'd look lovely on a hat, if they were only artificial. I wish I had a hat."

And she had. A large stiff hat that hurt her head just where the elastic was sewn on, and she had her stiff white frock that scratched, her tiresome underclothing, all of it, and stockings and heavy boots ; and Selim had his sailor suit—the everyday one that was too tight under the arms ; and they had to wear them always, and their fur coats were taken away.

They went sadly, all stiff and uncomfortable, and told the Bouncible Ball. It looked very grave, and great tears of salt water rolled down its red and green cheeks as it sat by the wet, seaweed-covered rock.

" Oh, you silly children," it said, " haven't you been warned enough ? You've everything a reasonable child could wish for. Can't you be contented ? "

" Of course we can," they said—and so they were—for a day and a half. And then it wasn't exactly discontent but real naughtiness that brought them to grief.

They were playing on the Downs by the edge of the wood under the heliotrope tree. A hedge

of camellia bushes cast a pleasant shadow, and out in the open sunlight on the Downs the orchids grew like daisies, and the carnations like buttercups. All about was that kind of turf on which the gardener does not like you to play, and they had pulled armfuls of lemon verbena and made a bed of it. But Selim's blouse was tight under the arms. So when Thomasina said :

" Oh, Silly dear, how beautiful it is ; just like fairyland," he said :

" Silly yourself. There's no such thing as fairyland."

Just then a fairy, with little bright wings the colour of a peacock's tail, fluttered across the path, and settled on a magnolia flower.

" Oh ! Silly darling," cried Thomasina, " it *is* fairyland, and there's a fairy, such a beautiful dear. Look—there she goes."

But Selim would not look—he turned over and hid his eyes.

" There's no such thing as fairyland, I tell you," he grunted, " and I don't believe in fairies."

And then, quite suddenly and very horribly, the fairy turned into a policeman—because every one knows there are such things as policemen, and any one can believe in *them*.

And all the rare and beautiful flowers withered up and disappeared, and only thorns and thistles were left, and the misty, twiny trim little grass path that led along the top of the cliffs turned into a parade, and the policeman walked up and down it incessantly, and watched the children at their play, and you know how difficult it is to play when any one is watching you, especially a policeman. Selim was extremely vexed: that was why he said there couldn't possibly be glow-worms as big as bicycle lamps, which, of course, there were in " Whereyouwantogoto." It was after that that the gas-lamps were put all along the parade, and a pier sprang up on purpose to be lighted with electricity, and a band played, because it is nonsense to have a pier without a band.

" Oh, you naughty, silly children," said the Bouncible Ball, turning red with anger, except in the part where he was green with disgust; " it makes me bounce with rage to see how you've thrown away your chances, and what a seaside resort you're making of ' Whereyouwantogoto.' "

And he did bounce, angrily, up and down the beach till the housemaid looked out of the cave and told the children not to be so noisy, and the policeman called out :

" Now then, move along there, move along. You're obstructing of the traffic."

And now I have something to tell you which you will find it hard to make any excuses for. I can't make any myself. I can only ask you to remember how hard it is to be even moderately good, and how easy it is to be extremely naughty.

When the Bouncible Ball stopped bouncing, Selim said :

" I wonder what makes him bounce."

" Oh no, *don't* !" cried Thomasina, for she had heard her brother wonder that about balls before, and she knew all too well what it ended in.

" Oh, *don't*," she said. " O Silly, he brought us here, he's been so kind."

But Selim said, " Nonsense ; balls can't feel, and it will be almost as good to play with after I've looked inside it."

And then, before Thomasina could prevent him, he pulled out the knife Uncle Reggy gave him last holiday but one, and catching the Ball up, he plunged the knife into its side. The Bouncible Ball uttered one whiffing squeak of pain and grief, then with a low, hissing sigh its kindly spirit fled, and it lay, a lifeless mass of paint and india-rubber in the hands of its assassin. Thomasina burst into tears—but the heartless Selim tore open the Ball, and looked inside. You know well enough what he found there. Emptiness; the little square patch of india-rubber that makes the hard lump on the outside of the ball which you feel with your fingers when the ball is alive and his own happy, bouncing, cheerful self.

The children stood looking at each other.

"I—I almost wish I hadn't," said Selim at last; but before Thomasina could answer he had caught her hand.

"Oh, look," he cried, "look at the sea."

It was, indeed, a dreadful sight. The beautiful dancing, sparkling blue sea was drying up before their eyes—in less than a moment it was quite flat and dusty. It hurriedly laid down a couple of railway lines, ran up a signal-box and telegraph poles, and became the railway at the back of their house at home.

The children, gasping with horror, turned to the Downs. From them tall, yellow brick houses were rising, as if drawn up by an invisible hand. Just as treacle does in cold weather if you put your five fingers in and pulled them up. But, of course, you are never allowed to do this. The beach got hard—it was a pavement. The green Downs turned grey—they were slate roofs—and Thomasina and Selim found themselves at the iron gate of their own number in the terrace—and there was

Uncle Thomas at the window knocking for them to come in, and Aunt Selina calling out to them how far from respectable it was to play in the streets.

They were sent to bed at once—that was Aunt Selina's suggestion—and Uncle Thomas arranged that they should have only dry bread for tea.

Selim and Thomasina have never seen "Whereyouwantogoto" again, nor the Bouncible Ball—not even his poor body—and they don't deserve to either. Of course, Thomasina was not so much to blame as Selim, but she was punished just the same. I can't help that. This is really the worst of being naughty. You not only have to suffer for it yourself, but some one else always has to suffer too, generally the person who loves you best.

You are intelligent children, and I will not insult you with a moral. I am not Uncle Thomas. Nor will I ask you to remember what I have told you. I am not Aunt Selina.

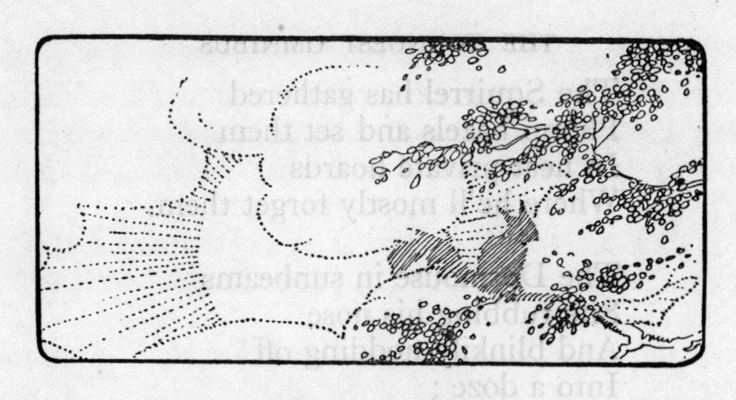

THE SLEEPERS

By Rodney Bennett

Autumn is here.
The year's growing older.
Evenings draw in.
Mornings are colder.
Bracken turns yellow.
Berries turn red,
And the Sleepers are secretly
Making their bed.

No more at evening
The Flittermouse wheels,
But in belfries and hollow trees
Hangs by his heels.

The Squirrel has gathered
Plump hazels and set them
In neat private hoards
Where he'll mostly forget them.

The Dormouse in sunbeams
Sits rubbing his nose
And blinkily nodding off
Into a doze ;
While the Hedgehog by twilight,
For such are his habits,
Spreads moss in a snug hole
That once was a rabbit's.

Soon they will all of them
Cosily creep
Into their bedrooms
And tumble asleep.
Even the Toad,
Now as plump as a mole,
Will decide he had better be
Toad in a hole.

The Squirrel and Dormouse
Will tuck in their toes
And make their tails counterpanes
Over the nose,
While the slumbering Hedgehog,
Since tail he has none,
Tucks *his* nose where *his* would be
If he had one.

Hardly they'll breathe
Or their hearts beat at all,
Hardly their blood
Through their bodies will crawl,
Yet, rain, frost, or snowfall,
Still cosy and dry,
They will all slumber safely
While winter goes by.

Then, one soft day,
They will dream of the sun,
And feel in their bones
That the spring has begun,

And, lean but alive,
They will waken, and then
Nose off down the hedgerow
On business again.

THE SEVEN SLEEPERS

By Alison Uttley

Snow fell softly on the world, covering the fields and hedges with a big white blanket. In the sky the Moon peered this way and that to find the house of the Seven Sleepers. At last she saw a little green cottage under the holly tree in Big Wood, nestling so close to the dark trunk that its thatched roof touched the low shining branches, and its small chimney pressed against the prickly leaves.

She gazed curiously at its tightly shut windows, and the door with its brass knocker, all dull with the rain and snow. Then she flashed her lantern through the end window, and saw the nose of a red squirrel who lay curled up in bed. Squirrel started slightly when the light fell on her, and pulled the sheet over her face.

" Safe as moonshine," said the Moon, and she peeped through all the little windows in a row under the eaves. In each room somebody lay asleep, and the Moon laughed to herself.

As she stared in at the tiny room with delicate blue curtains, the room which was so small she could scarcely get her moonbeam inside, she heard a slight sound, and a strange being came through the wood.

His face was glowing with light, and his kind brown eyes were like the eyes of a young fawn. On his shaggy back he carried a sack, and twisted round his short horns was a wreath of mistletoe. He danced along on his cloven hoofs, and played on thin reed pipes the sweetest music the Moon had ever heard.

The Moon bowed when she saw him, and shielded her lantern, for no light was needed when Pan the Friend was there.

" You are first," said Pan, resting the sack on the snow. " Are they all asleep in there ? " and he pointed to the windows.

" Yes, Your Majesty," replied the Moon, " but Squirrel is restless."

" She always is," laughed Pan, straightening out his broad shoulders, and stamping his hoofs on the ground. " She always is. The least sound, and out of bed she hops. She is the only wakeful one of the Seven Sleepers, and when she comes out in the Winter, woe betide her if I am not near ! "

" Is Your Majesty honouring them with a visit ? " asked the Moon.

" Of course," answered Pan. " It's Christmas Eve, you know. Animals as well as men must have their joy. I cannot do much nowadays, but this is one of the privileges left to me."

" It's cold for Your Majesty," said the Moon, flashing her lantern up and down, on the trees and hills and distant villages, where the dogs howled when they saw her. " Shall I ask the Sun to hurry up and warm things a little ? "

" Ah ! no," cried Pan quickly. " I must work at night now, there are too many eyes when the Sun awakes."

He slung his pipes round his hairy neck, pushed open the door and entered the cottage.

" It was a piece of luck to see him," cried the Moon to herself. " He slides along in the shadows so softly no one knows he is there, except for the sound of his pipes. I'll wait till he comes out again." And she pulled a cloud over her face and had a nap.

Pan busied himself in the kitchen for a few moments, and then ran noiselessly upstairs.

On the landing were seven little doors.

He listened, and a smile of contentment spread over his wise old face.

Little grunts and squeaks, sighs and shuffles, came from all the bedrooms, as the sleepers dreamed of summer days, of green hills and shallow streams, of flowery meadows and soft wet bogs. A hundred visions ran through their heads, and each one lived again in the country of his heart's desire, whilst Pan stood outside in the passage breathing happiness into all the little hearts beating within.

But there was no time to lose. He gently turned a door knob and walked into Squirrel's

room. There she lay, curled up with her bushy tail over her feet, smiling in her sleep, and at the foot of the bed hung her red stocking.

Pan dipped into his bag and pulled out a pair of curly-wool slippers, white and soft, woven from the fleece of a mountain lamb. He pushed them deep in the stocking, and then skipped lightly out of the room. Squirrel dreamed of waving beech trees, and great oaks, and little nut trees laden with brown nuts, but she did not know who had brought her the dream.

Then the god went into the next room, where, on a round soft leafy bed lay Snake, coiled in a ring, with her head on a pillow of grass. From a hook in the ceiling hung her long black stocking, for although she had no feet, she possessed a useful stocking, which she kept for sore throats, or Christmas Eve, or for a portmanteau when she was going on a long journey.

Into it Pan slipped a green silk dress, all frills and spickles and speckles.

" She'll want a new dress next Spring," said he, as he tiptoed out of the room on his pointed hoofs, and left the Snake dreaming of shadowy green glades, and thick wet grass, with deep hiding-places.

Dormouse slept in the next room. He was such a jolly chubby little fellow that Pan stood watching him for a precious minute. He lay in his cot with the eiderdown pulled up to his chin, grunting softly as he dreamed of a round nest under the hedge, with seven tiny babies in it.

At the foot of the cot hung a brown sock, and Pan put a little fur waistcoat inside it.

" Keep him warm when he wakes up, the young fellow," said he, and he touched the small head lovingly and gently closed the door.

Hedgehog's room was next. He lay in a ball at the top of the blankets, with a pink stocking tied to one of his prickles.

" He doesn't mean to lose it," laughed Pan, as he untied it and dropped inside a pearly knife with two blades and a corkscrew. Then he tied it up again and looked at the gently breathing animal.

" That's a fine present for a Hedgehog, for life will be none too easy for him," and Hedgehog dreamed of a hawthorn hedge, thick and leafy, with wood sorrel and sweet-smelling ferns growing at its roots, and

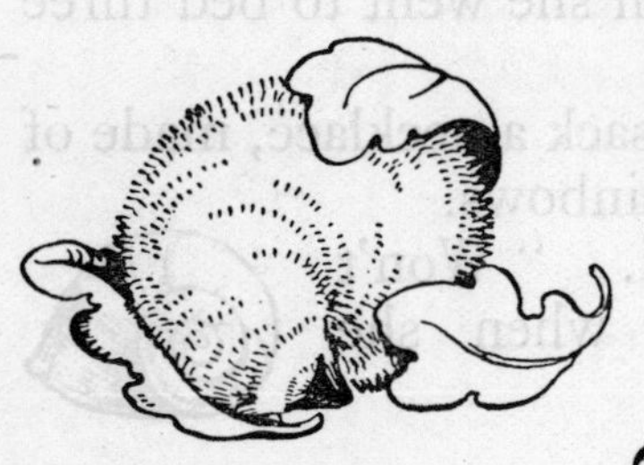

big white eggs laid by some stray hen in a hollow.

"That's four," sighed Pan, as he stepped into the next room.

Frog slept there, in a bed woven of reeds, with a wet sheet tied round his chin. He snored and snored and kicked his little legs about, but when Pan came near he lay very still as if he felt the presence of the Animal's Friend.

Pan took a pair of skates from his sack and put them in the green stocking which lay on the floor where Frog had kicked it.

"You can skate on dry land if there isn't any ice," he whispered, "and sometime you will be saved from an enemy."

And the Frog smiled as he dreamed of murmuring streams and lily ponds, of hard round pebbles and soft silky mud.

"Now for Snail," said Pan, as he opened the door next to Frog's. There, on a little white sheet, lay a shell, and inside it was Snail, fast asleep. But she had not forgotten to hang out her tiny grey stocking when she went to bed three months ago.

Pan brought out of his sack a necklace, made of dewdrops, the colour of rainbows.

"Ha!" he chuckled. "Won't little Snail startle them when she wears her jewels!"

There was only one room left, but that was his favourite, and Pan loved to see the neat beauty of that room. He opened the very small door at the end of the passage, and crept in on his shaggy knees, bending his horns to the ground to get through the doorway.

Such a warm, cosy room was Bee's! Its walls were hung with blue silk, and its blue velvet carpet was rich as a pansy petal. On the smallest bed in the world slept Bee, with a patchwork quilt over her furry body, and her head on a feather pillow as big as a pea. Tiny, tiny snores came from the bed, and her wings moved up and down as she breathed. But as Pan entered she dreamed of the wide moors with purple heather, of the great lime trees with golden flowers, of hedges with wild roses and honeysuckle, and a flicker of a smile crossed her face.

Pan searched for her stocking, but it was so small that even his quick bright eyes nearly missed it. There it hung, all feathery and fluffy, on one of the bed knobs. He could only just get a wee pot of honey into it.

" Good Luck to you, little Bee," he cried, as he crept back into the passage and shut the small door.

Downstairs he went, carrying his sack on his shoulder, and out into Big Wood, where the Moon was waiting to see him again. He put his pipes to his lips and played a tune, and the stars leaned down to watch him, and the trees bent their heads to listen.

"Good-bye, Seven Sleepers," he cried. "A Happy Christmas, and Good Hunting in the Spring."

Then away he went, to carry bundles of hay to the cows in their stalls, sieves of corn to the horses in the stables, and comfort and cheer to all the animals who were waiting for him in the byres.

The Moon leaned through the branches of the holly tree, and peered at the sleeping animals.

"Good-night, Seven Sleepers. Sleep well until Spring comes to waken you," she called, and then she sailed away to meet Orion the Hunter with his two dogs, who waited for her in the starry spaces.

PRINTED IN GREAT BRITAIN AT
THE PRESS OF THE PUBLISHERS